MW01036005

THE ROSES UNDERNEATH

A World War II Mystery

by C. F. Yetmen

Ypsilon & Co. Press
Austin, Texas
info@ypsilonpress.com

ISBN 978-0615868363
Library of Congress Control Number: 2013918345

Text set in Electra
Book design by Adam Fortner
Cover by David Provolo
Author photo by Samantha Eisenmenger

For my family,
especially E, then and now.

Also by C.F. Yetmen

What is Forgiven (Anna Klein book 2)
That Which Remains (Anna Klein book 3)

Tiefere Bedeutung liegt in den Märchen meiner Kinderjahre als in der Wahrheit, die das Leben lehrt.

Deeper meaning resides in the fairy tales told to me in my childhood than in the truth that is taught by life.

—Friedrich von Schiller

chapter one

Sometimes, especially in the mornings, Anna could pretend life was normal. That it was normal to eat a spoonful of lard for breakfast and to brush her teeth with her finger. That wearing shoes with more holes than actual leather was normal, and that a bath was a rare luxury. Since everyone else was doing the same, it was normal, in a way. The thing her mind had trouble with was that all this made her lucky.

The one really normal thing played out as it did every morning. Amalia refused to put on her shoes. She stared at her mother, chin pointed, waiting for the next provocation.

Anna tried to remain impassive. Patience.

"Child, *bitte*. We have to go. Mama will be late and you are coming with me today."

"I don't want to. I want to stay with Aunt Madeleine like before."

"I know you do but you can't stay at the hospital all day. Auntie needs to rest. Once she is better and comes home you can stay with her again." Anna shot another glance at the grandfather clock in the corner ticking away, oblivious. The morning sun streaming through the unopened window cast a feeble beam into the small room, lighting the sad scene. One bed, a sofa, small table, a large wardrobe pushed into the corner, the suitcase with all Anna's worldly belongings balanced on top. Home sweet home.

She smoothed the front of her blouse with the palms of her hands. "We will visit Auntie after I am finished working today. We can bring her something for dinner. Now, let's go. Shoes."

The girl sighed as if to empty every last molecule of air from her lungs and dragged the dusty brown shoes out from under the bed. Anna had cut the toes off to make them fit longer and now they showcased her mismatched socks with the holes in them. *If the sock has holes and the shoe has no toe, what is the point of wearing either one?* Anna wondered.

Amalia slipped on the shoes and stood up. "Is Auntie going to get better, Mama?"

"Yes, of course she is, my little Maus. She needs some medicine for her lungs. They will make her better at the hospital. Then you can stay with her again. But today you have to come with me. Are you ready?"

"Ready, Mama. Are we going to see *Amis*?" Amalia looked worried.

Anna took the child's hand and pulled her to the door. "Of course, little Maus. The Americans are everywhere. And don't call them *Amis*, I don't think they like it. Do you have Lulu?"

Amalia ran and pulled her doll from the bed. Lulu was dirty and missing one eye and some of her hair.

"Lulu hasn't seen an American yet. I told her not to be scared," Amalia said as Anna closed the apartment door behind them.

The day promised sunshine but a morning chill lingered and neither Anna nor Amalia had a sweater. The back court of the apartment building was still cast in shadow, the broken windows to the ground floor apartments boarded up like patches over injured eyes. A small path had been cleared between the piles of brick and stone and dust. The two made their way through to the big wooden gate that opened to the street.

"Let's see how fast we can walk," said Anna, hoping the exertion would warm them and that she could make up some time.

Emerging on the Adolfsallee, they turned left toward the Wiesbaden town center, Amalia taking off in a half-skip, half-run. People were out and about, beginning daily tasks of cleaning, clearing rubble, finding food, securing work or just walking the streets in search of something. A line of women—pails in hand—had already formed where the milk truck sometimes appeared. The Allied bombs had been comparatively gentle on Wiesbaden, but that was just a relative notion. Bombs were bombs. Anna watched Amalia jump over holes in the sidewalk, her green dress bouncing in the dust clouds she kicked up. *This is the landscape of her childhood,* Anna thought. *Mountains of rubble and rivers of blood.* The girl was only six and had seen so much misery and stomached horrible fear, and Anna worried that more was to come. The war had been over for three months already, but what had replaced it? What were they living in? A sort of provisional purgatory, she thought, with occupiers who had to sort the bad from the good, the guilty from the innocent, the past from the future. *We are damned; we unleashed hell on the world. And now we*

Germans must make good. She thought this every day. But to make amends for monstrosities perpetrated in your name and with your complicity, even if it was coerced? Was it even possible?

"Mama, look." Amalia was pointing at something on the ground and beckoning. As Anna approached, she saw what had caught Amalia's eye. Gleaming in the sunlight was a large metal button, the kind found on a Loden jacket or a dirndl or some other traditional dress, the kind the Nazis had been so fond of the German *Volk* wearing. It was heart-shaped and stamped with a scroll pattern. "Can I take it?" whispered Amalia, her eyes beaming as if she had found buried treasure. Which, Anna thought, she had, in a way.

"Yes, you may," said Anna, joining in the spirit. "What a prize."

Amalia picked up the button, now black with grime and held it on her flat palm. "Can we wash it, Mama? So it will shine?"

"Yes of course, little Maus," said Anna. "Now put it in your pocket and keep it safe. We need to hurry."

Amalia slipped her hand into her mother's and they walked on between the piles of stones that lay like sleeping prehistoric creatures along the street. Anna imagined them hibernating, waiting until they could be reanimated into something new, something hopeful. As they approached the Rheinstrasse, the bustle of the city flowed along the main thoroughfare and the Bonifazius church glowed in the morning sun, Gothic spires flanking its bombed out sanctuary like two sentries. The American MP directing traffic at the intersection whistled and motioned for them to cross. They turned and walked east into the sun, joining the people heading to whatever jobs they were lucky enough to have. Nearing the large, looming Landesmuseum, where the Americans had set up shop, they walked along the newly installed chain-link fence with the barbed wire on top until they came to the guard at the workers' entry outside the rear courtyard. The sign read *U.S. Army Monuments, Fine Art and Archives*, and the young soldier standing at the entrance looked as earnest and rigid as a statue himself. Anna sat Amalia down on a bench next to the gate.

"Listen to me, Maus." Anna squatted down. "Do you remember what I said? You wait here until I come out and get you. And what will you say if anyone asks you why you are here?"

Amalia exhaled and flatly recited the words: "My name is Amalia Klein. My *Mutter ist* Anna Klein. She *ist* in there. I wait for her?" She pointed at the building.

"Mother, not *Mutter*," said Anna, stroking the blond hair that threatened to escape from Amalia's braids. "Mother."

"Mother," said Amalia. She pulled the button from her pocket and studied it with scientific intensity.

Anna's stomach clenched. She wished she had some choice other than leaving her daughter here, on a bench on the sidewalk. But she didn't. "Look, Maus." She pointed at the GI. "See that American? I bet he comes from Texas, from the Wild West. Maybe he is the sheriff of his town and he has a big horse and he keeps all the bad guys away. That's probably why he's standing guard here now. What do you think?"

They stole a glance at the bulldog of a GI. His face was young but worn and tired. His white MP helmet was balanced precariously on his head, which seemed too large for his short, square body. The name on his uniform said Long, which almost made Anna smile.

"So he's going to need your help keeping bad guys out of the museum while Mama goes to work." Anna turned Amalia to face the three-story building and pointed to the top floor. "Count three windows from the end and that's where I'll be. I'll be watching you all the time while I am doing my job. Your job is to sit quietly here."

"But how long will you take, Mama?"

"Not long, only until lunchtime. Do you promise you won't move? You have Lulu to keep you company."

A pile of trash rained down from an upper window. GIs and German workers dodged the periodic showers of debris, old blankets, mattresses, pieces of wood, and building materials. These were the remnants of the hundreds of displaced people who had sought shelter in the museum at the end of the war. Now it would house the new offices of the Americans they called the Monuments Men. Anna was not altogether sure what their job was, it seemed to have something to do with returning items to people. But they had needed English speakers and typists and to her great good fortune, she was adept at both.

She hoped she could get away with this absurd arrangement at least for a day. The thought of her daughter out here all day and all alone made her insides seize up, but she could not afford to lose the job—it was the only thing keeping them from starving.

Deep breath. She kissed Amalia on both cheeks, stood, and approached the GI, who had been watching them with detached interest.

"Excuse me, sir? This is my daughter Amalia and she will wait for me here today while I am working inside. She will be no trouble."

He shot her an exasperated look. "Lady, I'm not a babysitter," he barked out of a crooked mouth. "You can't leave her here all day. This is no place for a little girl." He looked at Amalia who was pretending to ignore the two adults. Air hissed through his teeth with irritation as he saw a jeep overloaded with crates approaching. "I got things to do, lady." He saluted as the jeep bounced through the gate with a great revving of its engine.

Anna took advantage of the distraction and bolted toward the museum, waving her pass at the GI. "You won't even know she's here. It is just for today, sir. Thank you." She felt sick to her stomach but ran up the stairs to the back entry. Only then did she peek over her shoulder to see the small figure of Amalia, sitting on the bench where she had left her, knees pulled up to her chest, head buried, like a wounded animal playing dead. *She's hiding*, Anna thought and turned to enter the building, wishing she could do the same.

The small wooden desk had just enough room for a typewriter and a sheaf of paper. Two stacked wooden crates served as Anna's chair, and as soon as she sat down, she remembered that she had wanted to bring a cushion from the old settee in Madeleine's house, but had forgotten. She had forgotten it every day for the last three weeks. The room was large. Sunshine streamed through the windows overlooking the entry and its constant bustle of cars and people. From her desk she could see the bench where she had left Amalia, but only if she stood and craned her neck—an activity not encouraged in the typing pool. Frau Obersdorfer ran things with an exuberant military precision that annoyed Anna. She looked at her watch. Three hours until her next break.

"Good morning, Frau Klein. Here are the custody receipts for this morning. And we have good news! The plumbing is working now," Frau Obersdorfer bellowed. Anna took the stack of forms and placed them to the left of the typewriter, ready to be transcribed.

"I thought it smelled better," Anna mumbled. She put down the old, brown leather bag that held her papers, her empty wallet, a packet of rationed cigarettes and the photo she carried of her and Thomas, taken before they were married, when none of what her life had become had seemed remotely possible. She almost never looked at the photo anymore; there was little use in thinking of her husband and her former life now. She rolled the first form onto the drum and typed the date—9 August, 1945—and the place—Wiesbaden Central Collecting Point. The form provided receipts for the piles of objects, books, paintings, rugs, furniture and household items that were being secured by the Americans for safekeeping and protection. At least supposedly. Every item had to be accounted for—every saucer, every spoon, every lamp. Anna wondered why any of this mattered when everyone had lost so much. She typed list after list of items, none of it very interesting and all of it hard to read. The American officers had such bad handwriting, and it was slow-going deciphering both the script and the words. Two chairs (baroque), three Piranesi prints, four silver cups with matching saucers, one brass standing lamp, one table (Biedermeier). Received by: Joseph Foster, Capt. Anna pulled the form from the machine, placed it to her left and began on the next one. She documented the endless things left floating, homeless and without protection, which, like their owners, were now either dead, sick, or dispersed into the landscape like spores from a million dandelions.

Before she knew it, Anna had completed fifty forms and was ready for a new pile.

"Frau Klein." The voice pierced Anna's concentration and she jumped. Frau Obersdorfer loomed over her. With her was an American Anna had not seen before. She had not even seen them approach.

"Yes?" Anna stood up, out of habit.

"Frau Klein, Captain Cooper needs to speak to you," said Frau Obersdorfer. She turned on her heel and was gone. She did not abide interruptions well. Anna's stomach knotted up with a familiar, dull cramp. Any unexpected turn of events was almost always bad news, especially when it involved someone in a military uniform. She looked up at the soldier, who gestured for her to step out into the hall. She obliged and he followed, closing the door to the typing pool behind him.

"Anna Klein? You speak English?" he said, peering at her through eyes squinting with either anger or anticipation, she could not tell. She nodded.

"You have a daughter?" The American's voice was soft, but carried some force. His palms turned upward in a frustrated, questioning gesture. He was quite tall, so she felt at a disadvantage right away, but unlike so many of the Americans, he did not take up a lot of space, either with his voice or his demeanor. His hair was a mix of dirty blond and brown, and his features sat easily on a well-proportioned face. He was older—maybe close to forty—and looked like he had not been "in-country" for too long. Most of the Monuments Men didn't look like regular soldiers. This man looked rested and clean, like he'd been waiting in the wings of the great theater of operations for the last four years before making his entrance.

"Yes," said Anna in perfect English, the one enduring legacy she still carried from the secretarial school in London that had been her home until the Anschluss in 1938. Then Herr Hitler and Mr. Chamberlain had agreed, each in his own way, it was time for her to come home, only Hitler had decided her new home was Germany, not Austria. The annexation of her homeland into the German Reich had been a foregone conclusion that most of her neighbors welcomed. But

Anna's mother never got over the insult, and until she died, she refused to call herself a German. Anna had not seen the distinction herself. As far as she could tell, she and people like her were nothings, just pieces of a board game, beholden to some greater will they did not control.

She focused on the American's stare, trying to appear calm. "Has something happened?"

"You left her waiting outside the front gate?" His heavy eyebrows darted upwards, wrinkling his forehead.

"Has something happened to her?" Anna's heartbeat shifted into a higher gear, and she immediately thought the worst. The blood rushed in her ears and she cursed herself for making such a stupid decision.

"Listen, ma'am, you can't just leave a little girl sitting out on the street all day. It's just not safe. Are you understanding me? What kind of mother does such a thing?" He glared.

Anna nodded. "I understand. Captain, please tell me, what has happened?"

"Nothing happened." He gave the second word a generous dollop of sarcasm. "She is perfectly fine. She's just sitting there, bored out of her little mind. But I am telling you, it's not right to leave her there. She's just a kid. What were you thinking?"

"You are right. I am sorry, sir. But I had no choice. You see, I had nowhere to take her today and I thought at least this way she would be close by." Anna wished he would go away. Why was it his concern what she did with Amalia?

The captain's hands moved to his hips and he cocked his head. "Well the United States Army is a lot of things but it is not a babysitting service. This will not do at all. Don't leave her there again. This is no place for a kid." Having made his point, his body language softened, revealing something that could be nervousness. He was squinting at her again as if she were a puzzle he was trying to solve.

"Don't you know anyone at all who can take care of her?" he asked.

"Yes of course, I will find someone. I won't bring her again," Anna lied. Madeleine was in the hospital for at least another week. Even on a good day, it was a lot to ask of the old woman to keep up with a six-year-old.

"All right, see that you don't." Captain Cooper took a step back to indicate that the conversation was finished. Anna didn't know if she was supposed to go back to work or go fetch Amalia. She pointed at the door to the typing pool. "Shall I?"

"Yes, yes, go ahead," Cooper said with irritation. "I've got an eye on her for now. But just for today, you understand?" He turned and strode down the hall in that military way, his shiny boots squeaking on the stone floor.

"Thank you, sir," she called after him.

Cooper raised a hand in an acknowledging wave. "Just for today," he shouted over his shoulder.

She opened the door and walked back to her desk, avoiding the smirking stares of the other girls in the pool.

Sitting down she realized that she had sweated through the back of her blouse. Her heart was still pounding. She stood back up, pretending to straighten her skirt, and stole a glance down to the bench outside. Amalia was slouching with her head resting on her hand. She was bored. So far, so good.

chapter two

"Mama, what is this?" Amalia stirred the murky, tepid liquid in the tin bowl, her nose wrinkled at its briny smell. Her cheeks were flushed from sitting in the sun all morning. Several curls had escaped her braids and stood wiry along her hairline. The dank, heavy air of the mess hall had managed to dampen Anna's constant appetite.

"It's bouillon, Maus. Beef, I think," said Anna, peering into her own bowl. Dipping her spoon in, she recoiled at the lukewarm saltwater taste. "Yes, beef bouillon. It's yummy, so you better eat yours all up before I do." She smiled and threatened to swipe a spoonful from Amalia's bowl.

They sat at a long table inside the civilian mess hall, which Anna heard the American director of the Collecting Point—a Captain Farmer whom she had never seen for herself—had set up for his German workers. The dilapidated storefront on the Wilhelmstrasse had been furnished with rows of old tables and benches, mismatched and mistreated. Plaster peeled off the walls and electrical wires draped across the room like low-rent Christmas decorations. The one window that was not boarded up conceded a sliver of sunlight, but Anna sat too close to the makeshift kitchen at the back of the room to get any benefit. Steam from giant vats boiling on an ancient wood-burning stove wafted overhead and created a haze that might have reminded Anna of her early school mornings in England, if those mornings had been inside a sauna.

People began flowing through the front door and forming a line along the wall: young women in simple skirts and blouses whose fabrics bore tell-tale signs of their first incarnations as towels or bed sheets, and men in old trousers held on bony frames by suspenders or in hand-me down U.S. Army fatigues with the insignia torn off. It seems Captain Farmer had seen the sorry state of his workers and made a best attempt at clothing and feeding them with the limited resources available—a noble gesture that Anna wasn't sure they deserved.

She was glad they had arrived early. The lunch often ran out and since she had no food for dinner, she wanted Amalia to at least eat something. She watched her daughter drink up the rest of the soup and then pushed her own bowl across the table.

"Here, have mine too." She lit herself a cigarette instead.

Amalia took the offer without a word and scooped the soup with focused determination. Anna tried to think about dinner. She had three stamps left on her ration card; maybe there would be some bread today. The card had to last until Saturday—still three days away—but if there was any bread today she would use them up. They would cross tomorrow's bridge when they came to it. Maybe Madeleine still had some points left on her card.

"Mama? An American came and talked to me. He spoke German. He asked me my name, except he sounded funny when he said it." Amalia imitated an American accent, her mouth contorting around the exaggerated vowels. "I told him Amalia, but he said it Ameeelia. So I said no, Amaaahlia. I told him, like the *Herzogin*. He didn't understand me. How do you say *Herzogin* in American?"

"It's English, Maus, not American. And you say duchess."

"Duchess," Amalia said. "Duchess Amalia." She paused a beat as a shadow crossed her face. "When is Papa coming?" She asked this question every day, usually right after something good had happened, as if she wanted to tell him right away.

"Soon, I hope, Maus. We'll see him soon." Anna squirmed. Another lie. She no more knew where Thomas was—much less if he was safe—than she knew where the next meal was coming from. And he didn't know where they were either. Anna found it hard to believe it had only been two months since she left their little village, her house and her husband. The almighty Allies, puffed up in their Yalta armchairs, delivered them all into the hands of the Russians. Thomas had been against their leaving. There had been a big fight that Amalia had overheard, even though Anna and Thomas hissed at each other over the dirty dinner plates like two snakes trapped in a bag. In the end, Anna bartered all their firewood and rations, and even some of Thomas's medicines for an old truck and drove west. After two days the truck's axel broke and she and Amalia walked 20 kilometers to Wiesbaden, abandoning all but one bag of a few clothes and belongings along the way.

"Papa says we have to take care of each other." Amalia threw this accusation at Anna now whenever she wanted to get her way. Amalia, like Thomas, loved people, and liked to help others—a trait Anna did not possess in any conspicuous quantity. Where Anna was suspicious, Thomas was trusting, where she was cynical, he was hopeful. When she wanted to flee Germany, he wanted to stay and help. Anna had admired his affirming outlook when they met, but as the war brought monsters she never knew existed into their home, her opinion began to shift. It was slow at first, but one day, there it was, wholly formed, the new sentiment: She could not count on Thomas any longer. The knot gripped her stomach again and then gave a twist for good measure.

"I know, Maus. We will see Papa soon. I know he misses us, too." She stood. "Come on, let's go for a walk before I have to go back to work. The fresh air will do us some good!"

Back at her small table, Anna examined the new stack of custody cards that had appeared during her break. Frau Obersdorfer was known to not take a lunch, preferring to reload all her typists with fresh ammunition so that no time was wasted in the afternoon. She presided over the typing pool as her own fiefdom, setting and amending rules at will and appeasing the great American overlords, most of whom seemed happy to stay out of her way. She was not unfriendly; she just had no time for the messiness of people's characters or lives that tended to impede her progress. Short and round, with her bottle-dyed Aryan-blonde hair tied into a tight bun, she was always flushed as if she had been running, even when she was sitting at her desk, surveying her realm, which she did now.

"Did you have a nice lunch, Frau Klein?" she asked. With only the two of them in the room, the older woman took the chance to make conversation. "What are they serving today in the mess hall?"

"Beef bouillon, after a fashion."

"I hear the director's wife sends the cubes from America. Hot soup is quite the treat."

Anna wondered if this was a joke. The saltwater soup a treat? Frau Obersdorfer was looking at her papers and displayed no expression.

"Yes, my daughter was very hungry," she replied, but before she finished speaking, she regretted mentioning Amalia.

Frau Obersdorfer looked up. Her puffy little eyes stared at Anna over the half-moon glasses that hung around her neck from an old piece of cord. "Ah yes, your daughter. How is the little one? She came with you today?"

Anna paused. "Yes, she is waiting outside by the sentry. She's quite all right. It's just for today." She tried to cover all potential criticisms before they could be articulated. "I mean, I know sitting there is boring for her, but I will find a better arrangement."

"Yes. See that you do. Captain Cooper was quite distressed about her presence. He asked me if this was how we treat our children. I had to assure him as best I could that we Germans love our children as much as anyone. We aren't Russians, after all. Sadistic heathens." She straightened a stack of forms by slamming the edges on the table.

Anna tried to think of what to say. "Yes, the Russians, terrible," was the most she could muster. The door opened and three young women entered, chatting and laughing.

Grateful that the conversation with Frau Obersdorfer was at an end, Anna stood up to check on Amalia, whom she had left at the same spot. The sentry shift had changed so Anna had to explain the whole situation all over again and convince the new soldier, who did not seem any more pleased than the short Corporal Long from the morning. Amalia was still on the bench, but now a soldier was sitting and talking to her. The two of them were hunched over, elbows on knees. At first she thought maybe Amalia was sick, but then she realized they were looking at something on the ground. After a few moments the man straightened and turned to point up at the window. It was that Captain Cooper. Anna ducked down, even though he could not possibly have seen her. What was he doing? She straightened and peered over the windowsill. Now Amalia looked up and waved too. The Captain held something up and Anna squinted to see. It was Lulu, Amalia's doll. He waved the doll's floppy arm and smiled. Then they both turned around and resumed their conspiracy.

"Frau Klein."

Anna sat down and snatched the first form from the stack. She hadn't realized that the room was full and everyone was back at work.

Frau Obersdorfer approached her table. "Eyes on the keys, please," she said. "Little children should be in school so their mothers can work," she said.

The shadows were long in the courtyard when Anna re-emerged from the building to find Amalia sitting in her spot, looking at a picture book.

"What have you got there, Maus?" she said as she wrapped her arms around her daughter, thankful they had made it through the day.

"Captain Cooper gave this book to me. Look, isn't it so beautiful?" She sat up and grinned. "It's called *The Snow Queen*."

"Captain Cooper? He gave you a gift? Why would he do that?"

"I don't know. I can't understand what he says. I tried to tell him I can't read yet, and then he wanted to read it to me but it's in German, so he couldn't read it either. We just looked at the pictures." She giggled and ran her hands over the book's cover, its beige linen stained and worn.

Anna wondered where the book had come from. She picked up Lulu and tried to think of the last time Amalia had received a present. Christmas? Memories floated in her head—dates and occasions, seasons and celebrations. She could never seem to put them where they belonged anymore. When they drove away from their sunny little house they left behind everything that rooted them to their place. Of course, these were just things, Anna told herself, and not even valuable things at that. But things gave people a sense of being, of existing in the world. Maybe if the truck had made it all the way to their planned destination in Landstuhl, where Thomas's cousins had a farm, Thomas would have found them by now. Instead they had slept on the street in the Wiesbaden town center, lost and starving. The *Amis* tried to move her and Amalia to a displaced persons camp, but Anna begged the MPs to help her find Madeleine's house, on the Adolfsallee. When she finally saw it, the flood of memories of her mother's best friend, her beloved Auntie Madeleine, nearly cut her legs out from under her. Almost unrecognizable with age and frailty, Madeleine had taken them into her bombed-out apartment without a moment of hesitation. Now all Anna had were the clothes on her back and a key to Madeleine's home. And this job. Their new life had begun.

"Mama. Let's go." Amalia was on her feet, hopping up and down clutching the book to her chest with both arms wrapped tightly around it. She looked happy and was excited to get home. "Madeleine will be so happy," she said. "Can we read it tonight after dinner?"

There was the dinner problem again. Anna took her daughter by the hand and they waited for the MP to wave them across the street.

They walked up the hill of the Rheinstrasse and turned toward the old town with its narrow streets and dark corners. Clumps of people huddled, making exchanges and haggling over unseen goods. The black markets kept getting bigger. She considered seeing what was available, but didn't like to take Amalia with her on those shopping trips. *No place for a kid,* she told herself, repeating the American's words.

They walked on into the narrow passages with their empty shops and decapitated buildings. Twenty minutes later they were standing in a long line at the bakery. A line meant there was bread to be had inside. Anna craned her neck over the heads in front of her to see how much, if any, was left. Maybe they were in luck. The line lurched forward and women emerged from the small shop, each with one loaf of bread that Anna could smell as they passed. She was so hungry she felt like a hollow tree trunk, ready to fall face-first onto the street. She fingered the sleeve of the faded red dress that hung on her diminishing frame and could not believe there had ever been a day when she refused food in fear of losing her figure.

At the front of the line, she handed her ration card to a stern-looking woman with ruddy cheeks and a strong body odor. "Good evening, Frau Klein," she said with an exaggerated smile that appeared on her face as if from nowhere.

"Good evening," Anna returned the affectation.

The woman examined Anna's card with squinting eyes as if she was deciding the authenticity of a painting. She looked up. "You have your daughter with you. *Hallo,* Amalia." The woman winked. Amalia took a step closer to her mother and buried her face in Anna's skirt. Anna placed a protective hand on the child's head.

"Frau Wolf is doing well?" asked the woman.

Anna averted her eyes from the woman's stare. "Frau Wolf has been admitted to the hospital."

"Yes I know. She's been so ill. I do hope it's not the slow fever. Dear God in Heaven, after everything that's happened, that would be just too much."

Anna rubbed her hand against the fabric of her dress, as if to wipe off the invisible bacteria. "I am sure it will be all right." She was not about to reveal anything more, in case Madeleine really did have typhoid. She pushed the thought out of her mind. "Thank you for your concern, Frau. . ."

"Hermann," she said. "We are neighbors. I live downstairs at number 45, don't you remember? We met when you and your daughter arrived." Her eyes scanned Anna from top to bottom, landing on the hand bearing her wedding band before returning to her eyes. "You are working with the Americans now? With the artists or whatever they are?"

"They are not artists. They call themselves the Monuments Men," Anna said, feeling all ears in the shop on their conversation. "They are doing something with all the stolen art." She shrugged. "I am just a typist."

Amalia peeked out from behind her mother's skirt. "They gave me a book!" she said. "The American gave it to me."

"Oh did he? How nice of him." A sneer twitched on Frau Hermann's face, but she caught it, winking at Amalia instead. "Your Papa will be so happy, won't he?"

"My Papa's not here. We left him behind," Amalia mumbled.

"Yes, I know," said Frau Herman, not taking her eyes off Anna, who returned the stare. An audible sigh came from the woman next in line. Frau Hermann completed the transaction deliberatively, tearing off the last ration stamp from Anna's card and handing her the loaf of bread. "Well, that's all your stamps until Saturday," she remarked. "Please give Frau Wolf my best. Perhaps I'll stop for a visit soon. It is so kind of her to take you in." Another curl of the lip.

"Oh, yes, lovely," said Anna, thinking the exact opposite as she took the bread and herded Amalia out the door. "Thank you, Frau Hermann," she sang over her shoulder.

Outside on the street she stopped to put the bread into her bag. "Well, wasn't that nice?" she chirped, feeling stupid.

"That woman is horrible," Amalia said. "I don't like her. Do you like her?"

Anna sighed. "No Maus, not really." She began walking and Amalia ran alongside and slipped her hand into hers. Anna gave it a reassuring squeeze.

"How did she know my name?" Amalia's eyes were focused on the pavement.

"Who doesn't know the great Amalia Aloyisia Klein? I am sure word has spread far and wide about the bravery and beauty of Amalia the Magnificent." Anna laughed.

Amalia stopped and let go of Anna's hand. She clutched her book to her chest. "I still miss Papa. If he was here, he would read the book to me."

Anna sighed. "I know," she said.

"Do you think he's safe?"

Anna started walking to avoid looking her daughter in the eye. "Yes, I do." A lie. "I think we'll see him soon when he comes to find us." Another lie. She had not been able to contact him or anyone back home since they had arrived. The *Amis* kept promising that lines of communication would be up and running soon and then blamed the Russians for not cooperating. It had been weeks and she was at a loss as to what else to tell the girl, who didn't believe her anyway.

"You left him there. I wanted to stay with him." Amalia's stared at her shoes. "He's my Papa and you just left him. We are supposed to take care of each other." She stood rooted to the spot.

Anna made to scoop Amalia into her arms but the child resisted, pushing her mother away and then swinging at her, landing a solid jab on Anna's left cheek. Anna took a step back and put her hand to her face.

Although the blow stung only a little, tears clouded Anna's eyes. Amalia turned her back on her mother and began to sob, her head bent over her chest and her tiny body shaking. Anna straightened and wondered for the hundredth time if she had been right to leave. Maybe they should have stayed. But she knew deep down in her center that they had to leave, or it would have been the end of them. Everyone knew about the rapes and the murders. Thomas had promised to protect them, but Anna knew it was impossible.

She took a step forward and pulled her daughter toward her, then squatted down to look her in the eye, gently holding her face in her hands. "I know, little Maus. I wanted to stay with him too. But it was not safe for us." How to explain this world to a child? Even with her innocence already eroded, there was no reason to accommodate more horrors in her young mind. They had made it this far, and if they were very lucky, things would get better.

Amalia finally crumbled, allowing Anna to pick her up. The girl buried her face in her mother's collar and wrapped her arms around her. They both hung on to each other for dear life, and Anna welcomed the weight around her neck. It kept her feet from sliding out from under her.

She looked up at the glowing sky looking for some reassurance, but it only reinforced her insignificance. She blew her daughter's hair away from her mouth. "All right, Maus. Lulu wants to hear your new story and so do I. We'll go fetch some more food for Auntie and go visit her, how does that sound?"

chapter three

Opening the door to the hospital's public ward, Anna felt the warm, stale air and smelled the combination of urine and disinfectant; it made her grimace. She peered into the dim room, its long corridor formed by rows of beds and curtains lined up like some kind of waiting room for the afterlife. Nurses bustled from one bed to the next, moving trays and bedpans with no discernible purpose. At the far end, a small, fat nurse spotted Anna and Amalia and turned to the person lying in the bed near her.

"Frau Wolf, your daughter is here." The nurse's voice seemed to echo between the tiled walls and high ceiling. She gestured at Anna to come in.

"Wait here, Maus," Anna whispered and left Amalia standing in the open door as she crossed the room. They had devised the ruse that

Anna was Madeleine's daughter in order to secure visitation rights. Their papers were lost, they said, but the hospital didn't seem to care that much anyway. Anna walked past the beds of patients, some sleeping, others sitting with visitors, and a few lying dormant, eyes open but not moving, like porcelain dolls presented on beds of white linen.

The woman's wrinkled face sprang to life when she saw Anna. "Are you back again? Oh, I am so glad." Madeleine stretched out her arms to invite an embrace. Anna leaned into the woman's bony frame, cradling her like a newborn. Madeleine smelled of rosewater as she always had—a small constant that comforted Anna.

"Where is my girl?" Madeleine whispered, eyes sparkling. Anna straightened to beckon Amalia but she was already there. She jumped on the bed.

"Look at what I got, Auntie, a book. It's about the Snow Queen." Amalia held up the tattered book and ignored Anna's motions for her to be quiet.

Madeleine laughed and clapped her hands. "A book? Where on earth did you get such a treasure?" Madeleine looked at Anna.

"One of the *Amis* gave it to her," Anna said, sitting down on the bed. "It probably came through the Collecting Point with some other belongings. It's not worth anything, so I guess they didn't know what to do with it."

"Captain Cooper gave me the book, Auntie. But he can't read German, so maybe I will read it to him when I am big." Amalia wiggled the book in her hands so Madeleine would take it from her.

"Captain Cooper? Who is he? He sounds important." Madeleine pulled herself up onto her elbows, sparking a coughing fit that sent Anna for the carafe. She poured water into an old teacup, held it to the woman's lips, and helped her take a few sips.

"Madeleine you should rest. We just wanted to come and give you a hug. We'll only stay a few minutes."

"Nonsense. I have been resting all day." Madeleine shooed Anna out of the way to make room for Amalia to snuggle up. "Now, *meine Kleine*, my little one, tell me about everything you saw today."

It occurred to Anna that she had been so preoccupied that she had not asked her daughter about how she had passed the day, or what Captain Cooper had said to her. Between the mess with him and wondering what they would have for dinner, she had not even thought to ask.

Amalia giggled. "Oh Auntie, everything was so strange. I sat on my bench and at first the American at the gate, he didn't talk to me. I watched all those jeeps go in and out. I watched the men fix the windows. Then the guard smiled at me and gave me a wave. So I waved back. Then he started making silly faces. He was very funny. Then Captain Cooper came, and the first guard—he stopped and pretended not to see me anymore. Captain Cooper asked me my name but he talked very funny. He said *was ist deine name?*"

Madeleine smiled. "Well he seems nice. Anna, maybe he can help you find out about Thomas."

Anna snorted. "Oh, I doubt that. I met Captain Cooper today as well. He was not happy about Amalia being there. He thinks me a delinquent mother. He made it clear that she was not to come back." She shrugged. "Tomorrow will be interesting."

"Child, I am sure he is reasonable. If Amalia is not making any trouble. And he gave her a book. . ." Madeleine trailed off. "Well, perhaps that would give him cause to help you find out about Thomas. You know, to reunite the family."

"I don't want to ask them for a thing. And even if I did, and he agreed, which I doubt, that does not solve the problem for tomorrow. And anyway, why would he help me? He has enough to do. I'd be better off going to the Red Cross. That's their responsibility after all, no?" She picked her bag off the floor and dug around inside. "Let's not worry about that now. Let's have our dinner."

She pulled out the slices she had cut from their loaf of bread, spread with a bit of lard and wrapped in an old newspaper. Then the last boiled egg, which she handed Madeleine. For dessert there was an anemic, rubbery carrot cut into three pieces.

"What do you know about Frau Hermann? From downstairs?" Anna asked Madeleine as she handed a slice of bread to Amalia.

Madeleine peeled the egg. "Ingeborg? Not that much. But she was the worst informant during the bad years. Or the best, depending on your point of view. I guess you got the bread from her at the bakery?"

"Yes. She thinks I am trading favors with *Amis* so my child can have a book to read," Anna said.

"Oh she thinks everyone is trading favors. She thought that during Adolf's time too. Everyone was sleeping with anyone in a black uniform to get a tin of coffee or a piece of bacon. I think she's just jealous that no one on either side wants to trade favors with her," Madeleine laughed.

"So how is it that she's still in business? Did she lie on her *Fragebogen*?" asked Anna, considering the questionnaire the Amis gave all Germans as a way to sort the good from the bad. *What have you been doing for the last ten years? How many neighbors got sent away thanks to your watchful eye? How much did you love the Reich?* De-Nazification, the *Amis* called it, like de-lousing. As if that were possible.

"Oh she was never a member of the Party, not properly. She was one of those horrible women in the *Frauenbund*, a model of all that German motherhood nonsense, but nothing more. She was just a busybody. She would have sold out her mother as easily to the Nazis as to the Americans if she thought it would get her somewhere. The Americans don't care if you are an old fashioned fishwife of the first order. That's not on their questionnaire. Even they can't de-fishwife the world." Madeleine laughed again, this time with less conviction. "Some things will never change."

"Yes, I guess the fishwives will always be among us," lamented Anna. She shook her head as Madeleine offered the peeled egg. "You two share it."

"Child you must eat more. You are the breadwinner now. You have to take better care."

Anna waved her off and watched Amalia bite the egg in half. "Leave the rest for Auntie, Maus," she said. She leaned back on her elbows and looked at the late day sunlight streaking through the windows above. "Madeleine, what was the name of that sanatorium where Mother worked in Vienna? Do you remember?" Anna leaned back and chewed on her bread.

"Why do you ask that, child?"

"I was just remembering how Mother would read books to the patients—the veterans from the Great War—when she was volunteering there. She would pick books so carefully for each man to make sure it was something he would like, something that would lift his spirits or make him feel whole again, even just for a while. And she would always make those delicious little cream cakes that I wrapped in paper and brought to the hospital every Sunday. Do you remember?"

"Oh, they all loved her there. The patients, the nurses, the doctors. Especially that special doctor." Madeleine winked at Anna. She meant Thomas, the handsome young doctor who had just arrived from Innsbruck. He was trying some new psychological treatment on the patients to help them fight battle fatigue. The day Anna met him he had just sat all night at a man's bedside as he tossed in tormented sleep. Thomas spent his days on the ward talking and listening to the soldiers, always compassionate and kind. Where the practice had been to lock these men away, he brought their pain out into the open. As Anna would learn, he was never afraid to face the things that others turned away from.

"He caused such a stir when he arrived there at the hospital," Madeleine said. "He was very modern with all his talking therapies, or whatever they called it. Everyone thought so." Madeleine smiled at the memory. "I remember your mother telling me about him one day. We met at Herrenhof for coffee and she had just come from the sanatorium. She was delighted that someone was showing real compassion and concern for the men. I admired that about her, even when we were growing up. She was always concerned with the welfare of others. I think it was her true calling."

"I can't believe she's gone," Anna whispered. "I miss her so much."

Madeleine put a papery hand on Anna's and squeezed. "I know, my dear. I do, too. Kathrin was my best friend for fifty years, can you imagine that? Even with this damnable war I never thought we would lose her. Seems so naive now."

Hearing her mother's name spoken aloud made Anna wince. She bit herself hard on the inside of her cheek to stem the vision of fire and burning flesh that always accompanied her mother's memory now.

"Anyway, it was Heldenburg," Madeleine said, shaking her head and taking a bite of the bread.

"What was Heldenburg?"

"The sanatorium. The name just came to me. What brought this memory on?"

"It was the book that reminded me. The one the *Ami* gave to Amalia. And then I couldn't believe that I forgot the name of the place. I hate how memories just slip away like that. As if they never happened."

"Mama, can we read now?" Amalia's voice severed the thread of Anna's memories. Amalia crawled to the edge of the bed and threw herself down on her stomach, dangling her head off the side and holding the book down to the floor with straightened arms. Even though she'd pretended not to, she had been listening, as usual. "Captain Cooper can help Papa find us right Aunt Madeleine? The Americans know where everyone is, right?" She nodded in agreement with herself. "They can find anything. I watched them all day. Do they get to keep everything, Mama? Since they won? Are we going to be American now?"

"Do you want to be American?" Anna asked with a smile. "You would make a fine American, I think. They need smart girls like you on their side. And you are very good at finding things, too."

Amalia remembered the button she had found on the street that morning and pulled it out of her pocket. "Look what I have, Auntie," she said putting out her hand.

"Well, that's the most beautiful button I have ever seen." Madeleine looked at the small heart-shaped token and clapped her hands together. "I have just the thing for that," she beamed. She opened the drawer of her nightstand and rummaged among the papers, then pulled out a short length of green silk ribbon. "That one sweet nurse used this to tie my hair. Watch this, *Schatz*," she said, and strung the button onto the ribbon. She tied the ribbon around Amalia's neck and centered the button in the front. "There now. You look smashing. Just like a princess."

Amalia fingered her new necklace, her smile wide. "Like a duchess," she said. "Thank you, Auntie. Now I can wear it all the time." She threw her arms around the old woman.

"Oh! What's that sound I hear?" said Madeleine putting her finger to her lips. "I hear a terrible rumbling. What is it? Where is that coming from?" She spun her head dramatically around and put her ear to Amalia's belly. "It's in here. It's the belly monster that wants to be fed. We better give him some more bread before he gets angry." She gave Amalia her slice of bread. "Here, eat this."

"Auntie, no, it's yours. You have to eat so you can feel better. I don't want to eat it." Amalia pushed the bread away. "Please Auntie, you eat it."

Madeleine sighed. She took the bread and ate it as Amalia watched her. When she was done, she kissed the girl on the cheek. "You, *mein Kind*, are your father's daughter. You are a good little sausage. What a lucky old girl I am to have you looking out for me. I promise I will get better. Now, where did you put that book?"

As Madeleine and Amalia sat engrossed in *The Snow Queen*, Anna cleared the remnants of their tiny meal as she sucked on her carrot. She scooped the eggshells into the newspaper and folded it into her purse. She would put the shells into her barley coffee tomorrow. Then she lay across the foot of the bed and listened as Madeleine read. Fairytale visions floated in her head and she considered what would happen tomorrow, when Amalia turned up again at the Collecting Point. Soon the summer would be over and schools might start. First the Americans had to rewrite all the history books, or at least take out the biggest lies. *How long does something like that take, rewriting history*, she wondered. She looked at Madeleine who was putting on a brave front for Amalia, but seemed to be sinking into the bed as she wore out. Amalia, her head on the pillow next to Madeleine, stared wide-eyed at the pages. Madeleine's voice, a whisper now, told about the devil's mirror that shattered into a million pieces and covered the land like grains of sand so everyone in the world could see only ugliness in everything around them. As she mustered the energy to go home, Anna realized she couldn't remember how the story ended.

chapter four

"Frau Klein, a word, please."

Anna looked at the clock. Quarter of twelve. It had taken longer than she had expected. "Yes of course," she said as she stood from her table and walked through the door that Captain Cooper held open for her. Out in the hall, he gestured for her to walk with him.

"Let's go to my office. We can talk there."

Anna nodded and followed him toward the stairwell. She tried to read the American's demeanor and gauge how much trouble she was in. He seemed calm but she could never tell with the *Amis*. After so many years of barking and screaming from men in uniforms, the Americans' friendliness confused her. She walked down one flight of stairs and emerged on the second floor, which was being converted to makeshift offices. Metal desks hugged the walls in the open galleries while salvaged tables and chairs from the museum's better days teetered in uneven stacks. They made their way toward a small alcove on the far side where a desk and chair formed a small workspace. A telephone wire ran down the back of the desk and along the entire length of the floor before dropping down through the railing into the open space on the floor below. Cooper placed a chair facing the desk and motioned for her to sit. He took his seat opposite her, leaned back and folded his hands across his stomach. He looked at Anna, and blinked as if thinking of something to say. When he spoke, he sounded like a father scolding a child.

"Frau Klein, maybe I didn't make myself clear yesterday. What I said was that your daughter was not to come back here. I thought we had come to an understanding—or was I mistaken?" He flexed his jaw and waited for her to answer.

"Yes of course, Captain, you made yourself very clear." Anna tried a smile. "I've found a place for her to go on Monday. It was just too short notice for today." She closed her mouth before more lies could escape. Cooper looked at her skeptically. Anna tried to change the subject. "Amalia is very happy to have her book. That was a most generous gesture. She loves books, and actually that story is one of my childhood favorites. So, thank you. A book is a very great treat for all of us."

"All of us?" Cooper asked, leaning forward. "Who is 'all of us?'"

Anna shifted her weight. "The three of us. We live with an old family friend who took us in, in May. She is at St. Josephs—her lungs are bad—so that's why she can't watch Amalia. We came here from Thuringia, Amalia and I."

"Thuringia, that east of here, right? Weimar is in Thuringia, am I right?"

Anna nodded.

"You are widowed?"

"No. My husband stayed behind. He is a doctor, so he was needed. He plans to join us as soon as he can." She smiled as if to reassure him.

"A doctor. Was he at the front?"

Anna shook her head. "No, he was unable to serve. I mean, that's what they—the Army—said. He was in charge of the hospital in our district. That's what he's doing now." A group of German workers passed the desk, talking and laughing. When they saw Cooper at his desk, they fell silent and walked by. One of them, a slight young man with dirty, blond hair fixed his eyes on Anna as he passed and smiled, but Anna looked back at the American.

"Hmm. So he was in the Party, your husband? Most doctors were in the Nazi Party, as I understand it," Cooper said.

Anna straightened. "No, he wasn't. Not officially."

"What does that mean? Either he was or he wasn't." Cooper's palms turned upwards as if to catch her answer.

Anna shifted in the chair. "Yes, you see, ours is just a very small town and the hospital is really more of a clinic. He escaped attention. We kept to ourselves, mostly." A bead of sweat ran between her shoulder blades and she found herself longing for the relative pleasantries of Frau Obersdorfer.

"Hmm." Cooper wrinkled his brow and cocked his head. Anna bit her lip and waited.

"Thuringia belongs to the Ivans since Truman gave it back to Stalin. How does your husband plan to get out? He should probably hurry before things get locked down and *no one* gets out."

"Oh, I am sure he has a plan." She shrugged. "I guess you just set out and keep going, one foot in front of the other. That's what everyone does, right?" A nervous laugh gave her away.

"Well, you had better hope he gets out soon. Things are rough over there. And a kid needs her dad, especially if she's lucky enough to still have one. Anything I can do to help? If he needs a job, I am sure one can be arranged. I mean if he's really clean like you say. I can't do much if he was a Party member."

Anna felt a twinge of defensiveness, but decided to bury it somewhere under her discomfort and desperation. "No, no. Thank you, Captain. We can manage." She leaned forward. "Is that all? I must get back to work."

"Actually, no. I wanted to talk to you for a minute. I don't think you know about everything that's going on around here. You see the custody receipts up there in the typing pool, but do you understand what it is we are trying to do here?"

Anna shrugged. "You are gathering all the lost and misplaced valuables in case people come looking for their belongings."

"Well, yes, but it's more than that. You have heard that a lot of art was stolen and hidden during the war?"

Anna nodded. "Yes. You mean stolen from the Jews, here in Germany?"

"I mean from everyone and everywhere."

"I know Hitler had ideas for that museum of his in Linz," Anna said. "And he had that atrocious exhibition of German art every year. The art got worse every time. It was a joke by the end. All the good artists were gone by then. He had terrible taste in art." She smiled, mostly at the fact that she could say such a thing to a man in a uniform now.

Cooper nodded. "So that's what we're about. Retrieving the art the Nazis stole. And also safeguarding the monuments and buildings, checking for damage and getting them fixed up."

Anna felt something surge somewhere in her gut and fly out of her mouth before she could stop it. "Oh yes, first you bomb us, then you fix us, is that right? That's very clever. I suppose this is a way to create lots of jobs and give yourself something to do now."

Cooper's face hardened. "You can thank us for the bombs later. After all, if it hadn't been for them, you probably wouldn't be sitting here right now," he said. The rebuke lay on the desk between them like a cold stone. Anna threw it back at him.

"No, I wouldn't be sitting here now, you are right, Captain. I might be dead, I might be a prisoner, or be learning to speak Russian. My mother might even still be alive, but she is not and I am here, working for you, and trying to build a life that I don't recognize. And for that, I think I am grateful. I just don't know if this is better than any of those alternatives. So if you don't mind, I think I will thank you another time." She closed her mouth and tried to determine if the outburst had made her feel any better. *If I lose the job now, so be it.* She was tired and hungry. And now she was angry. No, she didn't feel any better.

Cooper leaned onto his forearms and looked at her. For a long time they sat, Anna looking out the window to avoid his stare. She tried to anticipate his next words and wondered how he was going to fire her. He would probably be friendly about it. After a long pause, Cooper inhaled loudly and she shifted her eyes toward him. He looked solemn.

"Let's leave this for another day, shall we? I know things can seem very black and white on this side of the table. Right now we have work to do and I need your help. I'm heading out to survey some buildings next week so I won't be around much."

"Buildings?" Anna said, relieved to move on.

Cooper nodded. "Churches, monasteries, historic stuff. Survey for damage and also check for valuables. It'll take all week to cover the sector they assigned me. I'm the only architect at the Collecting Point right now, so it's all on me."

"You are an architect? I thought you were all museum people or something."

"Lots are, but there are also artists and academics. Basically if you knew anything about any kind of art, you qualified. I guess that includes guys like me. The Army doesn't really know what to do with us. Anyway, I'm glad you found a place for the duchess because I'll be driving around the Rhineland every day." He paused. "And so will you. I need a translator to help me with the locals and I've put in for you to accompany me. So I'll see you at 0800 Monday morning and we'll head out. Meet me in the courtyard, Okay? And wear something comfortable." He gave a big smile. Anna felt the air leave her body.

The sun glowed overhead when Anna left the building for lunch. Amalia was lying on her stomach on the bench, resting her head in her hands and looking at her book when Anna approached.

"Is this little Maus hungry?" she asked as she tickled the girl's ribs. But as soon as Anna touched her daughter, she knew something was wrong.

Amalia sat up. "Mama do I still have to come here every day? I don't feel good." Her cheeks were flushed and her eyes hollow. Her arms had turned the color of smoked salmon. The day was hotter than normal and the humidity stuck the heat to them like a rancid warm washcloth. Anna felt Amalia's head. It was burning. She sat down on the bench and pulled the girl closer. Amalia put her head in her mother's lap and Anna felt her daughter's heat seep into her own skin.

"She doesn't look so good."

Anna looked up to see a man, hands shoved into the pockets of his baggy wool pants as if he were trying to hold them up from the inside. She squinted into the sun at his back.

"Excuse me?"

"Heat stroke. I've been watching her this morning. It's just too hot for her to sit here. I tried to get her to move into the shade but she refused. Told me her mama made her promise not to move. I guess that's you?"

He sat down. Anna stroked Amalia's hair. Somewhere a car backfired, making her jump. She wanted to run away, take Amalia with her and never come back. But she couldn't find the energy to move.

Anna recognized him now. He had walked past Cooper's desk earlier. He had been the one who stared at her. With his blond hair and cool eyes he might once have been the poster boy for Aryan masculinity, before the front had aged his baby face. He was maybe twenty years old but carried his withered body like an old man, hunched and depleted. Lines sprouted from around his eyes and mouth and a hollowness in his cheeks gave him a fragility that all the young men seemed to sport these days. It was the price they paid for being alive.

"Are you all right?" He smiled.

She nodded. "Yes, of course. I'll get her home and get her temperature down. She'll feel better soon." She made to stand but Amalia's limp body weighed her down.

"What's her name?"

"This is Amalia." She looked at him. "And you are?"

"Oh, I am sorry. Schilling. Emil," he said. "I am pleased to meet you, Frau…?"

"Klein. Do you work here?"

Emil nodded. "I was working on the plumbing, but now that it's all fixed I've been assigned to create perimeter lighting for security. There's a big shipment of art coming in a week. We have to have the place locked down by then. And you?"

"Typist. On the third floor."

"So she waits for you here all day?" He pointed his chin toward Amalia.

As Anna embarked on her explanation, she found her defensiveness had turned into anguish. "I have no one to leave her with during the day. The woman we are living with is in the hospital. The kindergartens don't open for at least another month if we're lucky. I have to bring her with me and let the *Amis* do a bit of childcare. But it's not really a good solution."

"I can see that," said Emil. "I mean, this is no place for a child."

"I am aware of that," Anna snapped. "I will find another solution this weekend. Surely the Red Cross or someone has made arrangements for people like me?"

"Oh you don't want to do that," he said. "That's no good. All the bureaucracy and papers and forms. Getting through them will take days and then what? She'll end up in one of those horrible American Army places. And anyway, I know somewhere she can go."

Anna exhaled. "And where is that?"

"My sister has been watching children of other workers from the Collecting Point while they get settled. At our house—my family's house.

It's just up there." He waved a hand toward the hills that protected the eastern side of the city. "I am sure she'll be happy to take one more."

Anna shifted her weight. "Well, I don't have any money. I can't really pay."

Emil waved a hand. "She'll trade food from your rations as payment. Just to have enough to feed the children."

More food, Anna thought. *I am always running after a carrot, like a dog on a track. Even when I get one carrot, I have to get the next one.* She sighed. "Oh I don't know. Amalia has always been with me, and I. . ."

She stopped as Amalia lifted her head and tried to say something before she vomited into Anna's lap, retching a few times and clutching her stomach.

"Mama?" she whimpered. "I want to go home." She began to cry, her body contorting into a bony ball. Anna stood and lifted Amalia to her shoulder.

"Yes Maus, we are going home now. Please excuse us, Herr Schilling."

"She can't stay here," Emil said, his head shaking. "Look at her. I am only trying to help. I understand, of course, you don't know a thing about me. Why don't you come visit tomorrow and meet my sister and see for yourself? I promise it's all well and good. Please, at least take a look." He looked concerned, which Anna resented. She hated that she needed help. But she knew she could no longer afford the luxury of pride.

She exhaled again. "When, shall we say?"

"How about tomorrow afternoon, at four o'clock? Do you have a bicycle?"

"Yes, I can get one."

"Good. I will give you directions."

◆ ◆ ◆

By the time Anna got Amalia home, the lunch hour was well over. Frau Obersdorfer would be wondering where she was. As she laid her daughter on the bed and began to pull off her dress, Anna debated what to do. She couldn't leave Amalia here alone—the girl was burning up. She dabbed her forehead with a cool rag.

"Here, Maus. Drink a little water." She held a glass to Amalia's lips and propped her head up.

"Mama, my head hurts so much," the girl wailed.

"You have sunstroke. It will be all right, we just have to wait for it to pass."

"But I feel too sick."

"I know Maus, I know. Just lie down and try to be still. You will feel better soon." She lifted the girl's head and turned the pillow over to the cooler side.

Amalia offered a weak smile. "That feels good." She reached for Anna. "Mama, will you lie down with me?"

Anna smiled and lay down next to her daughter, pulling her into the crook of her arm. For a while they lay in silence. The thought of Heide Gerber, her neighbor in Kappellendorf, floated into her consciousness. An enthusiastic young mother with three little ones and a husband on the front, Heide often shared her rations with Anna, bringing over an extra pat of butter or cup of flour. The children—two boys and a girl, all under five—were a handful, but they also brought valuable extra rations along with a useless commendation from the Führer. The boys played with Amalia in the garden and up and down the narrow street while Anna and Heide sat and talked on their front steps. When the news came that her beloved Herbert, a garrulous twenty-four-year-old with a crooked smile, had been shot through the head on a field in the Ukraine, Heide was stoic. Once, Anna heard her crying through the open kitchen window and sent Amalia over to fetch the children, so Heide could be alone. Amalia ran into the garden and returned with a bunch of wildflowers and her favorite green blanket in hand. When she came back without either, she told her mother that she had given the blanket to Frau Gerber to make her feel better. Six months later, in the nightmare January of 1945, when the food had run out and snow threatened to smother them as they froze, Heide had covered the bodies of her dead children with the same blanket. Then she lay on the floor alongside them and took the poison she had already fed them in a spoonful of honey. They lay there a whole day before Anna found them, silent and cold, and for a flash she had envied their peaceful escape. For them, it was over. Thomas had taken the bodies to the morgue and Anna had lied to Amalia, saying they had left to live with family in the city. Anna could see the shadow of doubt behind her daughter's eyes darken with every lie she told, the girl playing along with an adult game that made no sense to her.

She wondered what Thomas was doing at that moment. Maybe if she was very still and focused all her energy, she could make him appear at the door. Maybe right now he was walking down the Adolfsallee, tired and hungry, looking for number 45. If he were here, she might not need the job with the Americans, or a place for Amalia to go, or even to live in this one room with its one sad window and its dirty bed. If he were here, she would not feel lonely and they could be a family again. She would have her husband back. A physical pain rose somewhere in the back of her throat, a tightening that always signaled tears. She stopped herself. There was no sense in thinking that way. Things were the way they were, and nothing she wished for would change that. She closed her eyes and focused on Amalia's breathing, slow and restful now, like little waves of air caught in a tide pool, trying to escape into the ocean but always sucked back inside. She adjusted her breath to match the rhythm and, within moments, she was asleep, too.

chapter five

Anna woke with a start, her heart pounding in her ears. She sat up and tried to get her bearings. When she remembered the events of the previous afternoon, she fell back into the pillow and groaned. What would happen now? She had left the Collecting Point without notice or explanation and not returned. She could see Frau Obersdorfer's smile spreading across her face as she considered a more worthy replacement for Anna. Next to Anna, Amalia slept, her breath steady and her small body cool to the touch. *That Cooper might stand up for me*, Anna thought, but she hated the idea of being beholden to anyone, let alone an *Ami*. Then again, the job was the only thing standing between her and complete despair. She was earning all the money that fed Amalia and Madeleine. They depended on her. All three of them depended on the damn *Amis*. She closed her eyes. Thomas's face appeared before her, and she let it stay. In the morning quiet it was as if the two of them were alone and she inhaled his presence, taking in the memory of his smell, the feel of his starched collar against her cheek when she turned her face toward his. The sight of him was vague and shimmery; she couldn't make out the particulars of his face, which worried her. *I am forgetting him,* she thought, and tears burned the corners of her eyes.

Later she and Amalia sat at the little square table having a breakfast of leftover bread toasted on the stove. With some butter and a cup of real coffee it would have been a decent meal. *One out of three is better than nothing,* thought Anna. She was still in the green, flowery nightgown that Thomas used to say made her look like she had been swallowed by her mother's drapes. It was her favorite because she had worn it in the hospital after giving birth to Amalia. Now that her frame was considerably smaller she thought that both of them could easily fit in it together again. Amalia chewed on her toast and drew a picture on a scrap of paper. Anna felt the warm, late-summer breeze slide in through the window and stroke her face. It was going to be another hot day.

"Mama, look!" Amalia held up her picture.

Anna guessed it was a woman wearing a large headdress. Big circles hovered where ear ears would be "Very nice," she said, distracted.

"Mama? Who is Queen Nefertiti?" Amalia asked twirling the pencil between her fingers.

The question took Anna off-guard. "Queen Nefertiti? Well, she was the wife of an Egyptian pharaoh. Why do you ask about her?"

Amalia ignored the question. "What else?" she asked.

Anna racked her dormant mind. "People say she was the most beautiful woman to ever live." She squinted at Amalia. "Why do you want to know about her?" She took a hair clip from the table by the bed and began gathering her hair at the nape of her neck.

Amalia jumped onto the bed. "Because I think Captain Cooper told me she is coming here."

"That's impossible, Maus. Queen Nefertiti has been dead for thousands of years," Anna laughed.

Amalia giggled. "Not the *real* queen, mama. The statue. It is coming. Captain Cooper said." She played with Anna's hair. "Captain Cooper said he would let me see Nefertiti when she comes."

"Oh he did?" Anna's voice was at a low simmer. "Well we'll see, little Maus. You know, I want to tell you something." She tried to act indifferent to her own words, hiding her anxiety over what she was about to say. Amalia, as usual, sensed her unease right away and set her jaw, ready to defy whatever it was that was coming her way.

"Listen to me," Anna began. "Today we will go visit a nice lady who can maybe look after you while I go to work. So you won't have to wait for me anymore." She smiled a pained smile.

"What kind of lady?" Amalia fingered the edge of the blanket.

"A very nice lady I'm sure. We will go visit her together today, you and I. And then you can see for yourself." She reached out and stroked Amalia's hair. "And there will be other children there too, so you can make some friends. Won't that be nice?"

Amalia looked away, her bottom lip pushed into a scowl. "But what about Captain Cooper? He is my friend."

"Well, if you start going to this new lady's house then you won't be at the Collecting Point anymore. So you won't see Captain Cooper anymore either." Anna stood, surprised at her own irritation. She hadn't meant to sound so final, but it was true. And anyway, she probably didn't have the job anymore, after missing a whole afternoon. She would have to find new work right away. Amalia deflated and shot her an angry look.

"But I want to see Nefertiti. And Captain Cooper is my friend, not yours, so you don't get to say."

Anna sighed. She refused to use up her energy on a fight today and for sure not over some promise the *Ami* had made. "Yes, Maus, all right. We will talk about it later. Let Queen Nefertiti arrive in one piece and then we'll see, yes? Now let's have a quick bath. I'll go see if there's any water."

In the afternoon, after they had picked up their new ration book, Anna and Amalia rode around town on Madeleine's old bicycle. Heading north on the Wilhelmstrasse they cut through the park, stopping to sit by the pond for a while. Amalia ran in circles between the plane trees. Work crews made up of former Nazi party members organized the rubble into manageable piles under the watch of American guards. Because the rubble train did not reach this far, the piles were well picked over for anything that might be useful and now had to be transported by wheelbarrow. The wood was all gone—stored up for the winter or used for cooking—so all that remained were the dusty fragments of stone and concrete that had been the arcade of the state theater next to the park.

After a while they rode up to the casino and spa where the noble and famous had come for centuries to rejuvenate and revive themselves. Now it was the Americans' turn. They had requisitioned the place as the Eagle Club, exclusive to officers and dignitaries. Anna wondered how it looked inside and what luxuries were bestowed on those deemed worthy to enter. She and Amalia stood at the edge of the bowling green, the once great lawn that was the casino's welcome mat. Rows of jeeps were parked at the entry, and officers milled around the bombed-out arcades, chatting up German girls and showing off. Others sat on the edge of a fountain, their laughter rising in the air and floating past Anna's ears on its way somewhere else. She felt like a child with her nose pressed against the window of a pastry shop.

"Mama?" Amalia pulled at her skirt. "Being American looks better than being German."

Anna had to agree. It did look that way from where she was standing.

"Mama? Will you have to go to work every day?"

"Yes of course, Maus, you know that."

"But what if Papa comes? Will you still have to go to work?"

"I don't know. We will see. I need to earn money so we can put our life back together. Maybe get a new house. Wouldn't that be nice?"

Amalia nodded. "A new house with Papa?"

Anna nodded and took the girl's hand. They started toward the old city, pushing the bicycle through the Kaiser-Friedrich-Platz with the half-demolished Nassauer Hof Hotel, which Anna remembered having visited once when she had come with her mother to visit Madeleine before the war. It had been an elegant, storied old place. Now it was a badly wounded relic of another time, over which the Kaiser's statue still presided. Even he was looking toward the Americans across the street, watching them rebuild his beloved country. Anna had always thought that Friedrich's more liberal attitudes toward government and his hatred of war to be a kinship, but now she viewed him with disdain. He stood, one leg in front of the other, trying to take a step toward the *Amis*, but rooted forever to his plinth, forced to watch and accept his fate.

They turned back to make their way to the Schilling house through the narrow maze of streets that led to the Marktkirche in the center of the city. In between the burned and bombed façades, some semblance of everyday life had resumed. Here and there a makeshift shop was open, trying to sell whatever bare necessities were on hand. But the only people with any money were the *Amis*, who walked the streets in small packs like tourists on a ruined vacation. They wanted to spend their dollars on souvenirs, but the kind of souvenirs they wanted, the kind that proved they had won the war, were burned or buried in back yards all over the country. The people who had all the money didn't want what was for sale, and those with no money desperately did.

At four o'clock Anna and Amalia stood at the iron gate of a small Wilhelminian villa on the Gustav-Freytag-Strasse that did not look too much worse for wear. The neighborhood to the east of the old Landesmuseum that was now the Collecting Point retained a leafy nobility despite the occasional evidence of bombing. Anna double-checked the address and then leaned the bicycle on her hip to straighten Amalia's dress, which had become twisted during the ride up the hills. They had put on the best dresses they had brought with them: Anna's was a red one with little white flowers and a bow at the neck, Amalia's a too-short blue hand-me down with a sailor's collar. Anna tried to flatten the curls that had escaped from the girl's braids as they always did and then checked her own hair. Finally, she pushed the button next to the metal nameplate that read *Schilling* and looked at Amalia.

"Best manners please, Maus," she said. "Remember *please* and *thank you*. And don't take too much food, even if it's offered."

"Let's not embarrass ourselves." Amalia said, anticipating her mother's next words. Anna smiled into her collar.

A door at the side of the house opened and a tall, athletic woman bounded down the short run of steps toward them. She crossed the small yard in three long strides and opened the gate with a hard pull.

"Frau Klein? *Wilkommen.* I am Frieda Schilling." She offered a strong handshake and a warm smile. Her bright face was framed by blonde braids coiled on top of her head but her flowery dress was threadbare and faded. She seemed to Anna to be very young. "Please do come in. Bring your bicycle inside the gate too. We have to keep everything nailed down these days." Her voice was loud but friendly. She trained her eyes on Amalia, bent over, and cocked her head to one side. "And you must be my new friend. I am happy to see you. I hope you will like it here."

Amalia shrank behind her mother's legs and said nothing. Anna thanked Frieda and walked the bicycle and her daughter through the open gate. "You are kind to invite us," Anna said. "Thank you."

"Nonsense," said Frieda, guiding Anna to the front door. "Emil tells me you are in need of childcare, and that is the one thing I am good at. We must all pull together and get through this difficult time."

The door opened to a large foyer with a staircase leading up and down. A door on the left was closed. Frieda led the way up the stairs. "Emil has taken the downstairs apartment since he returned from the front but I live upstairs. It's much nicer. You can get some fresh air up there." The stairs creaked underfoot in a comforting, homey way and the smell of cooking floated in the air. At the top of the stairs a beveled glass door stood open. Frieda gestured them inside.

The upstairs was smaller than Anna expected, but well-appointed. Refined but well-worn worn fabrics in dark red and green covered the antique furniture and paintings were stacked two and three high on the wall. Amalia's wide eyes took everything in without blinking.

"You live here with your family?" Anna asked.

"Emil and I have the house to ourselves. It's been in our family for generations. Mother used to live upstairs on the top floor but she's passed on. It's been just us for a long time." Frieda motioned for them to take seats on the long sofa. Amalia crawled up next to her mother and leaned in close.

"I am terribly sorry," said Anna. "It must be very hard." Talk about people's families made her uncomfortable because it inevitably led to questions about hers. She changed the subject. "So the Americans are not interested in your house? How fortunate."

"So far, we've been lucky. There are much nicer mansions that are more their taste. I think they've overlooked us. But I suppose that could change at any moment." She took a seat on one of the end chairs. "You are not from Wiesbaden?"

"No, we came in June. We are staying with a friend until my husband joins us."

"He's a doctor, my Papa, is," said Amalia.

Frieda smiled at her. "How nice. I am sure he misses you very much." Frieda leaned in close from her seat in the armchair. "Amalia, may I ask you a question? Do you like *Apfel Strudel*?"

Amalia's eyes expanded. "I've never had it."

"Never? Well, I've just taken one from the oven, just for you." Frieda clasped her hands triumphantly.

"You made apple strudel?" Anna's mind ran down the list of ingredients for a strudel: butter, sugar, flour, apples. Frieda may as well have said she cooked magic beans in a pot of gold.

Frieda stood and made her way toward the kitchen across the hall. "Yes, we got a bit lucky and I got my hands on some apples this week. Not the best ones, but apples nonetheless. And the only thing apples are good for is strudel, as my mother used to say."

Anna wanted to ask how Frieda had acquired such a prize. Instead she said, "Will your brother be joining us?"

"Emil? Yes he should be here soon. He's gone out on one of his missions. I never know where he goes, but he usually comes back with something. Maybe he'll surprise us. Now, please excuse me while I fetch the tray."

Amalia tugged at Anna's sleeve and crooked a finger at her to get her full attention. "How many pieces of strudel can I eat, Mama?" she whispered. Anna could almost hear her mouth watering.

"Only one, Maus, we are guests," she whispered back. "Only one." She kissed her on the forehead.

Frieda returned with a wooden tray loaded with cups and saucers and plates, all of the same faded pink rose pattern. She distributed plates and cups around the oval marble-topped coffee table. "Miss Amalia, will you please help me bring the strudel from the kitchen?" she asked. Amalia nodded, hopped off the sofa and followed Frieda. When they returned, Amalia carried the pan of strudel wrapped in a towel. The aroma almost made Anna cry. That was followed closely by another that was almost too much to believe. It hung in the air the way a perfume introduces the arrival of a guest. Now Anna's eyes were wide. "Is that…coffee?" she asked.

Frieda snorted. Oh no, we haven't had proper coffee in months and months. This is only Nescafé. That's the best we can do, I'm afraid. Emil has made it his life's work to get his hands on real coffee and keep it. But you know how things are these days, coffee is worth more to barter with than to drink."

"Nescafé is wonderful," Anna said. "It's a thousand times better than that barley swill. Although I have gotten used to the taste, I guess."

"Never touch the stuff," said Frieda. "I'd rather drink puddle water." She poured a cup for Anna, and one for herself. Amalia squirmed in her spot waiting to get her hands on a piece of the warm pastry. She could barely contain herself when Frieda began to cut into it. "Now Amalia, as the guest of honor you will have the first—and the biggest—piece."

"I am the guest of honor?" asked Amalia holding her plate out.

"Yes, you are here to decide you'd like to stay here while your mama goes to work," said Frieda. "That's why I made you the strudel." She winked. "You must start eating before it gets cold. And you too, Frau Klein. Let's not stand on ceremony." She pointed at Amalia with a heaping fork. "After we've eaten I will show you the children's play room and the garden, and then you can decide if you would like to visit me here every day."

The strudel was just as Anna remembered. Warm, flaky pastry, rich with butter, apples spiced with cinnamon—actual cinnamon. She put the plate down to stretch the time between bites. "This is wonderful, Fraulein Schilling, really. What a treat. You are so kind. Amalia, what do you say?"

"I say this is delicious," Amalia said, her mouth full.

Heavy footsteps echoed in the stairwell. "Ah, that will be Emil," said Frieda. "You put out the pastry and he shows up, like a stray dog knows when the butcher throws out the scraps." She turned in her chair as Emil barreled through the door. "Emil, there you are, subtle as a herd of elephants."

Amalia snorted at the joke.

Emil kissed his sister on the cheek and reached over to shake Anna's hand. "Frau Klein, welcome, and Amalia, too. I am so pleased you are here. Are you getting to know Frieda? I hope she hasn't scared you away. I see she's made strudel."

Anna thought something about the two of them was carefully controlled even as they teased each other, as if there was a subtext she could not read. She took another bite of strudel.

"Finished!" Amalia said, setting her plate down and wiping her mouth with the napkin.

"Right," said Frieda as she stood up and held her hand out. "Let's go. Frau Klein you stay here and finish your strudel. Emil will help you find us." The two went off down the short hallway and Anna heard a door open and Frieda say, "This is where all the children play."

Anna hated having Amalia out of her sight. The fear of having to leave her in the care of a stranger felt as real and solid as if it were sitting next to her on the sofa. The fact that she had to admit that the strudel and the coffee, not to mention the lovely home, could maybe make her ignore it unsettled her. The whole scenario made her feel cheap, like she was being bought.

"How many children did you say your sister keeps?" she asked Emil, who had helped himself to a generous slice and was refilling his sister's cup for himself. He poured milk into the coffee with a shaking hand. Anna noticed the tips of three of his fingers on his left hand were gone just above the first knuckle.

Emil noticed her attention and wrapped his other hand around the affected fingers. "Frostbite," he said. "My souvenir from Leningrad."

"Oh, I am sorry," Anna said, feeling the war enter the room again. Its odor was always present, even when there were only *Amis* around.

But these young soldiers—the *Soldaten* that they were all supposed to ignore now—always brought the reality back.

"Bah, it's nothing. I got off easy." He kept his fingers hidden. "I think it's four now. Children, that Frieda watches," he said. "Two girls and two boys. It varies, people are so transient now, but it's mostly mothers who work at the Collecting Point like you. Well, like us both, I guess." He stopped speaking as if catching himself before saying something he shouldn't.

Anna nodded, feeling awkward. She tried to find something to fill the silence. "How are the Americans treating you?" was all she could think of.

"Oh the *Amis* are fine, most of them. I don't bother them, they don't bother me. I figure if they can clean up this mess then that's all right with me."

"I guess so," Anna replied. Her eyes landed on the paintings on the wall behind Emil's chair. "You have a lot of nice paintings." She wondered how they had survived all this time, not having been sold or traded for food, or their frames broken for kindling.

Emil exhaled. "Ah yes, my mother's paintings. She was a bit of a collector. I even bought a few things myself, before the war. They aren't really very valuable, mostly they are from local artists—Rhine painters, you know? But I like them. They are nice scenes of happy days."

"Maybe there will be happy days again," Anna said, but she didn't believe it. The didn't deserve it anyhow.

"For you, yes I think so," Emil said. "But not for me. Not for us soldiers. All we can do is hope that the children don't have to pay for what we did, right?"

"Is that why you are helping us? Me and Amalia?"

Emil shrugged. "I guess." He shifted his weight in the chair. "So, what do you say? If Amalia likes it, I am sure Frieda can arrange a workable payment for you."

"You have been most kind." Anna thought if she had worn a hat she'd be clutching it in her hands now, playing the part of the down-and-out mother, having just been bribed with strudel and coffee, ready to sign over her greatest treasure into the care of another. "Shall we go see the room?" *It's going to take more than strudel and coffee to buy me*, she thought.

But as soon as she peeked into the playroom, the deal was sealed. It was filled with toys and books that sat in an orderly fashion on low shelves lining the walls. A small chalkboard stood on an easel, flanked by a row of low tables that had been pushed together to make one long surface. Happily mismatched chairs were neatly tucked underneath. Amalia sat on one of these, working intently on a drawing, using three colored pencils. Frieda sat next to her on a low bench, her long legs pushing her knees up to her chin. A small metal train track ran along one side of the room, under a row of windows that flooded the room with sunshine. In one corner sat three dolls in various states of undress and in the other sat a pile of pillows and blankets formed a cozy nap-time corner.

"What do you do with them all day, Fraulein Schilling?" Anna asked.

"Oh, whatever the day requires. We go outside a bit in the cool morning—the children are helping me prepare the garden for fall vegetables. Emil just got hold of some carrot and turnip seeds. We have lunch, usually some bread and a soup. On Sundays I make a big pot of something that we eat all week. Then we have a rest, right here on the floor with our blankets and pillows. I usually fall asleep myself. They wear me out. And then in the afternoon we play with whatever we like, sometimes we dress up, sometimes we sing songs. Then when it's time to go, we tidy up and walk down to the museum—I mean to the Collecting Point. It's all easy and straightforward. They are just so young and they've been through so much, haven't they?"

"What did you do during the war, Fraulein Schilling?" It was the rudest of questions to be asked, but Anna had to do it.

Frieda didn't blink. "I was a nurse, Frau Klein. Here in Wiesbaden." She lifted her chin and held Anna's gaze. "For children," she added.

"And you have children of your own?" Anna asked.

Frieda shook her head. "No. Not of my own. It has been my calling to take care of others. That has been my life"

Anna nodded and turned to Amalia's picture. It was three figures, holding hands and smiling. A yellow sun shone overhead and an oversized butterfly floated in the sky. It was a happy picture.

Anna nodded and stepped back into the hall. "Shall we discuss the payment?"

chapter six

Anna stood in front of the wardrobe squinting into the darkness.

"Mama? What are you doing?" Amalia sat up in bed, her hair wild from sleep and eyes still clouded. She yawned.

"Looking for something."

Anna reached over and turned on the light, which made Amalia dive under the blanket. Now Anna could see what she was looking for. Her old, gray gabardine pants with the wide cuffs. *Suitable for days in the country, either family picnics or surveys of bombing damage on historic landmarks*, she thought. She pulled the green cotton blouse out of the drawer and finished getting dressed.

"You look funny, Mama." Amalia laughed.

"You don't like my pants?" Anna twirled and struck a pose.

Amalia giggled and shook her head as if she had finally seen everything. Then she remembered what day it was. "Mama! Today is the day, right? Today I get to go to Fraulein Schilling?" She jumped out of bed and pulled Lulu out from under her pillow.

Anna put her nerves aside. "And you know what else? We have strudel for breakfast."

Amalia squealed and raced Anna to the kitchen. Frieda had sent them home with a slice of strudel and a packet of Nescafé. Anna put the kettle on and cut up the pastry for Amalia.

Amalia climbed up on the small table under the window and swung her legs as she chewed.

"So my little Maus, did you sleep well?"

"I had a bad dream. About Papa." She looked up at Anna, waiting for her reaction. She was a good little bomb-thrower herself.

Anna feigned neutrality. "You did? Tell me about it."

"I dreamed that Papa was trying to come to us, but he was lost. I could see him walking the streets looking for us, and I called to him but he couldn't hear me." She swung her legs harder, and the table swayed under her weight.

Anna wiped her hands on the back of her pants. "That's a very bad dream. But you know it's not real. It's all over now."

"But what if Papa can't find us? What if he never finds us?" Amalia's chin began to quiver.

"He will find us. Don't worry. Your Papa is a very smart man. And I will try again to get word to him about where we are. It will be all right, I promise."

"You always say that. And it's not all right. Not at all. I miss my Papa." She began to cry, still chewing on the strudel.

Anna put her arms around the girl. "Oh, Maus. It's all right to cry. Papa loves us and he will find us. Until then we just have to be brave and take care of each other. And today you'll get to meet some new friends and have a lovely time with Fraulein Schilling. The day will go by in no time and then we'll be one day closer to the day when Papa is with us again."

Amalia continued to cry, and eventually the whistle of the kettle joined in. Anna stood holding her daughter. She again imagined Thomas walking up the Adolfsallee, she and Amalia leaning out the window waving at him before running down the stairs as fast as they could, laughing and crying at the same time. She knew it would not happen like this, but it was a nice story. Maybe it would happen. There must be a good reason why he had not answered any of the messages she sent.

The early morning sun already felt oppressive. Anna found a small spot of shade in the central court of the Collecting Point waiting for Captain Cooper. She wondered if she still had a job, after disappearing Friday afternoon. Begging for forgiveness when the topic of her absence came up was the only strategy she had thought of so far. She stood on the bottom step of the entry, her back against the wall, and tried to stay out of the way of the mad activity. Everyone had something to do or somewhere to go and she felt conspicuous. She tugged nervously at her pants, and then tried to tame her hair. In the rush to leave the house she had forgotten to pin it up and now it hung loose around her shoulders, dry as straw and just as straight.

"Hi there." The voice surprised her and she swung around to see the short Long, the MP from the guardhouse. He sauntered over, one hand digging in his breast pocket. "You waiting for someone?" He fished out his cigarettes and offered her one. Anna held up her palm and shook her head although she would have loved to have it to settle her stomach.

"I am to go with Captain Cooper to survey some buildings. I mean, I am to translate. I was told to wait here."

"You and the architect, huh? Well you've got yourself a nice day for it. Where's your sidekick?"

"I'm sorry?"

"Sidekick, you know, your partner in crime."

Anna looked puzzled.

"Your daughter, the cutie." He chuckled.

"Cutie?"

"I mean she's cute, you know, adorable. She's a smart one too, but I bet you know that. Anyway, where is she?"

"She is staying with a family up on the hill. They will bring her down this afternoon."

"You mean that lady who brings kiddies down here every day? What is it, some kind of school?"

"Not really. Just sort of a babysitting service."

Anna paused. She had left her child with someone she knew nothing about except that she had survived the war, just as Anna had. *What had Frieda done to make it this far?* Everyone who was still standing was suspect to Anna. When Amalia and Anna had arrived at the house that morning, Frieda had greeted them with a smile and taken Amalia to play with some dolls. Two other children—a little boy and his older sister—had already arrived and were happy to be there. It seemed everything was good and proper. But Anna knew appearances were not to be trusted.

"You okay, Fraulein?" Long was smiling again. He rocked on his heels as he took a drag from his cigarette and exhaled a plume of smoke straight into the sky.

"Yes, of course," Anna said. "And it's Frau. Frau Klein."

"I see. And where is Herr Klein these days?"

A jeep pulled up and stopped with a screech of its tires, inches away from Anna's feet. Long straightened and took two steps back.

"Corporal Long, did I just catch you fraternizing with this nice lady?" Cooper jumped out of the driver's seat and walked around the jeep to the MP. "I believe there's somewhere else you need to be, am I right?"

Long muttered a "yes sir," and ambled off across the courtyard. Anna tried to look ready for anything by picking up her bag and throwing it confidently over one shoulder.

Cooper grinned at her. He looked fit and rested and Anna wondered how the *Amis* maintained their continual energetic optimism. It made her tired.

"Good morning, Frau Klein. I see you are ready for our little field trip. Where is the duchess today?" Cooper relaxed as he spoke and turned his attention to digging around in the back seat of the jeep.

"She is well taken care of," Anna said. "She won't be coming here again."

"Well that's good, but I was just getting to like her." He smiled. "Maybe there's a chance she'll come visit me again. I did promise to show her some of the loot we've got coming in next week. Should be a grand day around here. You won't want to miss it. Anyway, she's feeling better?"

Anna shook her head to show she hadn't understood.

"Friday afternoon. You were gone. I asked your friend, that German fellow, the young one you were talking to, where you went.

He told me the girl was sick and you had taken her home. I figured you stayed with her."

Not my friend, Anna thought. "Yes, she was ill but she's much better," she said.

"Too much sun, am I right?" He shook his head. "I told you. Anyway, Frau Obersdorfer came looking for you and I told her you were working with me starting immediately. That did the trick. Here." He handed her an envelope that Anna recognized as her weekly wages. "But I'm sure she docked you for Friday." He grinned.

Anna took the envelope and nodded her thanks, embarrassed that he had lied for her and annoyed that she was now beholden to him, if only a little. "Captain, may I ask just what is it that I am to do today?"

"Ah, I was just getting to that. Here, jump in and I'll give you the full debriefing." He gestured her toward the passenger side of the jeep.

She climbed inside and felt a strange rush come over her. After seeing all the film reels of American generals driving around in jeeps and liberating the European continent, it felt surreal to be in one herself, as if she had crossed some invisible boundary into another world. The seat was as hard as a church pew and the floor was dirty. This was not at all what she had imagined.

Cooper slid into the driver's side. "Okay, so here's the story: You are going to be my navigator, my translator, and my go-between for the locals. I'll rely on you to explain to me everything they tell you and then to write it down in the report. Is that clear?"

"Yes." Anna tried to look like was she was up for the job but she'd rather have been sitting back on her crate in the typing pool with Frau Obersdorfer looming over her. She was not in the mood for adventure of any kind.

Cooper handed her a map and a folder with blank custody forms and notepaper. Anna stacked the papers on her lap as Cooper reached under the seat and pulled out a paper bag, which he held up. "Since we'll be out all day I got the canteen to make us sandwiches—I think it's real cheese. We'll have ourselves a nice picnic." He smiled, eyes twinkling. "Are you ready?"

Anna nodded and the jeep lurched forward. As they bumped through the gate, the sentry saluted. Within moments they were cruising south on the Wilhelmstrasse, away from the old city and toward the train station.

So this is how the world looks to Eisenhower, Anna thought as she watched the people and ruins fly by, removed from their immediacy. Now she was separated from her world, looking in from the outside. Cooper would never understand what it was like to be on the other side. Even when you got out of the jeep and walked around, if you were an *Ami*, you knew you could always get back in and drive away. That was the difference. If it weren't for Amalia, Anna might have liked to stay in the jeep forever.

Her hair whipped about her head as the jeep sped up. She tried to hold it back with one hand but this meant she had to let go of the papers Cooper had given her. She gave up and pretended not to care. They drove in silence and Anna looked around at her new hometown. When the jeep stopped at an intersection where an MP was directing traffic, a group of young women with children crossed the street in front of them. Two little boys turned and waved at Cooper and flashed the victory sign with their little fingers. Cooper chuckled and returned the gesture. One mother, wearing a faded cotton dress and men's shoes turned and looked blankly at the two of them. Her eyes locked with Anna's. The woman was holding a little boy of maybe three years by the hand. The child struggled to keep up and was crying. The woman turned away and Anna looked down at her hands.

"Let's move it please, Corporal," Cooper shouted. "We're not here to get a suntan." He returned the MPs salute as the jeep passed. Anna turned to watch the group of women.

"So much to do," said Cooper. "So much to repair."

"Yes, the bombs really hit hard here," Anna said.

"No, not that," said Cooper. "So many lives."

Anna swallowed hard and said nothing.

"Oh I'm sorry. That was—I shouldn't have said that." Cooper shook his head. At the next intersection, he turned onto the Mainzerstrasse and accelerated as the foot traffic and bicycles diminished. He hit the steering wheel with the heel of his hand and turned to her. "Oh, come on now. It's a beautiful day. We get to drive out and look at beautiful German architecture. We have cheese sandwiches. Maybe we'll get lucky and find some missing treasures and bring them back. You never know." He smiled a big American smile. "You gotta try to see the good that's left."

"And where is that? I don't see it anywhere." She gestured to the ruins of a bombed building to the right, its skeleton standing among the growing weeds. "Is this it?" Anna spat the words at Cooper but her anger was only there to cover the overwhelming sense of sadness that constantly lapped at her feet. She wanted to curl up on the jeep's front seat and cry.

Cooper didn't respond. He drove on, tipping a hand occasionally to a passing soldier, smiling at waving children. Anna felt childish and embarrassed. Why was this so easy for them? She looked at his face with its delta of laugh lines flowing out from under the frames of his sunglasses. She softened a bit.

"You are from Iowa?" she asked. "Where is that? Is it pretty there?"

"In Iowa? Oh sure, it's pretty if you like your country flat and fields full of corn. There's plenty of both." He looked at her. "My parents have a farm. But I left to become an architect." He shifted gears as they sped up. "Not to say I don't like farming. I still go back in the fall to help with the harvest. But I'm not right for the farm life. Chicago's where I work."

Anna felt the warm air on her face and tried to imagine a place called Chicago. "You are an architect there? What are you doing here?"

"You mean because I'm so old?" he laughed. "Yeah, well I was too old to serve in the regular army but I volunteered and they gave me a nice desk job. I helped plan barracks and design bases stateside. Not exactly high design but I was doing my part. I heard about the Monuments Men unit when they first formed it and how they were looking for architects and people willing to get shot at while protecting the landmarks of Europe. I applied for a transfer and next thing I knew I was in Tuscany, ducking from snipers and trying to keep some Renaissance church from being flattened. I always wanted to do a grand European tour, but the bombs really made it interesting. Still, it's a free trip, so I guess you get what you pay for." He exhaled as if to disperse the memory into the air.

He turned the jeep onto the sidewalk where it lurched to a stop in front of a three-story brick building as big as a city block. Piles of rubble gathered at its base underneath boarded-up windows. Like at the Collecting Point, there was much coming and going of building materials and workers.

"What is this place?" Anna asked as she squinted into the sun.

"State archive," Cooper said. "The structure took some secondary damage from that." He shot a thumb toward the nearly flattened train station to the west. "Leaky roof, blown out windows. Nothing major, but it's not watertight. I've already surveyed it and just need to check on the work. Come on."

Anna followed him inside, and stood by awkwardly as he talked with another American about things that sounded very bureaucratic—orders of glass and deliveries of roof tiles. Cooper stared at a clipboard and signed his name to papers that the other American slid under his pen. The place smelled musty, like an old library. Anna stared at a crate marked *Landgraf Hessen Homburg 1622-1699* that sat next to an open office door. She did the math. Three hundred twenty-three years. What were the last seven years compared to that? A blink of an eye. Pieces of paper documenting the mundane details of feudal life survived three centuries, but human life was as fleeting as a cloud and just as trivial. The wave of hopelessness rose to her ankles and she stamped her foot.

Cooper laughed about something and slapped his colleague on the back. "All right, let's go, Frau Klein. I'm done here."

That was easy, Anna thought and allowed herself to relax just a little. Her stomach rumbled in response.

Back in the jeep she tucked the papers under her thighs and tried to get a handle on her hair. They drove back toward the city but then turned west, following the scarred main artery of the Dotzheimerstrasse in the direction of the once-verdant outskirts. After a while, the city loosened its hold on the buildings and they became more spread out, as if they were trying to escape to greener pastures. A vast compound of barracks appeared, its enormous box-like buildings arranged around an open space so large it made the whole place look like the building blocks of some giant. The jeep took almost a full minute to pass the buildings.

"DP camp," Cooper said, pointing with his chin.

"I'm sorry?" Anna asked, shouting over the jeep's engine.

"DP camp. Displaced Persons. I think we've got about seven thousand in there. You can thank your lucky stars you didn't end up there. It's pretty miserable."

"Seven thousand? That's bigger than my town. What kind of displaced persons?"

"Mostly Germans like you. People fleeing the Reds—the Russians—they just keep coming."

Anna did thank her lucky stars as they drove on toward the rolling hills for several kilometers. Cooper slowed to a stop outside an iron gate that was propped open by a piece of scrap metal. He consulted a map that he pulled from under the seat. They were well and truly in the country now and Anna wondered what could possibly be of interest here.

"Yes, this is it." Cooper held his arms out as if to present the property to a prospective buyer.

The villa was small and charming, looking content on its little hill. Some damage was visible on the roof but, overall, it was in good condition. The long drive leading up to the main entry was lined with the stumps that remained after the firewood harvest. What looked to have been a charming garden with manicured hedges and pools of flowers was now an empty dustbowl with the odd patch of weeds adding anemic splashes of green.

"What happens now?" asked Anna.

"We go in, we say hello, we have a look around. See what's going on. If there's some people in there, you'll need to help me talk to them. And, I'll need you to help me secure the building. Any DPs in there need to move along and any damage must be documented. Anything valuable that can't be secured we take back with us. We leave a custody receipt, of course. Are you ready?"

"Ready, yes." Anna thought the job sounded straightforward enough.

Cooper put the jeep in gear and stomped on the gas.

chapter seven

Anna stood back as Cooper leaned into the heavy wooden door with his shoulder and then kicked the base with a dirty boot to loosen it from the frame. There was no need—the door swung open easily and he strode inside without hesitation. *Like he owns the place,* thought Anna. Which he did, technically. She followed at a distance as he checked each of the three doors that led off the main entry hall into smaller rooms. He had taken his Colt .45 from the back seat of the jeep and was carrying the gun awkwardly in his right hand. Anna had not considered that they would need to be armed. She hugged her papers to her chest to muffle her pounding heart.

"All looks clear." Cooper returned the Colt to its holster. "Okay. Let's see what we can find."

Just then Anna saw something move behind the balustrade of the second floor. She gasped and looked up.

"What?" Cooper whispered, his hand moving back to his holster.

"Something moved up there." Anna stepped back and leaned against the wall at the foot of the stairs.

Cooper bounded past her up the stairs, waving the gun in front of him. "Hello there? United States Army here. Come on out now." He motioned for Anna to come up. She took a deep breath and followed. On the landing, he took her elbow and pulled her alongside him as they walked down the corridor. Several closed doors ran along the wall to her right, but he was headed for the one at the end. He pushed it open.

The room seemed empty, abandoned to its fate. Drop-cloth-covered chairs and a large bed stripped of its sheets occupied the space at random. An old blanket lay rumpled on the bed and, in the corner, under an open window, lay a pile of rocks. Anna nudged Cooper and pointed to dust smudges on the floor that tracked between the bed and the bathroom door, and then to the large wardrobe that stood directly opposite them. Cooper nodded and strode across the room. He flung open the wardrobe door with one hand, the other pointing the .45 into the dark opening.

"Come out now, you," he bellowed. Then he took a step back. "Well, I'll be damned."

Anna squinted to see what the wardrobe had revealed. A boy huddled on the floor, bony blackened knees drawn to his chest. The three of them locked eyes for a moment, then the child bolted for the door. Anna dropped her papers as she caught him by the arm and spun around with the force of his escape. He tried to wrestle free but Anna held on, grabbing his other arm and pulling him close as hard as she could.

"*Um Gottes Willen*, for God's sake, what are you doing in there?" she cried. The boy thrashed and Anna hugged him as tight as she could. His head snapped back and hit her squarely on the nose, causing her to loosen her grip. He tried to get his footing on the wood floor but slipped and fell back. Anna grabbed him by the waist of his pants and held on. "Don't be scared. We won't hurt you."

Cooper stood rooted to the spot, pistol pointed in their direction. "Ask him who he is and what he is doing here," he whispered. "Go on."

"I was just doing that, sir. If you could put your gun away, it would help, I think," Anna said, sitting back onto the floor with the boy wrapped inside her arms. Cooper stashed the weapon and took several steps back, palms raised in sarcastic apology.

"What is your name?" Anna asked gently. "My name is Anna. I am your friend. Can you tell me your name?"

"Are you an *Ami*?" the boy snapped.

"No, I'm not. Only he is." She pointed to Cooper. "What are you doing here?"

"Let me go! I am not talking to him." His eyes shot at the American. "I don't like *Amis*. Who are you?"

"My name is Anna Klein." Anna loosened her grip to turn the boy around and face her. "Do you want me to tell him to go?"

He nodded and Anna used a free hand to wave Cooper out of the room. His eyes threw her a silent question, but he obliged and closed the door behind him.

Anna took a good look at the boy. His eyes were big in his hollow face, his lips dry and crusty. A small scar ran from the corner of his mouth down his chin and disappeared into a scrawny neck that was ringed with dirt. Anna could feel the bones of his shoulders in her palms. He seemed frail as bird and he couldn't have been more than ten years old.

"Now tell me *Kind*, what is your name?" she asked again.

The boy looked at the floor as if he wanted to dissolve into it. "Grünewald Oskar," he said under his breath.

"Oskar, where are your parents?" Anna took one of his hands in hers. "Do you know?"

"Yes."

"Well, where are they?"

He shook his head.

"No? Tell me please, so we can find them for you."

The boy snorted. "They are dead. My parents are dead." His eyes dared her to respond.

Anna pulled him close and eventually he softened and crawled into her lap. She rocked back and forth as they sat in silence. "You are safe now. Don't be scared," she whispered into his matted hair. After a few minutes, Cooper peeked through the door, eyebrows raised like question marks on his face. She shook her head for him to leave them alone, but he opened the door anyway. Anna sighed.

"He says his parents are dead," she whispered. Oskar turned his head to see Cooper enter the room and bolted from Anna's lap like Jesse Owens on fire. He was down the stairs before Anna could get to her feet.

"I said stay out," she shouted as she ran past Cooper and took the stairs two at a time. The front door stood wide open and Oskar's footsteps cascaded down the marble stairs. The sun blinded her and she put a hand to her eyes to shield them. Oskar ran along the path toward the road, his skinny legs spinning in panic. Cooper appeared at her side but she held her arm out for him to stop. "Let him be," she said. "He can't go far. He has nowhere to go."

Cooper let out a sharp breath. "Frau Klein, I am not in the babysitting business, I keep telling you. We are here to work."

"I *am* working Captain. I am being—what do you call it? Your go-between." Anna cocked her head. "What do you suggest we do now?"

"We go about our business and see if he comes back. Then we'll figure it out." His tone was neutral and hard to read. "Go get your papers and let's get started."

Oskar came to a stop outside the remnants of the iron gate, hands resting on his knees, trying to catch his breath. The run had worn him out. Anna sat down on the steps. "I'll just wait here until he comes back."

"Frau Klein, we are here to work, and you work for me," Cooper barked. "I can't stop for every waif and urchin running the streets. There are too many of them and that's the Red Cross' job. If you don't care for this job I'll be glad to find someone else who does. Now let's go."

"Yes sir, Mr. Captain," Anna said. "But just a moment, please." She went to the jeep and fished the brown bag from under the seat. She laid the two cheese sandwiches on the parapet by the front door. "For when he comes back."

They spent an hour assessing damage inside the house, which was minimal. Most of it seemed to have been caused by marauding soldiers. The roof leaked in the kitchen and the place had been cleaned out of any valuables. A few pieces of furniture hid under dust covers but nothing was very interesting. Cooper walked with purpose through every room and pointed out damage or lack thereof. Anna took notes but peeked outside to get a glimpse of the boy when she could. Oskar sat by the gate for a while, a small gray figure hunched with his back to them. When the sun was overhead and the air thick with heat, he started back up the path. He was halfway back when Anna saw him walking, hands shoved into the pockets of his too-short pants.

"He's coming back," she said. "Could you leave him alone this time, please? He doesn't trust you. Maybe I can find out where he lives and we can take him home." She straightened her papers on a little sideboard in the entry hall and put them back in the folder.

Cooper stood in the doorway and watched the boy approach, arms crossed across his chest like a vexed father. "Oh all right, Frau Klein. I guess he's going to get my sandwich too, right?" He smiled. "I'll stay out of it for now, but we have to move on soon." He stepped away from the door.

After Oskar had eaten both sandwiches, Anna sat with him on the steps. The color had returned to his cheeks and his body was calm. She stroked his hair. "Now, Oskar you must tell me how you came to be here. Tell me everything you remember. I won't tell the *Ami* anything you don't want me to, all right?"

Oskar stared at his shoes, mouth set firm in defiance. She sensed the fear returning to his body. He put his chin on his knees and began to play with the hole in the tip of his right shoe.

"Come on, child. Don't you want to go home?"

He turned his face toward her. "Why are you with that *Ami*?"

Anna bent over and put her cheek on her knees to put her face close to his. "You know, I have a little girl. Her name is Amalia. We came here and had nothing. The *Ami* gave me a job so we can have money and a place to live. That's what I am doing here. It's my job."

"Working for the *Amis*? That's not a job for a German woman." He looked at her with cold eyes. She recognized the well-drilled tone of disdain and contempt that was the mark of party members and the thugs they empowered. She inhaled. "Well, the *Amis* are the ones that have the jobs to give now," she said. "And I have to take care of my family. So here I am."

"Where is your husband?"

She decided to play along for a few more rounds. "He stayed behind in Thuringia. He is a doctor there, in charge of the hospital."

"You should have stayed with him. Your place is with him, not here with the *Amis*."

She knew he was only mimicking what he had been taught but his tone irked her. *Damned Nazis. Now even this had to be undone.* "Tell me Oskar, how old are you?" she asked.

He hesitated. "I am eight years old."

"You have been through a lot at eight years old."

He had never known a world where people didn't bark orders at others, shame them or belittle them, threaten, coerce or terrify them.

"I wanted to fight, but it was over before I got old enough." He sat up straight and crossed his arms. "I was going to fly airplanes. I was going to bomb *their* cities and *their* houses. So they would know what it feels like. But now I can't even do that." He slumped again.

Anna reached out to place a hand on his back, but he jerked away. "I would never work for the *scheiss Amis*. You are a disgrace."

Anna sighed. "Yes, perhaps I am. But for now let's worry about you. Why don't you tell me why you are here?"

Oskar stood up and walked down the stairs to the gravel path. He kicked at the stones and dragged his feet in the dust, making a scraping sound Anna had always found irritating. She settled in for the waiting game.

Cooper's American footsteps approached behind her. Decisive, confident. "So, Frau Klein, how's it going? He talking or what?" He smiled at the boy who glared up at him.

"Not yet. Give me some more time please, Captain. He's very upset."

Cooper sighed. "Frau Klein, we have to move on. You can talk to him in the jeep. We'll take him to the camp and they'll sort him out. Find his family or whatever he needs." He held a hand out to pull Oskar to his feet. "Come on son, we'll take you somewhere safe," he said, his voice too loud.

"What's he shouting about?" Oskar asked Anna.

"He says we'll take you to the American camp. They have doctors there and they'll take care of you."

"I don't need a doctor. I am not going with you." The boy shoved his hands into his pockets

"They can help you find your family," Anna said.

"I told you, my parents are dead," he said. "Thanks to his bombs." He pointed at Cooper, and before Anna could stop him, he jumped up and ran around the side of the building.

"Now what?" Cooper shouted.

Anna stood and started after the boy. "His family died in a bombing raid. Just let me talk to him, please." She turned the corner and stopped. Oskar had disappeared down a set of stairs leading to a basement. She shook her head and followed him into the dank blackness behind the door.

"Oskar? I know you are in here," she called out as she felt her way along a stone wall. "Listen to me, child. Your family died in the bombs? Well this is something we share, you and me. My family did too. My mother and my father." She paused but only silence responded. "So, now you can believe me. I can help you. We can find you a real home. You don't have to live here anymore. And you don't have to be alone."

Her eyes were slow to adjust to the darkness. She stood still and listened, but no sound came. A click, and then a dirty yellow light hovered in the center of the room. Oskar stood, one arm still raised to hold the cord of the bare bulb.

Anna blinked. For a moment she couldn't focus on anything but the boy, but then the details of the room sharpened. The space was small with a low ceiling and dirt floor. Rows of shelves lined the back wall and stacks of large, flat packages leaned upright against each other like files in a cabinet. To the right more crates were stacked on the floor almost to the ceiling, an empty gilded frame as big as a bed sat abandoned in the corner. Anna turned slowly. She had expected to find a stash of canned food, household goods, or some furniture hidden for safekeeping. The only furniture was a long table along the left wall, also piled high with paintings and frames. Underneath the table a large landscape painting leaned against the wall. Next to it, flat on the floor, a portrait of an elegantly dressed man stared up at her. There was a still life of flowers and a bowl of fruit against a dark background, a painting of a woman in a yellow dress twirling a string of pearls between her fingers, and a small painting of Christ on the cross with Mary at his feet.

Anna put her hand to her mouth. "Oskar, what is this place?"

The boy had not moved from his spot in the middle of the room. "They were here when I came. I don't know anything about it." He stepped back and knocked over an empty gold frame that leaned against the shelf.

Anna picked up the frame. "These probably all belong to the estate. Someone put them here for safekeeping."

The door creaked. "Frau Klein, get the boy and let's go. Or we leave him. Time's a-wasting." Cooper took three more steps and froze.

"Holy mother. What the hell is this?" He stared at Oskar and Anna, who was still holding the frame. "Frau Klein, what are you doing?"

"What? I am helping the boy. He says these paintings have been here the whole time he has."

Cooper's head swiveled one direction and then another. He put his hands on hips and chewed on his bottom lip. Anna put her arm around Oskar's shoulder.

"Well what do you know," Cooper said. "I mean look at all… Well this is something. This has to be the biggest stash we've found so far. Usually it's been a handful of paintings, but this has got to be hundreds of them." For several moments, the three of them stood rooted to the spot as if they were waiting for something else to happen.

Cooper looked through the paintings lying on the table. He pulled some out, leaned them upright along the wall and then stepped back to get a full view. "These paintings are the real deal, not some backwater weekend landscape dabbling. Just look at that one." He pointed at a large painting that showed a pudgy girl in a yellow dress. She stood on a chair to look out a window but had turned her face to gaze out of the painting directly at them, her plump hand under her chin. "Look, it must be something English, don't you think? Amazing!"

"That's not English, that's German." Anna said. "The English didn't paint people this way, at least the Romantics didn't. And this looks Romantic to me."

Cooper looked at her as if she'd just spoken Chinese.

"In fact I'd say this is probably by Runge. I don't know his work so well, but he painted children, and he painted them huge, like this one. See how she seems gigantic? Like a small adult, really. He tended to put them in foreground like this so they dwarf the landscape. The English did it more the other way around, the landscape absorbed the people."

"Runge? Who is Runge? How the hell do you know all this?" Cooper asked.

"Philipp Otto Runge. I am almost certain it's him. He was a German Romantic painter. Look at the composition, and the way the light streams through the window and onto her dress. The colors are definitely German, more toward the blue and green. And look," she waved her hand over the canvas, "the English didn't render such crisp depictions. They used more impasto—more texture. And there's a windmill in the background. He worked in Hamburg, I think. They have windmills there. Is there a label on the back?"

Cooper seemed amused. "Well, well," he said. "You've been keeping something from me, Frau Klein. Shame on you."

"What? Because I can tell an English Romantic from a German one?" she shrugged. "And, all right, my mother's brother was an art dealer. He let me work for him at his gallery in Salzburg sometimes on my holidays when I was young. He taught me a lot. I enjoyed it." She raised her hands to deflect Cooper's next question. "He left for America when the Nazis declared their war on art. He wanted no part of it and said he was too old to fight the bastards. So he left. What?"

"And where is he now? New York?"

"No, he died on the ship on the way to America."

"Oh. I'm sorry. And his collection?"

"He sold it all before he left to fund his emigration. Since he was, you know, 'Aryan,' it was easy for him. The Nazis were such art dilettantes. They bought anything they could get their hands on. But the Jewish dealers suffered terribly. My uncle quietly gave some of his collection to several Jewish colleagues to help them raise funds for their own escape, but the Nazis would force them to sell for ridiculous sums, nothing compared to what the pieces were worth, if they got anything for them at all. It was so terrible." Anna shrugged. "All because Hitler was obsessed with art. They all wanted to be like him. So, is there a label on the back?"

Cooper turned the painting over. "Just one. It says *Breuer Darmstadt*. Maybe a gallery in Darmstadt? I bet we could find who this belongs to." He bent down and ran his hands across the surface of the painting. "Why did you never tell any of us about your knowledge of art?"

"No one ever asked, and I wasn't going to volunteer anything. We've learned not to talk much."

"You didn't think it would be helpful, your knowledge about art?" Cooper was incredulous.

"Helpful to whom exactly, Captain? To the Americans?"

"Yes, to the Americans, Frau Klein. It would have been good to know there was a knowledgeable person in our midst."

"I would think the Americans can send their own experts to do this work. Why do you need our help?"

Cooper sighed. "We need all the help we can get. What I want to know is why was this art never registered or documented under Paragraph 51? All valuable property must be registered and inventoried, so we know what all is floating around out here. That should have been done ages ago. Who is hiding it? And why?"

Anna laughed. "I imagine the owners would like to keep their collection, not have you send it to America."

"America? Who says it's going to America?"

Anna paused. "Captain, everyone knows you are taking the art back to America. The spoils of war. Everything is yours now, isn't it?"

Cooper's eyes flashed and Anna was taken aback. She had expected a chuckle and a smart reply.

"Who says that?" he growled. "Tell me."

Anna rolled her eyes and repeated herself, speaking deliberately as if talking to a small child. "We all know that's what you are doing, you Monuments Men." She made a grandiose gesture like an emcee introducing the star of the show. "Why else would you even get involved in these details? "

Cooper took a step toward her, finger wagging. "Listen to me, Frau Klein, very carefully. You and I need to straighten a few things out. I have tolerated your attitude—hell, I can even understand it—but now I am going to say something so we can clear the air. Here goes: We are not like you, like the Nazis. We do not take things that are not ours just because they are shiny and pretty and we think we are entitled. This is cultural property that belongs to the people of Germany. I am here to see that it gets back to the people who are the rightful owners."

Anna held her ground but her blood simmered. She knew this moment had been coming and the words flew out of her. "Like us? No, you are not like us, Captain! You are the saviors. We are the sinners. We will pay for what we have done, what was done in our name when we looked the other way." She waved an arm in Oskar's direction. "Look at that. Look at our future. Look at what we did to our own children. No, you are not like us at all. And I hope you never will be." She turned her back to him and pretended to sort through the canvases on the shelf. "And just to be clear, Captain, I am not a Nazi and I never was." Her hands shook.

Cooper sighed and looked at Oskar, who shrank behind a cabinet. "Don't you see Frau Klein? That's why we are here. To put back the things that are beautiful. To give them back to you. To Germany. That's a start isn't it? I am not here to take anything." He shook his head and slumped his shoulders. "Do people really think we are here to take the art?"

"Can you blame us?" asked Anna. "After everything that's happened?" She smiled at the boy. "Everything's all right, Oskar," she whispered. "He's just yelling at me. Don't worry." She winked.

"Look, Frau Klein. We are not taking the art. But this is a major find. We have to get this back to the Collecting Point, prepare an inventory, and find out where it belongs. For sure this doesn't belong to this little old villa. There's something else going on here." He looked at his watch. "Damn, it's too late to get a truck out here today, so we'll have to lock up and be back first thing in the morning. We'll take the boy to the DP camp on the way back to town. Tell him to get his things. I'll get the camera and take some pictures in the meantime."

Once Cooper was gone, Oskar came out from behind the frame and scowled at Anna. "So what happens to me now?" he sniffed.

"We are going to take you to the camp where they will take care of you."

"I am not going to any camp."

"You'll have a bed and a nice meal and there will be other children there too. They will help you find a place to go."

Oskar shook his head, his eyes big as chestnuts. "I like it fine here. I won't leave."

"No, you can't stay here, who will take care of you?"

"I can take of myself already. I am all right. I can get a job."

Anna laughed. "What will your job be? Supreme Commander?"

"Don't be stupid," he snarled. "I can do things. I can stay here and guard the art."

Anna laughed. "No you can't. That's the *Amis'* job now. You are relieved of duty." She paused. "Is that why you are here? To guard the art for someone?"

Oskar kicked at the ground. "No, of course not. Who cares about some stupid pictures anyway?" He shoved his hands into his pockets and kicked at the dirt on the floor. Anna took him by the shoulders and pushed him to the door. "Go get your things. We have to go soon."

Cooper came back holding an ancient camera with an oversized flashbulb. "I think this might be okay," he said as he loaded the film into the chamber. He saw Anna's blank stare. "What? Something happen?"

"No. Everything's fine. Do you think maybe this is some kind of storage place for the black market?"

Cooper shrugged. "Could be. All this stuff is technically contraband. Not allowed to change hands under Paragraph 51. You think the kid is involved?"

Anna shook her head, but she was not convinced.

"Well, we'll get to the bottom of it. Right now I really need to get back." He pointed the camera at the shelf and clicked the shutter. In the brightness of the flash, the room with its camouflaged treasures was frozen for a moment in time. He turned and took several more photos in each direction. When he was done, she tugged the cord on the light and followed him to the door.

They found Oskar sitting on the front steps. "Where are your things?" asked Anna impatiently.

Oskar stood up and dug his hands into the pockets of his pants. He pulled out a pocket knife, a bottle opener and a pencil and showed them to her on the flat of his hand. "Here," he said. "But look, you can just leave me here. I'll watch out for the paintings for the *Ami*. Really.

Tell him." He fiddled with the bottle opener before putting it back in his pocket and looking at Anna with expectation.

"No, I'm sorry," said Anna. "Let's go." She pushed him into the back of the jeep and took her seat on the passenger side. She half expected the boy to make another run for the house, but instead he stared at his lap, as if waiting for a verdict to be handed down. Cooper threw the camera on Anna's lap and climbed in behind the wheel. As the jeep bounced down the lane toward the main road, Anna grabbed the dashboard and turned to smile at Oskar. He sat sideways on the back seat, bony knees pulled to his chest, just as he had been when she found him. Tears spilled from his eyes and washed his dirty cheeks as he stared back toward the house.

chapter eight

The ride was not long but every moment seemed taut and stretched to its limit.

"Will they really take good care of him at the camp?" Anna shouted over the noise of the engine.

"Oh, sure. There are doctors there, and other kids too. Really, I promise—he will be fine." Cooper smiled.

"But you told me how grim the camp is."

The American looked at her. "Well, it's not the Ritz, but being there beats him living out at the villa by himself, don't you think?"

On the outskirts of the city, the camp's endless barbed wire fence rose up and lined the street on the right, and Anna could understand the boy's reluctance. Cooper turned the jeep down the main entry road and then onto an alley between two rows of plain stone barracks.

People were everywhere, civilians and soldiers, children and old people. It seemed like a very organized town unto itself. A makeshift playground had been set up on a small patch of green with a swing made from an old jeep tire hanging from a tree. Children played happily, chasing a ball and then each other around the tree. The women who sat nearby stopped their chatter and turned to watch the jeep approach, their heads swiveling as if following a tennis ball across an invisible net.

"Who runs this place?" Anna asked.

"This is UNRRA's territory. United Nations Relief and Rehabilitation Administration. He'll be just fine here. As you can see, he's not alone." He sighed and Anna thought she saw a mournful shadow cross his face.

"See if you can find someone to keep an eye on him," Cooper said. "I'll deal with the paperwork."

Anna nodded and reminded him of the boy's name and age. She scanned the faces of the women on the bench and chose the one at the end, who looked about the same age as she, with wiry brown hair framing large, watery eyes and a sharp blade of a nose. She wore a tattered brown cotton dress and men's shoes. She looked weathered, but sat straight and tall, as if defying a weight bearing down on her shoulders.

Anna took a deep breath and shot a glance at Oskar, who regarded her with angry mistrust. "All right," she muttered. She got out of the jeep and approached the woman, her heart pounding.

"Hello. I hope you can help me." Anna tried on an American smile and extended her hand. She felt stupid but kept going. "I am Anna Klein. And this is..."

The woman recoiled as if Anna were pointing a gun at her. "*Was wollen Sie?*" she asked. Her head turned sideways but her eyes focused on Anna's.

Anna stopped and waved her hand toward the jeep. "This boy needs to stay here for a while. We just found him." She looked back at Cooper, who leaned against the jeep watching her.

"Tell her he came from the country," Cooper offered. "I'll go and get him registered with one of the nurses." He marched off to the nearest building.

Anna sat down next to the woman and leaned forward, elbows on knees. She looked at Oskar, who made a heroic effort to not look at her.

"The Captain would like to know if you could help take care of the boy, until we, I mean they, the Americans, or maybe the Red Cross, can decide what to do with him. Could you help us?" Anna smiled. The woman folded her arms across her chest.

Anna tried a different tack. "Look, he has no one at all to help him. His parents are dead." She paused. "I am a mother, too, and I will try to do what I can, but I can't keep him. Would you please help me? He is a sweet boy."

The woman shifted her eyes toward Oskar and chewed on the inside of her cheek. She pointed a skeletal finger toward a slight boy sitting at the base of the tree, scraping a stick through the dirt. "That's my boy," she said. "He's all I have left."

Anna stared at the little boy under the tree, trying to tune out the chatter of the women complaining about the *Amis* and lamenting the conditions of the shelter and the quality of the food. Somewhere a girl cried out and a woman bolted from the bench in response.

"I have a daughter," Anna said. She wondered if Amalia was all she had left, too.

"What is the boy's name?" the woman asked.

"His name is Oskar."

"He will need to be properly registered with the agency. Yes, I will do what I can, which is not much. But I will make sure he is looked after."

Anna felt a breeze on her face. "Thank you, Frau…"

"Niemeyer," said the woman. "Maria." She offered her hand.

Anna introduced herself and they shook hands. She stood and made a show of excitement as she walked toward Oskar. He stared at her from under defiant eyebrows. Anna held out her hand to help him out of the jeep.

"Come on now, Oskar. This is a nice place. They will take care of you." Her voice was too enthusiastic. She felt like a salesman on commission, trying to sell him an overpriced suit he didn't need.

The boy slid onto his feet but made no move toward the playground. "I don't want to stay here. I want to go with you," he mumbled, all the bravado gone.

Anna's heart tightened. She squatted down and squeezed his bony arms. "I promise you, Oskar, I will come back and help you. For now, you go with Frau Niemeyer and get settled. Everything will be all right. I know it will. She tried to hug him, but he pulled away, reapplying his tough veneer. She gave him a little push in the direction of the playground where Maria stood with her arm held out. "Go now, and I will see you soon."

He started to walk and then turned to look at her. "Tomorrow?" he said. "You'll come tomorrow?"

Anna nodded. Another lie. She felt as if someone had thrown a heavy blanket on her, blocking out the air and light. She put a hand on the jeep to steady herself.

The boy turned and shuffled away as Cooper came out of the building.

"All right then, I think we can call it a day." Cooper handed her some papers. "Here. The boy's registration information. You hang on to it. I got the paperwork started but he needs to go in and be interviewed and photographed. There's a doctor that will check him out too. You find someone to watch out for him?"

Anna nodded and took the papers. Oskar stood next to Maria and her son, hands in pockets, shoulders hunched. Maria rubbed his head and talked to him. When she saw Anna looking, she raised a reassuring hand and nodded. Anna returned the gesture.

"It's all going to be okay, don't you worry," Cooper said, looking at his watch. "Now let's get going. It's past your quitting time and I'm not authorized to pay overtime," he chuckled.

Anna turned away from the playground with a heavy heart. "What time is it now?

"It's almost six. I mean 1800. I still can't get the hang of that."

Anna gasped. "Oh dear God. I was supposed to be at the Collecting Point at five o'clock to meet Amalia." Her voice rose an octave.

Cooper rolled his eyes. "Take it easy. We'll go right now. I am sure she's fine. I mean you did leave her there by herself all day before, right?"

Anna ignored the low blow. "Let's just go now, please? Captain?"

Cooper grinned and jumped into the jeep. "Yes, yes, here we go. Hop in."

As they drove Anna conjured all possible scenarios of what had happened to Amalia. None was reassuring—at best the girl was scared and worried. She didn't want to think about the worst. She cursed under her breath. Cooper looked at her and offered a sympathetic smile. He reached over and made to pat her leg but then thought better of it and touched her arm instead.

"It's okay, Frau Klein. We'll be there in no time. You'll see."

Cooper accelerated and sped through the city streets, avoiding people on bicycles and clumps of pedestrians. He swerved around a milk truck parked at the curb, barely avoiding the line of women that had formed behind it. "Can I ask you something?" he said, as he righted the jeep and slowed down.

"Yes?" Anna said, but she meant, "No."

"I know you Germans like to be formal and all but if we are going to be working together I feel awful silly calling you Frau Klein all the time. Would it be okay if I call you Anna?"

Anna wondered why Americans were always so set on being informal. She liked formality. It made things clear. "Actually, I am Austrian. Or I was. But yes, I suppose we like to be proper in our dealings with others. It's just good manners. But you may call me Anna if it makes you happy." She did not like where this was going. "And what shall I call you?"

"Oh well, if you want you can call me Coop. That's what everyone calls me. But I guess probably you don't want to do that."

"But what is your first name?" asked Anna.

"Henry."

He did not seem like a Henry at all. "I shall call you Captain," she said.

Cooper snorted. "I figured. Look, the duchess is just fine, you'll see, Anna." He shifted gears.

When they arrived at the Collecting Point, Amalia and Frieda were nowhere to be seen. They had agreed to meet at the rear sentry gate, but no one was there. Cooper stopped the jeep and jumped out to speak to the MP. Anna looked around but saw only the workers and soldiers going about the business of preparing the museum for the coming shipment. *They must have added a second shift*, she thought.

"He says they were here but they left a while ago. Says they went up that way." Cooper pointed up into the hills.

"They must have gone back to the Schilling house," said Anna gathering her things together. She started to get out of the jeep, but Cooper stopped her.

"Hey, don't worry. I'll give you a lift. It'll be faster. Just sit tight." Before Anna could object, the jeep lurched forward. She gave Cooper directions to the Gustav-Freytag-Strasse and barely five minutes later they pulled up outside the Schilling house.

"Thank you," Anna said. "I am sure she's here. You don't need to wait. Do I report back to the typing pool tomorrow?"

"No, ma'am. You're mine now. We may have to go back and secure the villa if we can't get the stuff out of there. You're the only person who knows about it so let's keep it just between us for now, okay?"

Anna squinted at him. "Why? Isn't that breaking the rules?"

"Only a little bit. Trust me on this. I just want to be sure everything stays safe before we can get it back to the Collecting Point. It will be a day, two days tops."

Anna felt uneasy. "I don't like to break any rules," she said, staring straight ahead. She knew what Cooper would say next.

"Yeah, I know. That's a German thing right? Just follow orders? You need to loosen up a little. Relax. It will be just fine."

Anna smiled at her prescience. "Two days," she said. "Then I will have to report you." She turned toward him and raised an eyebrow to show she was joking. "And we'll check on Oskar? At the camp?"

"If that makes you feel better, sure."

Anna rang the bell at the gate and attempted a wave goodbye. "Thank you, Captain. See you tomorrow."

Cooper folded his arms across his chest and sat back, head tilted. Anna rang the bell again and waited a few moments. She looked up at the house but could see no signs of life. Cooper's stare poked at her back and she wished he would go away now, as if he was crossing some imaginary line into her life. She shook the metal gate but it would not budge.

"Here, let me get that." Cooper was beside her. He reached through the slats and pulled on the lock mechanism. The gate unlocked and he pushed it open. "Come on," he said. "Let's see what we can find."

Anna followed him through the garden and stood back as he knocked on the door. She did not think the Schillings would appreciate her bringing an *Ami* to their doorstep. But no one answered. For the second time that day Anna followed him as he pushed open a door and entered a German house.

"Hello?" he called.

"Frieda? Amalia?" Anna echoed. She started up the stairs to Frieda's apartment but noticed the door on the pied-a-terre ajar. "That's Emil's apartment," she said.

"Who is Emil?"

"Emil Schilling. He works at the Collecting Point. He's how I found this place for Amalia."

"Ah. Your friend that you were talking to the other day, the sapper." He pushed the door open and stuck his head in. "Hello? Herr Schilling?"

Anna wanted to tell him that he was not her friend, that she had no friends, but Cooper was already halfway down the hallway.

"*Ja? Hallo?*" Emil emerged, wiping his hands on a towel.

"Emil, we are looking for Amalia. Is she with you?" Anna said more amiably than she felt. Emil stared at Cooper. "You remember Captain Cooper, from the Collecting Point? We've been on a field visit today and were late in returning. Amalia was not where I expected to meet her, so I wanted to see if she's here."

Cooper returned Emil's stare with equal intensity. Anna looked at the two men sizing each other up.

"Of course, she's here with me," said Emil and gestured to a door at the end of the hall. "Please come in. She's in the sitting room."

Anna pushed past Cooper and hurried down the hall. She found Amalia sitting on a small green sofa, the *Snow Queen* book on her lap, a plate of bread on the table in front of her.

"Mama!" She jumped up and flung her body at Anna so hard that Anna lost her footing.

"Maus, I am so sorry," Anna whispered into her daughter's neck.

"I thought you weren't coming. I thought something happened to you." She squeezed her mother tight.

"It couldn't be helped. But everything is all right now." She released her grip and held Amalia in front of her. Red splotches around the girl's mouth told that she had been crying.

"Duchess, there you are." Cooper stepped into the room and Anna tensed. Amalia smiled and gave him a shy wave. Anna started to tell him that they were fine now and he could go, but Amalia held up her book for him to see and tugged at Anna's pants. "I am looking at his book. Mama, tell him." Anna relayed the message and Cooper gave a thumbs-up in response. Amalia giggled and dug her head into Anna's thigh.

Emil appeared in the doorway. "Anna, would you like to stay for dinner? It is late and you must be hungry. I have soup." He smiled a small, nervous smile.

"Oh, no thank you. That's very kind but we must get back and see to our auntie, right Maus?" To Cooper she said, "Thank you Captain, for your help. I'll see you tomorrow. We must be off now." She tried to make her way past him, but he blocked the space between the sofa and the door. There were suddenly too many people in the small room and Anna started to feel claustrophobic. No one moved one way or the other as Emil and Cooper each held their staked-out ground.

Anna looked around the room for the first time. Arranged around the sofa were a matching chair and a wooden coffee table. Under the window that faced the street was a small bookshelf, and along the far wall stood a small square table with two straight-backed chairs. There seemed to be no feminine influence on the space at all; even the paintings on the wall seemed haphazard and random with no regard to placement, as if Emil had hung them from nails already in the walls. She spotted the ubiquitous copy of *Mein Kampf* on the shelf. *Means nothing*, she thought. Everyone in Germany had been obliged to own a copy, although she had never read hers. That copy had gone into her oven sometime during the past winter and she had been glad to get rid of it. She wondered why anyone would still have a copy on his shelf when it made such excellent fuel for the fire.

"Emil, where is your sister?" she asked. Maybe small talk would get things moving.

Emil shrugged. "She had to meet someone. A friend. Amalia came to wait with me. We had a good time, didn't we?"

Amalia nodded but inched closer to her mother who placed a

protective hand on her head. Cooper finally moved and began to survey the room, inspecting the furniture and the paintings as he had done earlier at the villa. Anna felt a seething rise inside her. *Damn* Amis. She ventured an apologetic smile at Emil, who was happy to take it. He rubbed the knuckles of his missing fingers.

"All right, ladies, I'll drive you home." Cooper walked between them, forcing Emil to take a step backward.

Anna grabbed Amalia's hand and pulled her into the hallway. "Thank you, Emil. Good night," she said.

The three of them got into the jeep and Amalia climbed over the seat to the back. Anna wished Cooper would go away, but she decided to let it go—she was too tired.

"Well, Amalia? How are you?" Cooper asked Amalia in heavily accented German. "Was it a nice day? *Schoener Tag?*" His jovial mood had returned.

Anna disliked Cooper's taking the question that was hers to ask, but turned to her daughter and put on an expectant smile.

Amalia nodded. "Yes, it was. I got to play with all the toys. Mama, did you know that Fraulein Schilling has a whole trunk full of dolls? She let me play with one that had long blond hair and a pretty red dress. She is the most beautiful doll I ever saw." Amalia yawned and leaned forward, her elbows resting on the seat backs.

"And we had pea soup for lunch. It was good. I was hungry. And we had a rest. I fell asleep. Fraulein Schilling gave me a nice pillow and blanket and she laid down on the floor with us. And we dug holes for the potatoes." Amalia paused. "Then we went to the museum and the other mothers were there waiting, but you weren't." Her voice rose and then fell into the accusation.

"I know, Maus, but it couldn't be helped." Anna gritted her teeth. She did not want to have this conversation in front of Cooper.

"Tell her it was my fault," he said, as if on cue. "That we were late. I'll take the fall for that."

"Excuse me?" Anna said.

"I pick up more of the language than you think. I just can't make myself understood. My mother is German, you know. She speaks German around the house. So, tell the duchess it was my fault and I'll make sure you won't be late again."

Anna translated, happy to pass the blame.

Amalia looked at Cooper with intense eyes. "Okay," she said and laid her head on her forearms. If not for the jolting of the jeep, she would already have been asleep.

"Your mother is German?" Anna asked.

"Yep. Engel was her name. Elizabeth Engel. Her people come from the north, up near Hamburg. But she's never been back since she came over as a girl. Her family got out before World War I and she grew up in Iowa, where they settled. She met my dad in high school and they married."

"Is she still alive?"

He nodded. "She's on the farm. She and my dad still work the place. Probably my little brother will take it over. Me, I want nothing to do with it."

"The war must have made for hard times for her, no? As a German?"

"It's been hard for her to have me over here, that's for sure." He downshifted as they rolled down the hill toward the city. "Say, is she really named after a duchess, or was she pulling my leg?" He pointed a thumb over his shoulder at Amalia.

"Well, yes and no," Anna said. "Anna Amalia was the duchess of Weimar, which is near where we lived before we came here. So between the two of us we make one duchess. She just likes to claim the title for herself. Many places in Weimar are named after her--the duchess, I mean. Amalia loves to insist they were all named for her. How did you know this?"

Cooper laughed and his eyes crinkled in the corners. "I figured it out. She told me she was a *Herzogin*. So I looked it up."

Anna shook her head and laughed. She pointed to the address in the Adolfsallee and held on as Cooper pulled the jeep over and pitched to a stop. Anna got out, feeling depleted. She lifted Amalia from the back seat and set her down on the sidewalk.

"Thank you very much for the ride, Captain. Where shall I report tomorrow?" Anna stepped up onto the curb and took Amalia's hand.

"Oh, let's say we start at nine. I kept you much too late today and I have a bunch of paperwork to do. You can report to my office and help me sort through everything. Just remember, not a word to anyone."

Anna nodded. "All right. Thank you, Captain."

"*Gute Nacht*, duchess!" Cooper winked at Amalia, who waved. He revved the engine and made a flamboyant U-turn on the street, then drove back in the direction of the Rheinstrasse. Anna fumbled for her keys in her bag, willing herself to be upstairs inside her familiar walls, with the door to the world closed firmly behind her.

"Well, Frau Klein. How nice to see you! This is a pleasant surprise."

Anna turned to see Frau Hermann, the woman from the bakery. *How long had she been standing there?*

"Frau Hermann, hello. How nice to see you." Anna pulled Amalia toward the entrance.

"So nice of the American to drive you and the little one home. I went up to bring some eggs for Frau Wolf, but no one was home. I know you are quite…busy." She smiled, her face flushed and glistening in the heat like a pork roast fresh from the oven. She folded her hands in front of her round belly and shifted her weight onto her heels. Waiting.

Anna bristled. "That's very kind of you. Frau Wolf is still in the hospital but she is doing much better. I will tell her you asked after her." She pulled her daughter's arm. "Come, Amalia, let's go. *Guten Abend*, Frau Hermann."

"And to you as well, Frau Klein," the battle-ax chirped. "I do hope you will hear good news from your husband soon."

chapter nine

Lying in the lukewarm bath, Anna tried to erase the film of dust she had gathered in the villa's basement but the sliver of soap only seemed to move it around on her body. She wished for some lotion to smooth her hair and her dull skin. Her hipbones protruded from a concave belly and her legs looked like withered branches from a dying tree. Her feet, once delicate in pretty shoes, now looked like an old farmer's—the toenails yellow and brittle, the veins visible through her skin like rivers on an old map. She ran her tongue around her teeth, looking for the troublesome one, the incisor on the top left. It was still there, but wobbly. She wondered what she would look like when it finally fell out.

Sighing, she sank under the water, savoring its touch on her face, inside her ears, and enveloping her completely. She thought of Thomas. It had been a nightly ritual before Amalia was born, one of them in the bath, the other on the chair next to it. It was their time to talk, about their shared day at the hospital, about the patients, the successes and failures. Sometimes Thomas would read to her, either Rilke or Schiller, or they would find something to laugh about even on the darkest days. They were so intertwined that there was no space between them, as if they were held together by a magnetic force. They moved through the world as one being, seemingly untouchable. When Amalia came, the nightly bath enlarged to include her. It was a bright light in days that were growing inexorably darker and more frightening. Their little house began to feel frail and vulnerable in the swirling storm and she pressed herself harder to Thomas to keep the space between them from opening even the smallest amount. It had even worked for a while.

Anna exhaled loudly as she surfaced. He heart pounded and her temples throbbed. The bathroom was empty and the water cold. She was alone, and the Thomas she still loved was far away.

In the morning Anna and Amalia took the bicycle so they could visit Madeleine in the evening. Anna rode and Amalia ran alongside, swinging Lulu by one arm. As they passed the bakery, Anna peered in to see Frau Hermann back at work, the line outside already twenty-long. A truck full of laborers rumbled past, some of them old men, some wearing ties and hats. Party members, perhaps, hoping for a rescue and imminent return to a world more to their liking. The wind picked up and the faintest smell of breakfast floated past, escaping from the overflowing plates of American colonels at the Hansa Hotel.

Amalia ran ahead and Anna pedaled faster to catch up. They made their way up the hill to the Frankfurter Strasse and turned into the Gustav-Freytag-Strasse. At the Schilling gate, Amalia rang the bell.

"Mama, you can go now," Amalia said, turning her back.

Anna was taken aback, expecting a tearful good-bye. She leaned the bicycle against the stone wall and squatted down.

"Don't I even get a hug?"

Amalia obliged with one eye on the front door. It opened and a boy ran down the steps. Amalia let her mother go immediately. "*Hallo*, Fritz," she said as the scrawny kid used all his weight to pull the iron gate open. "Bye, Mama." With only half a wave, Amalia was gone. Anna watched her disappear into the house.

"Frau Klein, it's all right, I am here," Frieda called from the upstairs window. "We will see you this afternoon. Will you be on time today or should I plan to feed Amalia her dinner here?"

Anna stepped back to get the sun out of her eyes. "No need. I will be on time today." She tried to tamp down her defensiveness.

"Very well. I will bring them to the museum at five o'clock. *Tschuess*. Bye now." She waved a dish towel and retreated into the shadows.

Anna stood in the street, listening for sounds from inside the house. What sounds exactly, she was not sure, but nothing came, even with all the windows open to the warm morning. She turned the bicycle back toward town and gave the house one last look before swinging her legs over the saddle and coasting down the hill.

Anna was removing the clothespins from her pant legs when she heard Cooper approach. Not by his footsteps—American boots had rubber soles, not like the hobnailed German ones that still echoed in her head. As usual, it was his voice that announced him as he chatted his way through the workers in the courtyard. She straightened just as he spotted her.

"Pants again, huh?" he said. "Good idea. We have a visitor. I need you to translate." He turned on his heel and motioned for her to follow. "Come on. I don't want him to get away."

"Who is it?" Anna jogged a few steps to catch up.

"Schneider, he says his name is. Ludwig. Wants to talk to an arts officer. All the others are out in the field today or in Frankfurt meeting with the brass. So he gets me."

"What does he want?"

"Well, beats me. That's what I need you for." As they began to climb the stairs, he pulled Anna's elbow to stop her.

"Listen, I want you to tell me if anything seems suspicious, okay? Just tell me your honest impression."

"Yes, of course," Anna nodded.

Ludwig Schneider sat in the chair opposite Cooper's desk. His black fedora lay on his lap and a battered briefcase rested against the leg of the chair. As Cooper approached, he stood with some exertion and extended his hand.

"Please, I am Ludwig Schneider," he said with a slight lisp and hint of Bavarian accent. His thin hair stood up on his scalp in a halo effect, which added a whimsical quality to an angular face softened with the sagging of age. He was shorter than Cooper and his tie reached only to the middle of his round belly. Sweat stains permeated the armpits of his threadbare shirt and he gave off a smell of stale smoke.

Cooper returned the introductions, anointing Anna his assistant and translator, which earned her a raised eyebrow from Schneider. Cooper pulled a chair to his side of the desk for her and slid a pad of paper in her direction. He sat down heavily in his chair. "So. What can we do for you today, Herr Schneider?"

"Yes, Captain, I wanted to introduce myself to you and offer my assistance," he began in German, pausing to look at Anna, who translated.

"You see, I am an art appraiser and I also ran a small gallery before the war. Perhaps I can be of service in the work you are doing. And I would also like to apply to re-open my business. So as to support myself and my family."

Cooper regarded him coolly. "I see. And in what capacity would you be able to assist us?"

Schneider leaned forward and rested a hand on the desk. "I have knowledge of German artists and restoration practices. I have many connections in the art world here in the area. I am interested in helping return the pieces to their owners." He pulled at his collar, which was too tight, and licked his lips.

"We have people to do that, Herr Schneider," Cooper said. He cocked his head. "Tell me, what happened to your inventory, as a gallery owner. Did you manage to hang on to it?"

Schneider shifted in his seat and seemed taken aback. "Well, as a gallery owner I had very few pieces of my own, you understand. Most of the work was on consignment. The art was not mine to keep." He cleared his throat with a loud honk.

Cooper ignored the misdirected flattery. "Well, where did it go, the art that was not yours to keep?"

Schneider raised his chin and looked at Cooper. "If you are asking me if I sold to Party officials, yes, I did. I was under pressure. The National Socialists were very interested in collecting art, as you well know, and I was not in a position to refuse, of course. I was only a small dealer, not very important. The gallery was just me and my wife, who is now gone. In fact it was actually her gallery and not mine."

As Anna translated Cooper held Schneider's gaze. He rearranged a stack of papers on his desk. "Your questionnaire, your *Fragebogen* here says you were in the SA. I am curious as to why the U.S. Army should be putting thugs from the *Sturmabteilung* on our payroll?"

Schneider's forehead glistened. "Yes, I was SA but only for one year, and it was very early, in the 1930s. You will see also on my papers there that I spent four months in a *KZ*, in a concentration camp. I was not a good Nazi. My papers have all been examined. If I may..." He reached into his bag and produced a letter, which he handed to Anna. "It is from Major Phillips in Frankfurt."

Anna handed the letter to Cooper, who read it through smirking eyes. His attitude irritated Anna. She smiled at Schneider, who dabbed at his forehead with a dingy handkerchief.

Cooper slid the paper back across the table toward Anna, who read it without picking it up. It was a letter of introduction from Major Phillips in Frankfurt declaring Schneider to be a man with useful expertise who was interested in helping the Americans in their work. A hand-written note added a thought about possible employment as an arts advisor or consultant.

"That letter tells me nothing, only that you've convinced Phillips that you should have a job. What I want to know is why did the Nazis have against you?" Cooper crossed his arms. "After all, you were one of them."

Schneider seemed to anticipate the question. "Did they really need a reason? They were not happy with my work. At the Reichskammer, the cultural chamber that was responsible for furthering the arts—that was in Frankfurt—I was assigned to purchase art from the Jews. Forced sales, you understand. But I did not cooperate well enough. They accused me of offering too much money for the pieces and not documenting the sales correctly. It was a nightmare, to tell you the truth. After I came out of the camp, my health was never good again, and, well, needless to say, I kept my head down. Now that we have finally survived, I'd like to be useful again."

Cooper shot a look at Anna. "All right Herr Schneider. Thank you for stopping by. We'll call you if we need you, but I have to say we're fresh out of jobs today." He stood and extended his hand.

Schneider followed suit and shook Cooper's hand. "And my business? I must be able to earn a living. For my family."

Cooper shook his head. "You'll have to wait. We'll get set up and sort out this mess you and your friends created when you started taking everyone's belongings. Until then, no cultural objects may change hands. Paragraph 51—you must know it. You'll just have to sit tight until that gets lifted. Maybe you'll find some other employment in the meantime."

Schneider deflated. He produced a visiting card from his briefcase and handed it to Cooper. "My address and name, for you," he said in English. "Please, if anything comes up..." He bowed to Anna, and turned to go.

"Just a moment, Herr Schneider, I have a question," Anna blurted out. "Do you know the Gallerie Breuer?"

The old man stopped and looked over his shoulder. "The Breuer? In Darmstadt? Yes, I know it. Breuer was a friend." His voice was flat. "Why do you ask about him?"

Anna shrugged. "I just wondered what happened to the gallery."

"Breuer is gone," said Schneider. "I saw him last in summer of '42. After that he was probably taken away." He focused on her. "Where did you hear about the gallery?"

"What's he saying?" asked Cooper. "Anna—Frau Klein—What are you talking about?"

Anna ignored Cooper and Schneider's questions. "What happened to the gallery's inventory?" she asked.

"I don't know. I am sure it was requisitioned with the rest of his property. Taken to Frankfurt probably, but that was after my time there." Schneider raised his hat to his sweating head. "Good day, Frau Klein. I hope I can be of assistance to the Captain."

When Schneider was gone, Cooper turned on Anna. "What the hell were you doing just going off and talking to him without my permission? I asked you to translate, that was all."

Anna shrugged. "I thought he would know something about the gallery where the Runge came from. I mean with all his so-called connections."

Cooper shook his head. "I don't trust him. There's something shifty about him. He's not telling the truth. And how does he know Phillips anyway? That guy never leaves his office. What the hell does he know about art experts?" He scratched his nose. "What did he say?"

"Shifty?"

"Yes, you know, he was so groveling. The way he sniveled about his connections. I just didn't like it." Cooper picked up the letter Schneider had left behind and read it in a mocking voice. "*His reputation as an art dealer and restorer is well-established. I think he could be of service to you.*" He sneered and tossed the letter back on the desk. "As if I need ex-Nazis lurking around the hallways here. That's a hell of an idea."

"All professionals were required to join the Party if they wanted to keep working," Anna said. "It's not that simple to just dismiss him on that account."

Cooper looked at her from under his eyebrows. "Of course not. But he was in the SA. That doesn't even make sense as a professional choice for a gallery owner. He's not convincing as a brownshirt. What did he enforce, art auction etiquette? Please."

"The SA was easier to get into. They took pretty much anyone, after the Nazi Party got more selective."

"Okay, but I don't think that helps his case. Anyway, I'm sure as hell not going to start with him as my first hire, I don't give a damn what Phillips says."

"Who is Major Phillips?" Anna asked. "Wouldn't he be your boss?"

"Technically, yes. But he's out of his league. Has no background in anything to do with arts or architecture. Just a military pencil-pusher who landed himself a nice assignment in a fancy office."

"I didn't know you could disobey orders like that," Anna said.

"It's not an order. It was a suggestion." He sat down at his desk and leaned on his elbows. "So tell me what Schneider said."

Anna sat down in the chair opposite Cooper. "Just that the gallery owner, Breuer, the one whose name was on the back of the painting we found at the villa? He said he's gone. Taken away in 1942. Never seen again."

"Damn." Cooper tapped Schneider's card on the pile of papers in front of him. "And that inventory?"

"Taken too. He doesn't know where. Or he didn't say."

Cooper looked at Schneider's card. "No, of course not. Well, maybe he can help us down the road. I'll hang on to this."

Anna smiled and took the card from his hand, putting it in a folder along with the letter. "It will be here when you need it. Under S. For shifty."

By lunchtime Anna had helped Cooper finish his paperwork, typing his reports and creating a filing system for them. "Organization isn't my strong suit," Cooper had said and she'd agreed, surveying the stacks of papers and folders covering the entire surface of his desk. It was amazing how much paperwork an army generated. Orders for equipment required copies in triplicate: for the director, for the Wiesbaden headquarters and for the American command in Frankfurt. As soon as a piece of paper was sent out, one came back to inform you that the first piece of paper had been received. This went on and on. *Ridiculous*, Anna thought.

They spent the afternoon back at the villa, trying to document the stash that was still a secret. Starting with the paintings piled on the long table, they systematically took them down, leaned them against the table legs and photographed them. There were so many that Cooper photographed only the major paintings. He lined them up five and six at a time to make the limited film stretch. They studied artists' signatures and tell-tale labels on the backs for clues as to their origins. Anna identified a series of German Romantics she thought must belong to the same collection as the Runge, even though the rest were far lesser pieces. But she could not find any marks or detail that tied them together for sure. No others came from Breuer's gallery in Darmstadt, and most had no identifying marks on them at all. Cooper photographed, cursing the crack in the camera's viewfinder, and Anna scribbled on a pad. She described the painting and its frame, noted its approximate size and listed the artist's name where she could. She would type up the proper forms later. It was very slow-going.

They had only gone through about half the pile just on the table when Cooper made a big production of checking his watch.

"I know it's only three o'clock, but you know what? I'm beat. What do you say we put everything back like we found it and call it a day?" He rubbed the back of his neck.

"But we still have at least another hour," Anna said. "I was hoping to finish this pile today." She waved at a teetering stack of small paintings. "It won't take much longer."

"No, no, I need to head back. Can you put them back where they were? We can pick up where we left off. There's no way we can do this ourselves. We're going to have to haul everything back to the Collecting Point. I'll get a truck out here tomorrow."

Anna looked around. She was irritated at their lack of progress. She set down the landscape she was holding. "Have you reported that this stash exists? I didn't see a report in the paperwork today."

Cooper shook his head. "Not yet. I'll get to it tomorrow, don't worry. I'm just behind. You know what, let's go to the camp. I want to talk the boy. Before we move this stuff. Maybe he can tell me something else." He paused. "Actually, maybe you should talk to him. I don't think I'll have any luck."

Anna smiled. "Yes. I will." She began undoing all the sorting she had spent the afternoon on, putting things back where they had been when she and Cooper had arrived. "Why do we need to put them back if you are just going to come get them tomorrow?"

"Better that everything looks undisturbed, in case someone really is using this as their personal warehouse. Then we can see if anything's been touched. Hey, ask the boy about that again, will you? I think he knows more than he let on. I'll go load up the jeep."

Anna finished re-stacking her piles and then blew on the fingerprints they had left in the dust on the table. With her shoe she scuffed out their footprints in the dirt leading to the steps and then closed the door behind her. Back in the jeep, she rubbed her damp feet and closed her eyes against the sunlight.

Cooper climbed in. He had put on his sunglasses and garrison cap, the one that looked like an upside down paper boat with the silver captain's bars on the side. His tie was tightened and he was wearing the short Ike jacket, like all the *Ami* officers wore now. Anna regarded him as he put the jeep into gear and they bolted forward. The Americans looked like gods compared to the trampled and hollow Germans. Next to Emil, Cooper was a picture of vitality, even though he was twenty years older.

"You okay?" Cooper smiled at her.

Anna turned away, embarrassed that he had caught her staring. "Yes. I was just wondering why you would let the art be left unguarded like this. What if someone really comes and takes it?

"They won't," he said. "Trust me."

Anna shook her head and clenched her teeth. *Amis,* she thought. *Cowboys, all of them.*

When Cooper turned the jeep into the DP camp's gate, Anna grabbed the dashboard to keep from sliding into him. He saluted the MP and proceeded to the barracks without slowing down.

Anna scanned the playground. It was full of skinny children in dirty clothes running and playing. Their voices echoed off the building, the air sweetened occasionally by a dollop of real childhood laughter. A bundle of little girls sat together at the far end, fussing over a doll, their hair reflecting the sunshine. *Everything seems so normal,* Anna thought, but then her days at home in Kappellendorf over the past few years had mostly seemed altogether normal too. Even when the bombs fell, life went on. People cooked, cleaned, gossiped, had babies, went for walks, complained about the weather, complained more about the rations and oppressions. Children went to school, mothers folded laundry and fathers—the ones that remained—went to work, smoked their pipes, and read the paper at night. Take away the foundation of dread that their lives teetered on, and the loneliness that came with mistrusting everyone, and life—for her at least—had seemed tolerable. But she knew there was a price. A small memory of Thomas peeked into her consciousness. He sat, smiling at her across the breakfast table, his hair matted from sleep, his eyes soft. She wondered if he had sat at that table this morning, alone and missing her? Or was he somewhere else, looking for her? She stuffed the memory back down and got out of the jeep.

"I'll go check on his paperwork, see if you can find the rascal," Cooper shouted over his shoulder as he headed toward the main administration building.

Anna made her way to the barracks door, avoiding the wide arc of the tire swing. She could smell the mix of dirt and sweat that children playing outside always emitted. It smelled like a kind of freedom, she thought.

The heavy door groaned when she pulled it open to step inside the dingy foyer. Two hallways extended from each side and a metal staircase led to the second floor. The plaster walls were a sickly green, the paint peeling to reveal gray underneath. Signs with arrows and numbers were taped to the wall, but were meaningless to her. A young woman was walking toward her, scraping her shoulder against the wall. A tired cotton dress hung on her emaciated frame and her hair had been cut short, like a boy's. Anna tried to make eye contact but the woman's gaze was locked on the floor in front of her.

"Excuse me, can you tell where I can find Frau Niemeyer? Maria Niemeyer? I believe she lives in this building." Anna stopped and waited for a reply that did not come. The woman walked on without indicating in any way that she had heard the question. Anna watched her for a moment and when the woman reached the foyer end of the hallway, she turned, leaned her left shoulder against the wall, and started back.

"Frau Klein?"

Anna turned to see Maria in a doorway down the hall. She was wiping her hands on her dress and looked flushed.

"You are looking for Oskar? He is here with me. I am working in the kitchen today. Please." She waved Anna toward her. "That's just our Luisa. She walks up and down all day. I try to keep an eye on her."

"She needs help," Anna whispered.

Maria raised her eyebrows. "Of course she does. But the paperwork, it takes so long. The *Amis* are trying to find her family."

The young woman reached Maria, turned again without a word and started back down the hall, the skin on her arm glistening.

"Come on, come see Oskar." Maria pulled her gently by the arm.

The kitchen was an onion-scented steam bath of boiling pots and blazing fires. Several women worked at the tables chopping, some moved pots between stove and sink, and others washed. In the far corner, Oskar sat on a table next to a woman wrapping bread into pieces of paper, his legs dangling over the edge. He pretended not to see Anna.

"Well, it looks like you have plenty to eat at least," Anna said.

Maria shook her head. "This is for the whole barracks for today. One meal for six hundred people."

"Six hundred? This is not enough for that many people."

"Precisely. And that's just this building. There's ten more just like this here," she said. "Come on." She led the way to Oskar's corner. "Look who's here to see you, child. Stand up and say hello."

Oskar slid off the table and looked at Anna's kneecaps. She squatted down and hugged him. "Oskar, how are you doing?"

He refused to meet her eyes. "Are you coming to take me home?" he mumbled to the floor.

Anna shook her head. "No, *mein Kind*, I'm not. I wanted to say hello, and to see if you'd like to come play with my little girl this weekend? We could go up to the Neroberg. Maybe have a picnic?"

Oskar shrugged. "Maybe. I guess."

Anna straightened. "Well, good. Now, is there anything I can do here to help?"

Maria laughed. "Well if you want to wrap sandwiches, that would be good. Then maybe we can get supper out on time for once."

Anna put on the smock Maria handed her. It was so big that she looped the ties around her waist twice before making a bow. She began wrapping the sandwiches, taking one from the tray and rolling it into the top sheet of the stack of paper. It took her five sandwiches before she realized the papers were old Wehrmacht maps of Belgium. *If only old Adolf could see this. The bastard.*

After she had made a pile of twenty, Oskar took the tray into the dining room next door, returning with the empty tray in less than a minute. Anna started to work faster.

"Tell me, Oskar, how did you end up staying at the villa?" Anna tried to act disinterested, as if she had just asked him his favorite color or subject at school.

The boy fidgeted with the edge of the stack of maps. "I told you. I just stayed there."

"Yes, but why there? And where did you live before?"

"I came from Darmstadt. After the bombs fell I got a ride on a truck one day. I went to the door and it was open. So I went inside. No one was home and there was a bed." He shrugged.

"But that's been a long time." The bombing of Darmstadt had been the previous September, almost a full year ago. Anna remembered the day—September 11, 1944—because it had been her seventh wedding anniversary. There had been no celebration, only the furtive acknowledgement of the day with a kiss and a smile. There was no thinking of where they had been or where they were going. Only that they still *were*. The news from Darmstadt had trickled in through news from families of neighbors, the official news reports, then eventually through a letter from Madeleine. The bombing had lasted only 30 minutes but the fires raged for days. Bomb shelters became furnaces. Flames raced though the streets, finding entry through every door and window as the asphalt melted. The entire city was destroyed—a grim prelude of what was in store for more cities in the months that followed. Anna looked at Oskar and wondered what he was not telling her. She decided to play along with his story for now.

"How did you survive for so long on your own?"

"I took food. From the *Amis*. From people. It wasn't so hard."

"And you were all by yourself? Did no one ever come there?"

He nodded and puffed up. "I wasn't scared."

"No, of course not. I'm just wondering about the basement. How did all that art get there?"

"I told you, it was already there. And how should I know where it came from? Nobody ever came. I told you all this." He took the tray of sandwiches away. This time he didn't come back. Anna continued wrapping and tried to think of a better strategy to get the boy to talk. She would have to earn his trust somehow.

"Anna? I mean, Frau Klein?" Cooper called from the door. "We need to go."

"Coming." Anna looked at her meager pile of sandwiches. "I'm sorry, I didn't do much." She took off the smock as Maria patted her arm. "Thank you for coming. I know it matters, even though he's not letting on. It makes a difference."

"Tell him I'll be back this weekend and we'll go on the picnic I promised."

Maria assured her she would relay the message and Anna followed Cooper outside to the jeep. The sun was sinking in the west and a cool north breeze felt good on her face after the heat of the kitchen.

"I think you're right about Oskar hiding something about why he was at the villa," Anna said. "He's not telling me the whole story. And what he is telling me makes no sense."

Cooper leaned his elbow on the steering wheel. "Yeah? Well never mind that now. I did find out something." His intensity took Anna aback. "I checked on the kid's paperwork. Something's come up. About his family."

"Really? That was so fast. Did they find someone to claim him?"

Cooper shook his head. "Not exactly. But they found out who his parents were."

Anna slumped. "Oh?"

"Peter and Magda Grünewald. Residence: Heinrichstrasse, Darmstadt. Both deceased, September 11, 1944."

"So he's telling the truth about that part at least." Anna sighed. "How did you find out? Does he have any brothers or sisters? Other family?"

Cooper handed her a yellowing card with a Swastika emblazoned on the top. "Take a look for yourself."

As she scanned the form she realized it was a kind of death certificate for the Grünewald parents, listing their particulars: the father born 1914 in Passau, near Munich; the mother in 1917 in Mainz, the town between Wiesbaden and Frankfurt. *Both so young,* Anna thought. Under the father's name, his rank: SS Sturmbannführer. Children: Oskar Friedrich Grünewald. No date or city was listed in the space provided for information about his birth. She turned the card over, looking for more information.

"What you're looking for is on the front there." Cooper pointed his finger at a scribble on the form where Oskar's birth information should have been. *Adoptiert, Steinhöring, 1937* it read.

Anna turned the paper over again, as if some new information might have appeared on the back, but it was blank. "Adopted?"

"Didn't expect that did you?" Cooper grinned. It seemed to Anna that he enjoyed a good mystery.

She looked at the form again. "His father was SS. That explains his general world view. And I think Steinhöring is in Bavaria, where his father is from, so that would make sense too." She tried to picture the boy's parents. SS officers and their wives had to prove their Aryan heritage going back generations. No doubt Peter and Magda Grünewald were prime specimens of the Master Race—tall, blonde, and privileged, thanks to their racial value to the Reich. Oskar completed the picture, his straw hair and blue eyes, strong features and solid build all contributing to the perfect ideal of the Nazi family. Anna shuddered.

Cooper handed her a gray paper folder that was thick with pages. The letters UNRRA were stamped on the front. "I requisitioned this for you. You wanted to figure out the boy's provenance, see if you can find anything in there. Don't say I never gave you anything." He started the jeep and Anna clamped her hands down on the folder to keep the pages from blowing away.

Anna wondered if Oskar knew he had been adopted. Where had he come from? Maybe his mother had died in childbirth? Or when he was a baby? Even two mothers hadn't been enough to keep the boy safe. And now, both were probably gone, lost to him forever.

chapter ten

Madeleine was sleeping when Anna and Amalia arrived. Visiting hours were long over but the nurse—the kind one with the dimpled chin and splotchy face—let them sneak in.

"I am also a mother who has to work," she whispered. "But don't let matron catch you. Just a few minutes, please." Standing at the foot of Madeleine's bed, Anna thought they should let her rest, but Amalia was already at her head, whispering in her ear.

"Auntie? Auntie wake up. We are here to see you." Her little hand stroked the old woman's stringy hair, now matted to her head with several days' worth of sweat. Anna set down the small basket she had brought. She had boiled one of Frau Hermann's eggs and added it to some bread and the jar of quince jam. The hospital had little more to offer than broth and bread and even though bringing food was frowned upon officially, the reality was that it meant more rations for those patients who had no such outside deliveries.

Anna sat at the foot of the bed, which gave a low creak and tilted under her weight. The movement roused Madeleine, her eyes opened and focused on Amalia's face, poised inches from her own.

"*Mein Schatz*, is it you?" she smiled and took the girl's face between her hands. "All day I was waiting. I am so glad you came."

"Are you feeling better?" Amalia whispered.

"Much," said Madeleine. She peered into the darkness at the end of the bed. "Did you bring your mother with you or did you drive yourself?"

Amalia giggled and Anna reached across the bed to quiet her. She leaned forward into the square of light that came through clerestory high above the bed. "Here I am, Madeleine. How are you feeling? Did the doctor see you today?" She cradled the woman's icy hand in hers.

"No sighting today. I think they've given up on me. Which is really all right because I feel much better. I'd like to come home." Her eyes betrayed her lie. "They aren't doing a damn thing for me here. At least at home I have my own bathroom, which smells a lot better than this one here."

"That's for certain," said Anna. "Shall I talk to the doctor or do you want to sneak out in the middle of the night?"

"Your mother is feeling adventurous today." Madeleine winked at Amalia. "Tell me, what's been going on?"

"Oh, nothing much. Captain Cooper and I went out yesterday and surveyed some of the villas out west and down along the Rhine. Documenting damage and cataloging valuables. Nothing very interesting. Look here, I brought you an egg. Frau Hermann brought some from her sister's farm. I gave the other one to Amalia." She fiddled with the basket and held up the bread. "And this. Are you hungry now? I can fix it for you."

Madeleine looked at her. "So that's all, just driving around the countryside with the American? Nothing exciting? What about you, Amalia, where were you when all this was going on?"

"Mama was so late to pick me up that I had to stay with Herr Schilling," Amalia grumbled. "She and Captain Cooper were out until after my dinner time."

Anna shot Amalia a stern look. "Maus, I told you we lost track of time and it took longer to get back than we thought. We had to stop to drop off something we found." When Madeleine gave her a questioning look, she filled her in on the details of the new childcare arrangement. She found herself sounding much more confident in the set up than she felt. Madeleine appeared relieved and pushed herself up on her elbows. "See, I knew it would all work out and you would find someplace for her to go. Now tell me about what you and the American found."

Anna sighed. She whispered the story about finding Oskar at the villa, leaving out the repository, the Runge, the secret mountains of art. "So we took him to that displaced persons camp and that's why we were so late," she finished, beginning to peel the egg anyway.

"So where did he come from? Is he all alone, the poor child? How old is he?" Madeleine asked.

"You found a boy, mama?" Amalia perked up. "Can I play with him? What's his name?"

Anna put a finger to her lips to remind Amalia to lower her voice. "His name is Oskar. He came from Darmstadt. He says he's eight years old. He's got pretty fixed ideas about how this all should have turned out and he's not happy. A real *Hitler Jugend* poster boy."

"Well you can't blame him for that. He's just a child. His parents died in the Darmstadt bombing? That was nearly a year ago."

Anna nodded. "Last September. That's what he says. I've not had much luck getting more out of him. Captain Cooper says he'll try to find a place for the boy to go."

"Mama, he could come live with us," Amalia squealed. "We have a place to live. We should take care of him." She crawled over to Anna and grabbed her arm.

The door at the end of the ward opened and the robust figure of the matron marched toward them. "Frau Wolf? What do you think you are doing? Visiting hours are over. You are disrupting the entire ward." She glared at Anna. "Who are you?"

"This is my family, matron, they have come to visit me. Were we being loud? Did we interrupt your nap?" Innocence washed over Madeleine's face. Anna looked down at her hands to hide a smile.

The matron snorted. "Frau Wolf, I see you are feeling much better, hosting parties at your bedside. I suggest you return to the comfort of your own home and give this bed to someone who truly needs it. I have too much to do to play nanny to you. I will prepare your papers for the doctor."

"Don't bother. He won't miss me anyway." Madeleine waved a bony hand. "I'll let myself out tomorrow morning. Send me your bill."

The matron glared at Anna, turned on her heel, and was gone.

Madeleine's eyes gleamed and her face revealed her younger self. "I just love to let them have it. There's no medicine anyway. All they do is take my temperature and look at me accusingly, as if I am taking a vacation on their watch. And what can these old witches do to me now? Stupid woman."

Amalia wiggled. "Auntie you are coming home." She threw her arms around Madeleine and knocked her back onto the pillows.

Anna gave the old woman a motherly look. "Madeleine, you should be in the hospital where they can take care of you."

"You are assuming they are taking care of me. I've been here nearly a week already and I was better off at home." She winked.

Anna exhaled. "We'd better go, it's almost curfew. I'll come and get you in the morning and make sure you are settled at home." Anna kissed the old woman's forehead and tucked the basket onto the bed next to her with an admonition to eat. Madeleine sank back into her pillows and closed her eyes.

In the morning Anna and Amalia walked the three kilometers to the Gustav-Freytag-Strasse. The day was warm but the heavy clouds threatened afternoon rain. Anna was glad to return Amalia to Frieda's care, and when they arrived they found little Liesl already there. The two girls took each other's hands and walked into the playroom. Where Amalia was tall and thin, Liesl was short and round. Her blond hair was pulled into braids so tight they threatened to separate her hair from her scalp. She wore a pair of boy's overalls and a white shirt with little red flowers. Like Amalia, her shoes had the tips cut out to make them fit longer. No doubt this little indignity had bonded them together. Anna watched, standing in the doorway to the playroom. Amalia seemed happy to act as a big sister to the child, even though they were the same age.

"How wonderful to be a child, no?" Emil said as he looked over her shoulder.

"Why do you say that?" Anna spoke without taking her eyes off the two girls.

"Look at them. They are so resilient. It takes so little to make them happy."

Anna laughed. "Spoken like a man who's never lived with a six-year-old." When she turned to look at him, she saw that her remark had hit a tender spot.

Emil pursed his lips and looked away. "No, I guess I have not had that particular pleasure. Are you coming?" He pulled the door open.

Anna would rather have walked alone, but she nodded. "*Tschuess*, Maus." She waved at Amalia, who waved back and blew a kiss before returning to rocking a doll in its cradle. Anna took a deep breath and willed herself to walk away. "Yes, I'm coming." She took her bag from the bench next to the door.

Emil shouted a farewell to Frieda who was in the kitchen rinsing potatoes for lunch. She had greeted Anna and Amalia with smiles when they arrived and proudly shown off the potatoes, outlining how she would prepare them: sliced with the skins on and fried in the drippings of fat. Anna's mouth watered just thinking about it and she was happy Amalia would have such a good meal.

As they walked down the hill to the Collecting Point the morning dew was still heavy in the air and sun filtered through the canopy of the tree-lined street, creating a shifting mosaic on the ground. Emil seemed to relax, and Anna, softened by the warm breeze, wanted to make amends.

"I am sorry for what I said earlier. About living with a six-year-old. It's just that it's not all happiness and laughter. Amalia is the light of my life. She is everything to me." Anna's voice choked around the words, and she covered the emotion with a cough.

"It doesn't matter. Don't worry about it. Sometimes we forget how fortunate we are," Emil said.

They walked on in silence, their rhythmic footsteps echoing off the houses along the street. Anna thought of Emil's frostbitten fingers. "Are you doing all right Emil? I mean, really?" She suddenly wanted to know.

Emil bristled and said nothing for so long that Anna thought he had ignored her.

"I think of my friends. Every day. I guess I am lucky too."

"Your comrades from the Wehrmacht, your army buddies?" Anna's mind saw the rows of bright young faces from Göbbels's propaganda film reels marching toward an impossible promise. She always had this image when she thought of the Wehrmacht.

"Yes. I was in the first wave of Operation Barbarossa in '42. And you know how that all ended. We barely made it to Stalingrad. Then I got a load of shrapnel in my leg and got sent home. I was on the last transport out before the siege—on my twentieth birthday too. I never got back to my unit or saw my comrades again. They either froze to death or are starving now in some godforsaken Russian prison camp."

Anna searched for words but found only an apology.

Emil shrugged and exhaled. "No need. We all went through the shit didn't we? Each in his own way."

"Well, some of us more than others," she said, mostly to herself. Anna knew she had been spared. It was the *why* of her dispensation that gave her trouble. "That must have been very hard, the Russian campaign," she said. She felt useless.

Emil stopped and Anna passed him with several strides before she turned to look at him. He stood, hands in pockets, shoulders tensed as if supporting some invisible load.

"You are the first person to say that to me. No one wants to know anything," he said, his voice taut. "If we don't expect to be treated as heroes, no one will tell what we did. Isn't that the bargain?" His eyes darkened. "I was just a child when I went into Russia. What did I know? I was only a soldier. I did what I was told or they would have shot me, too. I was as dispensable as any one of those…people. In Russia. Those Jews. So I survived. For what? For this?" He spat into the street and sat down on the curb.

Anna stood by uncomfortably, regretting she had opened this door. She sat down next to him and placed a tentative hand on his back, but he pulled away.

"Don't," he said. He hid his face in his hands. "You know, Anna, I think my soul is already condemned because of things I did. Hell can't be any worse than what happened in Russia. I've already been to Hell." He lowered his hands and stared into the distance, reliving some unseeable specter. Anna sat in silence. She tried to envision Emil's horror but her mind wouldn't allow it. There was nothing to do but sit. She looked at the tree-lined street and wondered once again what it was in humanity that drove people to such unholy cruelties under such a beautiful blue sky. They sat for a good while.

"People like you, people that stayed here stoking the homefires of the *Vaterland*, you have no idea." He turned his gaze on her. He was breathing hard and his boyish face had contracted into something she didn't recognize. He spat again.

Anna wanted to make him feel better. He was still just a boy. "Emil, I…"

He held up a hand to stop her. "Don't even try. Don't tell me it will get better. Don't tell me anything." He exhaled and stood up, offering a hand to help Anna to her feet.

"I'm sorry I brought it up," Anna stammered. "That was stupid." She searched his face.

He wiped his eyes with the back of his hand and began walking. "I've made you late. Come on. Don't want you to get into trouble with that *Ami* of yours."

As they neared the Collecting Point, noise and activity echoed from the courtyard. At the back gate, a group of Americans were gathered, laughing and slapping backs. A radio had been brought outside with a long wire, and more Americans and some Germans were gathered around it. All at once cheers rose up from the crowd.

"What's all the fuss?" Anna asked a GI at the back of the throng.

"Truman says the Japs surrendered. The war is over! It's all over. And we won the whole goddamn thing!" He slapped Emil on the back and laughed into his face before turning back to his friends and being absorbed by the crowd.

Anna looked at Emil and was about to translate but he waved her off.

"I got it," he said.

She felt vacant, as if someone had scraped her insides clean with a dull knife. She searched for the place where the happiness, the relief, the joy should be, but couldn't find it. It was like turning a faucet only to discover there is no water. The moment she had hoped for, the one she had held on to for so many years, had finally come. And now it had passed just as any other. She simply felt nothing. Looking down at the worn shoes on her filthy feet, she wanted to cry but didn't dare. She looked at Emil. His eyes were as blank as hers.

"So that's that, then," he said. "Everything's back to normal." They looked at the celebrating crowd. Even Frau Obersdorfer seemed more flushed than usual as she stood, her hands to her cheeks.

"I don't feel much like celebrating," Anna said. "But I am happy the war is finally over everywhere."

"Me too," said Emil.

Cooper was crossing the courtyard, hands in pockets and sleeves rolled up past his elbows. He spotted Anna and Emil standing apart from the crowd and made toward them. Emil let out an extended sigh, like the air being let out of a tire.

"Morning," Cooper beamed.

"Good morning, Captain," Anna replied.

Emil straightened and gave a single nod. "Captain."

"So how about that? The whole damn thing is over. It's a great day. We made it."

"Yes, we did," said Anna glancing at Emil, who looked away.

Cooper looked from one to the other and tried to fill the silence. "Well. I guess we'd better get started. Big delivery still on schedule for Monday." He turned to Emil. "That perimeter security needs to go up ASAP. *Zaun?* Fence, yes?" He waved his arm in a circle and nodded expectantly.

Emil nodded back and offered formal goodbyes before heading toward his work crew, already busy at the far corner fastening wires to the fence posts.

"Well, congratulations," Anna said. She contracted her face into a smile.

Cooper studied her. "No need to congratulate me. I'm just glad it's over. Come on, let's get to work."

She followed him inside the building, dodging the manic activity. Inside, the sounds of hammers and men working echoed in the marble halls and the smell of paint lingered in the dense air. Paintings and other art objects leaned against the walls in the downstairs foyer, waiting to find a home.

"They've got to get the heating working by Monday or we'll be in trouble," Cooper said. "If we can't control the humidity, we'll do more damage than good to those paintings."

They went up the stairs, squeezing past two Germans repairing the banister. One of them nodded at Anna as she passed and she still felt strange to not be required to at least mutter the Hitler salute and make a perfunctory gesture. It was as if the whole country had it on the tip of their tongue but had to stop themselves every time. As if they all spoke a different language now.

"Oh good, it's quiet up here," said Cooper as they arrived at his desk. "I need to talk to you."

Anna preempted him. "Could I please have an hour off this morning? I can stay a bit later, but I need to see my aunt home from the hospital. She's just here at St. Josef's." She gestured toward the window. "I won't be long."

"Oh, she's feeling better, that's great."

"Not exactly. She was evicted. For bad behavior, mostly."

Cooper laughed. "Even better. Look, I'll give her a ride."

Anna flinched. "No, Captain, I can manage. Really. But thank you."

"Nonsense, I am giving the old lady a ride. You have to stop turning me down all the time. I'm just trying to help. Loosen up, will you?"

Anna sank into the chair. She decided to let his comment go, although she didn't understand just how much loosening up he expected of her. "Very well. Thank you. What did you want to talk to me about?"

"That's better. I found out something out about the villa. Did you know it was used as some kind of children's home during the war?"

"Why would I know that? I didn't live here, remember?" Anna paused. "You think Oskar's being there is connected somehow? How did you find out?"

"I tried to get hold of a truck to go over there today and one of the locals told me. Doesn't that seem strange? Of all the places he could go, he goes there?"

"There were so many orphans." Anna couldn't see a connection. The open window creaked as a breeze blew through and briefly moved the stifling air. "Maybe it's just a coincidence."

"Maybe." Cooper took a piece of chewing gum from his shirt pocket. He pulled the stick from its envelope and folded it in half and half again before tossing it in his mouth. He held the package out to Anna who shook her head. "But it sure seems weird, that's all. Anyway, I can't get a truck out there until tomorrow." He stood up and walked to the window, pulling a handkerchief from his pocket to mop his brow. The heat was becoming oppressive.

"Psst, Anna." He gestured for her to come to the window. "Look at this."

Anna looked down into the courtyard and searched for what Cooper had seen. A convoy of trucks was pulling in, drawing the attention of the workers who gathered to unload them. "What is it?"

"Look, over there, our friend is back."

Anna saw Ludwig Schneider, standing at the gate talking with a corporal.

"Maybe he wants back in? To talk to you?"

"More likely he wants to go over my head. That guy he's talking to, that's Miller. He's kind of shifty too," Cooper said. They stood and watched. Schneider nodded at the soldier and handed him a piece of paper. Then the two men shook hands and Schneider walked away in the direction of the park.

Anna suddenly became aware that she and Cooper were rubbing shoulders in the small window frame. She lingered for a moment, enjoying the connection, the feeling of another human close by her side. She realized she liked their shared objective, even the secret of the art stash between them. Cooper turned his face toward hers, and Anna could feel his eyes on her. When she turned to look at him, a loneliness rose up and squeezed her chest, making her inhale sharply. Their eyes locked, and she could smell the sweat on his skin mixed with the starch of his uniform. Her feet took several clumsy steps back, and she pretended to look in her bag for something to hide the color rising in her face.

"I wonder what that was all about," she muttered.

Cooper cleared his throat and turned his face away. "Who knows? People are always trying to bribe the guards." He mopped his forehead again and looked at his watch. "Why don't we go fetch your friend now?" The air between them had gone very still, and Anna could not meet his eyes.

"Yes, let's," she said, and shouldered her bag.

Madeleine did not look like someone who should be coming home from the hospital. Cooper carried the old woman up the flight of stairs to her apartment and laid her gently on the bed. Madeleine pretended to swoon and he indulged her by holding her hand and propping her against the pillows. When she was settled, he opened the windows and then stood in the middle of the living room, waiting for something.

Anna checked the faucet in the kitchen. "Water's running at the moment. Can I make you a coffee, Captain?" Having him in the apartment felt strange—her two worlds were overlapping. It was disorienting. She peered at him through the small pass-through between the kitchen and living room.

Cooper caught her eye. "I have to get back. Why don't you get settled and I'll see you back at the museum. In an hour, say?" He saluted at Madeleine. "I hope you'll be feeling better soon, ma'am."

"I'll make up the time I missed," Anna said as she followed him to the door. "Thank you, Captain."

He pulled the door handle and turned to her. "Don't mention it. I'll figure out a way you can make it up to me." He winked and then was gone, down the stairs. "See you later, Frau Klein," he shouted behind him. Anna could hear the neighbors run to their peepholes as she closed the door. *Damn* Amis.

"Well, that was fast," Madeleine said when Anna brought her a cup of water and sat down on the bed. "He seems very nice. How kind of him to bring me home. I never would have made it on my own." She sat up and sipped some water. "He didn't want to stay? I suppose he's very busy."

"Yes," said Anna. "The whole place is working like mad to prepare for the art coming from Frankfurt on Monday. All the art the *Amis* found in the Merkers mine, back in April. Did you hear about that?"

Madeleine shook her head. "You mean up there near by Bad Salzungen? Wasn't that where they kept all the gold? The *Reichsgold*, I mean?"

"Yes, but you remember, the *Amis* also found art in the mine. The Nazis hid it there—I think it was all from the national museum in Berlin."

"I do remember hearing about that. Well that's exciting, isn't it? I wonder what the *Amis* will do with all of it."

Anna lay back on the bed, her legs hanging down the side. Her stomach rumbled. "Who knows. I don't really care. I miss Thomas, Madeleine. Do you think he's all right?"

"Of course, my child. He is just fine. He will be here as soon as he can. You mustn't worry about him." She patted Anna's hand. "Come on now. Up you get. I am going to nap and you need to get back to work. Did you eat?"

Anna shook her head. "I'll have some bread before I go." She kissed the old woman's cheek and stroked her hair. "How about you have a bath tonight?"

Madeleine nodded and patted her cheek. "That would be lovely. Now go, and don't worry about me."

Anna returned to the kitchen and sat on the small stool by the black cast iron stove that always smelled of bacon fat. She imagined that somewhere in its bowels lay a forlorn slab of bacon waiting to be discovered. She lit her last cigarette and inhaled deeply as she looked out the window. Blue sky. She could hear sparrows. The rustle of the plane trees signaled the warm breeze before it stroked her face. She thought of Oskar and wondered how he must really feel under that toughened exterior. What happened to his real parents? He had lost two mothers already. She had only lost one and that was when she was already an adult. To be a motherless child in this world? She shook her head to dislodge the idea. The sounds of the city—voices, motors and footsteps—trickled into the room and fell on the floor around her feet. She felt completely alone.

The late afternoon sun had put the entire rear courtyard of the museum into shadow, providing a long-awaited respite for the day's heat. Anna stood at the gate, peering up the Frankfurter Strasse, to see if Frieda was bringing the children. The afternoon had been very busy with organizing papers and setting up the office. Cooper had found a table and chair for Anna, and she now had her own workspace under the window next to his desk. He sent her up to requisition one of Frau Obersdorfer's typewriters, which had gone about as well as expected. Anna carried the machine, a ream of paper and some loose-leaf carbon sheets down to the second floor and set up her desk. It wasn't much. The typewriter, paper and some pencils. But it was a spot, and that mattered. From there she could look out onto the front entry, the Wilhelmstrasse and the Rheinstrasse straight ahead. The Collecting Point director, a fastidious American named Captain Farmer with weight of the world on his shoulders, had stopped by. Cooper introduced Anna as his translator and praised her knowledge of art. "Nice to have you working with us," the director said, eyes darting behind his thick glasses, before he moved on down the hall.

Anna felt an unexpected swelling inside her. For the first time since leaving her home she felt truly present, like a real person, and not just a lost desperate face in the crowd—a DP, a German, a *Kraut*. She had seen so many desperate faces along the road from Kappellendorf as she drove the truck with Amalia's head in her lap. After Anna had told her over and over to close her eyes and look away, Amalia had decided to lay down for most of the trip. Once in a while they would pick up women and children walking alongside the road and drop them in the next town. A rotting stench hung over the countryside—animal carcasses rotting in the sun, here and there a dead body, desperate people begging for food. An intermittent trickle of hollowed men walked in the opposite direction, fleeing from the Americans, their army haircuts and averted eyes betraying their true identities. On a small country lane near

Eisenach, a young woman, half naked and screaming, had run from the underbrush and stepped without flinching in front of the truck. Anna swerved and missed her by a hair, sending the truck and their meager belongings into the ditch. For her efforts Anna was rewarded with a tirade of curses and insults from the woman who charged at her, knocking her to the ground and pummeling her with rage. "I want to die," she had screamed over and over. It took the three other women who had been on the back of the truck to pull her off Anna and run her back into the forest by throwing stones at her. Then it had taken the rest of the day and the help of a passing American patrol to get the truck out of the ditch. The memory revisited Anna nearly every day. She wondered what had become of the wretched woman.

"*Hallo*, Anna."

She spun around to see Emil, his face red and glowing, hair matted against his head. His face was relaxed and open, the way it had been when they met at his house.

"Emil, *hallo*. You've been working hard," she laughed.

"Yes, we're almost ready. Almost all the windows are in now." He jabbed a thumb over his shoulder. "We still have to work on the humidity. But were are getting there." He looked at the ground and bit his lip. "Anna? I am sorry about this morning. I should not have—"

Now Anna cut him off. "Don't," she said. "You have nothing to apologize for. Let's not speak about it again."

"Please let me invite you to dinner. Today is an auspicious day, and we should celebrate." He held her gaze with an intensity that made her nervous.

"Actually, I don't feel much like celebrating, Emil. You are kind to ask," she replied.

"I'm not being kind," he said. "I am asking you to dinner."

"Emil, you know I am married."

His eyes flashed. "Yes, of course, I know that. I just thought we could..." He stuck his hands in his pockets and looked up at the sky. "Listen, I don't mean anything by it. I like you. We survived. Doesn't that put us in the same boat?"

Anna reached for his hand. "Emil I like you, I do. But you must understand, I have Amalia. And now that Madeleine is home, I need to take care of her. I can't have dinner with you. Besides, where would we go? What is there to eat? No, it's not possible. I am sorry."

Emil pulled his hand away. He looked at her with a shroud of sadness covering him. He seemed to shrink in front of her eyes. "All right. I understand. I won't bother you again."

"You are not a bother, for heaven's sake, Emil. You have helped me so much. It's just that I have to take care of other things now."

She spotted the undersized phalanx of children marching down the hill, with Frieda at the rear. Amalia was still holding hands with Liesl and they tugged each other's arms playfully. Frieda saw Anna and waved.

"Here they are now," said Anna. "Emil, will you be all right?"

He shrugged. Anna was nearly knocked over by Amalia's tackling hug.

"Mama! Pick me up," Amalia giggled. "*Hallo* Herr Schilling. Are you coming with us?"

"No, Maus, he isn't," Anna replied. "He has to go home, too. He's had a hard day of working." She lifted Amalia to her hip. The other children ran to meet their mothers, who had emerged from inside the building. Some lit cigarettes; others talked with the soldiers loitering in the yard. Anna recognized one of them from the typing pool and another from the filing offices downstairs. The mothers all went their separate ways without any casual after-work chatter. Anna too turned to leave, but bumped into Frieda who had come up behind her.

"Ah, Frau Klein. It's good to see you. Everything is well?" Frieda smiled and waved to another mother over her shoulder. She looked at her brother. "Emil, what are you doing here?"

Emil shrugged. "I'm just leaving." He waved a hand at Amalia but held Anna in his gaze. He turned and walked away.

Frieda sidled up to Anna, standing closer than Anna thought was comfortable. "I hope he's not bothering you," she said with tight lips and eyes darting at her brother's back. "I think he's taken to you a bit. Just misplaced emotion, you know. I've told him to let you be, that you are married and not interested in the likes of him anyway. He'll have to find his happiness somewhere else."

Anna shrugged off Frieda's intimation. "I do feel strangely protective of him. He's just a boy, really. He needs proper treatment. For his mind," she said. *Thomas would help him*, she thought.

"Oh, he'll be all right. He has a hard time, with all the Americans taking all the women. All the good German women are gone now. With all the bombs it's a wonder any of us is still standing." She looked at Anna and added, "I mean *most* good German women, of course. We are still here, you and I." She laughed. "But, of course, the Americans have so much more to offer a woman, don't they?"

Anna wondered what Frieda was trying to say. She wanted to let the comment roll off but it stuck to her. Did she want to be thought of as a 'good German woman?' Was she one? Did she care? She didn't think she did, but what did that make her? "Yes. Well, we'll be off," she said and took a step back.

Frieda fumbled with the belt of her dress. "When did you say your husband would be joining you?"

"My Papa will be here very soon," Amalia said. "I told you *Fraulein*, he's getting closer every day."

"That's right," Anna mustered. "Any day."

"Oh, so you've heard from him. How wonderful! I'll tell Emil. That will make the situation clear to him."

Anna decided to leave it alone and turned again to go. "Goodbye, Frieda." She paused to let the question that was percolating rise all the way to her mouth. "Were you ever married? I mean, are you waiting for someone, Frieda?"

Pools of roses surfaced on Frieda's cheeks. "Me? No, I never…well the war, you know." She bit her lip. "No, that was not to be for me."

"Maybe it still will." Anna smiled. "You never know."

"No, you don't. You never do," Frieda exhaled. The two women parted, Anna setting her sights on home and another night spent waiting for her husband to return from the war.

chapter eleven

The water in the tub was murky. Anna threw a remnant of the bar of soap in the water, and Amalia dumped the pile of clothes in. Anna leaned over and pulled pieces out one by one, hung them on the edge of the tub, and began to scrub them with the wooden brush. Her back ached after only two minutes and the soap burned her already dry hands. When she had washed all of the dresses, blouses and underwear, she took off her pants and added those to the water. Sitting on the edge of the tub she wrung out each item as best she could, then threw it in the sink. She could have gone down to the wash kitchen in the basement, but she'd rather not encounter any of her neighbors. She didn't feel like talking to anyone, and anyway, this way she could wash all the clothes at once.

"Here, Mama, these are Madeleine's." Amalia threw more clothes into the tub.

Anna sighed and knelt back down on the floor and washed the old woman's nightgowns, which is all Madeleine wore anymore these days. The soap transferred its salt onto the clothes so that even straight from the wash they already smelled sweaty. The edge of the metal tub cut into her armpits and her arms wailed. She brushed her hair from her eyes with the back of her hand.

"What is Auntie doing?" she asked.

"We are playing Snow Queen. She is reading the words and I am acting out the parts."

Anna was so glad to have Madeleine home, even as sick as she was. She liked the soothing presence of her mother's best friend. She was the closest thing she had to her own mother, something that rooted her to her life before. Without that, she thought she and Amalia would float off into the sky, alone and untethered. They owed Madeleine their lives, she knew that. They had arrived on her doorstep without even one suitcase, Anna following the vague directions of the forlorn people in the streets. When Madeleine had opened the door, Anna was shocked at the sight of her: frail and dirty, hair hanging in threads from a snowy scalp, her body racked with age and sickness, the air in the apartment hot and rancid. Amalia had already been crying for most of the day, her hunger and confusion and fear their constant companions. The reunion brought them all to tears and they stood for a long time on the landing in a huddle, their grief and joy sharing what little room was left for any feeling. Madeleine said their coming had saved her life, but Anna knew it had been a reciprocal act. Maybe one day Anna could repay her.

Anna was draining the tub when a knock at the door snapped her back to awareness. She looked down at herself, standing in the bathroom in her underwear. All her clothes were wet. The knock came again.

"Mama, I'll see who it is," said Amalia, skipping past the bathroom door.

Anna heard the door creak and then a man's voice.

"Yes, it is," said Amalia. "Yes, I will give it to her. Thank you."

As soon as the door closed, Anna stepped into the hallway. Amalia held a large basket filled with food: bread and butter, jars of jam, vegetables, eggs. There was even a sausage and two packs of Lucky Strikes. Real American cigarettes.

"It's from Herr Schneider. He said to tell you, Mama. Look there's cookies." Amalia squealed with delight and ran past her into the living room to show Madeleine.

"What else did he say?" Anna asked as she followed. "Anything?"

"He said to tell you he is very..." Amalia searched for the word. "Grateful. For your help. Did you help him Mama?" Amalia was spreading the contents of the basket onto the bed to show Madeleine.

"No, I did no such thing." Anna sat down and put her hand on her rumbling stomach. Schneider was bribing her? Why? If she'd gone to the door she could have turned him away. Now it was too late.

"Who is Herr Schneider?" asked Madeleine. She held the sausage under her nose and inhaled.

Anna began to recount the visit with the old man when Madeleine interrupted.

"Ludwig Schneider? The art dealer? He showed his face to the Americans?"

"Yes, why would he not?"

Madeleine snorted. "He was fat and happy during the war, dealing art to the Nazis, those criminals. Last I heard he was working for the culture chamber—the Reichskammer—in Frankfurt. As an 'art consultant.'" She rolled her eyes. "What did he tell you?"

"That's pretty much what he said. And that the Nazis sent him to a concentration camp. He made it sound like he was some kind of principled resister or something. Cooper didn't like him so he sent him away."

"Well he's right to do so. I never liked that man. We used to travel in the same circles and see him at parties. He'd always be angling for some advantage or seeking some favor from whomever he thought had the power. It was embarrassing. My Otto hated him. He would pretend to be hard of hearing when he was trapped in a conversation with him." She chuckled at the memory. "Of all the people to crawl out from under the Nazis, he had to be the one. A resister? Never."

"Well, what do I do now? I have to send this back. I can't take favors from him." She looked at Amalia, who was clutching the packet of cookies to her chest. "Come on Maus, we can't keep it. I am sorry."

"No, Mama. It was a present. You can't give presents back."

Anna sighed. "It's not a present little Maus. I can't take this. I could lose my job!" She reached for the cookie, but Anna pulled her hand away.

"Mama!" she wailed.

Madeleine patted Anna's knee. "Now, let's be practical. He didn't give the food to you; he gave it to the child. You did not accept anything and you never saw him. You can't return the basket—you don't even know where he lives." She batted her eyes.

"I could find out," Anna said.

Madeleine held up a hand. "Now, you could give the food away, but what good would that do? Schneider already thinks you have it. Really, the Americans don't have to know about this. And, Schneider can't be sure you even received the food, given that he didn't see you. What a shame it would be if he made the delivery to the wrong house."

"But Amalia…"

"Hungry children presented with a basket of food might say anything to get their hands on it, mightn't they? You can't go by the word of a child. So unreliable." Madeleine grinned and Amalia looked at her mother with the expectation of Christmas Eve on her face.

Anna swallowed. She wanted Amalia and Madeleine to have the food; they both needed it desperately. Her stomach joined the conversation with a loud grumble that made Amalia giggle. Anna stood up. "Oh, all right. Someone has to eat this food, I guess. It might as well be us."

"Just think, Schneider doesn't get to eat any of it. That seems right and good to me." Madeleine clapped her hands and looked pleased with herself.

Amalia jumped up and flung her arms around her mother's neck. "Thank you Mama. I love you."

Anna hugged her back and allowed herself to enjoy the moment. She put the girl down and returned to her washing. The food would have to wait a while longer.

Anna hung the wash on the line at the far end of the living room and then prepared a nice meal of buttered bread, sausage and cucumbers. She sliced everything as thinly as possible so the cucumbers were nearly transparent but still delicious. It was much too extravagant. *But what the hell*, she thought. *The war is over. We can celebrate a little*.

After they had eaten, the three of them lay around like beached seals, the rhythmic drip of the washing lulling Anna into feeling happier than she had in months. Even Madeleine had a rosy blush in her cheeks. Outside, the sun was finally setting, and the day was winding down. Anna turned on the radio. She still half-expected to be assaulted with the shouting, the absolute righteousness and the hateful lies that had been spewed at them for years through the radio waves. Every time you turned on your receiver it was Hitler or Göbbels or that fat Göring screaming at you. She never believed any of it, instinctively, but without having access to any alternate reality, the Nazi world view, their *Weltanschauung*, became so normal she no longer knew what was real and what was not. The Americans now controlled the radio, but her cynicism continued. Official voices, no matter whose they were, still made her suspicious. But, for now, the radio played American big band music and its rhythms glided through the air without leaving a mark anywhere.

This time the knock on the door was loud and insistent. Anna jumped from the couch where she had fallen asleep and instinctively looked for Amalia. The girl was fast asleep next to Madeleine. Anna pulled the clock from the small side table and held it up into the moonlight: four-fifteen. The street outside the open window was silent. She stood still and waited. The knocks came again, this time more insistent. She tugged her damp bathrobe from the line and pulled it on. Creeping down the hallway, her breath tightened her chest like an inflating balloon.

The knocks came once more. This time Anna heard a voice, whispering. She put her ear to the door.

"Anna? Let me in. Goddammit. I'll wake up the whole building. Come on, I know you're here," Cooper's voice growled.

Anna opened the door a crack and Cooper pushed his way in, nearly falling on top of her. In the dark she felt his breath on her face and put her arms up to catch him. His shirt was wet and his footing unsteady. "For God's sake, Captain, what is going on? Are you drunk?"

Cooper slumped on the floor. Anna closed the door and bolted the lock. She flipped the light switch, but the electricity was out again. The room was pitch dark and she could only make out his shape on the floor. He pulled himself up to sit with his back against the door.

"No, I'm not drunk, damn it."

"What's happened?" Anna knelt down and tried to focus her eyes on his face.

"I was out at the villa, and someone ambushed me. Beat the hell out of me. Christ." He dabbed at his head.

"Mama?" Amalia stood in the doorway to the living room like a ghost in a thin white nightgown.

"It's all right Maus, go back to bed. Everything's all right," Anna whispered. She turned to look at her daughter. "Go on," she hissed. The girl darted back into the darkness.

"Come on Captain, let's get you into the bathroom. Can you walk?"

She pulled him to his feet and leaned her shoulder into his side. In the bathroom she lit the candle by the sink and held it up. "Oh my dear God," she gasped. His right eye was swollen nearly shut and a gash above the eyebrow poured blood down the side of his face. The left side was in better shape, but the ear was encrusted with dried blood. More blood had flowed from another gash at the base of his skull down his back, soaking his shirt.

Cooper took the candle from her and held it up to the mirror shard that hung over the sink. "Holy Mother," he said. "That's gonna be hard to explain." He smiled at her with a fat lip.

Anna held a rag under the running water and began to dab at the cuts without much effect. Cooper winced and took the cloth from her, wiping his cheeks and forehead.

"Careful, you'll open them up again," she said. "I don't have any alcohol to clean them. You should really go to the hospital."

"Can't," Cooper said. "I'd have to go to the base hospital and then there'd be a whole ton of paperwork explaining what I was doing and with whom, why, when, where, and how. I'd rather just skip all that if it's all the same to you."

"Well what were you doing out there in the middle of the night? Maybe you could explain it to me," Anna said.

Cooper smiled over her shoulder. "Duchess! You're up late."

Amalia stepped inside the bathroom and regarded him with frightened eyes. "Is he hurt?" she asked with a mosquito voice.

Anna knelt down and put her arms around her daughter. "He's a little bit hurt. He had a car crash." She switched to English. "You had a car crash, didn't you, Captain?"

Cooper nodded. "Jeep drove right into a tree. I never could see in the dark." He smashed his hands together and made a face. "Don't worry, duchess. I'll be right as rain. *Alles okay*."

Amalia hugged her mother's leg. "I'll be right back," Anna said. She picked the child up and went into the living room. She put Amalia back in the bed with stern instructions to stay there, softened with the promise of a cookie for breakfast. Madeleine continued to snore softly, oblivious. Amalia lay down and snuggled her body next to the old woman. She didn't close her eyes.

In the bathroom, Anna took the washrag and dabbed at the cut at the back of Cooper's head. His hair had hardened with the drying blood. She rinsed the rag and worked at the wound until finally she could see the cut.

"Well, I don't think you need stitches, but you do need a some proper medical attention."

"Ah, forget it. Just give me that bar of soap."

Anna gave him the sliver left over from the washing. He ran it under the tap and rubbed the wet bar on his face and neck. Anna winced. "This is how you do it on the farm," he said. "I'll be fine."

Anna sat on the edge of the tub. She felt icy in her wet bathrobe. The adrenaline was starting to wane and she clenched her teeth to keep them from chattering. "Tell me again, what happened?" she asked.

Cooper shrugged. "Well, the thing is, I don't sleep well. And it was bugging me, what you said about the villa maybe being a store room for the black market and that the boy is acting all squirrely about why he was there. So I drove out there to have a look around. I was in the basement when I heard the door open. I pulled my weapon, but the other guy was too fast. Next thing I knew, I was down, and he was cracking me on the back of the head with my own gun." He reached down to touch the holster on his hip. "Oh shit." He spun around as if looking for something behind him. "Oooh shit. He took it. God damn it." He closed his eyes. "That's gonna be real hard to explain."

Anna's teeth freed themselves and began to jabber, telegraphing her anxiety despite her best efforts. She pulled the robe around her body, making the damp cold on her skin worse.

"They took your gun? Damn it, Captain. Why did you have to do go out there?"

Cooper smiled at her. "Now take is easy, sister. Everything will be fine. Don't you worry. This has nothing to do with you."

"So tomorrow you'll secure the repository and we'll start doing things, how do you say it…by the book?" Anna asked.

"Well, no."

"No, I didn't think so."

He sat on the edge of the tub next to her. "The guy that hit me took the Runge."

"What? How do you know?"

"What do you mean, how do I know?" He pointed at his head. "I was there."

"You saw him take the painting?"

"No, it was there when I got to the basement. But when I left, it was gone. I must have passed out for a while. I checked everywhere. The painting is definitely gone."

Anna closed her eyes. Part of her wanted him to walk away. She could go back to the typing pool and type up other people's reports. Thomas would come and they would restart their little life together. The other part of her asked Cooper, "Why would they only take the Runge, I wonder?"

"Anna?" a voice came from the living room. "Are you all right? What's going on?"

Anna sighed. "Well, we might as well go into the living room and be comfortable. Everyone's up now." She took the candle and led the way. She lit more candles before remembering that the room was decorated with her dripping underwear. She shook her head and decided not to care.

Madeleine was sitting up in bed with her arm around Amalia. "Captain, you've had an accident?" she said in her best English.

Cooper smiled and sat down on the couch, his arms reaching back onto the seat to steady himself. "Yes, ma'am. Nothing to worry about." His eyes fell on the basket on the table and then traced the laundry hanging like misshapen and tattered banners in the dark. "I like what you've done with the place. Did you have a nice dinner today?" He pointed at Schneider's basket.

Anna reddened and pulled her bathrobe around her legs as she sat down at the end of the bed.

"A present." Amalia piped up in English before Anna could speak. "From a man." She tugged at her mother. "*Sags ihm*, Mama, tell him."

"It was misdelivered," Anna lied. "Amalia answered the door and he was gone before I could stop..." she sighed. "Oh, what the hell. It came from Schneider. He wants me to help him get a job at the Collecting Point, I guess."

"We decided to eat the food anyway," Madeleine said. "Would you like some sausage or maybe some bread? We have cucumbers too. Anna, fix him a plate. The poor man."

"No thanks, I'm good," Cooper said. "So, Schneider was here?" He pointed at the floor and looked at Amalia, who nodded.

"I was doing laundry," Anna said. She felt the escalating embarrassment warm her.

Cooper leaned forward. "So he knows where you live. Isn't that interesting. But you didn't talk to him?"

"He's a horrible little man. I've known him for years," Madeleine whispered.

Cooper put a finger to his inflated lip and pointed to the open window. Anna nodded and crossed the room to close the shutters. When they were alone with the dripping laundry, Cooper gestured for Madeleine to go on.

"He was such a little weasel. My husband and I never bought a thing from him but many of our friends did. Then the political situation began to separate us from our friends. People we thought we knew, and even liked, turned out to be nothing more than ignorant and hateful beasts. And greedy, too. When Hitler took power in March of '33, all of a sudden being a Nazi was the fashionable thing. People were afraid to be caught on the wrong side. March Violets the old Nazi guard called them—late bloomers. So many people applied for Party membership that they had to stop taking them. You know, having a low Party membership number was a big honor in those circles. I guess people liked to prove that they were idiots before most others had caught on. After the Nazi Party stopped taking members, people joined the SA since it wasn't so particular. As long as they had some paper with a Swastika on it to identify themselves, they were happy."

"Like I said, that explains how Herr Schneider ended up in the SA," Anna said. "He didn't want to be left out in the cold."

"So you would consider Herr Schneider an enthusiastic follower?" Cooper asked as he dabbed at the nape of his neck with the wet rag.

Madeleine stroked Amalia's hair. "Of course. He became one when he saw which way the flag was waving, so to speak. And it worked, too. I heard he had the job of appraising the confiscated Jewish property. Of course, all those things were obscenely undervalued. And only Aryan buyers were permitted. Schneider once wanted to buy what few pieces we had—nothing important—but my Otto had the sense to sell it in '38, while it was still worth something. Probably the Nazis got their hands on it in the end anyway. We took the money and sat on it, kept it in cash." She waved her hand over her head. "It's what helped me survive. I'm down to one room but I have a kitchen and a bath, and I am grateful. Our old apartment isn't even standing anymore."

"Uncle Otto died in 1942," Anna said. "A heart attack. He was a banker. The greed and the corruption were too much for him. He was always trying to do the right thing. The insurance refused to pay because they said he had not kept up the premiums. That was a lie. He just wasn't a good Nazi. Before he died they moved into this small apartment. He bought it for her before things got really bad—the rations, the hunger, the bombs. Of our two families, we are the only ones left now."

Cooper looked at Madeleine. "Do you have children, Frau Wolf?"

Madeleine nodded. "A son. He died at the Somme, in the Great War. Anna's mother was a great champion of the soldiers of that war because of him. She was my best friend." She smiled, but her eyes flitted.

Anna rubbed Madeleine's back. Cooper glanced at his watch. "I should go. People will be up soon. Better if I'm gone before the wagging tongues wake up."

They are already awake, Anna thought. No one in Germany slept very deeply anymore, and everyone was trained to jump at the sound of banging on a neighbor's door in the middle of the night. It was not the kind of thing you got used to, no matter how often it happened, or who was doing the banging. She helped him off the couch.

"I hope you feel better, Captain," Amalia said. "Tell him, Mama."

Anna translated and Cooper gave her a thumbs-up, which Amalia returned halfheartedly. She lingered behind her mother's bathrobe as Anna ushered Cooper to the door.

"Tomorrow you will explain to me why you were out at the villa in the middle of the night," Anna said.

"I thought I already had," Cooper said. "I told you, I thought something fishy was going on there. I guess I wanted to just go there and think, but maybe I wanted to find something, too."

"And now you'll prepare the report and have the art brought to the Collecting Point, yes?"

"Well, I could do that, but I'd have to leave out some parts. And now one of the pieces is stolen. And so is my gun."

"Because you didn't report that you found the stash when you should have."

"Right."

"Right. So what happens now?"

"I'll figure it out. Let's talk tomorrow."

As soon as he was gone Anna closed the door and bolted it. It was five o'clock. They could maybe get two more hours of sleep. She pulled off the damp robe and crawled into bed with Madeleine and Amalia. The bed was warm and dry but sleep eluded her. Questions danced together in her head: Why was Cooper not following protocol? Who took the Runge painting? And why, of all places, had Cooper come here in the middle of the night?

"Frau Klein?"

A whisper startled Anna back to reality. She had been bent over a pad of paper, doodling the name Ludwig Schneider, Reichskammer, Frankfurt. Then she wrote: *Breuer, Darmstadt, Runge*. She looked at the page and drew circles around all three sets of information and pondered all that had happened. *Isn't this how the detective would solve the crime in one of those English mystery novels?* In the middle of page she wrote the name Oskar Grünewald and tapped her pencil as if to elicit some response from the paper itself. Now she turned to see Cooper limping to his desk. She jumped up and pulled out his chair.

"Captain. Is everything all right?"

He sat down. "Oh sure. Fine. I told my CO I got into a bar fight with some enlisted men. He rolled his eyes and told me to go get cleaned up. Gave me a warning. The nurses fixed me up and I even got some aspirin so things are looking up. I didn't mention the case of the missing side arm. You okay?"

"Yes. Of course." She took a step back and straightened as a group of GIs walked past the desk. "Is there anything I can do?"

"Sure—go down to Records and get the list of galleries that have filed to reclaim property or asked to re-open or just declared themselves to still exist. We can take a look and see if any claims or gallery names match our find."

"And you'll send someone to retrieve the art today? And file your report?"

Cooper sighed. "Yeah. I pulled together a couple of guys and got the trucks. We'll go out there today. You okay to stay here?"

Anna breathed a sigh of relief. She wanted nothing more than to sit at her desk and scour lists all day.

"Oh yeah, one more thing." Cooper winced as he shifted his weight in the chair. "I meant to ask you last night. Have you ever heard of some Nazi department called Lebensborn?"

Anna searched her memory and come up with only a vague idea relating to mothers and children. "I think it was some kind of program for pregnant women. There were some homes where women went to have babies? I'm not sure. Why do you ask?"

"I inquired downstairs about adoptions, you know—how that worked and if there were any records of birth parents or things like that. I figured you people keep such good records, there had to be a paper trail somewhere. One of the girls in the personnel department said Lebensborn, as if everyone should know this, but when I asked her what that was, she clammed up and turned red as a radish. Wouldn't say another word about it."

"So you think maybe it had something to do with Oskar's adoption? I do remember Himmler was always going on about how women should give the Führer a child. The more the better. So I think Lebensborn was some kind of SS program? It was all sort of secret and mysterious. And, of course, we didn't ask any questions. Maybe I'll see what I can find out." She turned to go, but Cooper grabbed her hand.

"Hey, listen. Thanks. I know you didn't really sign up for this. I'm sorry I've dragged you into the mess I'm making with the art and all. And I'm sorry about last night. I had nowhere else to go." He looked genuinely apologetic and the gesture took her aback.

"I am glad you are not seriously hurt," she stammered. She tried to remove her hand but Cooper squeezed it, just once, before he let go. She smiled for an instant and made her exit.

Walking down the hall, Anna was aware of the remnant sensation of his hand around hers. A ripple of something warm pushed its way though her body. She closed her palm as if to hold on to the invisible hand in hers. *Damn* Ami. She wiped her palm on her pants and quickened her pace toward the stairs.

chapter twelve

Anna stood up and stretched her back. She closed her eyes and took a deep breath. The Collecting Point had only been open for a few weeks, but already the claims for lost and stolen property amounted to reams and reams of papers. Some claims were itemized, with the owner's information typed and their belongings meticulously listed to the point of tedium. Three silver teaspoons. One Wedgwood plate. A set of silver salt and pepper shakers (antique). Other claims were vague and inscrutable, especially the ones written in longhand. None matched the items from the villa, not even close. It was already after two o'clock. She had worked through lunch, preferring to keep to herself and make up the time she had lost. Cooper had vanished, saying something about checking on the fence. She hadn't seen him for hours.

Anna leaned on the balustrade in the hallway and looked down into the main foyer. Americans and Germans were busy working on the building, the wiring, the windows, the furniture. Everywhere there was cleaning and scrubbing, moving and organizing. The place was like an anthill. She was on the south side of the building, which had housed the archaeological collection before the war. The northern windows across the foyer had been damaged more severely in the bombings and workers were still replacing them. A continual ribbon of tiny shards of broken glass tracked throughout the entire building and sometimes the constant crunching underfoot made Anna's teeth stand on edge. Two thousand little panes, Cooper had told her. Captain Farmer, the Collecting Point director, had received a tip from a German worker about several tons of glass that were abandoned by the Luftwaffe at a barracks under construction near the Wiesbaden airfield. He found it under a pile of garbage and managed to get away with it, stealing the precious glass out from under the Air Force. Cooper loved telling this story, which had become a small legend around the building, saying that brawn may win the war, but brains will win the peace. The director had also taken the cots and other equipment abandoned by the Luftwaffe at the museum to UNRRA and traded them for food. The Army cast-offs that the German soldiers now wore were also his doing, since the Germans were forbidden to wear their old uniforms—often the only clothes they still owned.

Anna went back to her desk and picked up where she had left off. A knock on the wall behind her made her turn. A GI with blond hair and a serious face stood in the opening.

"Excuse me, Frau Klein? Anna Klein?"

Anna nodded.

The soldier checked something off his clipboard. "Great, come with me, please." He stepped aside to allow her to pass.

Anna didn't move. "Where am I going, may I ask?" she said.

He smiled apologetically. "Personnel. We have to tighten up the place before Monday, so I need you to fill out some paperwork and get you a proper ID. Everyone's getting one." His name tag said Bormann. Anna smiled and wondered how much grief he'd gotten for sharing a name with Hitler's top adjutant. She picked up her bag and followed him downstairs to the records section.

The new pass they gave her had her name and the photo the *Amis* had copied from her paperwork at the Arbeitsamt—the official employment office where all Germans had to register. Bormann stamped her papers with the flourish only the terminally bureaucratic could produce and presented them with a smile. Anna hated identity papers. Sooner or later they always got used against you. But this one, which read "U.S. Military Translator/*Dolmetscherin*," was an asset for now.

Back in Cooper's quasi-office, the heat of the day had taken hold, and Anna lowered the blinds in the window above her desk to reduce the glare. There was no breeze anyway. Returning to her lists, she saw a note had been placed on top of the pile.

Anna, I'll be at my apartment this evening after work. I must talk to you. Please stop by before you pick up Amalia. Yours, Emil.

Anna crumpled the paper in her fist and threw it into the bin under Cooper's desk. She considered how much longer she could fend Emil off without offending him and upsetting his sister and thus endangering the babysitting arrangement. There were rumors that the schools would restart within the month, once the *Amis* had approved the textbooks and purged all the history books of their so-called Nazi truths. All that would be left would be a pamphlet about the glory of the Weimar Republic, the hapless old Hindenburg who handed power to Hitler like a tray of biscuits, and the American saviors who rescued them. Everything in between still needed sorting out. But at least then Amalia could go to a real kindergarten. Anna would hold her breath until then.

She was trying to focus on the details of a claim by one Albert Ritter of Eberstadt, regarding the loss of, among other things, twelve porcelain cat figurines, when she felt hands clamp down on her shoulders. She jumped.

Cooper laughed. "Sorry. Man, you are wound tight."

"Don't do that," she hissed. "You scared me half to death."

With his fat lip and swollen eye Cooper looked half-crazed. He sat down at his desk and leaned back. "Guess where I've been?"

"Retrieving the repository from the villa?" Anna turned her chair to face him.

"That's being taken care of. I got sent to survey a church, out in Erbenheim."

"And?" Anna tried to seem interested.

"And, there were some nuns there. They ran a school there during the war. At least some of the time." He began to examine the scab forming on the back of his hand with great interest.

"So?"

"So, one of them, an older one who started off kind of grumpy, she spoke English. *Schwester Gerlinde*. We got to chatting, and I asked her how many kids they had in the school and what happened to them. She told me things got pretty chaotic in about '43 with the bombs and the shortages. She said the official children's home, the one out at our villa? It was an SS home, like you said. Sometime in '42 it began overflowing with all these blonde orphans. So sometimes the nurses there sent them some kids that were waiting to be adopted. He rubbed the back of his head and winced. "Here's the part I don't get. She said the kids were brought there by the SS. Apparently they had nurses in the SS?" He chuckled. "SS nurse seems kind of oxymoronic doesn't it?"

"Oxymoronic?"

"Yeah, you know a term that contradicts itself. Like military efficiency. Or world peace."

Anna squinted at him.

Cooper shook his head. "Anyway, the nun said the nurses brought them. Then eventually the families—who were also always SS by the way—would show up with the paperwork and take their new kids home. You see what I'm getting at?"

Anna shook her head no.

" SS? Nurses?"

"Oh, you mean the Lebensborn program?" Anna said.

"Yes, that's what I mean," Cooper said with mock irritation. "So the SS was adopting out kids. I doubt they were doing it out of the kindness of their hearts. There's got to be more to the story."

Anna agreed. "There's always more to the story with those people. Oskar must have some connection there. Maybe they took him in again after his mother died? It can't be a coincidence that we found him there." Anna chewed the inside of her lip. "I guess I need to go talk to our boy again."

Anna hurried Amalia along the Gustav-Freytag-Strasse. She had left work five minutes early and run almost the whole way to the Schilling house to get there before Emil did. Now she wanted to avoid him on the way home, which took her back past the museum. Amalia was carrying the doll with the red dress from Frieda's playroom tight under her arm. Frieda had given it to her to keep and Amalia had named her Lili. "Because she is Lulu's little sister," she explained.

Anna scanned the road ahead. "What did you do today, Maus?" she asked.

"We played in the garden. We dug holes."

"Dug holes? For what?"

Amalia rolled her eyes. "For the onions, Mama. We are planting onions. Look at my hands." She held out her left hand to show the black fingernails. "I look like a real farmer!" She giggled.

Anna rubbed the girl's head. "You are a city farmer. Maybe you can plant some potatoes in our bathtub."

They turned onto the Frankfurter Strasse where the traffic picked up and they had to sidestep people coming toward them. Anna picked the girl up to keep her from getting separated.

"Anna!" The voice came from in front of her, but her view was blocked. She pretended not to hear and kept walking upstream.

"Anna?" Emil's smiling boy face appeared. "Anna, didn't you get my note? *Hallo* Amalia." He reached out and patted Amalia's back.

"Emil, *hallo*. I am sorry, but we are in a terrible hurry," Anna said and kept walking.

"Oh I see. May I walk with you?" He fell into stride with her. "Are you all right?" He poked Amalia in the belly to make her laugh.

"Yes, of course. I am fine."

"Listen, I need to talk to you." Emil lowered his voice. "But I really don't want to do it out here."

Anna looked straight ahead. "I'm sorry, Emil. We really have to go."

"Anna, it's not what you think. Please…" He grabbed her arm. Anna froze and turned her head toward his face. Then she looked down at the fist wrapped around her bicep, fingers pushing into her flesh. Before she could resist, he pulled her into an alley behind the nearest row of houses.

She tried to pull her arm away. "Let go of me. I'll scream," she threatened, looking up at the open windows. She felt stupid, but it was the only threat she could think of. Blood rushed like a waterfall behind her ears.

Emil released his grip but took up a position between her and the street. Amalia's arms were clamped around Anna's neck, her head buried.

"What the hell do you want? I told you we are in a hurry," Anna fumed.

"I told you. I just want to talk to you. You don't even have time to talk to me?" Emil leaned in, his voice low and coarse, as if he was talking through sandpaper. "I need to tell you something. But not here."

"Yes, here," Anna said.

Emil looked at her, then at the houses on each side, considering his options. Anna shifted her weight and wondered if she could get around him before he could grab her. Not if she was carrying Amalia.

"Look, Anna. I have not been entirely honest with you. And now I need to tell you something because, well because I like you. And Amalia too."

The girl peeked out from under Anna's arm. Emil smiled. His face returned to its normal boyish character, but his eyes betrayed something darker. Anna wanted no part of whatever he was about to confess.

"Emil, really it's all right. You don't need to…"

"Herr Schilling? Did you see my doll?" Amalia held up the new prize. "*Fraulein* gave her to me. As a present. Because I was such a good helper. Isn't she pretty?"

Emil's gaze bounced between Anna and Amalia. "Yes, she is. Very pretty. You must have been very good."

"Yes, I was. Mama, can we go now?" Amalia whispered. "I want to go home."

Anna put on a maternal smile. "I really must go, Emil."

She started to walk but he stepped in front of her. "You know something? I hate when you look at me that way. Full of pity and charity. Don't think I don't see it. You never look at the *Ami* that way." He leaned in closer and Anna caught the smell of alcohol on his breath. She held her ground but put a protective arm over her daughter's ear. "I don't want your goddamn pity. You think you are better than me? You think your hands are clean now that you work for them?"

Anna flared. "Pity you? For what? For surviving? Why do you earn my pity for that?" She pushed him away and began to walk, pulling Amalia by the wrist. Emil pulled her arm again and she struck at him, just missing.

"Let me tell you something," she said, turning back toward him and pushing a finger into his shoulder. "For six years I have been the only thing standing between this creature and the hell that was brought down on all of us. I am the only thing that protects her. You think I could have stuck my neck out so my head could get cut off and she'd be all alone in *this* world? Yes, my hands *are* dirty. You know how I know? Because I am still here. Because a lot of people got dragged away—people just like me, Germans, or people who thought they were Germans—and they never came back. Mothers taken from their children. Every day, Emil. And I did nothing. You saw it too, didn't you? Or maybe you were one of those doing the taking?"

Instantly she regretted her words. She regretted accusing him and she regretted giving voice to her worst fear in front of her daughter.

Emil's expression shifted slightly to something she did not recognize, but he said nothing.

"Everything all right here?" An MP loomed over both of them looking first at Anna and then Emil with practiced authority. He was so tall he blocked the sun from Anna's view.

"Yes, thank you, officer." Anna tried on an embarrassed laugh. We were just having a talk." Emil stared at the ground. "And now we are leaving. Let's go, Maus." She set Amalia on her feet and made to leave.

"I think you'd better move along too, *Fritz*." The MP jabbed Emil's shoulder. Now Anna recognized the emotion on Emil's face. Humiliation. By her and by the *Amis*. By the war and by his fate. She bit her lip.

Emil jerked away from the American and shot her a frozen look before walking away. Anna wanted to tell him things would get better, but she knew that they probably wouldn't. That he would have to reconcile his war with this sprouting peace or he would surely sink. But she couldn't tell him because she didn't even know how to do it herself.

Amalia's little hand into slid hers and they turned toward home. Anna willed her feet to walk.

"Why did you say those things, Mama?" Amalia's voice was small and far away, as if she were talking to someone else.

"What things?"

"About mothers getting taken away from their children? Why did you say that? Is that true?"

Anna squatted down to look the girl in the face. "No little Maus, it's not true anymore. The bad people are all gone now and we are safe. No one can take the mothers away." She pulled her close. "Don't be scared."

Amalia looked sideways and chewed on her lip. "But they killed that boy's mother. The one you found. I heard you tell Auntie. And your mother died too. And..." Tears rose in her eyes and one escaped down her cheek, as if warning of more to come.

Anna wrapped her arms around the little girl, wishing she could collapse her body into something small enough to keep her arms around forever. "Yes, that's true. They did take them away. But all that is over now. And I am still here. Now come on, let's go for a walk. Maybe we can get some tea for Auntie."

At the Bonifazius Church, instead of turning left into the Adolfsallee, Anna turned to the right, toward the old city. They passed the glassy-eyed veterans sitting along the old wall of the square and walked into the weaving, narrow passages. Americans strolled down the middle of the street, in groups of two or four, laughing and smoking. Some smiled at Amalia, others made off-color comments at Anna. She looked straight ahead, gritting her teeth.

In the Friedrich Strasse, near the Neugasse, they went into a tiny apothecary. The shop was no bigger than a bedroom and its tall shelves were only partly stocked with jars of dried herbs and teas. A short round woman stood behind a table on which were displayed baskets of various leaves, blossoms and twigs. The place smelled of earth and was cool and damp inside, like a cave. Amalia sneezed.

"What will be it be today?" the woman behind the counter asked.

Anna asked for a tea for cough and lung infection. The woman nodded, but before she moved she said, "And how will you pay?"

"I have dollars," Anna said, opening her purse. "I work with the Americans," she added unnecessarily. The woman gave the knowing look that usually implied her money came from less than honorable work and then turned to the jars behind her. She made a mixture of sticks and dried flower buds on a piece of paper, which she folded into a flattened triangle. On it she wrote the instructions for brewing with suggestions for drinking the tea three times a day. "Each spoonful is good for three pots, just let it steep a bit longer each time. This should be enough for a week, and that will help. I grow these myself; they are very good."

Anna nodded and handed over her money, which the woman tucked into the front of her blouse. "I thank you very kindly," she said.

Anna smiled and turned to leave. Reaching for the door she saw someone she recognized walk past the window. It was Ludwig Schneider, carrying a large flat package wrapped in brown paper, walking in the direction of the Schwalbacher Strasse.

Anna took Amalia's hand and waited for him to get a decent distance past the shop. Then she stepped outside. "Come on Maus, we need to go this way."

Schneider walked at a good clip, and Anna pulled at Amalia's arms to keep up with him. The girl was more interested in looking around at the mix of rubble and empty storefronts.

"Mama, slow down," she whined. "I want to look. Why are we going so fast?"

"See that man up there, the one carrying the big picture? I want to see where he goes.

Amalia's eyes grew wide. "That's Herr Schneider. What's he doing?"

"I don't know Maus," Anna whispered. "Let's just see where he goes. But we can't let him see us, do you understand?"

"Why not?"

"Because we are playing detective. Will you help me?"

Amalia nodded and skipped to keep up with Anna's pace. Schneider turned right into the Schwalbacherstrasse and Anna stopped at the corner. She stood on her toes to see over the bobbing heads making their way along the street, but Schneider had disappeared into the crowd. She picked Amalia up and set her on her hip. "Maus, can you see him?"

Amalia couldn't see him either so Anna let herself be carried along with the flow of people. Every third building along the street was gone. In between the rubble people set up shops, even a café here and there, defiant of the destruction. The approaching *Truemmerbahn*—the small train cars that used the tram tracks to clear the rubble from the city—shook the ground, but no one took any notice. The cars passed, loaded to the brim with pieces of concrete, brick, shards of glass and all the other building dregs the bombs had left behind. The human remains had been dealt with long ago—all that was left were just the symbols of their lives. Bricks and mortar, doors and windows had suffered the same fate—shattered into fragments, broken and unrecognizable.

"Mama there he is!" Amalia shouted. "I see him."

Anna cringed. "Shh! Not so loud."

"Oh, sorry, Mama. He went into a house. That one right there." She pointed to a plain residential building that was mostly intact. The door to the inner courtyard was patched together from wood remnants. As people jostled her, Anna looked up to see closed shutters. Some windows were broken or boarded over. One was open, its white curtain blowing out with the breeze. Anna sidestepped the cross traffic to get closer and read the nameplates on the door frame. None of them read Schneider and none meant anything to her.

"Maus, listen. I want you to remember these three names, do you think you can do it?"

Amalia nodded and stood up straightened as if awaiting orders.

"All right listen, here we go: Fromm, Schenk and Knopf. Can you remember that?"

"Fromm, Schenk and Knopf. Yes, I can," the girl shouted in a tiny soldier voice.

"Good girl. Now remember them until we get home and I can write them down." Anna made a mental note of the other three names: Vogel, Buchholz, and Mueller.

The door opened and a tiny old woman stepped into the street. Anna moved Amalia out of the way. The woman smiled and closed the door behind her. "Can I help you child? Are you lost?"

Anna nodded. "Yes, well I think I am a bit lost." She pulled Amalia closer to her leg and put a firm hand on her cheek. "I am looking for a friend of my mother's. Her name is Vogel, Gerda Vogel. Does she live here?"

The old woman squinted at her with milky eyes. "Oh child, there's no Vogel here anymore. The nameplate is old. There are only three families left now."

"Fromm, Schenk, and Knopf!" Amalia shouted again.

The old woman smiled at her. "What does she say?"

"So the Vogels are not here?" Anna lowered her head. "I see."

"I don't know where they went. I can ask my neighbor, Herr Fromm, he might know. He's lived here the longest and took an interest in the neighbors. I keep my door and mouth closed. I don't think that Herr Schenk would know anything—he only arrived in the building a few months ago. By then the Vogels were long gone."

"Mama?" Amalia tugged at her sleeve.

"Just a minute, Maus." Anna stroked the girl's head with a firm hand. She smiled at the old woman. "I see. You have been so helpful.

Thank you, Frau..."

"Mueller. If you'd like, I can ask. And if you come back in a few days I can tell you what I find out." She smiled at Amalia. "Such a precious child."

"Yes, we will try. Thank you again." Anna pulled Amalia's hand and they walked back in the direction they had come from. A clock somewhere rang six o'clock. The streets were clearing after the workday. Anna crossed over at the intersection, then backtracked until they were directly across the street from the house Schneider had entered. The evening sun cast long shadows on this side of the street. She sat Amalia down on the ledge of a shop window. "Right. Now we wait."

"What for, Mama?"

"For Herr Schneider to come out."

"But what if he doesn't? I am so hungry."

"I know, Maus. Me too. But he'll come out soon enough. We just have to be a bit patient."

Amalia kicked her heels against the wall and hunkered down into a long sulk. "Fromm, Schenk, and Knopf," she said under her breath.

"Vogel, Buchholz and Mueller," Anna added and put an arm around her daughter's shoulder.

chapter thirteen

And?" Cooper leaned in closer.

"And, nothing. He came out with a painting and walked to his house—at the address he gave on his card. Then we stopped following." Anna shrugged. "Amalia was hungry."

"Damn. And we don't know anything about who lives in the apartments where Schneider went?"

Anna pulled a piece of paper from her pants pocket. "Vogel, Heinrich, Mueller, Fromm, Schenk and Knopf. Frau Buchholz is the old woman I talked to. She said only Fromm and Schenk still live there."

"Are you telling me this is the only apartment house in Germany that's got rooms to spare?" Cooper scrunched his eyes.

"Maybe it's more damaged inside than it appears. There is heavy damage on the street."

Cooper looked skeptical.

"Anyway, I am going to check those names and addresses with the claims list and the list of collectors, to see if anything matches. I don't think Schneider came out with the same painting he went in with, but there's no way to prove that except that the second package looked smaller than the first. He must have left the first package there and exchanged it for something else. Which is illegal, right, under your paragraph?"

"Paragraph 51. Right. No cultural property may change hands, not even among relatives. But a flat package does not cultural property make. It could have been something else."

"Oh please, what else would it have been? And what will you do about it?"

Cooper placed his palms on the desk and straightened in his chair. "Someone needs to go have a look at that apartment and find out who lives there and how they know Schneider. But that's going to have to wait until after next week. There are no off-site surveys allowed until the Frankfurt shipment is all taken care of. This afternoon I need you to pick up some supplies. Miller will drive you." He handed her a pass and some paperwork. "Don't forget the film for the camera. Oh, and our stash at the villa? It's finally here. I got a truck out there yesterday. But we can't inventory it until things settle. We just don't have enough manpower. I can't even find anyone to get film developed so we can start sorting through the photos we took of those paintings."

Anna nodded. "I'll get the newest claim forms and at least type those." She stood. "Uh, we are going to see Oskar tomorrow, Amalia and I. Would you maybe like to come too? I was thinking we'd go up to the Neroberg, if I can borrow a bicycle for him. The weather has been nice, the fresh air will do us good."

Cooper tilted his head and squinted, and, for a moment, Anna wondered if she had spoken in German and he hadn't understood. He shook his head. "Can't do it, not this weekend. Plus, you know the fraternization rules. Sounds like fun, though. Oh, remember you're going to bring the duchess by next week to see the treasures. How is she?"

"She's doing well." If Anna were being totally honest, she'd have to admit the arrangement with the Schillings made her uneasy. Instead she changed the subject. "That reminds me. I need to find out when the schools are going to be ready to open. Do you know anything about that? I think she really needs to be in a proper school."

"Nope. But I hope it's soon. Having all these little urchins running around makes me nervous. There are these little monkeys that dig through the trash at the canteen, stealing the table scraps. Little tiny ones, littler than your girl. Some of the guys chase them away. I can't stand it. Like it's better to throw the food out than to let German kids have it? Not right. It just makes me sick." He leaned back in his chair and cradled his neck in his hands. Something wistful washed over his face and he turned toward the open window. "You know what, on second thought, maybe I will join you this weekend. I miss the duchess. You are right, the fresh air and the view will do me good."

Anna smiled. "What about the fraternization laws?"

"Ah hell, who cares. I am the last man in Germany obeying that order. Besides, you're a happily married woman, am I right? And I'm just a harmless old bachelor." He flipped the cover of his ledger closed and stood up.

On her lunch break Anna stopped at the makeshift post office and message board to send another *Lebenszeichen* to Thomas. She had already sent two of the little postcards, the Signs of Life that sent word of survival between scattered family. First she scanned the messages pinned to the board, but they were the usual: people looking for jobs, household items to buy or trade, or transportation to various towns in the region. Someone offered tutoring services in "all languages," which made Anna smile. Another was looking for a supply of zinc tubs of very particular dimensions. And then there were the photos of orphans and displaced children. Each one held a paper with a name written on it under the headline, "Do you know me?" Their faces were like an accusation. Many of them were from the Wiesbaden DP camp, and Anna assumed that Oskar's face would soon appear on the wall as well. Each one was more heartbreaking than its neighbor. Sweet little girls gave big hopeful smiles, teenagers wore tired, mistrustful expressions, and the toddlers looked confused and scared. So many lost creatures floating about, needing a soft place to land.

She took her postcard to the counter and wrote her message in clear, large print. At least it looked confident. *We are at Wolf home. Adolfsallee Wiesbaden.* She counted the words. Three more to go to reach the ten that were allowed. She tapped the pencil on the paper. *Please come now*, she added.

It was a version of the same thing she had written both times before, but she could not think of what else to say. She handed the card to the woman behind the counter who looked at the address through a pair of glasses she held up with her hand.

"Kappellendorf? Where is that?"

"Just east of Weimar. Twenty kilometers." Anna replied.

The woman made a sucking noise through her teeth. "Not much getting through to that sector since the Russians took over. It's all locked down. I heard no one was coming or going. This is some kind of peace we have on our hands, isn't it? My sister's mother-in-law, she's been trying to get out for weeks. Poor thing. She's eighty-two years old. You'd think they'd just let her go." She shook her head. "Anyway, this will go out next week, but I wouldn't hold my breath."

Anna thanked her and walked back out into the day feeling alone and small. Whenever there was a pause in activity, a moment to think, the hopelessness returned, a wave lapping at her feet, threatening to pull her under. Maybe her photo should be pinned up alongside the children on that wall, she thought. "Do you know me?" it would ask. "I am lost."

After her lunch break Anna met Corporal Miller in the courtyard so he could drive her to the supply store. The drive took them away from the town center toward the airfield where the Americans had all their logistics facilities. They did not speak for the whole twenty minutes, Anna clenching her teeth to keep from gasping at the American's terrible driving. She studied his profile as she braced herself for his erratic turns and weaves: He had a slack jaw that melted into his neck and the flattened face of a boxer who had gone a few too many rounds. Behind his Army-issue sunglasses, his eyes were deep set under thick brows. A fly landed on his cheek and he slapped himself hard, then wiped it away.

When they arrived at the vast complex of warehouses and boxy office buildings she exhaled with relief. Miller weaved the jeep between clumps of GIs and parked trucks and came to a stop outside a long, low, windowless building. He jumped out and lit a cigarette. "Meet you back here in thirty minutes," he said before shouting a hello to another *Ami* and catching up with him.

Anna was glad to be rid of Miller and went inside, flashing her papers at the MP as she saw others do. A tall blonde woman in an immaculate Army uniform sat at a metal desk guarding a black binder and a cup of pencils. Anna asked for the office supply storeroom and the woman gestured to her right.

In the supply room, Anna handed the list to the clerk behind a counter who noted each item with an authoritative "uh-huh" until he got to the bottom of the list. "Yep, we've got all of this, except I've only got three of those typewriter ribbons left. I'll give you all of 'em." He winked.

Anna thanked him and looked around. The clerk's name strip said Bender and his insignia designated him a corporal. His puffy cheeks and rounded features gave him a cheerful bureaucratic quality that was matched by an easy bounce in his step. A long, tall counter stood between Anna and several rows of shelves that stretched like cliffs into the darkness beyond. The room was dingy and hot, and Bender's uniform showed sweat stains under his arms. Anna fanned herself with her papers.

"Have a seat. Sorry it's so hot." He turned on an electric fan in the corner before being swallowed between the shelves. Anna was lulled by the hum of the fan and the breeze it blew at her with every rotation. Bender brought reams of paper, packs of carbon paper, and all the forms and blank custody cards Cooper had asked for. There were also several boxes of pencils, stacks of file folders, and the typewriter ribbons.

"Here's some photographic film, too. More ribbons are coming end of next week but until then I got no more to give you." He held up his palms in apology. "Tell Cooper you'll need to come back. How is old Coop? Haven't seen him in ages."

"He's well."

"You got a car outside? Here, I'll help you. Sign here first." He pointed to a line at the bottom of a form and Anna obliged. "And here. Here. And then here." He produced three more forms and stamped each one after Anna signed. He took the reams of paper under one arm and tucked the boxes of pencils and packages of forms into the space under his armpit. With the other he took the remaining papers. Anna took the folders and typewriter ribbons and pulled open the door.

"Tell Coop 'Hi' from me. I'm Corporal Bender. We were in Italy together for a while, before he went off with those Venus fixers. The arts guys. Haven't seen him since. Makes sense that he'd end up here. So, you Coop's secretary or what?"

"Translator," Anna said. "And secretary too, I guess. I do whatever needs doing."

Bender nodded. "Well, you got lucky. He's a great guy, Cooper. Saved my tail more than once. I'll have to come by and have a visit with him."

"I'll tell him you said so," Anna said, holding the door open. She helped unload everything into the jeep and thanked him.

Bender shook her hand. "Real nice to meet you, Anna Klein. You take care. Come see me again."

Miller saw her from across the parking lot and nodded. He threw his cigarette on the ground and got into the driver's side. "Got everything you came for?"

Anna nodded but Miller made no move to start the jeep. He spat onto the pavement next to the driver's side. "So, Frau Anna Klein can I ask you something? It is Frau, right?" he asked, leaning an elbow on the steering wheel and turning toward her. He sucked on his teeth as he pulled a cigarette from the breast pocket of his shirt. Placing the smoke between his lips he let it hang there. Anna wondered if he expected her to light it for him.

"You and Cooper. What's going on there?"

"I'm sorry?" Anna knew what he meant.

"What's going on there? You two seem awful close."

Anna felt the heat rise in her cheeks. "I don't understand."

"Oh come on. You understand just fine. Me and some of the guys, we were just talking the other day and we made a bet. I said I was pretty sure I had seen Cooper going into your house—over there in the Adolfsallee, right? And leaving at real strange hours. They didn't believe me. They said you were too stuck up. A real icebox. But I don't think so. You're not fooling me."

Anna's head spun around to face him "I don't know what you are talking about," she said, trying to sound convincing. How could Miller have known that Cooper was at her house at four o'clock in the morning? Was he watching her? She stared at her own reflection in his sunglasses. "What concern is it of yours?" she added. Perhaps he was bluffing. It was clear that everyone from the workers at the Collecting Point to Frieda Schilling to the meddlesome neighbor Frau Hermann thought that her job had progressed to something more quid-pro-quo in nature. Maybe Miller was just shooting in the dark.

Miller snorted. "Oh I'm not concerned. I'm just asking. There's a law against fraternization, you know." He leaned his head toward her. "Not that we don't all do a little of that here and there. Lots of German girls are willing, you know what I mean? And you all sure are a pretty bunch. Makes our jobs so much nicer," he laughed. "Such a funny word, ain't it? Fraternization. Sounds like we're all going to college." He pulled a lighter from his pants pocket, lit the cigarette and blew the smoke out of the side of his mouth with a loud hiss.

"I really need to get back, Corporal."

Miller nodded. "I just wanted to mention it. I ain't the only one who's seen you two in his office, whispering. People notice that stuff and they talk. You know how it is. I know it would be a real shame if Cooper got nailed over something as stupid as sleeping with the enemy. He'd get a transfer and you'd be out of a job. He's already on thin ice."

Anna fumed. "I don't know what you are talking about." She wanted to ask Miller what he knew about Cooper, but didn't dare. She thought of the report that Cooper hadn't filed. His refusal to hire Schneider. The stolen gun and the missing painting. What exactly was Miller insinuating?

"Sure you do." He blew a stream of smoke at her face. "I can tell you are a real by-the-book kind of girl. What you don't know about Cooper is that he tends to get himself in trouble. If Cooper's got you involved in one of his harebrained schemes, I'd watch out. You're getting set to take a real big fall. I'd say it's better to play by the rules."

Anna said nothing. The sun on her head felt like hot liquid.

"Everything all right there?" Bender called from the open door.

"Oh yeah, we're fine. No problem," Miller called back. "We were just leaving."

"Captain Cooper called from the CCP. He's expecting the *Fraulein* back. Wondering what's taking so long. You better step on it."

Miller gave a wave and settled in his seat. He started up the jeep and turned it in the direction of the city. They backtracked the route they had come and Anna relaxed a little as they got closer to town, even with Miller bobbing and weaving the jeep all over the road.

She wanted to trust Cooper. He could have fired her that first day when she left Amalia outside. Or the second day. He had been understanding and never crossed any line with her, not really. He had even tolerated her outbursts. She liked him, despite his bull-in-a-china-shop way of doing things. The thought of him using her in some scheme and throwing her to the wolves made no sense, but she knew it was possible. After all, what did she really know about Cooper? He was kind, she knew that for sure. Kindness was enough, she decided. For now. She closed her eyes and let the wind blow the doubt from her mind. In its place she put Amalia's smiling face and the sensation of her daughter's little hand in hers. As long as she had that, somehow everything would be all right.

One block away from the Collecting Point all traffic was stopped. Miller stood up in his seat to get a better view of what was ahead but sat back down. "Might have to be here a while. Looks like they're setting up the security perimeter for the delivery. You got your papers? You can walk if you're in a hurry. Don't want to keep the Captain waiting." He threw her a sideways look. "I'll bring the stuff when I get there."

Anna was grateful for the release and picked up her bag. She reached into the back seat and took the typewriter ribbons from the top of the pile of supplies.

"Think about what I said, why don't you? It's good to know who you can trust. And you can always come to me if you got a problem." Miller snorted and then spat to his left onto the street, into the path of a stooped woman walking past the jeep. *Schwein*, Anna thought as she walked away. *Pig*.

When she came over the little hill, Anna saw the cause of the back up. Three Sherman tanks sat on the street in front of the Collecting

Point. Her heart gave her a kick as the familiar gasoline smell drifted her way. One of the tanks rumbled to life and began to move. A handful of Americans shouted and waved their arms, trying to direct it into a small open patch at the southwest corner of the new fence. The tank lurched back and forth in the tight space like an overgrown bear trying to roll over in its cave. The same back and forth had happened when the American tanks had rolled into the narrow streets of Kappellendorf. One had gotten stuck in a tight corner and the Americans had simply run it into the offending building, sending its facade crumbling to the ground. The whole town had gathered to watch the arrival, hanging white sheets from their windows and standing in solemn observance. The Americans had stumbled on the Buchenwald concentration camp in the forest on the other side of Weimar only days before. Confirmation of the rumors of its atrocities had raced through the town. The Germans, no longer shrouded by willful ignorance or fear or even fervent support, absorbed the contemptuous and accusing stares of the Americans. There was nowhere left to hide, after all.

Days later the Americans rounded them up and marched the good Germans of the area through the camp to see with their own eyes what their complicity had wrought. Anna and Thomas had been separated during the march and she walked through camp without him, following a fat woman with a feathery hat. How this woman could have put on her Sunday best for this journey Anna would never understand. The memories of what she saw still flashed in her mind daily, sometimes hourly, searing and unbidden. Men so emaciated that their skin barely covered their bones, their mouths contorted in painful death, stacked more than a meter high, unfathomably neatly, head to toe, like firewood. The bodies were a translucent green—from starvation, Thomas had told her later—and the stench of rotting flesh permeated everything. She saw the crematorium with its half-burned bodies buried in ash; the bunks that resembled morgue drawers; the cellar where prisoners had been hanged or tortured, blood stains still on the walls underneath the meathooks. A bloody club was leaned against the wall in the corner, as if ready for its next victim. Anna vomited more than once, and an American photographer had taken her photo as she convulsed, her empty stomach forcing up nothing but shame and fury. She had known about the camp, of course; everyone knew about it. For years there were whispers and glimpses of emaciated prisoners being marched through the streets. It had been very easy to avoid any confrontation with the truth and Anna had been all too willing to turn away. But even having seen the truth with her own eyes it was beyond human comprehension. And to think it had been happening under her nose in the countryside she had so loved. It was no coincidence that Himmler had placed the camp exactly in the place on the Ettersberg where Goethe, the father of all German culture and civility, had liked to write his poetry. It was a calculated annihilation of all that had been beautiful about Germany. The Nazis had always been so good at symbolism.

Anna found a shaded spot and sat down on the ground to clear her head. Packs of little boys ran around and others sat on the curb in little rows, watching and elbowing each other. Above her, women leaned out of windows: the younger ones looked expectant, the older ones worried. The tank screeched back and forth, inching its way into the designated spot until coming to rest at the edge of the fence, its turret pointed toward her. American soldiers climbed up the side of the tank and thumped each other on the back, laughing and lighting cigarettes before moving on to the next one, which she presumed they would park at the opposite corner. Anna took the opportunity to make her way through the traffic jam to the main gate. There was now a jeep parked across the opening and an MP stepped into her path with hand raised before she was even close.

"No entry, Ma'am," he shouted.

Anna pulled her new papers from her bag and waved them at him. "What's going on?" she asked.

He held up a finger to silence her as he inspected the small card with her picture. His eyes met hers and she waited for the ritual to be over. He looked up and smiled at her. "Thank you, Frau Klein. Just stepping up security. You can go on in." He held his arm out and stepped back. Anna wondered if this *Ami* was friends with Miller, and if he, too, had an opinion of her and Cooper's relationship.

Inside the fence, the courtyard was less frenetic. Cooper stood in the middle, talking with a group of workers and waving his arms around his head like a dry-docked swimmer. Seeing her, he smiled, and Anna felt self-conscious, as if everyone was watching them.

"Oh thank God you're here, finally. I am trying to explain to them that we need more lights. The whole courtyard needs to be lit at night. Bright as day. We can't have any dark patches. Can you tell them?"

The faces of the workers all turned expectantly to Anna who relayed the instructions.

"Ah, okay!" One of the older men pointed a finger to the sky and beamed at Cooper who replied with his thumbs-up gesture. Everyone nodded and dispersed.

"Thanks. You were gone forever. I can't seem to get a damn thing done without you anymore. Don't leave me again." He laughed and spun around on his heel. "Where's Miller?"

"Stuck in that traffic. I walked. He'll bring the things up when he gets here." Anna followed Cooper into the building. "I got everything, even the last three typewriter ribbons in the city. Don't tell anyone." She held the box up and shook it.

"Great! And Miller's driving didn't kill you; that's good."

"No, the driving wasn't too bad," she lied. "But..."

Cooper turned toward her. "But what?"

Anna shook her head. "Oh nothing. Never mind."

Cooper cocked his head and narrowed his eyes. "Something happen? He make a move on you?"

"No, he didn't," Anna replied. Glad to be able to tell the truth. "Not at all."

"So, what's the problem?"

"I was just wondering how well you know him. You seem so different from each other. Are you friends?"

"Friends? Me and Miller? No I wouldn't say that. He is my subordinate and I try to keep those lines clear. We'd never met before I ended up here in Wiesbaden. And, anyway, we've got nothing in common. You sure he didn't make a pass at you or grab you? You seem strange. You need me to knock some sense into him?"

Anna smiled at the thought of Cooper punching Miller's flat face. "No need," she said. "Everything's fine."

Cooper seemed relieved. "So, guess what?" He twinkled at her. "I got a bike for me and one for the boy. And I got a day pass. For tomorrow."

"That's wonderful. How did you manage that?"

"I traded two packs of smokes for the use of two bikes for a day. And the day pass, well, that's all about who you know."

"Are you sure it's all right for you to leave tomorrow?" She wished she hadn't asked him to come along. It had been an innocent invitation, but now it was just more fodder for the rumor mill. She hated that people were talking about her.

Cooper stopped to let a group of men carrying a crate pass. "They won't miss me for one day. This is all exciting isn't it? I think we'll be ready for the shipment on Monday."

Anna frowned. "Are the tanks really necessary?"

"Better safe than sorry. We need the firepower. Just in case."

"I think they make people nervous," Anna said.

Cooper laughed. "That's the idea."

"As long you don't get dogs. Please tell me there won't be any dogs."

"No, no dogs." He softened. "Just guns. We're Americans after all."

Anna chuckled at his joke. "That fellow Corporal Bender is very nice."

"You saw Bender? Is he out at the airfield? He's a great guy. I need to pay him a visit. Haven't talked to him in months. Hell, a year, probably. Nice guy." Cooper smiled and shook his head, remembering some shared joke.

"He said the same about you. You haven't talked to him at all?" Anna considered Bender's claim that Cooper had called the supply store looking for her.

"No. Last time I saw him he was setting up post in some Italian village. I got my orders to move on. I'm glad to hear he's okay."

Anna watched Cooper as he shuffled through the papers on his desk. Was he lying about the call to the supply store or had Bender simply tried to save her from Miller? Did Cooper know more about Miller than he was letting on? She pulled the cover off the typewriter and wiggled the mechanism loose to change out the ribbon. If Cooper was lying about the phone call, what else was he lying about? She tightened the new ribbon on its spool and clicked it back into place.

"Oh, before I forget, see if you can't get that film roll developed downstairs. It's still in the camera around here somewhere. And tell me when and where to meet tomorrow. We should probably get an early start, don't you think? I am looking forward to it."

Anna nodded and fed a blank field report form into the typewriter. "Yes, me too," she said.

chapter fourteen

Anna pulled on her pants and the yellow cotton blouse with the green metal buttons then washed her face and brushed her hair. She rubbed toothpaste on her teeth with her finger and wiggled her loose tooth. Still there. Regarding herself in the mirror shard above the sink, she turned her head this way then the other to get a composite picture. Gray interlopers infiltrated her hairline like wires among the dull brown strands. Her eyes looked flat and the creases between her eyebrows had gotten deeper. She wondered if she would ever again recognize herself in the mirror. Then again, it was hard to look herself in the eye for very long. She faked a smile at her reflection. Unconvincing. Her face sank back into the comfortable contours of the constant frown she had acquired. She felt like an old sofa with faded upholstery and sagging springs. She pulled her hair away from her face and pinned it into a twist at the back of her head. A haircut would do her good; maybe Madeleine could do it for her tonight. When she decided she was presentable, Anna closed the bathroom door and rummaged through the drawer of the cabinet in the hall.

"Maus, I have something for you." She walked back the living room and sat down on the bed.

"What is it, Mama?" Amalia jumped up and down with one shoe on, eyes wide with excitement.

Anna held out a fist and smiled. Amalia cupped her hands underneath and Anna dropped a key tied on a loop of red ribbon into the girl's palm. "You wear it around your neck. So, if you ever need to leave the house when I am gone you can lock the door and also get back in. Or you can come home on your own if I can't come pick you up. Since you are almost seven years old, I think you are big enough to have it now."

Amalia's eyes dimmed. "Where will you be, Mama? Will you not come home?"

Anna slid to the floor and pulled the girl close. "Oh, Maus, of course I'll come home. I'll even pick you up every day just like always. But this way you can come home if maybe I am late. It's just for emergencies. I will tell Fraulein Schilling to let you walk from the Collecting Point if I am not there. You know your way home, don't you?"

Amalia nodded and bit her lip.

"But you must never lose the key and you may never give it to anyone or tell them you have it, do you understand?"

"I won't, Mama. I promise." She put the key around her neck and shuffled to the bed. She lay down on her stomach, *The Snow Queen* between her elbows, face toward the wall.

Madeleine patted Anna's hand. She nodded her reassurance. "Did you find out anything else about the people in the

Schwalbacherstrasse? Where Schneider took that painting when you followed him?" she asked.

Anna shook her head. "I looked at the lists yesterday, but so far no luck."

"I remembered last night that I knew a Schenk who lives on the Schwalbacherstrasse. I think he had a shop there. Antiques and restoration, that kind of thing. Very small operation."

Anna perked up. "Really?"

"Yes Konrad Schenk. His wife ran the business with him. He was nice enough but she was always pushing him and belittling him. He was an artist but she wanted a businessman. We didn't know them well. Maybe that's the man Schneider visited?"

"It would make sense, especially if he is a restorer. Madeleine you are a living address book!" Anna smiled.

Madeleine waved her off. "You sit in one place long enough you see a few things."

"Do you remember when he lived there?"

"Oh years ago, back in the thirties, I would say. He was already quite old then, come to think of it. It could be he is no longer alive."

Anna's face sank. "The woman I spoke to at the apartment said the Herr Schenk who lives there only arrived a few months ago. So it couldn't be the same one. Damn."

"A son, maybe? Returning from the war?"

"Yes, maybe. I will ask Cooper to look into it." Anna looked at the clock. "We'd better get going. She went into the kitchen to wrap the odds and ends of food and put them into the old shopping bag.

"Mama, is Captain Cooper coming too? And Auntie, are you?" Amalia asked over her shoulder.

Madeleine waved her arms. "No *meine Kleine*. I am staying here. That hill would be the end of me."

"But Auntie, fresh air is good for you," Amalia whined.

"There's fresh air enough down here. I'll sit by the open window a spell."

"And look for Papa?"

"Yes, of course. Don't I do that every day? If he comes today I'll send him up the Neroberg straight away."

Anna twitched. She took the basket and hurried Amalia, who took her book and tied her button necklace around her neck, carefully adding it to the one with the key. She kissed Madeleine on the cheek and followed Anna out the door.

At the front gate, Anna leaned the bicycle against the wall while she rolled up her pant legs. Frau Hermann was sweeping the pavement.

"Frau Klein, how lovely to see you. The ladies are going on a ride today?" She tapped the broom on the ground to shake loose a twig.

Anna nodded. "Yes it's a lovely day isn't it? We are going to the Neroberg."

"Oh, so lovely. With a picnic. How lucky for you to have a day just for yourself. I hope Frau Wolf is better, then?"

"Yes, she is doing very well." Anna gestured up to the window. "Aren't you, Auntie?"

Madeleine's smiling face appeared above. Amalia giggled.

"Yes, doing well, thank you, Ingeborg. I hope you are well also. How is your boy?"

Frau Hermann took a step back and looked up. "I expect him home any day. He's been released and I hear they are marching home. Shouldn't be long now."

"Well, that is good news. We can be very grateful for that," Madeleine said.

Anna swung a leg over the bicycle seat and held it steady while Amalia climbed onto the small luggage rack in the back. Anna put the picnic basket in the wire crate tied to the handlebars. Amalia slipped her arms around Anna's waist as she pushed off, leaving Frau Hermann nattering at Madeleine. Anna smiled, knowing how much Madeleine enjoyed toying with her neighbor. The breeze felt good on Anna's face and she savored the feeling of her daughter's arms around her waist and the weight of the girl's body behind her. Today was a good day.

They met Cooper in the park by the Collecting Point near the Villa Clementine, one of the stately old homes along the Wilhelmstrasse, now home to some American colonel. Cooper sat by a tree stump, two bikes leaning against it. He jumped up and waved at Amalia when they approached.

"You've got Oskar?" Anna asked, walking her bike across the dirt lawn. Cooper hooked a thumb over his shoulder. The boy sat at the edge of the small pond, scraping a stick through the dirt. Women scooped buckets into the clear spring water while children chased each other between the few trees and lampposts that remained.

"There he is, Maus. Let's go meet him." Anna took Amalia by the hand and pulled her along. "Good morning, Oskar. How are you?" she called.

Oskar punished her with silence.

Anna persisted. "This is Amalia. She's my daughter that I told you about."

Amalia took a step closer to Anna.

"You know something I thought of, Oskar? Do you know the stories by Karl May, the ones about the Indian in America, what was his name again?"

Amalia rolled her eyes. "His name is Winnetou, Mama. You know that."

"Yes, of course. Amalia likes Winnetou stories too, like you do, don't you Maus?"

Oskar shot her a sideways glance. "Winnetou is not for girls. How stupid," he sniffed.

"Yes, he is too!" Amalia said and let go of her mother's skirt. She sat down next to Oskar and regarded him with expectation. "My favorite is *The Treasure of Silver Lake*. What's yours? I had two books at my house. My Papa read them to me."

Oskar stared into the distance. "*The Treasure of Silver Lake* is all right but everybody knows *The Black Mustang* is better. I had *all* the books at my house. But my house got blown up. And so did my Papa." He jabbed the stick into the dirt and it snapped in half.

Amalia picked up a piece of the stick and rubbed it between her hands. "My Oma and Opa got blown up, too. In their house in Vienna, where they lived."

They sat in silence, side by side, their backs hunched over their knees.

"Were you there?" Oskar finally asked. "When they got blown up?"

Amalia shook her head. "No, I was at home. In Kappellendorf. Its about a million kilometers away from Vienna."

"I was," Oskar said. "I was in the basement. With my Mama. My Papa went upstairs to make sure everyone in the building had come down into the shelter. When the bomb landed, he died. And then the basement fell down on us and burned and my Mama died. But I didn't."

Amalia hugged her legs to her chest and rested her cheek on her knees. "That makes me sad," she said. "Are you very sad?"

"Sometimes. But mostly I'm mad."

"Because you miss your Papa?"

"Because it's not fair."

Amalia drew in the dirt with her finger. "It's not fair," she said.

Cooper touched Anna's shoulder. "We should get going. Today's gonna get hot."

Anna nodded and gathered the children as if she had heard none of their exchange. Amalia stood and reached down to pull Oskar to his feet. "I'll beat you," she said, and took off running.

They rode along the Wilhelmstrasse and then turned up into the hills in a small orderly column: Anna and Amalia in front, Oskar in the middle, and Cooper at the rear. As the street became more narrow and the incline steeper, Anna lifted Amalia off the bike so she could push it. Eventually Amalia fell back to walk with Oskar. Anna heard her telling Oskar all about her house, the things and friends she left behind, and her Papa. The street was quiet and the garden walls hid the residents, but windows were open and the sounds of domestic life rose up in the clean air. They trudged up the hill another twenty minutes before arriving at the top, hot and sweaty.

"Tell me again why we didn't take the little train? The one you sit in while it climbs the damn hill?" Cooper panted as he mopped his brow.

"Because you bombed it," Anna said. "Besides, walking is better."

"Okay, if you say so. I'd like to point out that I personally had no say in whether or not the train was bombed. Not my area of control, you know."

The shade offered by the dense thicket of trees was pleasant, and they found a level spot within view of the Russian chapel that perched on the top of the hill overlooking the city. A few people strolled around the once lush and manicured grounds that now seemed a relic of another era. The beautiful swimming pool—the Opelbad—further along and slightly below them on the ridge, sat empty and deserted, its lawn now a brown rectangle and its fountains and pool dry. A childhood memory of a day spent splashing in the shallow end with her mother and Madeleine—when they had come to Wiesbaden for a visit—hovered just outside Anna's conscious mind. She tried to pull it toward her but it wouldn't come. Like all the memories of her parents, this one had faded into a distance that Anna could not reach. She turned her back to the view and leaned the bike against a tree.

"Let's eat," she said to no one in particular. Amalia cheered and threw herself down on the cool ground. Anna unpacked the basket and spread everything down on an old bed sheet she had brought. She put the food in the middle and gave each of them a napkin. "Help yourself," she said.

"Women and children first," Cooper said, lying back on his elbows.

Oskar and Amalia dug in, Oskar inspecting each item with disdain but eventually eating it. Anna chewed on a soggy carrot and Amalia concentrated on peeling a boiled egg.

"Mama, you can have half," she said.

Anna shook her head and suggested she give it to Oskar. She looked down at the view of the city. The intact roofs of the hillside villas in the foreground, the shattered inner city in the distance, like dense forest giving way to an open, pockmarked plain. The steeple of the Marktkirche presided over the remnants and shards of the city at its feet. The sky was a deep blue, like liquid, and not a cloud interrupted its expanse. It reminded Anna of her total insignificance, at least beyond the handful of people in her life. She tried to enjoy the moment, but this new life away from her husband in a strange city, and now as a working mother, still did not suit her. It felt as if she were wearing someone else's clothes that were too big in some places and too small in others.

Amalia and Oskar finished eating and wandered into the trees to explore. Cooper took a piece of bread and pulled the crust off with his teeth. "So, how are you, Anna?" he asked.

She ignored the question and jutted her chin in the direction of the chapel. "What do you think of that church? You're an architect."

"It's beautiful," Cooper said.

"It was built for the Duchess of Nassau by her husband, the Duke. She was a Romanov, one of the Russian royal family."

"That explains the Russian architecture. Nice of him." Cooper smiled.

"She was dead. She died in childbirth. He built the chapel to house her remains and those of the baby, who also died. That's all I know about it."

Cooper squinted into the sun. "I do like it up here. Come on, let's go for a walk." He stood and offered a hand. "Leave that stuff."

"Someone will take it," Anna argued, but Cooper pulled her by the elbow toward the path to the church. She punched her hands into her pockets and followed as he strode ahead.

The chapel loomed large, its five towers and their golden domes gleaming in the sun like enormous candles signaling to the heavens: We're still here. Several windows in the tallest tower were boarded up and damage was visible on the delicate arches. It looked like a tarnished jewel or faded royalty clinging to an outdated role. As if to underline her thought, Cooper walked to the front and searched for the entrance.

"Not there," Anna called, waving her hand to indicate the side of the building. "That entrance is sealed. They sealed it in 1917 after the fall of the Czar in Russia. We have to use the side door."

"That's dumb," Cooper said. "This has such a great view." He held his arms out to the panorama of the valley below.

"Exactly," Anna said. "Only worthy of the nobles. No Czar, no view."

"No wonder the Russians had a revolution," Cooper grumbled.

"Is that not how things are done in Iowa?" she teased.

He smiled. "In Iowa we only have one door. For everybody. We got our revolution out of the way early. But still, the architecture is fantastic, don't you think? Look at those domes. Why do you think the Russians like these onion domes so much?"

Anna shrugged. "I don't know. Because you can see them more clearly when you are freezing to death out on the Russian steppe?"

"You are so bourgeois." He winked.

"Or maybe so the snow wouldn't pile up on them," she offered, ignoring his jab.

"I think it's to symbolize the fire of the soul reaching toward the almighty. Or something like that. I mean, just look at it." Cooper put his hands on his hips and leaned back. "Now *that* we don't have in Iowa."

"There's something to keep you warm when you are buried in two meters of snow," Anna scoffed. She actually liked his version, but the sport of arguing with him was more appealing.

Even on this warm day the inside of the church was cold. It felt damp and smelled of cloves. Icons of Russian saints rose up the wall that divided the small nave from the sanctuary. Two marble pilasters, their pediments scrolled like wedding cakes, flanked the central opening to the sanctuary. Several icons were covered with sheets and the small crypt of the mother and child was boarded up. Mottled sunlight filtered through the tower's windows and cast a cold, gray shroud over them. Anna folded her arms across her chest. She thought of the young mother and her baby whose deaths were worthy of such an extravagant remembrance. Sitting down on a chair along the wall, she waited for Cooper, who explored the small space like Lord Carnarvon opening Tutankhamun's tomb.

"Amazing. I never thought I'd get to see something like this," he said. He was lost in his own world, walking slowly around the space, seeing things that Anna could not see. She watched him run his hands over the marble carvings and inspect details near the floor, where she would never have thought to look. He walked to one place and then another to regard the nave from different vantage points. She half expected him to barge into the sanctuary secluded behind the wall of saints. Instead, he pointed straight up to the dome where the sunlight illuminated a ring of saints that guarded the entry to a glowing eternity beyond. "That'll make you believe in heaven." He nodded at her, waiting for a comeback.

Anna stood. "I am going back outside."

The warm air comforted her as she squinted into the sun and walked to the picnic spot. Oskar and Amalia were running between the trees and small clumps of people had settled in on patches of grass with meager lunches and tattered blankets.

"She's around," Cooper said coming up behind her. "Don't worry, they're just having fun. You think you'll get any more information out of the boy?"

"I hope so. I'll keep trying. Maybe he'll soften a little. I want him to trust me, but he really has no reason to. I can't promise that nothing bad will happen to him. And to him, I am still the lowest of the low, fraternizing with the enemy."

Cooper smiled at her and patted her arm. "He has to get used to the new world order. Come on, eat something." He sat down and opened the metal box he had brought, pulling out two small apples. "Look here. Have one of these—they're actually pretty sweet. And for the kids..." He pulled out a Hershey chocolate bar and wiggled it between his fingers.

Anna rolled the apple around in her hand before biting into it, avoiding the loose tooth as best she could. The taste exploded in her mouth: sweet and crisp and fresh like a cooling rainstorm on a summer day.

"You didn't like the church?" Cooper asked.

"Why do you say that?"

"You just seemed unimpressed, that's all."

"It's just a building. I have become unsentimental about buildings. Anyway, I would think a building like that would offend your American democratic sensibilities, given what it represents." She took another bite.

Cooper looked innocent. "What does it represent?"

"The rule of the few over the many. Domination by the ruling classes. Some lives being of greater value than others."

"Oh, that. I thought you meant the blind faith in an all-knowing and possibly benevolent God. But if it's just the ruling classes you have a problem with..."

"I only have a problem when the few take from the many. I think things should be spread around more evenly."

"Better keep your voice down. Someone will take you for a communist." He laughed and caught her eye. "You're not a Red are you?"

Anna's cheeks burned. "No."

"Why are you blushing?"

"I said I am not. That is the truth," she said, her voice dry.

"Well, you sure have some opinions. Better keep those to yourself. Where'd you get them anyway? I thought the Nazis hated the communists?"

"I hate the communists and the Nazis both. I can still have an opinion about people's rights." Anna bit the core of the apple in half and chewed slowly. "The Nazis hated everyone who had an opinion that didn't match theirs. But that doesn't automatically make everyone who disagreed with them right, either. People could be against the Nazis and be for something that's equally bad."

"Like the communists?"

She nodded. "Communists were thrown into concentration camps too. From the very beginning."

"Right."

"Right," she said.

Cooper sighed. "Okay, Anna, just tell me. What's upsetting you?"

Anna listened to her heart pound for a few moments. A breeze whispered through the trees, twirling dust and leaves around them in a short dance that died down as quickly as it started. Cooper looked at her with anticipation, the same expression he'd had the day he'd found Amalia sitting on the bench.

She thought of Thomas, his slightly off-center smile and the deep-set eyes that grew darker with worry and fear and anger. The kind hands that used to stroke her face, even when she began to rage against him. The last time she saw him, through the truck's rear-view mirror, he'd been standing at the gate to their garden, hands shoved his pockets, receding into the distance. She could still hear the sound of Amalia wailing, and taste the bile rising in her throat.

"All right. I will tell you. My husband, you know, he's a doctor. And, well, he's also an idealist. That is what first drew me to him. He was so passionate and caring—really caring—for people. And for a while I thought he might make a difference. But, of course, the world changed in every way with the Nazis. He refused to see the reality of the danger that he was in. Or he didn't care. He just continued on. And it became very dangerous—the meetings, the pamphlets, his friends coming to the house. The damn radio broadcasts and secret messages to Moscow. It put us all in jeopardy. Even when Amalia was born, he just became more committed. The Nazis started stringing his comrades up on wires in the middle of town. The Gestapo hauled him in and nearly killed him. He was gone for a week and I pleaded with them to spare Thomas for the sake of his patients, that they had the wrong man. Water torture, beatings, they knocked out half his teeth and then dumped him on the street. But that didn't stop him. I tried to be understanding, but things became impossible between us. Because we didn't agree. He thought it was worth dying for his beliefs, for a better world. But, for me, the world could not be better if he was dead. So things got bad." She waited for a reaction.

Cooper leaned in close. "Are you telling me your husband, the doctor, is a Red?"

Anna let the words hang for a few seconds and then nodded. "After the *Amis* came I thought everything would be all right. I breathed a sigh of relief. But then Truman gave Thuringia back to the Russians at Potsdam, and Thomas was overjoyed. Everything he had risked his life for was coming true. It was the future he dreamed of: the communists taking control, everyone getting their fair share, overthrowing the powerful. He was delirious with happiness. But he saw only what he wanted to see. I knew we had to leave, Amalia and I. I knew what the Russians did to women. So I made arrangements. I bought a truck and packed our things." Her voice shivered. "We had a terrible fight over Amalia—tugging and pulling her between us like animals until I could grab her and get her in the truck. She and I drove off and well, to tell you the truth, I am not sure if he's ever going to come."

She had finally said it out loud. Anna looked around, feeling very conspicuous, sitting on the grass having a picnic with the *Ami*. *How ridiculous*. She was wrong to have asked him to come. And now she had told him her secret.

Cooper whistled through his teeth. "Wow, I did not see that coming. That's a terrible situation. It never occurred to me you could be married to a Red. Nazi, sure, but a Red? Does anyone else know about this?" His face was serious. It made Anna nervous.

She shook her head. "No one. Not even Madeleine. I never told anyone, not even my parents. It was too dangerous. The Americans never asked me about communism, they just wanted to know if I was a Nazi. So I said nothing. But now I know Thomas's politics are a problem." She pulled at the grass next to her knees. "If he comes here I'll lose my job, won't I? The Americans won't tolerate having the wife of a communist working for them. And what will happen to us? We'll all get sent back to the Russian zone, won't we? I can't go there. But I can't stay here either and take Amalia from her father. I have no right. He's a good man, despite everything." Her eyes teared. "And, of course, Amalia blames me for leaving him. She doesn't understand any of this. She just misses her father."

Cooper sat and looked at her, working at a thought with his jaw. "Talk about going from the frying pan into the fire," he said finally.

"What's that?"

"Nothing. It's just incredible how you survive one nightmare and find yourself smack in the middle of the next one. People can't just be people anymore. Everyone has to pick a side. And you, my dear, have got a real problem. I won't tell anyone, but you're going to have to figure out what to do before someone figures it out for you."

"What do you mean?"

"I mean you're neither here nor there right now. You'll have to make a choice sooner or later. Things won't stay in this in-between way much longer. Either you decide or someone else will."

For a while neither of them spoke. Oskar and Amalia laughed as they chased each other, oblivious to everything. The sun glowed and a bird sang its tiny song into the big sky. The world continued, but Anna felt frozen. She could see no way forward, but now there was no going back.

"Look, I need to tell you something, too," Cooper said suddenly. He looked at the horizon, avoiding Anna's eyes. "I've got a problem at the Collecting Point. Frankfurt really wants me to bring on our friend Schneider, as a restorer. I told them no, and now Farmer—the director—and I are taking heat for it. Apparently our friend Phillips in Frankfurt is real hot for us to hire Schneider. I can't figure out why he's pushing so hard for him and ignoring my opinion. Farmer's a good man, and I don't want to make problems for him. But, at the same time, I know Schneider stinks and I don't want him anywhere near all the art we've got coming in."

He looked sad, his bright American optimism marred and tarnished. Anna felt sorry for him. She crossed her legs and leaned in to whisper, "I think so too. I don't blame you at all."

He nodded. "I know I'm right. His joining the SA doesn't seem to bother the brass. They said it was a formality for him to stay in business and that Special Branch has examined the *Fragebogen* and that there's no suspicion attached to him. Did you ever hear such a flimsy excuse? That rationale would pardon every Nazi in Germany. A *formality*? Please. Did you know he put his business in his wife's name? And now she's dead, so he'll get it back, no matter how long I stall his paperwork. But during the war, it was mostly hers and she was never a member of the Party, so we can't touch his assets or lay any claim to them. Any painting he can document as hers, he gets back, period. Then there's his trip to the concentration camp and getting himself kicked out of the Party. As if that proves anything." He paused. "Maybe he's a communist, too." He shot Anna a sarcastic look.

"If the Nazis thought he was a communist he'd have been hanging from a light post on the Wilhelmstrasse years ago," Anna said.

"I was kidding. Truth is, we are desperate for experts and we do need locals like him on our team. When we first started up, Farmer inadvertently hired a bunch of ex-Party members to work with the art. They had the best qualifications, you know? When the brass found out who they were, he had to fire the lot of them, and rightfully so. But it's nearly impossible to find anybody with the knowledge we need who has completely clean hands. So I guess now the higher ups are ready to make concessions. They sit up there in Frankfurt pushing papers around and looking important, but nobody gives a damn—not really—about what we are trying to do." He pulled out a handful of grass and tossed it into the breeze. "There's no way someone like Schneider just decides to change out of the goodness of his heart. I know he's up to something. I just have to prove it." He leaned toward Anna. "Will you help me?"

Anna straightened. "What do you mean? What can I do?"

He waved her closer and they leaned toward each other like children sharing a secret on the playground. "I thought of this when you tailed Schneider the other day. Didn't you say he sent you that basket of food?"

Anna nodded.

"See, he thinks of you as a potential friend. Why don't we make him think the bribe worked. That you are ready to help him if he'll just do one little thing for you first. Kind of a pact with the devil. Like us with Stalin."

"I don't know," she hedged. "What do you want me to do?"

Cooper looked around. "I want you to sell him a painting. Tell him you need the money and that you're on his side. I'll give you one to use. You won't really sell it of course, it'll be a sting. If he takes the bait, we'll arrest him and the case will be closed."

"And if he doesn't?"

"Then I guess I'll have to hire him. But I know he'll flunk the test. Once a thief, always a thief. And maybe the brass can forgive what he did before, but they can't look the other way if he's breaking their own laws now."

Anna looked around. "I agree with you, I really do. But you are setting him up. Is that legal?"

Cooper shrugged. "Sure it is. Paragraph 51 states that no cultural property may change hands. Period. If he gets an offer and he takes it, he's broken the law. If he's as upstanding as he says, the worst that will happen is he'll be offended."

"If he's as upstanding as he says, he'll denounce me!" Anna said. "Have you thought about that? *Me* being arrested?" She dug in her bag for the Lucky Strikes and Cooper obliged her with a light.

He waved her off. "Don't worry about that. You'll be acting as an agent of the great United States Occupying Forces. With my considerable authority." He waggled his head and grinned.

"What about Frankfurt's authority? What if they don't like it?"

"I'll deal with Frankfurt and I'll take the fall if I have to. Look, the stakes are too high. If he's crooked, he has no business working with us. It's too important. We are trying to clean up the mess that people like him made. These pieces need to get back to their rightful owners. And that's not so easy when most of them are dead or, if we're lucky, displaced. It's such a mess. I need people I can trust one hundred percent." He rubbed the back of his neck. "Look, I already can't sleep at night, with all this business about the shipment and the security. Shit, I haven't slept since I got here. The whole place has me jumpy. Come on, you gotta help me with this."

Anna pursed her lips and watched the smoke curling from the cigarette in her hand. "How exactly do you see this working?"

"We'll figure it out. You find him and tell him you've got something for him. See if he bites. If he does, you can set up a meeting. I'll follow you there of course, and I'll bring back-up. You walk in with the painting, he walks out with the painting, we arrest him. Easy as pie. I promise you won't be in any danger. These are greedy art dealers, not..."

"Brownshirts?" Anna volunteered. She thought about Cooper's blood on her bathroom floor. The swelling on his lip had just started to go down.

Cooper snorted. "Look, I've got no one else who can do this. You are the only one." He paused. "Here's a chance to make yourself useful." He waited another beat. "It's the right thing to do, Anna. And..." he put his hand on her arm, "I wouldn't ask if I didn't think you could handle it."

She looked at the ground. *Bastard,* she thought. She knew what he was doing. She had to pick a side. She waited a moment to see if maybe the ground would swallow her. It didn't. "All right," she said loudly enough to drown out yesterday's warnings from Miller that still buzzed in her ears. "I'll do it."

chapter fifteen

Oskar was running around inside the communal hall, where a few women supervised several dozen children who would rather be playing outside. Cooper was right, Anna thought as she spotted him. They really were little feral creatures. All the structure gone from their lives and with the fear slowly ebbing, the ones that had survived this long were letting out all their pent-up energy. She stood in the open door and watched for a few minutes until Maria saw her.

"Anna, how nice to see you." She walked toward her and extended a hand.

"*Hallo,* Maria. I see you have your hands full."

"Well, the weather is no good for them, but I have to say I like the rain. It's a nice change from the heat." She motioned for Anna to take a seat on one of the chairs that lined the walls. "I think Oskar enjoyed himself yesterday. It did him good to get away from this place for a few hours."

"Yes, he and my daughter played well. She was worn out."

"I asked him if he wanted to come to church with me this morning, but he refused. He just misses his mother so much. The poor boy, I wish I could help him. The Red Cross came on Friday to take his photo and it should be in the papers and the post office in the next week or so. But these things take so long." Maria sighed. "I would take him myself if I could but..." She raised a hand toward the room to acknowledge her circumstances.

Anna nodded. "I know. He's a good boy. Someone will remember him and come forward. I feel sure of it. They just need to know he's here." She felt no such thing, but she said it anyway. She waved at Oskar who had broken away from the group of boys and jogged over to her. He even smiled.

"*Hallo,* Frau Klein." His cheeks were red and his hair stood every which way like overgrown grass. His big eyes blinked at her. "Where's your American?"

Anna reddened. "I don't know. I don't see him every day, you know. Amalia sends her greetings."

Oskar smirked. "I think he likes you."

"Don't be silly. He's my boss that's all."

"You both sure talk a lot. Who goes for a picnic with their boss anyway?"

Anna held out her hand. "Come on, let's go for a walk."

"In the rain?"

"Sure why not? It's only drizzling now. Come on."

She took his hand and stepped outside. The rain had slowed to a fine mist that pushed a thousand little pinpricks into her skin. She hunched over and pulled Oskar closer as they walked to the playground. He sat down on the tire swing and Anna pushed it a little to make it go. Oskar lifted his feet.

"How are they treating you here? Everything going all right?"

The boy wrapped his hands around the rope and said nothing.

"I know it's not a proper home, but it's only temporary, I promise."

The tree branch creaked under the weight of the swing. Anna tried another approach. "Will you tell me about your mother? I'd like to know more about her." She gave the swing another push. A clap of thunder in the distance made them both jump, but Oskar stayed silent.

Finally, he said, "My Mama was beautiful. She was the most beautiful lady I ever saw." He dragged his feet through the mud, splattering Anna's pants and soaking his socks.

"What did she look like?" Anna asked.

Oskar stared at his feet and leaned his cheek against the rope. "She had long blond hair and she always wore pretty dresses. She never got mad at me, not even when I did something bad. She told me I was her gift from God."

"She loved you very much."

His blond head nodded. "She would take me swimming and for walks in the woods. We ate ice cream in the summer. And we read books. She always did things with me. She would stand outside my school and wait for me, and she was the prettiest mother there. Everyone thought so. She would have a treat for me every day. An apple, or sometimes a cake. She liked to make me potato pancakes. With applesauce. That's my favorite." His voice cracked.

"What about your Papa?" Anna knew she was picking at the boy's wounds.

Oskar shook his head. "Papa? He was gone a lot. It was mostly me and Mama. She said Papa was an important man so he was very busy. He had lots of medals on his uniform."

"Really? Your papa was an important soldier, then."

"No, he was not a solider. He was in the SS." He glared at her to let her know she had made a stupid assumption. He was insulted.

"Oh, he sounds very important."

Oskar puffed up. "He was very important, my Papa. We always had important people come to visit. I had a photograph of me and the Reichsführer, from when he came to one of our parties."

Anna imagined what Oskar's life had been like. Coddled and adored by a loving but willfully complicit mother, the Aryan pride of his murderous father, living a life of privilege on the suffering and persecution of millions. Tables covered with food, drawers full of soft clothes, presents for his birthday and warm baths before bedtime. All at the price of other children's lives. It was better for the world that his father was dead, but Anna felt a pang for the boy's mother. She couldn't help herself.

Oskar was on a roll. "Papa went all over, to Poland and to Czechoslovakia. He always brought me presents. Toys and things. He told me that when I grow up the world will be a better place than it is now. That Germans will rule the world and I will be a important man." He kicked at the dirt.

"What else did he tell you? Did he tell you things about when you were a baby? Where were you born?"

Oskar stopped swinging and stared at her. "I was born in Steinhöring. That's why Mama always called me her little Bavarian." He waited for the next question.

"And did you have any other family? Grandparents? Or maybe an aunt or uncle?"

"I keep telling everyone. I don't have any family. No one is going to come for me. Everyone I know is dead."

Anna sighed. He was probably right, or at least it was unlikely any close relative of a known SS officer was going to come forward and declare themselves to the *Amis* willingly. But there was nothing else to do. She walked around and squatted in front of him to look at his face. "If you tell me more about you, maybe we can find people who are your family. Didn't your parents have any friends?" She tried to stroke his arm but he pulled it away to wipe his nose.

"Sure, they had friends. Officers and people like that. They're all dead too. "

"All right, how about you tell me again how you ended up at the children's home? I mean, at the villa, where we found you."

Oskar's gaze shifted. "What do you mean, children's home?"

"Just a guess. I knew there was a children's home there. Or some kind of orphanage?"

"Not an orphanage," he snapped.

"No? It was like a school or something?" Anna held her breath.

Oskar rolled his eyes. "No not like a school. It was a place for mothers and children, and it was only for us, for the families–" He stopped.

"I see. So maybe you had friends there? Maybe that's how we can find someone who knows you?"

Oskar rocked the swing from side to side. "No, I was never there. I told you I just went there by myself after the bombing."

"You mean the bombing of Darmstadt last year? Can you tell me more about what happened after the bombing?"

He looked down at his knees. "I don't know. It was just really hot in the basement, like a fireplace. People were coughing and screaming, and it was like there was no air. My Mama, she held me close and told me to keep breathing, but then she fell over on top of me. The big metal door exploded and you could hear things blowing up all around us. It was so hot. People were trying to crawl out, but I was under my Mama. Her face was right next to mine. I just looked in her eyes until they dug me out."

Oskar said nothing else for a long time. Anna held her breath. The rain created a delicate curtain between them, as if each was separated from the other just enough to feel protected.

When he continued, his voice was small. "The smell was really bad. Like that smell from burning tires, but even worse. And people were crying and screaming, and I just laid there with my mama. I thought a beam had just hit her on the head and that she would wake up. But her eyes were looking right at me and they didn't move. They were empty and cold looking. It scared me really bad." He kicked the mud. "After a long time, someone called, 'is anyone under there?' And I said 'yes, I am.' And then my mama started to move. Like she was alive. But it was only them pulling her off me. The whole cellar had crashed in, the fire had come through on the other end, and people were burned dead, right where they sat. The lady from downstairs, Frau Winkel, she was sitting with her back on the wall, only her skin was gone, like a plucked chicken, and the bones of her hands, you could see them between the red and black. All her hair was gone and her lips too, so her teeth looked really big. I thought she was dead, but maybe she wasn't because she looked right at me. She was like a monster." He paused again. Anna waited.

"When they took my mama out, they laid her on the street. Right there on the street with all the others. There was ash everywhere, falling from the sky like rain. She laid there for a whole day and I sat with her and rubbed the ash off her face and her hair. They told me Papa was burned so bad they might never find him for sure. Because he had gone upstairs to make sure everyone had come down. But my Mama, she still looked beautiful. I stayed with her until they came to take her away. I told them I had an aunt who lived close by. I lied so they'd leave me alone. Then I walked though the city trying to find my friends, but it was all gone. Dead people were lying everywhere. They just lined them up next to the tram tracks so they could get picked up. All the buildings were gone. When it got dark, I walked to the woods and slept there. I stayed there until I got too hungry." He shrugged. "Then I went back into town and lived in a bombed-out building for a while."

"But, Oskar, that was almost one year ago. How did you survive?"

"Sometimes the soldiers would give me their food. Sometimes old ladies would give me bread or lard. Sometimes I just took it. Climbed in the open window and took whatever was there." He stopped and looked at her, as if calculating her reaction. "But of course then, when it got too cold in the winter, I caught a ride on a truck with some troops and I came back here to Wiesbaden. To the villa. And that's where you found me."

"And you mean to say that you were at the villa all that time?"

Oskar stopped the swing and looked up at her. "Frau Klein?" he said sweetly. "Can I go inside now? I don't want to talk anymore. It makes me too sad."

Anna stood and nodded. "Of course," she said. Oskar jumped up and ran to the barracks. Anna shivered in her soaked clothes.

The air had turned chilly and a wind was picking up. She followed Oskar and waved to Maria who was corralling a handful of little girls playing a game of ring-around-the-rosie. After retrieving her bike, she pinned her pants legs and headed into the gray toward the Adolfsallee, feeling drained. Why was no one coming forward to claim this boy? If his family was so well-connected, so high up in the ranks, surely someone, somewhere, would know of him. How could he just have been abandoned? What was he not telling her? And what did he mean when he said he came *back* to Wiesbaden?

When Anna arrived at the Adolfsallee, Madeleine was up, cleaning out the drawers of the old desk. Amalia sat on the floor by her feet, her old chocolate box of treasures open. Madeleine looked better than she had in weeks.

"It's that damn tea, I think," she said. "I hate to admit it, but I think it works. If I had any sherry I'd pour it in. Then it would *really* work." She sorted through a pile of postcards on the desk. "Look what I found here. A postcard I got from your mother in 1937. When you were all visiting Bad Gastein." She held it out to Anna.

Anna shook her head. "I can't," she said, averting her eyes from the card and busying herself with undressing. All the talk of mothers with Oskar made the idea of seeing her own mother's handwriting too painful. She dug in the pile of clothes on the bed for her robe.

"I want to see, Auntie," Amalia jumped up. The two of them bent over the writing and Madeleine lowered her voice to read the card.

"Mama, Auntie says I can keep this." Amalia waved the card. "I'll put it in my box."

Madeleine handed her the stack of cards to let her take her pick of more. "So, did you find out anything more about the boy?" she asked, only half-interested.

"Oskar? Just a little," Anna replied. "It sounds like he was adopted by a high-ranking officer's family." She looked at Amalia who was focused on reorganizing her box. "SS," she mouthed.

Madeleine made a face.

"But his mother seems to have been very loving and kind," Anna added.

"She was very beautiful," said Amalia to the floor. "Oskar's mother was."

Anna nodded. "Yes, that's what he told me. I think she loved him very much."

"She liked to do things with him a lot. He told me. And she had lots of friends. They had lots of parties. It sounds like fun." Amalia's eyes were wide. "I wish we had parties."

Anna sat down on the bed and rubbed her feet. "Yes, it does sound like fun, Maus. We will have a party, too, one day."

"When Papa comes we will have a party," Amalia cheered. "Oskar's mama liked to paint pictures of him. And take photographs. Maybe I can be an artist too, when I am big."

"Really? What else did Oskar tell you?"

Amalia sighed. "Mama, you already asked me yesterday. I told you. He's too sad to talk about it." She went back to her box of treasures.

"You know, that reminds me," Madeleine said. "I meant to tell you this earlier. About Ludwig Schneider."

Anna had been trying not to think about Schneider. "What about him?"

"I remembered my Otto did have a run-in with him once. You know the Nazis, they were taking all the art from Jewish collectors, even in the early days. Forcing them to sell it for nothing. Otto got together with a few of his friends, the ones he could still trust. I think this was in 1934. They bought up a few pieces belonging to some of our Jewish friends. Not much, just some things here and there so it wasn't obvious. I remember they bought each one for just under one thousand Reichsmark each, because if it was more than that you had to have the transaction certified by the local official. And then Otto and his friends turned around and sold the art as their own property for twice what they had paid. Because if the work was labeled as Aryan property they could get more for it. Then they gave the profit to the Jews to help fund their emigration. It worked for a while if you didn't get greedy and kept it all very small. Every little bit helped."

"So what does Schneider have to do with it?"

"Schneider was the auctioneer. Because the Party only allowed auctions through their sanctioned people. I remember he and Otto argued afterwards because Schneider suspected what Otto had done and threatened to report him. Otto had been very clever to cover his tracks. Bankers are good at that kind of thing. But Schneider couldn't prove it—he was never that smart. Families were desperate to raise funds, and the Nazis gave them pennies for what their pieces were worth. I know of one family that lost their entire collection. Significant pieces they were, German painters, right in line with what the Nazis liked. The Nazis must have liked Schneider's work because soon enough he became a fully fledged crazy like the rest of them. But still, after that auction I was so terrified. For weeks every knock at the door sent me into a near heart attack. If Otto was even five minutes late coming home from the office, I was beside myself. The poor man. I nearly drove us both insane. But nothing ever happened. And then much later Schneider himself got sent to a KZ, I think to Dachau, to the concentration camp. When he came back, he was never the same. Eventually he was kicked out of the Party, and we never heard from him again. I really thought he was dead."

"Do you know why he was sent to the camp?" Anna asked.

Madeleine shook her head. "No. It was in '42 or '43. By then we didn't ask questions anymore. And I didn't much care anyway." She looked tired now and Anna suggested she lie down. The rain picked up again and the afternoon was as dark as a winter evening. Anna closed the window where the rain was beginning to splatter the floor and turned on a lamp to provide dim light for the room. As Madeleine crawled into bed, Anna sat back on the sofa, putting her feet up on the arm. She tried to think of what Schneider could have done to get crosswise with his Nazi bosses. People who did short stints in concentration camps were usually being taught a lesson. If he was doing something to help the Jews whom he was assigned to rob, that would have been enough to get his bosses' attention. Maybe he wasn't so shifty after all. Or maybe he was even worse than the Nazis. Was that possible? The rain tickling the windowpane soothed her mind and she allowed it to wander until she fell into a light sleep.

Footsteps and voices in the stairwell jolted Anna back to consciousness. She had dozed off on the sofa as Amalia played with her dolls. The knock on the door was followed by Frau Hermann's voice.

"Frau Klein? I am sorry to bother you, but there's a woman here looking for you. She says she knows you." She repeated the knock.

Anna swung her legs to the ground and tried to gather herself. The clock said six thirty. Madeleine was asleep in her bed. Amalia had curled up next to her and was playing with her dolls. She gave Anna a worried look.

"It's all right, Maus. Just stay there." Anna called out that she was coming and tucked her shirt back into her pants. She stepped into her shoes and patted her hair down into its clip.

"Who is with you, Frau Hermann?" she said to the door, one hand poised on the handle.

"It's me, Frau Klein, Frieda Schilling. I am sorry to disturb you on a Sunday, but could I speak with you?"

Anna pulled the door open to see Frau Hermann, arms folded across her shelf of a chest, mouth configured into indignation. Behind her stood Frieda, her hair and clothes dripping.

"I am sure Frau Wolf is resting. I told her." Frau Hermann shook her head. "The woman needs her rest."

"Frau Hermann, thank you for showing Fraulein Schilling the way." She stood back to make room for Frieda to enter. "Please, won't you come in?"

"Thank you. I won't keep you long." Frieda puddled past her into the apartment and Anna closed the door with a deferential gesture that left Frau Herman stewing on the landing. Behind the closed door Anna rolled her eyes and smiled at Frieda.

"I apologize for her. She has given herself guard duty. She means well, I suppose. Please, try to get warm." She led the way into the kitchen. "My aunt is resting but we can sit here by the stove. Can I offer you a coffee? It's the real thing," she beamed, proud to have something to offer.

"Oh, well, I don't want to stay, but I guess under the circumstances, that would be lovely. I should have thought to bring you some, but if you already have your own, that's even better. Anyway, I already have my answer." Frieda bent around the corner and waved into the living room at Amalia.

"I'm sorry?"

"I am out in this rain looking for my brother. I thought maybe he was with you. He went out last night and hasn't come home. It's not really like him. I mean he does go off on his benders but usually he's back by now. He hasn't been here, has he?"

Anna shook her head. "No, why would he come here?"

"Well, sometimes when he drinks, he gets impulsive. And I know he thinks of you, still. I told him to stop, but anyway, I thought maybe he had paid you a visit."

"When he drinks?"

"He gets his hands on some liquor now and then. It doesn't last long with him. Luckily it's hard to to come by. I think he inherited this from our father. He was a drinker, God rest his soul."

"Well, he hasn't been here." She turned off the flame underneath the shrieking kettle and poured the steaming water into the coffee pot. The small talk annoyed her. It was tiresome and she always felt she should be on her guard: residue of the many years when no one could be trusted. She wished she hadn't offered the coffee—now she was stuck until they finished it. "I hope you find him. This weather can't be helping."

"I'm sure he's holed up somewhere, but I've already looked everywhere I can think of." She took the cup Anna held out and looked around. "So, this is where you are staying?"

Anna nodded. "Yes. We are very lucky. Most of the time the electricity works and the water runs. And there's room for all of us to sleep."

"But when your husband comes, you'll need to find something better. It's not right that our children have to grow up living this way."

Anna changed the subject. "You were a nurse during the war? In the Red Cross, I suppose?" Anna took a sip of her coffee.

"Yes, I got moved around quite a bit but I ended up back here. My family has been in Wiesbaden for generations."

"Really? Well, I wonder if you know my aunt? Madeleine Wolf? She has lived here all her life."

Frieda made a show of searching her mind and coming up empty. "No, I don't think I do. But I am sure we know some of the same people. Perhaps one day when she is feeling better we could talk." She took a drink. "How do you think Amalia has enjoyed her first week with us? She's a wonderful child. So sweet and pretty. And clever. She's the smartest of the bunch. I'm sure of that."

"She seems to be enjoying it very much. I think you have a future in this work. And there will be a lot of it, with the women all working now."

"I just love being around children." Frieda shrugged. "I guess it's my calling."

"And you're still young. You'll have your own children too, one day."

Frieda said nothing and drained her cup instead. She placed it into the sink and exhaled.

"I'm sorry. I've upset you, I didn't mean–"

"Not at all. But I really must get home. I want to be there when Emil returns." Frieda walked toward the door and then turned back. "With all that business happening tomorrow at the Collecting Point, no doubt you'll need to work late. If you'd like, Amalia can stay with me tomorrow night. Save you having to feed her and deal with all of that. It's not any trouble of course, we have plenty of room. And I do love having the little ones with me."

Anna stole a look at her daughter by way of the small pass-through to the living room. The girl was sitting on the sofa playing with her dolls.

"Oh, that is very kind. But really, my aunt will be able to watch her in the evening. It's all arranged. I am not worried." She paused, then heard herself say, "My aunt is feeling much better, so she can help me a little more, too."

Frieda nodded. "Very well. If you change your mind, just say so. But you mustn't need to be afraid of Emil. I will keep him in line. He's not a danger. He's just confused. And don't worry about Amalia either. I look out for her as if she were my own. I feel that way about all my children. I can do that, since you aren't with her."

Anna bristled at Frieda's insinuation, that she was somehow lacking as a mother. She turned on the water and began to rinse her coffee cup. "Of course, the schools will be starting soon and she'll be going to kindergarten. And, when my husband comes, we'll likely be on our way anyway. I don't know what will happen."

"Oh? Emil said you were a translator for that Captain. I thought it was an important job that you'd want to keep. I must have misunderstood. But I hope you are happy with the arrangement for now."

Anna gestured Frieda toward the door. "If Emil turns up here I'll be sure to send him home." She pulled on the door. "Amalia, come say goodbye to Fraulein Schilling."

Amalia appeared in the living room door and mumbled a goodbye, her eyes fixed on the floor.

"If it stops raining tomorrow we can finish planting the vegetables," Frieda said, her voice a sing-song of enthusiasm. She thanked Anna and made her way down the stairs. Anna closed the door and locked it.

Anna stared at Amalia. "Maus, is something wrong? You seem upset." She reached for her daughter but the girl turned away.

"I am not staying there tomorrow am I, Mama? For the night?" she asked.

"No of course not, Maus. I would miss you too much." She scooped the girl off her feet and carried her into the living room. Madeleine was sitting up in the bed, brushing her long white hair. Anna deposited Amalia on the blanket.

"Who was that? You could have introduced us. I am almost presentable." Madeleine played at scolding Anna.

Anna explained Frieda's visit as she straightened up around the room, expelling her nervous energy. "Madeleine, do you think it will it be all right with you to watch Amalia tomorrow evening? I think I do have to work late with the big delivery coming."

Madeleine nodded. "Of course, my dear. It's all right with us, isn't it?" She reached for Amalia. "I am feeling much better."

"Maus, you just come straight home in the afternoon you understand? Do you have your key?"

Amalia nodded and pulled it out from under her blouse and held it up. "But Mama, will you be very late? Who will tuck me in?"

"I shall be tucking in this week," Madeline sang. "I have been known to be a very good tucker-inner in my day. We'll have fun. You'll see."

Amalia furrowed her brow but said nothing. Anna pulled her daughter into her embrace and staggered backward to the sofa, where they fell in one pile, legs entangled. Amalia giggled as Anna tickled her armpits.

"I am just going to be a little bit later than normal. Auntie will take good care of you. Will you take good care of her, too?"

Amalia nodded and buried her head into Anna's shoulder.

"And what about if in a few days you can stay home all day with Auntie again? Would you like that?"

Amalia nodded. "But what about Herr Schilling? Where is he?" she whispered and stroked Anna's hair between her fingers. "Who will take care of him?"

chapter sixteen

Anna had fallen asleep without setting the alarm clock and all three of them overslept. After running nearly the whole way from the Adolfsallee she'd sent Amalia to run up to Frieda's house on her own. "Don't worry, Mama, I can do it," Amalia said as she ran up the hill. Anna watched her disappear into the shadows of the tree-lined street before going through the sentry gate.

The big delivery day at the Collecting Point was well underway. Dozens of GIs and German workers milled around the courtyard, all looking up the length the Frankfurter Strasse as if waiting for a parade to start. Anna made her way through the crowd and into the main foyer of the museum. The building was deserted. She went upstairs and deposited her bag under her little desk, pulled up the blind, and opened the window. As she looked down on the scene, she pulled her hair into its clip and re-tucked her blouse. The soft breeze and remaining cool night air helped settle her down.

She went downstairs and passed the administrative office near the front main entrance. It was deserted. An old table doubled as the reception desk and behind it were several rows of filing cabinets—some American Army-issue, others left over from the museum's pre-war days. She looked at the front door, then down the length of the entry foyer. The plaster walls were silent; no sounds of activity reverberated in the double-height arches. Before she knew what she was doing, she found herself tiptoeing past the desk and into the file room.

She scanned the small paper labels on the front of each drawer. She had no idea what she was looking for. Endless drawers marked the various levels of operations at the Collecting Point: personnel records, field reports, building operations, restitution claims, military correspondence, and on and on. The cabinets went all the way to the open window that faced directly onto the perimeter chain link fence and the street beyond. She hunched down between the cabinets and crept to the last row, pausing under the window to get on all fours.

These cabinets held civilian personnel records. She ignored the itch to look up her own file and instead ran her finger along the row until she got to the end. A tag on the last drawer on the bottom row read *Art Dealers: Hesse*, which would cover everyone who had made themselves known in the entire region, including Darmstadt. The tag was freshly typed and held on with a piece of tape. She paused and chewed on the inside of her cheek. Waves of excited voices floated in from outside. She put her hand on the metal pull and gave it a tug. The drawer was half empty; only a few files lay inside. She examined names: Arndt, Dornberger, Kranz, Proch, Heinrich, and then, there it was: Schneider. She pulled out the file and opened it.

A handful of papers fell out and scattered on the floor. She picked up the one closest to her. It was the letter of introduction for Schneider, recommending him for an advisory role at the Collecting Point based on his "vast experience in matters of art and restoration," signed by Major James E. Phillips. Copies had also been sent to the Collecting Points in Munich and Offenbach. Underneath, someone had scribbled a note: *Capt. Cooper, interviewed, declined 15 August.* Attached to the memo with a paperclip was another report, this one noting a repository of paintings at a villa west of the city. Anna felt a jolt. This memo came from a Lieutenant Colonel in the Regional Military Government in Darmstadt and noted that the repository had been inspected by MFAA officer Cooper and accompanying civilian translator Anna Klein on 14 August 1945. The second part of the memo requested an explanation of the fact that the repository had not been reported in a timely manner, as required, to the regional military headquarters. Anna turned the page over, looking for an annotation, a reply, anything that indicated a next step. She leaned her back against the wall. How did Cooper's late reporting of the repository get attached to the memo about Schneider? She scanned the words again, looking for a clue, but there was no mention of Schneider or any claims on the repository. Just that she and Cooper had been at the villa and had not properly reported what they had found. So who else knew about the art in the basement? Whoever had attacked Cooper and taken his gun did, that was for sure. But what did Schneider have to do with it?

"Frau Klein? What on earth are you doing down there?" A voice came over the top of the cabinet. Shrill, high pitched: Frau Obersdorfer. Anna looked up at the red face.

"Frau Obersdorfer, hello. I was researching something for Captain Cooper. He wanted to make sure his report had been filed."

"These are not the field reports. Those are over there. She pointed a finger to the next row of cabinets. And besides, you have no business being here. If you need a file, you ask the clerk." Frau Obersdorfer cocked her head in the direction of the empty desk at the front.

"Oh yes, of course." Anna nodded. She shuffled the pages into the folder and pushed it back into the drawer. Standing up, she straightened her pants and looked the woman in her beady eyes.

"Everyone is to be helping with the delivery today. That is what is expected," Frau Obersdorfer said.

As Anna walked out of the file room—with the woman close on her tail—the sound of applause skated in from the courtyard, followed by the rumble of engines. Three GIs ran past her and Anna followed them to the door in time to see the first of a phalanx of trucks and tanks crawling down the Frankfurter Strasse at a funereal pace. Along the street, people who had gathered began to cheer. Little boys ran alongside the tanks and waved. There was Cooper, waving his arms to direct the first truck as it turned into the courtyard, taking the bumps at the entry slowly. Behind that one, another truck waited and behind that, another and another. Anna counted fifteen trucks, but that was only until the tree canopy obscured her view.

The first truck sighed to a stop at the loading dock and an American jumped out to open the tailgate. Cooper sent several others to the back door where they stood guard while a small band of skinny Germans unloaded the truck. They formed a line and began handing crates from one to the other until it reached the building entry. Officers Anna had never seen before stood in small groups chatting and pointing. With their hands on their hips and caps askew on their heads they carried the air of victory, the jovial camaraderie over a job well done. Captain Farmer, the director, stood earnestly in the shadows, clipboard in hand, making annotations.

People clamored to be close to the action, and the crowd carried Anna forward. On the outside of the fence another crowd gathered. MPs patrolled the perimeter as women, children and old men pushed against the chain link fence, hands grasping the wire, faces eager.

Cooper jumped from the back of the truck and called instructions to two GIs who edged a large rectangular crate toward the lip of the truck bed. A buzz rose up and the visiting American officers shook hands and thumped each other on the back.

Anna turned to the old man next to her. "What are they saying?" she asked.

He gave her a toothless grin. "It's the painted queen. Nefertiti. She is safe again!" He wiped his eyes with a shriveled hand.

Out of nowhere, a chill ran down Anna's spine as she envisioned the ancient sculpture, witness to millennia of human affliction, emerging from her tomb in the Merkers salt mine. Anna joined the round of applause that rose from the crowd as the news spread. A tall American with a scruffy mustache in a sweat-stained uniform shouted for people to get out of the way and the crowd pushed back a bit. Anna wanted to help, but it seemed unloading was the first order of business. She went back inside and upstairs to her alcove, sat down at her desk and looked out into the courtyard. As the first truck pulled away, another stood ready to take its place. Anna let the feeling of participating in a greater cause wash over her. She couldn't remember the last time she felt that sensation.

"Anna—Frau Klein—come help with these, will you?" Cooper shouted as he passed their office. Anna jumped up and left the lists she had been scouring to follow him to a bathroom at the end of the hall where three women were filling bowls and buckets with water.

"Take one and follow me," Cooper said. He was sweating through his shirt but his face was in a state of bliss, transformed. She took a porcelain bowl from one of the women and caught up with Cooper down the hall.

"Here, put that in the corner there." He pointed to an empty spot in a room already crowded with stacks of crates taller than she was. "Then get another one and put it over there. Keeps the humidity up."

Anna retrieved another bowl and squeezed through the narrow canyon of crates to put it in the corner he had indicated. An odor of something she could not identify hung heavy in the air.

Cooper's head appeared in the gap between two rows of crates. "It's the salt. The smell." He inhaled. "From the mine. It's all over everything. Awful." He thrust a clipboard at her. "Here. I need all hands on deck. You can inventory this room. No need to open the crates. Just note the markings on every item and its dimensions. The brass want to be here when things are opened, but we need to at least keep a count. It would have been nice if Frankfurt had sent a pro forma or at least a list to go with all this stuff. We don't even know what all we have."

"All this was in that mine? For how long?" Anna asked.

"Oh there's plenty more, this is only the start. I think the Nazis moved it all when the bombs started, so it's been a good few years. It's the entire collection of the National Gallery in Berlin. And I'd like to make sure it stays intact."

"Was that really Nefertiti, in the crate?"

"Sure was. They put her in the first truck and marked her clearly. That driver felt every bump between Frankfurt and here, I guarantee it. I think I felt them too, and I wasn't even in the truck. But she made it."

"How many truckloads do you think there will be?"

"Frankfurt said they think somewhere around fifty. This will go on for a few days yet." Cooper smiled. "Pretty exciting, don't you think? Makes our little stash in the villa pale by comparison."

"Fifty trucks? Full of art?"

He nodded. "And that's just one repository. There's a bigger one at Heilbronn. And Neuschwanstein, that's mostly private property taken from Jewish collectors. Those will go to Munich. And there are still more than that. Göring's collections alone are enormous. He took everything he could get his hands on. It's gonna be a long time before this all gets sorted out. The Nazis didn't just take art for Hitler's dream museum, they took whatever they wanted for themselves. And if they went down, they were planning to take it with them. I've never known such systematic plunder of cultural objects. Gold and valuables, sure, but going after paintings and sculptures for the sake of the art? Never. You gotta hand it to them. Those guys sure knew what they were doing." He elbowed her and grinned. "Should we take a look?"

Not waiting for an answer, he led her toward a small rectangular crate that had a series of numbers stenciled on the side, like all the others. "Here, this looks as good as any," Cooper said as he wedged the blade of his pocket knife between the slats along the top and popped the frame off.

It took a moment for Anna's brain to register what her eyes saw. An old man sat at a table bathed in a half moon of golden light. He inspected a gold coin that he held into the candlelight. Books and papers were piled precariously behind him like a landscape that disappeared into the shadows. The color, the composition—it was unmistakable.

"Is that…" She put a hand to her mouth.

"Rembrandt. Am I right this time?" Cooper whispered.

"This is most definitely Rembrandt," Anna said. "I am speechless."

They stood for several moments, basking in their find and letting the chaos of activity around them fade away.

"I've never even seen a real Rembrandt in person, much less had a private viewing," Anna said. She stroked a finger along the edge of the canvas.

Cooper smiled. "This, *this* is why we are here, do you understand now?" he asked. "This is what matters. It's how we remember who we are." He leaned his face close to hers and whispered, "This will heal us. I know it."

Anna nodded. She was seeing a fragment of a world she thought was gone forever.

Cooper lowered the painting back into its crate. "Now, don't tell anyone I showed you that. I'll get in more trouble than I already am." He winked. "You okay?"

Anna took a deep breath and picked up her pencil. "Tell me where to start."

It was well past seven o'clock when Anna stepped out into the courtyard. The Collecting Point was still bustling, with workers staying into the night to unload and sort. Guards were now on duty around the clock. Anna felt both exhausted and exhilarated; it took her a while to recognize that this was a happy combination. She took in a deep breath of the summer evening and savored it. Her hands were dry and scraped from handling the wooden crates, and her blouse was dirty with their grime. She had counted more than one hundred crates in her room alone, sorted them, and lined them along the walls. Cooper checked on her a few times but he had been mostly occupied with maintaining some order amongst the chaos. Here and there she heard more cheers when another treasure was discovered. But she had stayed on her own, happy to be alone with the shrouded works, to let their presence soak in.

Anna shouldered her bag and walked toward the front gate into the setting sun. As she walked along the Rheinstrasse toward the Hansa Hotel, the traffic of American officers became heavier. A long line of jeeps was parked along the curb and strains of music floated out from the open doors of the hotel bar. She peered inside through the row of windows open to the street. *Amis* raised glasses and poured generously from bottles. She stopped, gazing on the scene. Cooper should have been there celebrating, she thought, but he was still at the Collecting Point, working into the night. "I won't be able to sleep anyway," he had said. "I'll see you tomorrow." They had exchanged tired smiles and Anna had told him to remember to eat something, like a mother or a wife. She cringed now thinking about the conversation.

The Americans inside the bar—the ones visiting from somewhere else to witness the Monuments Men's great success—stood around with drinks in hand congratulating themselves. Maybe they had been the ones to find the hidden masterpieces, Anna thought. Maybe they had stumbled upon the Rembrandt in a salt mine and gotten it out safely. Among the cheering *Amis*, Anna spotted a familiar face at the bar toward the back: Ludwig Schneider stood talking to a tall younger man who was wearing a well-cut gray suit. The two of them toasted and threw back their drinks. They fit well into the scene, as if they belonged there. It was the *Amis* who had all the power now, and there was Schneider, once again in the thick of it.

Anna debated with herself. If she talked to Schneider here, she'd catch him off guard and possibly put him on the back foot. On the other hand, she had no idea what to say to him. Ignoring her trepidation, she pulled her identification papers from her bag and walked to the door without any plan for what to do if she managed to get inside. A smiling soldier held up a hand to stop her but stepped aside when she waved her papers. She had half hoped she wouldn't be allowed in the door.

Inside the small Art Nouveau lobby it was almost as if she had stepped onto another planet. American officers stood and talked in soft voices while aides and staff scurried around them. Others sat with drinks or the newspaper. One well-fed American civilian held court in a stentorian voice around a group of uniformed men, who burst into exaggerated laughter as if on cue. *Politician*, Anna thought. She tried to look as though she had a reason to be there and made her way to the entrance to the bar. A waiter stopped her at the door.

"May I help you?" He looked down his nose at her pants.

Anna flashed her papers. "Yes, I just need to get a message to my boss, the colonel. Just over there." She waved a hand toward the back of the room. "It's urgent. A military matter."

The waiter looked over his shoulder and back at her. "Who is your boss?"

Anna looked past him and waved as if she had spotted someone. She smiled and nodded. "He says it's all right. Thank you very much." She pushed past the waiter and was absorbed into the crowd.

As she made her way into the middle of the crowd she hoped her smelly clothes and film of dirt wouldn't draw attention. Peering around the well-padded shoulders and neatly trimmed heads she could see Schneider and the other man still talking at the bar. Schneider raised two fingers at the barman for another round. From what she could tell they were the only Germans in the place. Such establishments usually were off limits to Germans, unless maybe they had almighty dollars to spend. She squeezed her way to the far end of the bar.

"Herr Schneider? Is that you?" She feigned surprise.

"Frau Klein? What are you doing here?" Schneider said.

"I came to leave a message for…for someone," she said. "I was just leaving. And you?" She threw a glance at Schneider's companion.

"Oh, I am so sorry. Frau Klein this is Herr Schenk. My colleague."

Schenk cocked his head and gave a half bow. "My pleasure," he said.

Anna returned the greeting with a half smile. She turned her smile toward Schneider to cover the recognition that she felt was obvious on her face. *Fromm, Schenk, and Knopf* she thought, remembering the nameplates at the apartment Schneider had visited.

Schneider was happy to have her attention. "Well, since you are here, may I buy you a drink, Frau Klein? Maybe a little schnapps? Or they have American things too. A whiskey perhaps? It calms the nerves."

Schneider's speech was thick with alcohol and he was even more flushed and sweaty than the last time she had seen him. His eyes were glazed and his face slack. Anna declined the drink although she would have loved to have one.

"Very well." Schneider raised his glass to his lips. "I thought you'd want to celebrate the big day with us."

"What are you celebrating?" Anna asked.

"Oh, you know, the return of what's rightfully ours," Schneider slurred. "At least for now."

"Come on, Ludwig, that's enough," Schenk snapped. "Keep it down."

Whatever Schenk's wartime activities had been, he had come through in good shape. With his muscular build and ruddy complexion he looked like he'd just returned from a hiking trip in the Alps, all aired-out and well-circulated.

"Herr Schenk, are you also in the art business?" Anna asked. "Are you related, perhaps, to Konrad Schenk the restorer? I think he used to have a small place on the Freseniusstrasse," she said, remembering the card Madeleine had given her.

Schenk gave her a cool smile for several moments before speaking. "Yes, he was my father. Did you know him?"

"Ah, yes of course," Schneider interjected. "Of course. I should have put this all together the other day. The address, it seemed familiar. And the name. You are staying with Frau Wolf. Funny how I didn't make the connection sooner. I have known Madeleine Wolf for many years. Such a lovely woman. She is your…?"

"My aunt," Anna lied. "My mother's sister. She mentioned that she knew you, Herr Schneider. I think you also knew my uncle, Otto Wolf?"

Schneider sipped his drink. "Yes, yes, of course. Such a dear man."

"Then you must know my aunt too, Herr Schenk?"

Schenk shook his head. "No, I've only just returned to the city. And, of course, my parents are gone now."

"Oh," Anna said. "My aunt will be sorry to hear that."

"Well, I am so glad to see you." Schneider lowered his voice and patted her arm like a father getting the attention of a child. "I was wondering if you received the items I delivered to your house last week? Were they to your liking?" He looked around, pulled his dingy handkerchief from his back pocket and began to mop his brow. He looked like he might slide under the bar at any moment.

"Yes. I am glad to be able to thank you in person. Your gift was most generous." Anna waited.

"It was my pleasure, of course. And it's been such an auspicious day today. So exciting, really. I watched a little from the sidelines. It's all I can do for now," Schneider said.

Anna shifted her weight. "Yes, it's really quite unfortunate that you've had no luck at the Collecting Point so far. They could certainly use a man of your expertise." She looked around and leaned in to whisper. "They really have no idea what they are doing."

Schneider nodded.

Anna continued. "Not to mention that all those things must be returned to their rightful owners in Germany. Not taken to America—stealing what's rightfully ours!" She looked around again. No one in the room paid any attention to them. It was getting more crowded and the air was warm. A line of sweat ran down her back.

Schneider took another drink. "Yes, I agree completely. We can't allow them to take our property. But what can we do?"

"I have some ideas," Schenk muttered. "But I am told they are too extreme for peacetime." He finished his drink and hailed the barman for another.

Schneider waved his hand for Schenk to be quiet. "So, what are they having you do in there, Frau Klein? Have you seen any treasures so far?" he asked.

"Well, the first painting I saw today was a Rembrandt," Anna whispered.

"A Rembrandt?" Schneider lit up. "Which one?"

"It was *The Money Changer*. Really, the place is just swimming with old masters and anything you can imagine. And so little security. Well, I don't know." She tilted her head. "It really would be such a help to have a man like you there. I wish there was something I could do. Maybe I should talk to Captain Cooper again? Or should I go over his head? I know he is resisting pressure to hire you. You have friends in Frankfurt, is that right?"

Schneider sucked on his teeth. "I've *made* friends in Frankfurt. You know how it is, my dear. One day your bread is buttered on this side, the next day it's buttered on the other side. I am a flexible man."

Anna pretended to consider this as a profound thought. "Well, perhaps I can have another word with Captain Cooper. He can sometimes be easily swayed. And it's possible, of course, that the situation will play itself out. If Cooper refuses to hire you, it may mean the end for him. Then you'd be hired for sure. Maybe as a restorer or an appraiser." She let the temptation sink in before continuing. "But first I wanted to talk to you about a personal matter. I wonder if perhaps I could impose on you to help me with something somewhat delicate?"

Schneider studied her. "Go on," he said. Schenk leaned in closer.

"Oh, not here, I am not comfortable discussing it with all these *Amis* around. Would you mind if we walk? I need to get home."

Schneider held his ground. "It all depends, Frau Klein. What is the nature of the matter?"

Anna felt like she was playing a role in a bad play. "Well, all right, Herr Schneider, it's my husband. He's caught in the Russian sector, you see, and would like to join me here in Wiesbaden. That was our plan, once I got settled. He's a doctor and could not leave his patients. But now that things are falling into place, it's time for him to join us here. Of course we do not have the funds for a train ticket or even the gas needed for a car. He could get transport through the Red Cross or the UN people, but that could take months. Right now he can't even afford the travel papers he would need to leave the Russian sector. It all costs money, as you know." She clutched her bag and sighed. It really was a bad performance.

Schneider looked at Schenk and nodded. "Go on."

"So I was wondering if you could—would—help me divest of a valuable in order to raise the funds we need."

"What kind of valuable?"

Anna leaned in. "A painting. A landscape. I think it would be of interest to you. And I'd be willing to let it go for very little in order to have my family back together. I mean it's just a painting after all. It's useless to me."

Before Anna knew what was happening, Schenk grabbed her by the arm and pulled her toward the door, holding her close with a painful grip. Schneider followed behind, fumbling with his hat and muttering apologies.

Anna's heart pounded in her chest. No one seemed to care or notice that a man was dragging a woman out onto the street. She tried to keep up with his stride but his hand twisted the skin on her arm and made her contort to keep her balance. He pulled her up the street until they were well away from the hotel's lights and activity.

"Keep on walking," he said as he let go. "Don't stop."

Anna was glad to oblige. He walked alongside her looking straight ahead. "Surely you were not so stupid as to attempt to discuss such a matter under the noses of the *Amis* just now. Please tell me you are not that dumb, Frau Klein," he snarled. "In your job you must be familiar with the rules of Paragraph 51 of the United State Military Code? Our new law of the land? Cultural objects may not change hands. Not even among friends," Schenk said. "I can't imagine why you would ask us to participate in such a transaction."

"I wasn't asking you. I was asking him." Anna jerked a finger over her shoulder at Schneider, who came panting up behind them. She stopped walking. "If you don't mind, this is between me and him. I don't much appreciate your manners."

Schenk chuckled. "Silly girl. All right, you talk to him. Ludwig, fill me in later. I'm going home." He held up a palm and turned north toward the old city.

When he was gone, Anna exhaled. "Look, Herr Schneider I am desperate. I know I could lose my job and end up in jail, but my daughter needs her father. Of course I would be forever in your debt if you took on such a risk on my behalf."

Schneider snorted. "In my debt? My dear girl, in such a transaction it would be standard for me to receive a percentage of the sale."

"Of course, yes, I didn't mean to imply otherwise."

"Look, Frau Klein, this is dangerous. The *Amis* are policing cultural property very closely. Well, I don't need to tell you that," he laughed. "How do I know I can trust you? How do I know you are not setting me up?"

Anna stepped in closer. She towered over the little man. "Setting you up? Why on earth would I do that? Herr Schneider, I'll be honest with you. The *Amis* are done with you. Your file is closed. I saw it myself. They have no intention of hiring you. But a few good words, perhaps even from my aunt, an affidavit, could help you. Any day now they are going to realize they are in over their heads and they'll be looking around for help. You know how it is. You get desperate, you break the rules. And you could find yourself working with the greatest art in the world. I held a Rembrandt in my hands today. Don't you want to make sure those masterpieces stay in Germany? That these valuables get returned to the right hands? To German hands? You can tell them what you know. Make it up, they can't tell the difference. You tell them something belongs in the Nationalgallerie in Berlin or the Staedel in Frankfurt or to some private collector friend of yours, what other authority do they have? The records are all gone," she lied.

Schneider looked skeptical but there was a glimmer of something in his eyes. Anna hoped it was greed. She kept going.

"But if my husband can't get here, I will have to leave and be with him. Maybe as soon as next week. So if you want my help, you will have to do this for me first. But time is short and there are only so many jobs available at the Collecting Point." She looked at the clock on the storefront behind him. "Now, I really have to go." She turned away. "Good evening Herr Schneider. Please let me know what you decide. You know where you can find me." She began walking, taking long strides to put distance between her and the little man.

The grunting and snorting took a good minute to catch up with her. "Frau Klein, just a moment, please." Schneider took her elbow. "May I see the item?" he asked.

"You may see it if you agree to the transaction," Anna snapped. "I am coming to you in good faith. As a friend."

"Perhaps you can tell me more about it? In case I were to know a buyer?"

Anna paused. "It's a landscape, as I've said. That's all I will tell you." She looked over his head and waited for the next round.

"How do I know the *Ami* didn't put you up to this?" he said.

Anna grit her teeth. She waved her hand for him to step closer. "Trust me, Herr Schneider. No one over there is thinking about you or me. They've got what they came here for. You think the *Ami* gives a damn about you or what you do? They just want to get their hands on the art. But if you help me, I'll help you. Maybe you can still make a difference." She sounded like Cooper.

Schneider let the offer lie for a moment. An internal debate distorted his face into a series of grimaces, as if he was trying to dislodge something stuck between his teeth. Finally, he waggled his head and negotiated himself into agreement.

"All right. You bring me the item tomorrow at the Nassauer Hof. You come alone. If I even smell the hint of a rat or an *Ami,* I will deny everything, and I am not above denouncing you. I have come too far through this mess to be tripped up by some half-baked scheme. This is not a game. You want to put your family back together, you'd better be on the up-and-up. Do you understand?" He spat the words from a contorted mouth and for an instant, Anna saw the Ludwig Schneider of 1939, all self-interest and desperation.

Anna nodded. "And this is just between us?"

"Just between us."

Anna squared her shoulders and extended her hand. "Shall we say seven o'clock? Tomorrow?"

chapter seventeen

When Anna entered, the apartment was quiet and dark. It was 7:45, nearly Amalia's bedtime, but no one was home. The bed was made and the dishes were put away. *The Snow Queen* lay open on the sofa. Anna looked around and felt disoriented. She wondered what she should feel. Alarm? Concern? Nothing? She went to the window and looked down onto the street. Long shadows contradicted the bright sky above. There was no sign of either Amalia or Madeleine. She stood for several minutes, hoping they would turn the corner from the Rheinstrasse, maybe with a loaf of bread or some other explanation for their outing. When they did not appear, Anna turned back to the room, looking for a note or some other clue. She looked at the clock again. Maybe they were visiting Frau Hermann downstairs. As she fished her key out of her bag, a knock at the door startled her.

Relieved, she walked to the door, ready to give her daughter a stern talking to.

A second knock came. Authoritative.

"Frau Klein? Anna Klein?" a voice called. *Americans.*

"Yes?" Anna felt the air go very still.

"Open up. United States Military Police. Open this door right now."

She froze. For a flash she hoped maybe it was Cooper playing a joke on her.

"Right now, ma'am. I'm not saying it again," the voice barked. She heard footsteps and then a second voice, consulting quietly.

She pulled the door open and peered through the crack. The MP on the other side was built like a tank, all bottom-heavy with a tiny turret for a head.

"Yes?" Anna's throat tightened. "What's happened?"

"You'll need to come with me. Down to HQ. Someone needs to have a word."

"What? Why? Is this about my daughter?" She took a step back and held on to the door frame with her right hand.

"Just come with me, ma'am. Bring your papers." The MP shifted his weight and the old wooden floor of the landing creaked. His colleague stepped into Anna's view. He was a taller, thinner figure, his face long and heavy with disdain.

"Let's go, Fraulein," he said and moved his hand to his holster.

Anna lifted her chin. "It's Frau. I must leave a note for my family. Is that allowed?"

"Yes, ma'am. Just make it quick," the short one said.

"Where are you taking me?"

The tall one sighed. "HQ at Paulinenstrasse. Hurry it up."

Anna scribbled a note for Madeleine and left it on the small table next to the door. She took her bag and went out, locking the door behind her. The tall MP grabbed her arm and pushed her to the stairs. "Let's go. Jesus Christ."

"Take it easy, Matthews, she's coming," said the other one.

Anna could feel condemning eyes peering through the peepholes and cracked doors as they went down the stairs. Outside, the tall one gripped her arm harder, as if she would try to escape, and pushed her into the waiting jeep.

"All right," Anna snapped. "I'm coming." She pulled her arm free. As she righted herself, she saw Frau Hermann standing in the gate to the courtyard, wiping her hands on a towel as if she had just come straight from her kitchen sink. Anna tried to call out to ask about Amalia but the jeep pulled away and made a u-turn toward the city. Anna's heart thrashed in her chest and her hands went hollow. These were not the MPs from the Monuments Men unit. She had never seen these men before. She clutched her bag on her lap and planted her feet to keep from sliding around the back seat. People on the street looked at her, some with pity, some with barely concealed triumph. They turned onto the Wilhelmstrasse, passed the Collecting Point, and then drove down the Luisenstrasse. Anna looked for Amalia and Madeleine's faces in the long evening shadows

"Excuse me, sir?" She tried to lean forward as the jeep lurched. "You know I am the only guardian of a small child. I can't be away all night."

"Tell it to the judge," the bad-tempered one grunted.

She tried again. "Also, I work at the Collecting Point. For Captain Cooper? Henry Cooper? All my papers have been checked."

"Lady, I can't help you. We were just told to pick you up."

"Who? Who told you to pick me up?"

"Look, I did you a favor and didn't cuff you in front of your neighbors. But you need to shut up and stop asking questions." His head swiveled and he shot her an angry look.

Anna slumped back in the seat. Cuff her? Her mind was frantic. Had someone denounced her? People denounced each other, telling the Americans about some Nazi past of a former friend or neighbor that may or may not be true, just to get revenge, she knew that. But who? And why? She tossed around the possibilities. Maybe they had the wrong Anna Klein. It was a common enough name. She exhaled and tried to calm herself.

When the jeep came to a stop in front of an old estate, now the plush headquarters of the U.S. Forces European Theater, she dared to breathe a small sigh of relief. With its gardens and colonnades it was hardly a prison or torture chamber. Still, it was very high level. The big MP with the small head pulled her out of the car and marched her inside where he deposited her on one of a wooden chair, one of many lined up along the wall of a large entry foyer. "Stay here," he said and walked to the front desk. He talked with the young officer, gesturing toward her and signing some papers.

Anna looked around. The place was spotless with all new chairs and desks—a far cry from the hodge-podge of the Collecting Point. A large American flag hung from the ceiling and a smiling Eisenhower gazed down from the photo on the wall. His peacetime portrait. The new American president, Truman, was next to him, looking earnest but benign, like a kindly uncle. People in crisp starched uniforms came and went—the women in WAC uniforms and men with squeaky shoes.

Next to her an old man sat resting his hands on a wooden cane. A threadbare suit hung on his frame and threatened to swallow him. He caught her eye and glared. The clock ticked just past 8:30. Anna hoped that Amalia was now home safe and sound and that Madeleine was comforting her, maybe lying in bed and reading her book. That was the best-case scenario. If they got picked up after curfew they would be taken to some police station overnight. Maybe Madeleine had fallen ill and Amalia had tried to get help. Or something could have had happened to Amalia. They could be at the hospital. Or worse. Anna's insides wrenched.

She forced herself to sit in the chair even though every molecule in her body was fighting for her to jump up, to run for the door. Her fingers made a pitter pat sound as they tapped her bag. Her teeth threatened to bite through her lower lip.

"Can you stop that damn noise?" the old man growled.

Anna regarded him through a sideways glance and then ignored him. She stared at the clock on the wall, watching the minutes tick away and take her deeper into the night. She thought of going up to the solider behind the desk and asking if would be much longer, like patients did when Thomas kept them waiting too long. She decided against it. Maybe they had found out about Thomas. Maybe they thought she was a communist? Maybe they wanted her to denounce her own husband? Her mind had run away from her and she could not still it. She forced her eyes closed.

When she opened them again, fifteen minutes had gone by. Nothing else in the room had changed. The man was still there, the soldier still sat at his desk and the occasional uniform crossed the room as if on cue to make things look busy. She stared at Eisenhower and considered offering up a prayer to him, asking him to intercede. Maybe he had that power. He was the supreme commander, after all.

Another twenty minutes later she decided to go and ask the soldier how much longer it would be and was just mustering up the nerve when a squarish woman in a green uniform appeared in front of her.

"Frau Klein, come with me. You speak English, yes?"

Anna nodded and stood up on weak knees. She followed the woman through a small half door and down a hallway into an office. A large table with four chairs stood alone in an otherwise empty room. The woman motioned for her to sit. Anna chose the chair facing the door and sat, clutching her bag on her lap.

The woman sat across from her, opened a file and ran the tip of her pencil along the margin of densely handwritten text.

"You work at the Collecting Point, correct?"

Anna nodded again. "May I ask what is this about?"

The woman held up her hand "Let me ask the questions, okay ma'am? We'll be done a lot faster."

Anna looked at the woman. She was firmly into her middle age and had the earnestness of someone who had been given responsibility she was not sure how to meet. Her face was round with fat cheeks but her nose was pointed and turned upward and looked like it belonged on a much thinner face. She tore off a blank piece of paper from a pad and sat with pencil poised.

"You work with Captain Henry Cooper, is that right? As his assistant?"

"Yes, and translator. He needs a translator when he goes in the field."

The woman began writing. "And you've worked at the Collecting Point for how long?"

"Two months. Since the beginning of July. I was one of the first people they hired. In the typing pool." She volunteered this for no reason at all.

"I see." The woman scribbled. "Were you present when Captain Cooper found the repository of artworks at the villa in Dotzheim on 14 August?" She looked Anna in the eye.

Anna paused. "Yes. I was there."

"And were there any caretakers present at the site of the repository?"

"No. Well there was a little boy. A lost little boy. We took him to the displaced persons camp." Anna shifted in her seat.

"And his name?"

"Oskar Grünewald. But I don't think that's really important."

The American made the face again, indicating that she was the arbiter of what was important. "Are you aware that the captain did not follow procedures when he failed to secure the repository immediately?"

Anna waited. "I am not sure I know what the proper procedures are. You see it was my first site visit, and–"

"He did not secure the repository immediately by either retrieving the art and delivering it to the Collecting Point or appointing a caretaker or U.S. military guard for it, is that what you witnessed?" the woman droned.

Anna slumped. "No, he did not. I mean, yes, that's correct. He did not."

"And were you present when Captain Cooper met with a Ludwig Schneider at the Collecting Point on 15 August?"

"Yes, I was the translator."

"And he refused to give Mr. Schneider a position at the Collecting Point despite the recommendation from Major Phillips that he do so?"

"I didn't know anything about a directive. Captain Cooper was concerned about Herr Schneider's qualifications, as far I understood the situation. How is Herr Schneider connected to the repository at the villa?"

The woman ignored the question. "So you corroborate that he refused to hire Mr. Schneider?"

"It was not clear to me that Herr Schneider was looking for a job," Anna lied.

"Why else would he be there?" The woman looked up.

Anna shrugged. "I don't know. People are always trying to curry favors. It was a very short meeting. I thought it completely inconsequential."

"And had you met Ludwig Schneider prior to the meeting on 15 August?"

Anna shook her head no.

"Were you aware of his credentials as a gallery owner and art dealer?"

"Yes, but only what he explained to me. He admitted that he had worked for the SA. I think that's why Captain Cooper refused to hire him. Despite the referral from Frankfurt."

"Yes. We are aware of Mr. Schneider's wartime activities. Have you had dealings with, met, or spoken with Mr. Schneider since the meeting at the Collecting Point on 15 August?"

Anna blinked. "Excuse me?"

The woman repeated the question, slowly and with irritation. She looked at Anna. "Well, have you?"

"No, of course not," Anna said.

The two women fixed eyes. Anna was careful to not make a move. She held her breath.

"All right, then." The American looked back at her paper. "I'd like you to be aware that at this time Captain Cooper is under disciplinary review. It is also imperative that the policies and procedures set in place by the United States Military and Occupational Government are followed to the letter by our personnel and the German civilians in their employ. We will not tolerate any deviation. As an employee of the United States Military Government, you can, and will, be held accountable if you become aware of any criminal or illegal activity undertaken by Captain Cooper or anyone else. And of course you yourself are subject to the same laws. Do you understand?"

Anna furrowed her brow. Americans said a lot of words that seemed to go nowhere.

The woman sighed and rephrased the lecture, this time pointing her pencil in Anna's direction. "If you are aware that he is doing something illegal and you fail to report it, you too will be held accountable by a military tribunal and face legal action. Is that understood?"

Anna nodded slowly. "Yes."

"Likewise, if you are aware of illegal activity by another civilian, as an employee of the U.S. Military you are obligated to report it to your superior. This was a preliminary questioning. Please keep in mind that the U.S. Military does not tolerate rogue behavior by its enlisted men, officers, or their civilian staff." She pushed her paper toward Anna and laid the pencil down on it. "Look over your testimony and initial here and here if you agree. You'll need to wait outside until the report is typed and then sign and swear an affidavit."

"Preliminary questioning?" Anna asked. "What does that mean?"

"Only that it's part of an ongoing investigation."

"Into Captain Cooper? By whom?"

"I am not at liberty to answer any questions." She gestured for Anna to sign the paper. "You can have a seat outside and wait for them to call you back after the report is typed."

When Anna slid the key in the lock on the door to the apartment, footsteps ran to the door on the other side. Amalia pulled the door and jumped into her mother's arms. She clung to Anna as if her life depended on it.

Madeleine appeared in the doorway to the living room. "Oh my dear girl, *Gott sei Dank*. Thank God, you are back. Are you all right? I can't tell you…" She patted her chest with the palm of her hand.

"Oh yes, of course." Anna tried to sound convincing. "It was all a big misunderstanding. Were you worried?"

"Yes," Madeleine said flatly. "When you come home to a note that says you've been taken to headquarters with American Military Police, it is a little worrisome. Especially now that it's so late."

Anna looked at the clock in the living room. It was nearly midnight. "Where were you two anyway?" she asked.

"We went for a stroll to the park and sat to watch the sunset. I hadn't been out for so long and I wanted to see a sunset. We thought we'd be home sooner." She cocked her head. "Were you worried?"

Anna raised her eyebrows.

"I am sorry, my darling, of course you were. Come in here and sit down. You must be exhausted. Look, I'll make you some of my tea."

Anna staggered into the living room and fell onto the sofa, Amalia still stuck to her. Anna peeled her off and held her daughter's tear stained face.

"I am so sorry I scared you."

"You said you wouldn't be so late. You promised me. When it got dark I thought you were gone forever. You are always late now."

"I know, my little Maus. I am so sorry. I had to go with the Americans. They wanted to talk to me."

"I thought the Americans were good guys."

"They are." She stroked Amalia's hair.

"But why do they take you away?"

Anna sighed. "Because they wanted to ask me some questions. They let me come right back home, though. It won't happen again, it was all a mistake. Don't worry." She pulled Amalia off her lap and settled her down on the sofa. "Can you guess what amazing things I saw today?

Amalia shook her head.

"I saw Nefertiti. She's really here."

"I don't believe it," Madeleine shouted from the kitchen. "She's really here? In one piece?"

"Yes, it was incredible. Cooper unloaded her from the truck and we all watched. I almost couldn't believe my eyes."

"And how does she look?" Madeleine handed Anna a steaming cup.

"Oh they didn't open the crate for us. They are waiting for the big-wigs from Frankfurt to come for that."

"Captain Cooper told me he'd show me Nefertiti when she came," Amalia whispered.

"I know," Anna said." You should remind him next time you see him."

Amalia played with the frayed edge of her nightgown, rolling it between her fingers. "Will you be late again tomorrow? I don't like it when you are late."

The meeting with Schneider pushed its way back into Anna's consciousness. She had willed it out of her mind to make lying to the Americans more palatable. Her stomach fluttered. "Maybe I will. But if I am, I'll just be at work. You'll know exactly where I am and that I will be home as soon as I am done. There's no need to worry."

Amalia waited as Anna drank the foul smelling tea Madeleine had delivered. "Did you send Papa a letter? Like you said you would?" she asked.

"Yes, Maus, I did. Just like I promised. Now we just have to wait." She squeezed Amalia's shoulder. "And you need to go to bed. It's very late."

A note from Cooper was waiting for her when she got to her desk:

In the field this AM, back after lunch. Please set up a filing system for the inventory lists and type up the handwritten notes on my desk. Hope you can read my chicken scratch. HC.

Chicken scratch? What was he talking about? Anna looked at the stack of papers on his desk: a mess of official forms, notepaper and scribbles on the backs of envelopes. She started to sort through it as best she could, making several piles according to topic and content. Eventually she had to use the floor as well. She sat down in Cooper's creaky chair to have better reach and to soothe her aching back. After about an hour she had all the papers organized and put away. Leaning back in the chair she surveyed her work with satisfaction. A corner of paper stuck out from the desk's center drawer, as if it had been pushed in absentmindedly. Anna tried to push it in, but it was pinched between the drawer and the frame. She pulled the drawer open a crack and tried again, but something still blocked it. She opened the drawer all the way to reveal a jumble of pencils, pens, loose paperclips, nails, American coins, a pair of broken sunglasses, and a spool of thread. She shook her head and pulled the offending paper out to see if it needed filing with the others. It was a memo from headquarters in Frankfurt from the same Major Phillips who had recommended the hiring of Schneider. He had summoned Cooper to go to Frankfurt for a disciplinary hearing. The meeting was scheduled for Tuesday 21 August at 11:00. She looked at the clock on Cooper's desk. It read 11:10. So that's where Cooper was.

Footsteps squeaked along the hallway and Anna became aware that she was sitting in her boss's chair, looking through his desk. She pushed the letter into the drawer and closed it. Then she bent down and pretended to be looking for something under the desk. She waited for the footsteps to pass but instead they stopped at the opening to the little alcove. From under the desk Anna saw a pair of American issue army boots, scuffed and dirty.

"Anna? You okay?"

Anna poked her head around the side of the desk to see Cooper in his field uniform, sleeves rolled up and sweat stains under his arms.

"Did you lose something?"

"Um, no. Just dropped a hairpin somewhere. It's not important." She crawled out from under the desk and stood to face him.

"What's wrong?" Cooper smiled.

"I thought you were out this morning?"

"I was, but now I'm back. Didn't take as long as I expected. It's getting hot." His eyes fell on the desk. "Hey, look at that. I knew you'd whip me back into shape. That's looking much better." He looked at her again. "What's wrong?"

"You're supposed to be in Frankfurt," she said.

"What? No, I've been out in Erbenheim this morning. Small find. Had to go check it out first thing. It wasn't anything important at all. I already brought it all back. More reports for you, though."

Anna flared. "Stop it, Captain. You are supposed to be at a hearing right this very minute. In Frankfurt, with Major Phillips." She pulled open the drawer and pulled the letter out to wave it in his face.

Cooper's face fell and his eyes went cold. "Are you snooping in my desk?"

"No, not at all. The letter was sticking out and I thought it might need filing. Why aren't you there? And what do they want with you?"

Cooper pushed her aside and sat down in his chair. She stepped back and pulled her own chair closer to the desk so they were sitting face to face.

He sighed. "Look, here's the thing. They're mad at me for not following their procedures. It's all Army bullshit, a technicality. I'll sort it out with them."

"Don't you think it would be better to sort it out by showing up at your own hearing?" Anna hissed. He was like a child that was unable to follow the classroom rules.

"Probably, but then we got this call this morning about a repository in an old mill. Someone had to go check it out and I was the only one around. So I went. I'll explain it to Frankfurt." He picked up a stack of papers and fanned himself. "It's fine. By the way, have you seen the camera? I was supposed to take some pictures, but I–"

Anna's temper surged. "Listen to me. It is not fine. Do you know I was pulled in last night and questioned about your activities? Four hours I was there. Amalia was scared to death. I was scared to death. They told me I am culpable if I go along with your 'rogue behavior.' And now you don't even show up for your hearing? Should I just go and turn myself in and save everyone the time and trouble?"

"Wait, wait, whoa. Back up." Cooper sat forward and leaned on his forearms. "They dragged you in? Who did?"

"How the hell should I know? Some very bad-tempered people from the great United States Military."

"They didn't hurt you, did they?"

Anna shook her head. "Hurt me? No. Just scared the devil out of me. Look, I don't want anything to do with this anymore. I just want to have a job, take care of my daughter and live my life. You can just leave me out of your adventures."

"What did they ask you?"

Anna recounted the questions and her answers as Cooper listened, wringing his hands and shaking his head.

"So you told them the truth, so what? You've got nothing to hide, right?" He sat forward. "I wonder who's behind this. Did they give you any clue? Was it Frankfurt? Or maybe Schneider is making trouble?"

"Are you listening to me? I don't care! Leave me out of it. I want to go back to the typing pool." She tried in vain to keep her voice down.

"No, I'm listening." Cooper grabbed her arm. "But you need to get it in your head. Your days of see nothing, hear nothing, do nothing? Those are over. You're in it now. We're in this together, you and me."

Anna pulled her arm away and stood up. "Find somebody else. I am not doing this. If you want to fight your own army and play by your own rules, go right ahead. Maybe it was that Major Phillips who is trying to get you, but who can blame him? You don't follow orders or protocol and you are dragging me down with you. I can't afford to get involved. I need this job." She bent to pick up her purse but Cooper jumped up and pulled her toward him. His breath was hot in her face.

"You can't afford to *not* get involved. Not anymore. Don't you want a future for that wonderful kid of yours? Do you want her to look at you every day of her life and ask, 'what did you do, Mommy? Why didn't you do anything?'"

Anna tried to push him away but he held on. "You idiot, I did what I had to so she will have a future," she said.

"That's no future, don't you see? She needs to look up to you. She needs to be proud of you. Otherwise she's a casualty just as sure as if she'd been shot up on a battlefield. This is the last chance you've got to save her. She needs to know you fought for something. *That's* her future. That's her start. I hate to tell you this but you've got no choice." Cooper let go of Anna's arm and took a step back. Anna shook with rage.

"I'm sorry. I didn't mean to…Are you okay?" He held up his palms.

Anna's head vibrated with a sudden clarity. It was as if a switch had turned on in her brain. She saw Cooper standing there in his sweaty, dirty uniform, his brown hair matted to his head, eyes aflame. But now she noticed something different: He was angry. All his bravado, the carefree, can-do spirit, it was a cover for a profound and deep anger. The same anger she felt. The difference was he had found the way out.

She sat back down and dropped her head in her hands. She saw Thomas's earnest face, smiling at her. He had believed in something enough to die for it. And she had hated him for it. She had believed only in surviving.

"Why do you care so much about what happens to me?" she asked, keeping her eyes on the floor.

Cooper pulled his chair around and sat down next to her, resting his elbows on his knees and staring at the same piece of floor. She watched his hands with their long fingers and broad knuckles as he rubbed his flattened palms together.

He cleared his throat and paused for a long time. When he spoke his voice was very soft and even. "Because I don't for one second pretend that what happened to you, what happened here, to Germany, can't happen to us Americans too. We all act like there's something that separates us from you, that we are not like you, but deep down we all know we are very much alike. It scares the hell out of us. Most guys can't admit it, but I do. And the only way I know how to deal with that is to look it straight in the face. What happened here can happen anywhere. It may not look the same and it may not sound the same, but that evil, that fear, it's in all of us. And if I see something I can make better then I'll do my best to help. And that's what I see in you and the duchess."

Anna couldn't bring herself to look at him. They both kept their eyes down, looking at their feet lined up in a neat row. He was right. She had done nothing. And now it looked like she might actually make it out of the nightmare alive. She had not ever really considered what would happen next. It had been too easy to let others decide what happened, or better, what didn't happen to her. She tried to picture her life in one year, in five years, but could see nothing. Her future was a void, like the night sky: seemingly empty but full of things she could only see in sparks. She wanted nothing better than to be worthy of her daughter's love and to make life better for her. For years that had meant surviving, living though another day. But now it meant something else.

She inhaled. "I saw Schneider yesterday. I got him to agree to a meeting. I think you are right. I think having him work here would be a terrible idea," she said, her voice low and steady. "The *Amis* last night asked me if I had seen Schneider since the meeting with you. I lied and said no. I lied on my sworn testimony."

Cooper rubbed the palm of his hand with his thumb and said nothing for several moments. He looked out the window and then toward the hallway. He sat up and let out a long breath. "When is your meeting?"

"Tonight. Seven o'clock at the Nassauer Hof." Anna ran her fingers under her eyes and rubbed her face as she sat up. "I am going to need a painting."

"Anything in particular?"

"A German landscape, if you have one."

Cooper looked at her sideways. "I think that can be arranged."

chapter eighteen

The lunch of watery lentils and bread was not sitting well with Anna. Her stomach churned and threatened to mutiny at any moment. She smoked two cigarettes in a row to try to at least calm her mind if not her stomach as she waited for Cooper on the delivery dock at the back of the Collecting Point. The last truck of the day had just pulled away and most of the activity had shifted inside. The afternoon was stifling hot and the breeze was so intermittent it provided no respite. Anna felt even worse than she smelled, which was saying a lot. Cooper thought this would be an inconspicuous place to go over the final plans for the meeting at the Nassauer Hof, but she thought it couldn't be more obvious. People would think they were sneaking away for a few private moments. Anna sighed. She had resigned herself to the gossip and rumors.

She considered how much her life had transformed in the last two weeks. From the typing pool to translator, to amateur undercover agent. The events that had led her to this point seemed unreal. And yet, here she sat, in her old gabardine trousers and the blue checked shirt she had worn a thousand times. Her tooth still wiggled and her stomach rumbled, but she felt somehow changed. She could almost make out a path ahead where previously there had only been darkness.

She and Cooper had worked out the details of the plan over lunch in the commissary, huddled at a table in the corner, taking care to speak in a poorly masked code that made her feel silly. They arranged a meeting point at the Marktkirche from which Cooper would tail her. He would bring MPs with him. Once she was inside the Nassauer Hof, they would pretend to inspect the rubble across the street at the Four Seasons or to be tinkering with old Kaiser Friedrich out front. When Schneider came out, the Americans would pounce. Cooper was confident that all would go according to plan and that Anna would discover her hidden talent for undercover operations. His confidence rubbed off on her a little, but her stomach was unconvinced.

Cooper came around the side of the building and pulled himself onto the loading dock. They sat side by side, their legs dangling over the edge like two children waiting for a bus.

"The whole place thinks we're having an affair you know," he laughed.

"I know."

"I hope that doesn't make you uncomfortable. I mean, I hope I haven't done anything to compromise your reputation."

Anna shrugged. "People will talk. They have nothing better to do." The thought of intimacy with anyone, much less this crazy *Ami* was laughable. She ached for a bath.

"Okay. So listen. I got you a good painting. It's a nice scene of the Rhine so there's some regional significance. The label says it's from a gallery in Mainz. There are no claims on it so no one will miss it for a day. It's pretty small, too, so you can fit it in a shopping bag, but it's too big for Schneider to hide easily once you hand it over. I borrowed a bag from one of the girls downstairs.

"Will that really work?"

"Sure. He only has to agree to buy it, or even just take it. That's breaking the law."

Anna was doubtful. "Why would anyone want to buy a painting by some local artist? Who cares about things like that now?"

"Nostalgia for better days? I don't know. Look, it makes more sense that you've got a landscape by a local artist that's been in your family. You can say it belongs to Madeleine and just play dumb as to its value. The idea is to make it easy for him to bite. If you show up with a more important piece and show any sign of knowing anything, he'll get twitchy. Just get him to want to help you out and buy the thing."

Anna nodded. "All right. Who is the artist?"

"Hard to tell from the signature. Just say you don't know. It's in the bag under your desk. When you leave, just pick it up and go. We'll return it tomorrow after we nab him." He exhaled and waited a beat. "Is the duchess going to be okay tonight?"

"Oh yes, Madeleine is feeling much better these days. She's got enough energy to watch her for a few hours."

"You didn't tell them anything?"

Anna shook her head. "No, not a word to anyone."

"Not even your friend, the sapper with the sad eyes?"

Anna turned to face him. "Emil? He's not my friend."

"If you say so. I don't think he'd agree."

"I just feel sorry for him, you know? I think he's got a long road ahead of him. He is suffering all the after effects of the war. He needs help."

"Don't we all," Cooper said. "But first things, first. I will see you at 18:45?"

"18:45. I'll be there." Her confidence was ebbing. She rubbed her protesting stomach.

Cooper chuckled. "Keep your head in the game, Frau Klein. I am depending on you." He patted her back and jumped off the dock. "See you later."

At home, Anna had just enough time for a quick sponge bath to make her feel human again. Playing dumb was one thing, but going into the Nassauer Hof smelling like an overripe fruit basket was another. She had not fallen that far. Once cleaned up, she pulled the black dress with the pleat down the front from the wardrobe. She held it up in the light. Too prim. Too desperate. She put it back and took out the green wool skirt. Too warm and it didn't fit anyway. Her remaining two items, the faded red dress and the yellow blouse with the puffy sleeves, were too flouncy. She sighed and sat down on the sofa to collect herself. Looking at her filthy pants gave her a thought. She went back to the wardrobe and dug around until she found a pair of Otto's old pants, light wool with a pale pinstripe. She pulled them on and smiled when the length was just right. Another dive into the wardrobe yielded ankle boots, a white button down shirt, and a belt, all clean and in immaculate condition. The boots fit pretty well, a little big, but the wide leg of the pants hid it well. The shirt was tight around her breasts and loose in the stomach but she folded it around her and tucked it into the pants. She rolled the sleeves up and took the belt into the kitchen to add another notch with the knife.

Madeleine came out of the bathroom wiping her hands. "Ah, my darling you look splendid," she clasped her hands together. "Very modern."

"Thanks, Auntie. Is it all right for me to wear Uncle's things? I reallly need something clean."

"Otto would love it. Wait, I have one more thing." She hurried to the desk and pulled something from the bottom drawer. Turning with great flourish she held it up. It was a man's wristwatch with a worn black leather band. You'll need this too. You are a working woman now. Here, put it on. It still works. I checked it the other day. Go on."

Anna put the watch on and they both admired it.

"Auntie, I don't know what to say."

Madeleine smiled. "All this time I kept it and wished I had someone to give it to. Now I do. So, where are you going?"

Anna busied herself with the boot's buttons and avoided her gaze. "Just back to work. There are some things yet to do today. I volunteered." She looked up and smiled. "But I won't be long."

"Mama, don't leave!" Amalia said. She was perched on the windowsill, her knees drawn up under her chin.

"Maus, please get down from there. You make me so nervous!" Anna shook her hands at the girl.

Amalia sighed and slid down. "You are no fun. I just like looking out the window."

"It's my job to be no fun." Anna put her hands on her hips. "How do I look?"

"Like a boy." Amalia wrinkled her nose.

Anna laughed. "As long as it's just a boy and not an old man. Now, come here and give me a hug." She squeezed the little body tight around the middle and whispered into her ear. "Be a very good girl and remember that I love you very much. Will you do that?"

"Yes, Mama." She pulled away and looked her mother in face. "Are you all right?"

Anna smiled. "Yes, of course I am. I have to go now but I'll be back before too long. Be a good girl, listen to Auntie, and eat your supper."

Anna stood and waved Madeleine to follow her into the kitchen. "I think there's some bread left over and some lard too. That's all until tomorrow."

"We'll be just fine, child. You seem nervous. Is everything all right?"

"Yes, of course. Everything's fine." She kissed Madeleine on the cheek and picked up the shopping bag that she had stowed under the table by the front door. "Bye-bye Maus, see you in a while." She blew a kiss and walked out the door.

Outside the front gate she leaned against the cool plaster wall and collected herself. Otto's watch read a quarter after six. Still plenty of time. She had left early so she could walk and calm her thoughts. Turning north toward the old town, the Marktkirche and the Nassauer Hof, she walked slowly, the bag heavy on her arm. She thought about what Thomas would be doing now. Probably still doing rounds at the hospital or maybe paperwork. Probably he hadn't eaten anything proper in days. She wondered what the food situation was like in the Russian sector. She thought of him thinking of her. He would think she was maybe doing the washing or giving Amalia a bath. He would never believe what she was about to do.

The sun tickled her left cheek when she emerged onto the

teeming Luisenplatz. She cut over into the narrow passages of the old city, emerging on the Schlossplatz. She paused to look at the Marktkirche glowing red in the setting sun, its beautiful Neo-Gothic architecture spared by the bombs. With extra time left before the meeting, she decided to go inside.

The cool air smelled of ritual and reckoning. Heads punctuated the rows of pews here and there, mostly alone but some in pairs. Anna picked a pew halfway to the front and slid in at the end. Sunlight streamed through the stained glass and bathed the interior in a comforting light. With its ornamentation and statuary removed, the church was stripped down, but dignified, its architecture standing in willful endurance.

Anna propped the shopping bag at her feet and slid her hand inside. She pulled the painting up halfway and saw its simple frame first. She separated the sides of the bag to get a better view. The scene was a river, as Cooper had said. The Rhine, a deep blue diagonal streak across the canvas, was flanked by jagged, tree-covered mountains on the distant side and open grassland with patches of splotchy, yellow wildflowers in the foreground. The sky was an anemic blue with scattered strips of flat clouds. The brush strokes were all rendered with hard edges, which made the painting seem flat and stagnant. It was not a bad painting, exactly, it just wasn't very interesting. She checked the back. A small faded label on the bottom indicated a Gallerie Neustadt in Mainz. No other marks revealed its origin. She slid the canvas back into the bag and sat for a few minutes before checking her watch. It was time. She stood and exhaled, willing the anxiety out.

Stepping out into the square Anna was hit squarely between the eyes by the setting sun. She squinted and looked around for Cooper, who should have been waiting near the church entrance so he could follow her. The square was busy with people. From her vantage point she could see almost all the way down the Friedrichstrasse, which Cooper should have taken if he was coming from the Collecting Point. But he was nowhere. She wanted to spin around in all directions, run around the corner to see if he was coming, call out his name. Instead, she stood rooted to the spot, listening to her heart pound. *I'll count to one hundred*, she thought. *If he's not here by then, I'll decide.*

When she landed on twenty she slowed down. By the time she reached fifty, she knew he wasn't coming. Sixty, seventy-five, then ninety, and one hundred. Cooper was a no-show. *Damn him*. She began to walk in the direction of the Nassauer Hof. There would still be time to back out. As she stepped into the shadows of the Spiegelgasse, her resolve strengthened. *For God's sake, you're going to try to sell a painting to an old man, nothing more*, she scolded herself. *Have a little courage*. She picked up the pace and held out hope that Cooper would be lurking in the Kaiser-Friedrich-Platz outside the hotel. But when she got there, he was still nowhere to be seen. She stopped to catch her breath.

"Ah, there you are, Frau Klein." Schneider was upon her before she could react. He took her elbow and walked her toward the hotel door. "I thought perhaps you'd lost your nerve." He smiled at her, his lips stretching over small yellow teeth.

"I hope you haven't been waiting long," she said as he held the door open for her.

"Not at all. I have only just arrived myself. Please." He gestured for her to go into the lobby, such as it was. The hotel had sustained a direct hit in the bombing of early 1945 and was only partially rebuilt. Mostly Americans and local VIPs congregated in its dining room, and she'd heard a few rooms were available to rent, if you could pay. She had last seen the hotel in newsreels in 1940 when delegations from France and Germany met here to negotiate the armistice; they had split France among themselves like greedy children. She and Thomas watched in a movie theater in Weimar and she let the tears run down her cheeks in silence. And now here she stood in the same lobby as those men, who had played chess with people's lives and never gave a thought about people like her.

"Where shall we sit?" she asked, looking into the dining room.

"Oh no, not here, my dear. We are meeting upstairs."

He guided her down the hall toward the stairs that circled the elevator. Anna steadied herself on weak knees. Schneider wheezed his way up alongside her, and when they reached the first floor, he directed her down the deserted hallway.

"Here we are." He opened the door to a guest room and pushed her inside with a firm hand.

The room was spare, with only a bed, a chair and a small wardrobe. It was a far cry from the plush accommodations enjoyed at the hotel by SS officers and their mistresses during the war. Standing at the window was Konrad Schenk. He smiled and crossed the room, hand extended.

"Frau Klein, a pleasure to see you again." His ice-cold hand strangled hers in a firm grip. This time he wore a dark suit and plain brown tie. He gestured for her to sit in the chair while he sat on the edge of the bed. Schneider stood in the alcove leading to the door, leaning against the wall, his hands behind his back and eyes on the floor.

Anna backed into the chair and sat down hard, pulling the shopping bag onto her lap. She had not considered that Schenk would be there. She wanted to tell Schneider the deal was off, that it was only to have been between the two of them as promised, but Schenk leaned forward and rested his arms on his thighs. He clasped his hands and seemed to be settling in for a speech.

"Frau Klein. Ludwig has told me all about you. I understand you have a very good job with the Americans."

Anna started to reply but he cut her off.

"I am sorry we didn't have time to talk more last time we met. I've wanted to meet you ever since I saw you and your daughter talking with my neighbor, Frau Buchholz. When was that? Was it last week, Ludwig? When she followed you? Ludwig was curious as to why you would follow him but clearly you wanted to talk about the painting and just lost your nerve. You were so patient to wait for him outside my apartment. You could have just rung the bell. And what a sweet little girl you have. Amalia, yes? You must be very proud of her." He leaned back and crossed his legs, waiting.

The mention of Amalia hit Anna like a blast wave. Schenk had seen the two of them outside his apartment when Schneider had gone inside. Or she and Amalia had been followed. But by whom? And why? Anna squeezed the painting inside the bag on her lap and looked at Schneider, but she knew he was no longer in charge. "Excuse me, but I thought I was only meeting with you, Herr Schneider."

"I invited Herr Schenk, because, frankly, he has access to more resources than I do in my current diminished state, which you are aware of." Schneider said it as if his circumstances were Anna's fault. "Together we are likely to offer you a better deal and I wanted you to get as much as you can for your painting."

Schenk tossed her a toothy smile, like an animal baring its teeth to its prey. "Of course we will make a deal with you, Frau Klein, there's no doubt about that. It's just that we'll need to see if what you've brought is of enough interest and, well, frankly, value, to provide what you need. It's travel papers for your husband, is that right? From the Russian sector?" He let out a whistle. "Those are pricey, as you know. The Ivans run a pretty tight operation. If he wants out, he'll have to pay."

Anna made a face of agreement, feigning exasperated solidarity against the Russians. She wasn't actually sure who was good and who was bad anymore.

Schenk chuckled. "Ludwig, perhaps you could go and fetch us some of that swill that passes for coffee these days. A coffee for you, Frau Klein?"

Anna shook her head.

"Very well. Just two then, Ludwig. See if they have any milk too."

Schneider closed the door behind him, turning the key in the lock. Anna smiled at Schenk and sat forward in her seat in an effort to move things along. The air in the room was stifling and she wished for a breeze, but the open window only let in sounds from the street below. They seemed very far away and Anna wondered if Cooper was outside. She tamped down her irritation at him and focused on Schenk, who had stood and was now pacing at the foot of the bed.

"Frau Klein, before we look at your painting, I'd like to discuss another matter with you, if you are amenable." He continued without waiting for a reply. "Herr Schneider and I, we've been colleagues for a number of years now. Well, even since before the war, to be honest. You can understand that we've been very busy. There was so much to do."

"I'm sorry, I don't follow," Anna lied.

"So many artworks became…available." He smiled and his nostrils flared. "All of them had to be sorted and properly redistributed."

Anna snorted. "That's one way of putting it."

Schenk sighed and shook his head. He set his teeth into a bored smile. "Look, Frau Klein, you need my help. I am willing to see what I can do. If you'd prefer to argue the finer points of provenance, we can do that instead. But it seems to me you are in no position to cast aspersions on what I do, given that you are prepared to break the law in order to help yourself." He held up his palms and made a face that suggested world-weariness, as if the hard work of plundering had exhausted him. "It's so very easy to sit on the side of the pool. But when you have to get to the other side, you jump in and swim like everyone else." He walked to the window. "Unless of course, you are here at the bidding of your American friends? I know you are very close with that Captain Cooper, no?"

He looked out the window. Anna guessed the view was of the Wilhelmstrasse and the bowling green across the street. She thought of all the *Amis* at the Eagle Club, downing drinks and enjoying their victory. Just the distance of a shout and the world was totally different. Sweat beaded along her hairline and on her upper lip. Wiping it with her hand, she stole a glance at Otto's watch. Twenty minutes past seven and they still hadn't looked at the painting. She decided not to respond to Schenk's question. Instead, she leaned back in the chair and crossed her legs. It was her turn to wait.

Schenk provided his own answer. "No, I think you are smarter than that. That would be foolish." He grinned. "Lucky for us, the value of art remains high. Or we'd both be out of a job. Isn't that right?" He laughed, but only in the back of his throat.

"You understand, of course, that we will be taking quite a risk on your behalf. Ludwig, he seems to have a fondness for you. He wants to help you and your pretty little daughter. Me, I am not so sentimental. When I pay for something, I like to know exactly what I am getting. Especially when the price I could pay is as steep as it is these days."

Anna wanted to punch him in his smug face. She reminded herself that she was not really asking him for money, that she was not at his mercy at all, that she had the upper hand. "I understand, Herr Schenk. I know we must help each other."

The key turned in the lock and the door opened. Schneider held a tray of two steaming mismatched cups. "No milk," he said and handed the tray to Schenk, who set it down on the bed and took a cup for himself.

"All right then, let's have a look at what you've got for us. This has been in your family, you said?"

Anna straightened. "Yes, it's a landscape of the area. I think it could be worth at least a little something. It certainly holds no sentimental value for me." She bent down, pulled the painting from the bag and rested it on her knees so Schenk could look at it.

As Schenk's eyes landed on the painting, his face sank, like a child disappointed by a much-anticipated birthday present.

"Is this a joke?" he asked. Schneider's curious face appeared over Schenk's shoulder.

Anna looked down at the canvas. "No, of course not. What do you mean?"

Schenk reached forward and pulled the painting from her hands. He and Schneider put their heads together as they examined it. "Frau Klein, you had better be honest with us. I will give you only one chance. Where did you get this painting?" Schenk said, without looking at her.

Anna swallowed and considered her options. Play dumb, she decided. She laughed. "Gentlemen, what do you mean? I've brought you a painting from my family's collection. Now, please tell me what you think it is worth, under the circumstances." She folded her hands across her stomach to keep them from shaking. "As I told Herr Schneider yesterday, I am only doing this so my husband can join me and I can keep my job at the Collecting Point. And I would certainly remember how you helped me. I would be in your debt."

Schenk handed the painting to Schneider and took a sip from his cup before tapping a cigarette out of the pack he took from his pocket. He lit it and leaned forward. "Frau Klein, here's what we are going to do. I know without a doubt that this is not your painting. In fact, I know who the rightful owner of this painting is. So no, we do not have a deal."

Anna could feel every drop of her blood rush through her body as if a dam had been released. Schenk and Schneider knew far more than she had realized. Maybe Schneider really was a hapless opportunist, but Schenk was a miscreant of a much higher order. She thought she might vomit all over his shiny shoes but mustered a reply. "Herr Schenk, if you think I am doing this for the Americans, I assure you that's not the case. This painting belongs to my family."

Schenk smiled as he fingered the rim of his coffee cup. He took the last drink and set it down. "You and I both know that's not true."

Anna decided she no longer cared about the painting or Schneider or even the Americans. She tried to think of a way out of the room, out of this whole mess. They knew the painting, that much was clear. But they also knew she could still be valuable to them. *Make yourself useful*, she thought. *Do something.*

She straightened in her chair and looked Schenk in his pointy face. He was in his element, with the intimidation and the threats. It was a language he spoke fluently. She steadied her voice. "Look, Herr Schenk. I've already told you I need the money. What I can give you in return is my assistance in getting Herr Schneider the job he wants. But in order to do that, I need to keep my job. And for that, I need my husband to come here."

Schenk shook his head and stubbed the cigarette into his coffee cup. "Spare me the nonsense, Frau Klein. There are only two ways that you got your hands on that painting. Either the *Amis* gave it to you to trap us, or you helped yourself to it. Either way, I know it's not a painting from your family and that you are lying. But I am going to forget about that for the moment. In a way, I should thank you, because you've shown me your hand. You've made my life a little easier. The important thing now is that you don't mess things up. You should know I have many friends." His face expanded into a smile. "In fact, we may even have a few friends in common, who knows? Maybe we could all have a nice dinner party sometime." He lit another cigarette. The smoke hung in the air between them like a dirty shroud. He blew it into her face. "You go to work tomorrow. Keep your mouth shut and we might be able to help you. But now we'll decide how you help us first. So think about it carefully. In any case you should consider yourself already in my debt." He stood. "Now, we are finished. Keep your eyes open. You'll be seeing me soon."

Schenk grabbed Anna's arm, yanking her to her feet. His other hand clamped onto the back of her neck, pushing her across the room and out into the hallway. He threw the painting after her and slammed the door. Anna stood in the dark corridor holding the empty shopping bag. The painting lay face down on the floor. Voices from the lobby drifted up inside the dim light of the stairwell. She walked to the railing and steadied herself with her free hand. Trying to not make a sound, she retched her lunch onto the worn carpet.

Anna pushed the heavy wooden door closed behind her. Even though it required no key to enter the courtyard of her building, she always felt a little safer inside her little fortress. Thoughts swirled in her head like water circling a drain. Taking the stairs slowly, she tried to make sense of what had happened. When she turned the corner of the second flight, Cooper was sitting on the top stair, smoking and grinning at her.

"I told Frau Wolf I would wait for you out here. That we had some business to discuss," he said. "You okay?"

Anna flared. "Where the hell were you? How could you just let me go alone? You were supposed to be there."

Cooper patted his hand on the step next to him, indicating for her to sit down. "You were being followed. They were onto you before you even got to the church." He offered her his pack of cigarettes.

Anna pulled a cigarette from the pack and waited for him to light it for her. Her hand was shaking."Who was?" she asked.

"Some guy Schneider put on your tail. When you turned onto the Bahnhofstrasse, Schneider was waiting in the Ludwigsplatz with some goon. He pointed at you and the guy started after you. I watched for a minute and decided to cut around on the Wilhelmstrasse to try to catch you before you went in and call it off, but Schneider got to you first. I figured if he saw me anywhere near there he'd know it was a set up, so I sat on the bowling green across the street and waited. I saw you go in with Schneider. The goon hung around for a while. Schneider came out after a few minutes and they talked and the guy finally left.

"He was getting coffee," Anna said. "Schneider. That's what he said."

"I figured they were satisfied that the coast was clear and decided to give you thirty minutes. So he didn't bite, huh? What happened?"

"You let me go anyway? You knew they were following me and you let me go?"

"Hey, look, they were after me, not you. If I had shown up it would have really messed it up for good. Anyway, I grabbed a jeep from one of the guys at the Eagle Club to get back here before you, in case they were still following you."

"Oh they're following me, make no mistake. Apparently that's been going on for a while." She shook the bag at him. "Where did this painting come from?"

Cooper knitted his brow. "From the Collecting Point. I mean, from the stash we found at the villa, because it hadn't been inventoried yet. No one would miss it for a few hours."

Anna groaned. "They knew that painting. That's why they refused to buy it. They knew it wasn't mine."

"What to you mean, *they*?"

"There was another man there—Konrad Schenk. He's the one Schneider went to see the day I followed him. They work together. Schenk makes Schneider look like a cuddle toy. I thought about it as I walked back," Anna said. "I snooped in Schneider's file the other day and there was a report in there about the find at the villa and how we—you—hadn't properly reported it. And I got questioned about both the villa and Schneider last night. So someone else knows about it already and somehow they've connected the two. *And* they know we found it."

Cooper nodded slowly, processing the information. "Schneider only knows that we don't realize it's his stash, if it even is. Otherwise, why would you have brought him his own painting?"

"Maybe to find out if he'd confess it was his? Or to double cross you?"

"Maybe. That seems like a long shot. I knew there was a note in my file about me not securing the repository. But I didn't know it was in Schneider's file, too. Who else would know and make that connection?"

Anna sat down on the stairs next to Cooper. She tossed a furtive glance at the door to the apartment, but it stayed closed. She lowered her voice. "Could it be the director? Who gets to say what goes into the files?"

Cooper shrugged. "I can see Farmer putting a note in my file, but why would he put something in Schneider's file? That just makes no sense. It must have come from somewhere else."

"Maybe whoever it is thinks you are in league with Schneider? Or someone is trying to make it look like you are?" She tugged at a loose thread at the hem of her pants. "And then there's Oskar, too. We still don't know what he was doing out there at the villa in the first place. This can't all be a coincidence—the orphanage, the art, Oskar. There must be a connection somewhere."

Cooper rubbed his forehead. "Okay, wait. Back up. Tell me exactly what happened at the meeting."

Anna recounted the story. Her adrenaline was still pumping and she tried to remember every detail now that it was over. Cooper listened and regarded her with raised eyebrows.

"We still don't know why the art was in the villa or whether it's legitimately Schneider's. And Oskar, well, we don't know what the hell his story is. And now we have this goon Schenk, who sounds like the brains behind the operation. And someone is following you and me both, it seems. I daresay you, Anna Klein, are getting the hang of this. But I don't like that they threatened you."

"It's all right," Anna said, surprising herself. "I don't think they closed the door on my helping them completely. They still think there's a chance that I can be useful. They are too greedy to let the opportunity go. If no one comes after them, they'll think I kept my mouth shut and maybe we can buy a little time." She took hold of the railing and pulled herself to her feet. "I need to get inside now." As she took her key from her pocket, Cooper reached for her hand.

"I guess I should apologize for getting you into this. I am sorry everything's gone to hell." His voice was quiet, eyes soft, but he didn't look at her. "I just don't have the patience for the wheels of military justice to turn our way. Time is not on our side, you know? It's just how I do things. Sometimes I get into trouble, but you have to believe that I would not let anything happen to you."

Anna felt a charge surge up her arm. She held onto his hand for half an instant before pulling away. "Don't apologize. I am all right. I do want to help," she said. "I think I like this job," she added, and then felt herself blush.

He smiled and started down the steps but stopped. "Have you heard any news? From your husband?"

Anna shook her head.

Cooper rubbed his chin with the palm of his hand. "I am sure he's very worried. I hope you hear from him soon."

Anna raised her palm to wave good-bye. "Don't let anyone see you leave. Be careful."

chapter nineteen

Anna climbed the marble stairs to Cooper's office as she put her identification papers back into her bag. She scolded herself for forgetting Cooper's landscape painting at home. She wanted the thing out of her house. The building was quiet. Most everyone was already outside waiting for the next convoy of trucks, and she wanted to put her things away before lining up to help unload crates. She tried to put the worries about Amalia out of her mind. She was perfectly safe and Frieda would not let anything happen to Amalia. A small voice tried to remind Anna that she did not really know this to be true. She only believed it because she wanted to, like a child who believes in St. Nicholas because it makes her happy. She gritted her teeth and paused on the stairs to catch her breath and set the worry down. She could pick it up again later. For now, she had work to do.

"Goddammit, I won't let this bullshit stand," a voice bellowed from above. "Who the hell is calling the shots around here anyway? Last time I checked it wasn't you."

Anna froze and instinctively pressed her lips together. She held her breath.

"I'll tell you what, let's do it my way for a while and see how that goes. Maybe that way we won't be losing paintings and side arms and God knows what else. We'll get some actual experts in here instead of you Keystone Kops. Jesus Christ. Do you have any idea who's breathing down my neck? The goddamn State Department. They're not even sure what the hell the point of this whole operation is. I've got one of them coming here next week to take a look at where all their money is going. And you're not helping the case one damn bit. Christ."

The voice was thick and congealed, with an accent Anna hadn't heard before. The words came slow and wet, and the talker breathed loudly through his nose. It sounded like the voice of a fat man, Anna thought.

"Major, if you'll just let me explain, I'm sure I can make you understand my objections to having Schneider work here." Anna recognized Cooper's voice. He sounded reasoned and steady even under the attack, but Anna knew he was boiling. "I have real concerns about his story and I respectfully ask that we wait just a few more days until we can check out that what he's telling us is true." His voice was taut and airless, as if he was trying to keep it inside a box that was too small.

"Listen, Cooper, I had to come all the way from Frankfurt to get this straightened out. You think I have nothing better to do?" The voice seemed to come closer and Anna ducked.

"Dammit Major, this isn't a game," Cooper said. "I take this seriously. Don't you think there are people who want to get their hands on what we've got here? Are you sure when we hire someone that they're on our side? Did you know that the Germans think we are here to take this art back to the States? That we are going to steal it from them? Have you considered that maybe someone got the idea to steal it back from us first? What's a few days, just to be sure?"

"Look here, Cooper, I don't give a damn what the Krauts think. Don't make it worse. Here's what's going to happen: You'll take a break from all your Lone Ranger bullshit until we get this all sorted out. I've found a nice little job for you out at the airfield, supervising incoming supply shipments. No intrigue, no excitement. Consider it a paid vacation courtesy of Uncle Sam. You can get used to following orders again. Once we deal with the highly interesting case of your missing sidearm and everything else you have been up to, we'll get things moving properly again and maybe we can find a place for you. I know Farmer likes you a lot, and I like Farmer—he's doing a good job as director—so that counts for something. But I won't promise anything. For now, you're out of the game. Consider yourself benched."

Heavy footsteps approached the top of the stairs, with a second set squeaking alongside. Anna tip-toed down the stairs as fast as she could and made it to the bottom before the footsteps started down from above. She backed up several paces toward the main entry door before reversing course and starting back toward the stairs as if she had just entered the building. She pretended to bump into the two *Amis* as they rounded the bottom of the stairs. Cooper's face was flushed and sweat beaded on his hairline. His eyes were angry and unsettled, his jaw set. Next to him was not the fat man Anna expected, but a tall, dark-haired man with angular cheekbones and a movie star mustache. He stopped to look at her as if she had no business being there. Anna wondered if she was expected to step aside to let him pass, but she stood her ground. She didn't like the way he talked to Cooper.

"Frau Klein, good morning," Cooper coughed. He took a step down to stand between Anna and the other American. "Major Phillips, this is my translator Frau Klein. She's one of our best civilian workers." Cooper stared at Anna, trying to convey some message she couldn't decipher. Anna decided to play dumb.

"A pleasure to meet you, Major. Captain, I hope I haven't kept you waiting," she said.

"You speak English?" Phillips grunted. Anna shot a look at Cooper, who rolled his eyes.

"Yes, I am the translator, after all." She smiled through her clenched teeth.

Phillips plowed on, oblivious. "All right, well, Captain Cooper has been relieved of his duties here. I'll talk to the folks up front about getting you reassigned. Why don't you go upstairs and get that mess of an office straightened up? I'll send someone up to get you." He pushed past her. "Cooper, you come with me. Nice to meet you, Frau Klein."

Anna stood on the bottom stair and watched the two men walk the length of the gallery, Phillips marching ahead and Cooper following, his back stiff as a board. She waited for Cooper to turn back and give her a look, something to reassure her in his usual way, but he didn't.

Below the window by Anna's little table, the trucks pulled into the courtyard, one after the other. She had cleaned up Cooper's desk and put away all the files and notes and looked once more for the camera in all the places it should have been but wasn't. After surveying her work, she took Schneider's file from the drawer, folded in half and put in her bag, although she wasn't sure what use it was. She wondered what to do now. Pulling out Cooper's squeaky chair, she sat down and rested her elbows on the desk. Her mind floated back to the events at the Nassauer Hof and she realized with a jolt she had left the painting Cooper had given her back at Madeleine's apartment. The thought that she had contributed to Cooper's troubles made her cringe, but then she remembered it had all been his idea. "It will all be okay," she muttered, affecting Cooper's round vowels. She wanted to slap him and then herself for going along with his stupid plan. Still, she did mostly believe him and it was obvious that Schneider was, at the very least, a liar. He was clearly used to finding ways around the rules if it suited him. But for Cooper to prove that to Phillips, he would have to confess about the meeting at the Nassauer Hof, and that would be the end of his job for sure. And Anna's too, she realized. She put her head down on the desk and tried to think. Cooper's angry face floated in front of her eyes and she tried to push it away. *This is all his fault,* she told herself. But she knew he had kept his mouth shut at least in part to protect her and she softened. It was hard to stay angry with him, which worried her.

The floor in the hallway creaked in the way that usually announced someone's approach. Anna lifted her head to see Schneider, sweating and looking taken aback, as if he had read her thoughts.

"Frau Klein! I was…I was looking for…" he stammered and looked around. "I think perhaps I am in the wrong place." He turned to go.

"Are you looking for Captain Cooper?" Anna asked. She stood up from the table and walked around to confront the little man. "He's not here at the moment."

Schneider laughed. "Well, as it happens, I am here to meet with Major Phillips. He is visiting from Frankfurt."

"Ah, yes. That makes sense," Anna said.

Schneider shrugged innocently. "I received a letter asking me to be here at nine o'clock this morning. So here I am. You've met him?"

Anna ignored the questions. "A letter? When?"

"I guess it was yesterday." As soon as the words left his mouth he tried to reel them back in. He coughed.

Anna nodded slowly. "You knew yesterday that you would be meeting with Phillips here today?" she asked. Now it was clear. Phillips was here to make sure Schneider got the job he had recommended him for. And he had gotten rid of Cooper to pave the way. Anna folded her arms. "You didn't even need my help to get the job. You knew that yesterday. And yet you let Schenk treat me like some criminal, let him threaten me? That's not very gentlemanly, Herr Schneider."

Schneider's eyes darted left and right. "No, no, not at all my dear. We wanted to help you. Well, I did. Schenk, he's wound pretty tight, but he's very good at this sort of thing and really not a bad fellow." He lowered his voice. "I must tell you he wasn't happy at all with that…item. He's convinced you were trying something funny. But I calmed him down, don't worry. And now I'm here, so it's all water under the bridge anyway."

"Why is Phillips so hot for you to work here?" Anna asked. "Why does he give a damn about you? Does it have something to do with the art the *Amis* found at the villa outside of town?"

Schneider stared at her. Anna stared back, holding her breath.

"I don't know what you are talking about," he finally said.

"But you do, of course. I guess you've already convinced some *Ami* higher up that the art at the villa is legally yours. I saw it in the paperwork. And we both know who the *Ami* is."

Schneider began to sputter, but Anna kept going. "Yesterday, I wanted to see if you would recognize the painting I brought you. But you didn't. It was only your friend who recognized it. That seems strange to me, since I thought it was supposed to be one of your paintings from your gallery inventory. The one from the villa."

Schneider stepped toward her. "My art? I don't have any art. I have nothing." He steadied his beady eyes to underscore his attempt at sincerity but the lie was as obvious and shiny as the sweat on his brow. *For a crook, he is a terrible liar*, Anna thought. *Better to let him go for now.* She tried not to smile as she pretended to backtrack. "Oh, I'm sorry. Yes, you said that before. You ended up with nothing. I thought I saw some papers that said you were placing a claim on the art from the villa. I must be confused. But maybe something of yours will still turn up and the *Amis* can prove it's rightfully yours."

Schneider tried a different tack. "So you don't need money for your husband's papers? Because it certainly seemed to me the other day that you were eager to reunite your family. Or was that a lie too?"

"No, that's no lie," Anna said. "I am still trying to raise the money to bring my husband here. I will figure something out."

"It's possible we can still help you with that," Schneider said in a lowered voice. "Now that we are all on the same team."

A pair of GIs squeaked passed them with long strides and Schneider pretended to wind his his watch. "I should probably go." He coughed. "Frau Klein, I am sure it's in our mutual interest to keep yesterday's meeting to ourselves, wouldn't you say?"

Anna smiled and nodded thoughtfully. "Of course. I would be very grateful to you, Herr Schneider, if you didn't mention it, since I was quite out of order with my little scheme. I had no business tricking you that way." She held out her hand. "After all, I do need to keep my job."

When he was gone, Anna wiped her hand on her pants leg and sat back down. *Bastard.* Maybe she could worm her way into working with Schneider, to align herself with him, at least in appearances, to keep track of him. He seemed to have a soft spot for her. And maybe he knew something about Oskar's family, if he was so well-connected. She kicked herself for not asking about the boy. Not that Schneider would have told her anything anyway. Still, he might have given some clue if he knew something about how and why the boy came to be there. Now that she was without Cooper at the Collecting Point, she would have to figure out a way to prove his instincts had been correct. She was angry that he had been so unceremoniously dismissed by Phillips. Maybe she could still make herself useful without him.

That notion flew out the window as soon as she saw Frau Obersdorfer's head come up the stairs and the accompanying body march toward her. The woman's flushed face could not conceal its owner's glee in Anna's demise. Anna put on a defensive smile and leaned back in her chair.

"Frau Klein. You'll be coming back to the typing pool," the woman twittered. She pointed to Anna's table. "Take that typewriter with you. And you'll need new identity papers. Give me your translator documents, please." She held out her hand like a mother waiting for a child to return a stolen chocolate bar.

Anna folded her hands in her lap. "I gave those to Captain Phillips. He said he would turn them in." The lie slid out before she could stop it and she almost smiled.

Frau Obersdorfer sighed and shook her head. "Very well. Get your new papers before you leave today. And, of course, your wages will return to what they were before." She snorted. "Almost as if none of this foolishness ever happened, isn't it?" She rocked back on her heels and regarded Anna over her half-moon glasses. "You are lucky. We desperately need typists to record all the pieces in the shipment from the Merkers mine. Otherwise the *Amis* would have sent you packing. I told them they should, but they never listen to me."

Anna nodded. She picked up her bag and pulled the typewriter off the table. "Yes. That is just my luck," she said and followed the woman to the stairs.

After lunch Anna sat down at the small table in the back row of the typing pool. She was by the window, which meant she at least got a bit of breeze but also the glare of the afternoon sun, which made her skin burn. The room was stifling. She wiped her forehead with her palm and moved another custody receipt from the right side of the typewriter to the left. Her back had gone from aching to something like numbness and her arms throbbed. She sat up straight and tried to turn her head as far as she could one way and then the other, keeping an eye on Frau Obersdorfer to anticipate the scolding that would come. Her eyes fell down to the street, onto the bench where she had left Amalia the day she met Cooper. It was empty and she recognized the same sentry stationed by the gate. Trucks were still coming at a steady pace and, no doubt, endless numbers of masterpieces were being unloaded right under her nose. A twinge of something—jealousy?—shot through her as she considered her regained position. Two weeks ago she was happy to sit here, type up the *Amis*' reports and go home. Now she was not so sure.

Anna was about to turn back to the typewriter when something caught her eye. By the fence at the corner, near the stationed tank, stood a lone figure. Anna squinted. The jumble of blond hair and the slouched posture were familiar. She leaned toward the window slowly so as to not draw attention to herself. It was Oskar, standing with fingers hooked into the chain link, face pressed against the wire, looking into the courtyard. Anna scanned his surroundings for anyone who might be accompanying him but saw no one. Oskar stood without moving, as if he were looking for something.

She fed a form into the drum of the typewriter and set up the first field for typing. What was the boy doing here? She looked again. He had not moved from the spot but was now standing with his back to the fence, hands in pockets, head turned down. Anna began typing absentmindedly. The DP camp was several kilometers away. How had he gotten here? There was no bicycle with him, nor anyone who looked to have brought him here. It was impossible that the camp would have let him leave there alone. Had he run away? Was he looking for her? She took one more look but he still had not moved. There was no break for another two hours—at the end of the day. She couldn't take the chance that he would still be there then.

Anna pushed her chair back and jumped up. As she ran toward the door she put a hand over her mouth and shook her head at Frau Obersdorfer. With her other hand she grabbed her stomach and doubled over, pretending to be in pain. Before anyone could stop her, she pulled open the door and ran down the hall toward the ladies' washroom. She stopped and looked back. When no one from the typing pool came after her, she continued down the stairs.

Downstairs she ran through the front entry toward the gate. But the boy was gone from his spot. Her eyes scanned the long perimeter. She ran though the gate and along the fence, looking down the street and across it, back toward where she had come from, and all the way around the corner. When she came to a stop, she was out of breath and frantic. Where had he gone? Had she imagined seeing him? Anna rested a hand on the fence and tried to collect herself. A group of people gathered at the intersection to cross the Wilhelmstrasse, but Oskar was not among them. When the MP waved them across, another group approached from the other side and Anna saw one head towering above the others. As the clump of people loosened, she recognized Konrad Schenk, his black hair shining in the sun, his robust presence diminishing the shoddy, gray people around him even more. Anna tried to shrink into the shadow of the tank and hoped he would pass her. For a moment, she thought she could follow him, but then remembered her noticeable absence from the typing pool. Her days of sleuthing for Cooper were probably at an end. She stared at the ground, as if lowering her eyes provided camouflage, but it was too late.

"Shouldn't you be on the other side of the fence, Frau Klein? Isn't that what you were so proud to sell yesterday?" Schenk asked in his practiced dismissive tone.

Anna said nothing and made to leave, but he took hold of her arm.

"Wait just a moment. I may have something for you. First of all, I should apologize for my disposition toward you yesterday. I was disappointed, yes, but I was also rude, and for that I am sorry."

The words did not match his demeanor. Even standing in the shadow of an American tank, he was threatening. Anna knew all she had to do was shout and the sentry that was standing twenty meters away would at least look their way. But she wouldn't make a scene and Schenk knew it.

He smiled with false benevolence. "So, please, allow me to give you a small compensation. I am happy to tell you I've looked into travel papers for your husband. They are not so hard to acquire. A small fee should cover it. And, for me, perhaps a token of your appreciation." His eyes shifted toward the Collecting Point.

Anna felt the sweat build on her scalp as if she'd walked into a sauna. She looked around nervously. "Perhaps we could discuss this another time? I am due back at work and I—"

Schenk interrupted. "Of course. I understand. I just want to show you." He pulled a folded document from his jacket pocket and opened it to reveal a set of papers. Anna scanned her surroundings but no one paid them any attention. She looked at the documents without touching them. They permitted travel from Weimar to Wiesbaden train station, which would be the fastest route for Thomas. The earnest face of a young man stared from the photo that was fastened with a metal ring in the paper. Anna tried to recall if she had told either Schenk or Schneider about Thomas's specific location. Schenk pointed a manicured finger at the page. "These have not been stamped. They can be used again. With your husband's photo of course."

Anna stared at the paper. "Where did you get this?"

Schenk shrugged. "There are so many pickpockets at the railway station. They have such fast little fingers. Much faster than standing in line for hours. I can let you have these for three hundred American dollars. You can even pay me over time. I know you don't have the money now, but perhaps you can get it." He folded the papers and returned them to his pocket and then spoke again as if he had just remembered something. "You know, it makes no sense to me why you would want to bring your husband here. He's a known communist after all—the *Amis* won't like that one bit. I imagine it will be difficult for him to find a job; they won't hire him, that's for sure. More likely they'll arrest him. It's a wonder they hired you. Did you tell them the truth about your background? I mean, I assume you are a communist as well?" He grinned. "We all have to pick which side of the table we want to be on, don't we?"

Anna felt her blood run cold. It was the same thing Cooper had told her: *Pick a side*. She stammered a protest but Schenk continued. "Perhaps it would be better for you to return to Thuringia instead. I could help you with papers of course. Just think about it. It would be a shame to see the Americans come after you. Travel papers for the Russian sector are considerably easier to get, of course, so three hundred dollars would take care of both you and your little daughter. You can tell Ludwig what you decide. He knows where to find me." He chuckled. "I forgot. So do you, don't you?"

He clicked his heels and walked in the direction of the tree line on the Frankfurter Strasse. Anna looked around, self-conscious. Three hundred dollars was a fortune. But wasn't it worth it to have her family back, if it worked? If they got away with it. She raised her eyes toward the row of windows on the third floor of the Collecting Point. Through the open window on the corner she saw Frau Obersdorfer staring back at her.

chapter twenty

What do you mean you invited Herr Schilling to dinner?" Anna put her bag on the sofa. "I don't understand."

Amalia bounced on the bed and Madeleine sat up. "What? Tonight? *Ach du Schreck.* Oh dear, I am not presentable."

"Maus, why would you do such a thing?" Anna asked.

"Because he is nice and I like him. And he said he would bring food. Maybe some sausage, even. Aren't you hungry Mama?" Amalia was oblivious to her mother's irritation.

"Of course I am hungry. But I…" She trailed off, too tired to put up much of a fight. Frau Obersdorfer had said nothing when Anna returned to the typing pool. No doubt she was biding her time to build a final case against Anna. The day had ended with Schneider taking up his position at a desk on the ground floor near where the art pieces were beginning to be sorted and photographed. When Anna was leaving, he was talking with the appraisers and photographers, smiling from ear to ear. To keep up appearances, she congratulated him and tried to make amends one more time. But the thing that weighed most on her was Oskar. Without Cooper's jeep she had no reasonable way to get to the DP camp to visit him until the weekend, which was still two days away. She tried to convince herself she had just imagined seeing him standing outside the fence. The streets were full of little boys running loose like packs of blond two-legged dogs. Maybe she had seen someone else. Her mind drifted to thoughts of Cooper. She wondered what his new assignment was and whether he would ever return to the Collecting Point. She knew he was probably frustrated and irritated at his transfer. She could see him raging against the system in his affable way. *Is he thinking of me? Does he wonder how I am doing?* She stopped herself. *What nonsense.* She focused her attention on Amalia, who was tugging at her sleeve.

"Don't be mad, Mama. Herr Schilling is nice, really. Why can't we make new friends?" Amalia came and stood next to her. She stroked Anna's arm, which was her usual way of pulling her mother's strings.

Anna bent down and kissed her daughter's head. "Of course we can make new friends, Maus."

In the kitchen she pulled out bread and jam and dug around in the basket for the remaining vegetables—some wilted greens and carrots. She rinsed them in the sink and filled a pot with water, not knowing what else to do. It wasn't enough food for one person, let alone four of them. What a ridiculous idea, to have a dinner party.

The knock on the front door was soft and timid. Anna approached the door. The painting from the botched hotel sale leaned against the wall in its bag. Not knowing what else to do, she pushed it behind the small table. How could she return it to the Collecting Point now? With Cooper gone, she was stuck with it. *Maybe I can get arrested for art theft as well*, she thought. *Why not?*

She took a deep breath before pulling the door handle. Emil stood back several steps on the landing, his arms hunched around an old cloth bag that he hugged to his chest. He smiled sweetly, revealing the youth that still lived underneath his battered exterior. Anna warmed and returned the smile.

"Emil, please come in." She stood aside and gestured him into the apartment.

"Is it all right? I wasn't sure I should come."

"Of course. We are glad to have you."

Amalia bounced up behind her and giggled. Emil greeted her with a wave and pulled something from the top of his bag. "I brought you something, Amalia. For your collection."

Amalia took the small box he offered her and ran into the living room, barely able to contain her joy as she called out to Madeleine. Anna closed the door behind Emil and he followed her into the living room. Madeleine sat propped on the sofa, her silver hair pulled into a loose bun at the nape of her neck, her eyes lively as she watched Amalia open the box. Anna performed the introductions and Madeleine put Emil at ease by patting the cushion next to her and inviting him to sit.

Amalia squealed as she held up a small wooden pin carved into the shape of a bird, its wings spread in flight, a long tail feather curving gracefully over its head.

"Just a little trinket from the box Frieda keeps for the girls to play with. I thought she'd like to have it since she is always finding little treasures," he said, warding off Anna's inevitable protest.

Anna nodded and bit her lip. Amalia beamed her thanks.

"Oh, and this is for you," Emil said. "Some things to eat. I got them this weekend so they are still pretty fresh." He held the bag up to Anna.

Anna was embarrassed, but accepted the gift and carried the bag into the kitchen.

"It's just some bread and a little cheese," Emil said following her. "Some milk for Amalia, and some Nordhäuser for us." He reached into the bag and pulled out a half-empty bottle. He held it up next to his face like a school boy who just broke into his father's liquor cabinet.

"Schnapps? Amazing," Anna said. "Where do you get these things?"

Emil shrugged. "Everything can be had. You just have to know who to ask. And be able to pay the price. There are some American cigarettes in there for you, too. I know you like them."

Anna had not had much luck on the black market so she respected those who could work the rules of that system to their advantage. One day she would figure it out.

"Anytime you need something, just ask me. Really. I will get it for you." He smiled as he pulled two coffee cups from the shelf and poured each of them a generous serving with a shaking hand. Anna noticed for the first time the resemblance between him and his sister. But where Frieda had turned out all strong-jawed and sharp angles, Emil's face was softer and well proportioned, as if his features had been honed by a kinder sculptor. She desperately wanted the drink but she could tell Emil wanted it more. Still, it was only one drink, and the bottle was already nearly empty.

"*Prost*," she said as they clinked cups. The schnapps seemed to catch fire in her mouth and burned its way into her empty stomach. The rise to her head was almost instantaneous. Emil drained his cup and poured himself another. Anna turned her attention to cutting the full loaf of dark bread with the long kitchen knife. Madeleine and Amalia chattered in the living room and for a moment the world seemed a little more normal. Anna considered the possibility that she liked having a dinner guest, even if it was only for bread and cheese.

"Thank you for bringing the food," she said. "We really had nothing at all to eat. I would have had to send you home hungry." She scooped the slices onto the wooden board they used as a serving platter and fanned them out.

"Anna, may I apologize for the way I acted the other day? I feel terrible."

Anna looked at Emil and felt the blood run to her cheeks. "No need to apologize, Emil. I regret the way I behaved, too. I think I made assumptions that were unfair. I am sorry."

He exhaled and looked at the floor, nodding his head.

"You wanted to tell me something and I didn't let you. Will you tell me now?" Anna sliced into the cheese to give herself something to do.

"No, it's not so important right now. I don't want to spoil the evening for Amalia by talking about those things. I will tell you another time." He cleared his throat. "How is your job?"

"The job is all right," she lied. She didn't want to talk about her demotion to the typing pool, although Emil would find out anyway. She added the cheese slices to the board. "How about you?"

Emil shrugged. "Same. The *Amis* kind of grow on you, don't they? I mean, with their big ways and their view of the world, like it's all going to get better. I guess that's how things look from where they stand."

"Things are going to get better, Emil. Haven't they already? At least now we are free."

"Free and hungry and poor."

Anna stroked his arm before she could stop herself. We have to take things as they come. We will see this through and life will get better."

"You don't know that. Lots of people thought that, and what did it get them? A bullet in the head, and that's if they were lucky. Funny how your thinking changes so much when you see what men can do."

"That's all done now, Emil." She changed the subject. "Do you have someone in your life, a special girl who will take care of you?"

Emil's head snapped to the side as if Anna had slapped him. "No, there is no one like that. There was someone, before the war, but she is dead and gone. I don't want anyone else. Even if I did, no one will want me. All the girls only have eyes for the *Amis* anyway. I'm the one who came back a loser, remember?" He rubbed his frostbitten stubs and filled his cup again.

"I don't think that's true," Anna said. "But your sister is worried for you. She says you are drinking too much." She tried to catch his eye but he avoided her.

"She told you that? Why would she say that? Just to worry you? To make me look bad?"

"She is worried for you, Emil. She cares about you."

He snorted. "I don't drink too much. Not more than anyone else. And why can't I drink after all that's happened? *I'm* not hurting anyone. *I'm* not keeping secrets. Everyone already knows what *I've* done." He was agitated now and Anna wished she hadn't brought it up. Her pulse fluttered, but she tried once more to reach him.

"You know, Emil, you can always talk to me. I am a pretty good listener. And you can tell me anything. If you want to get something off your chest, I will listen to you."

"I don't drink too much," he repeated. "Just sometimes, to help me sleep, you know? Or to help me get out of bed. Or mostly just to pass the time. There's not much else to do."

Anna nodded. "I know. I understand."

"It makes my head shut up, is all," he said. "I feel more like myself when I drink. Not like what I've become. But, for you, I'll stop for tonight. I don't want you to worry."

"Thank you. Things will get better, Emil, they really will." The words sounded empty and she knew it. She stroked his arm again. "You have been very kind to me. I would have lost my job without your help. So it matters a lot to me that you are here. Amalia adores you. And we are friends again, no? So that is good too. We can help each other."

He nodded and took hold of Anna's hand, interlacing their fingers. He squeezed. "Friends, yes. That is enough for me. Thank you."

Anna felt the tears rise and the surge of emotion surprised her. She leaned into Emil and rested her head on his shoulder. He felt solid and warm, despite the bony bumps. "Thank you," she whispered.

"You know I will do anything for you and Amalia. I do want to help you. I know my way around and I can get you things. Will you tell me? Don't ask anyone else, they may not have your best interests at heart. And it can be dangerous." He stepped back and put his hands on her shoulders. "Will you promise me?"

Anna was taken aback at his intensity. "Yes, I promise." She reached up and touched his cheek before turning to pull plates from the shelf. "And you promise me you will go easy on the drinking. I am depending on you. And the *Amis* need you too. They can't even get the water running. What good are they?" She handed him the stack of plates.

"Damn *Amis*." Emil's face thawed into a smile.

"Damn *Amis*," Anna laughed.

The Collecting Point was thankfully quiet. The heavy wooden door to the administrative offices was closed. A few workers were milling around outside, awaiting the day's shipment, and it was still early enough that many people had not yet arrived. Anna wished for a shot of Emil's Nordhäuser. Her head ached and she felt shaky, even though she had only drunk her one cup. On her way to the washroom to splash water on her face, she passed the file room. The usual clerk was not at her desk. Instead, an old German man sat in the spot, wearing an oversized jacket and an earnest expression. Anna considered the opportunity. If she could just get one more look at the files, maybe she could find some missing piece of information. There were still fifteen minutes until start time, before Frau Obersdorfer would rap her typing brood to attention. This could be her last chance.

She approached the man, who began to deliver a well-rehearsed speech he had prepared to deter unannounced visitors.

"The file room is temporarily closed. Please come back another time," he sputtered.

Anna stopped in front of the desk and tried her best to loom over him. "What do you mean, closed?"

"Closed. Because all the clerical staff is in a meeting with the director. I was told to tell everyone who needs a file to come back after lunch." His dialect was thick Hessian, his voice gruff and his skin pleated with deep, weather-worn grooves. Several upper teeth were missing and the ones left behind had spread out along his gums, trying to fill the empty space.

Anna cheered silently. "After lunch? I cannot possibly wait that long. Captain Cooper has asked me to research some gallery files. I'm his translator. It's very urgent." She paused. "Do you know Captain Cooper?"

The man shook his head and tried to deflect her by getting irritated, but Anna cut him off. "Well if you did, you'd understand why I have to get to the files right away. He does not like to be kept waiting. You know how these *Amis* are. I'll just go in myself. I know where it is, I've been in here many times." She walked around the side of the desk.

"You can't go back there, *Fraulein*. I was told to let no one in, under no circumstances. You'll have to come back later. They've got the operator sending all the telephone calls to me, like I know anything about anything. I don't even speak English. The damn machine is ringing like crazy." He swung his hand at the phone and it obliged him with a loud metallic ring.

Anna took her chance. "I'll just be one second," she said as the man cursed the interruption. He answered the phone in officious German, relishing his temporary importance. Anna walked quickly to the last bank of files and ducked down to the bottom row. If he wanted to come get her he'd have to leave his post. Kneeling, she examined the drawers, selecting the one marked *Gallery Owners Hesse*. She began sifting through the files and found a few new ones had been added since her last visit. She ran her fingers over the tabs to find the S section. Schneider was still there but there was no file for anyone named Schenk. The clerk hung up the phone but seconds later it rang again. He answered it and sputtered his speech into the receiver.

At the front of the cabinet was a new file, a kind of master list. She ran her finger down the paper. So many Jewish names. A chill seeped to the surface of her skin. She turned the page. No

Schenk here either. When she got to the end, she started over, this time checking the names by city. There were only two names from Mainz—a Gerhardt Heinrich, who was noted as deceased, and a Karl Rosenfeld. There was no gallery listed anywhere named Neustadt, the name on the label on the back of the Runge painting. Anna flipped to the beginning of the list once more, looking for Neustadt under the people listing. No luck there, either. She stared at the list. She was sure she was missing something. Setting the list aside, she opened Schneider's file and leafed through the papers. The same papers remained: the letter recommending Schneider for work at the Collecting Point, and the memo from Darmstadt stating the stash found at the villa had not been reported to the authorities. Anna paused, listening for the clerk's voice, to ensure she still had time. He was giving directions to the Collecting Point in an argumentative tone, as if only he knew the right way to get there. When he hung up, he muttered to himself. Anna continued through Schneider's file to the pages that had been added at the back—a letter from Schneider himself, dating back to June, requesting permission to reopen the business. It was addressed to the military government in Frankfurt this time, and a quick scan revealed a self-pitying tale of Nazi pressure in the face of his fervent opposition to the oppressive and shameful treatment of the Jews, culminating in his arrest and imprisonment in 1941, "for helping many Jews." The purpose of his business, he said, would be to save and restore the many works of art currently rotting in damp cellars throughout Germany. The memo was a translation signed by Schneider with the original German document attached to it by a clip. Anna re-read the German version, which sounded even more pitiable. She didn't believe any of it, but she realized that her own story condensed into ten simple lines of facts would sound just as disingenuous and hollow. She wiggled her tooth and turned the page. There was one more paper.

The clerk's footsteps clicked down the row of file cabinets toward her. She took the last paper and the list of names, folded them in half and pushed them into the waistband of her pants. Untucking her blouse, she stood up, just in time to see the clerk's flushed face.

"I was just leaving," she said.

"Never mind that. Do you speak English? Didn't you say you are a translator?"

Anna nodded.

"Good. Then you come and tell this *Ami* lady on the phone what she wants to know. She keeps talking louder and louder like I'm going to understand better if she shouts my ear off." He pulled her by the arm the way Amalia did when she wanted to show her something urgent.

"All right, sure," she said. "Who's the *Ami*?"

"No idea." He handed her the receiver.

Anna held it up to her ear. "Hello? I speak English. May I help you?"

"Okay, finally," the female voice on the other end said. "I need to get some information here. The Major is looking for someone... well, he told me to take care of this and I didn't really know where to start, so I figured I'd start with you guys. You're the arts people in Wiesbaden, right?" The voice was high pitched, slightly nasal and flustered. She over-enunciated her words and spoke too loudly. Anna held the receiver away from her ear.

"Yes, we are," Anna said. She smiled and nodded at the clerk, who sat back in his chair, happy to be relieved of duty.

"You keep lists there of people who can estimate the value of things?"

"Do you mean appraisers?"

"Yeah, appraisers. That's right. You have someone like that? The major is looking for someone in the area to come take a look at... Well, he just needs an appraiser."

"What does the major need appraised? People specialize in different things. Is it furniture, or a sculpture, or a painting maybe?"

The voice hedged. "Oh, okay, well, it's a painting."

Anna motioned to the clerk for pencil and paper, which he retrieved from the drawer and pushed across the desk. "It might be best if the painting came here. We have several appraisers on staff. I know they would be well qualified."

"No. I'm pretty sure he wants someone to come to him. It's just one painting."

"Very well, can you tell me what kind of painting?"

There was silence on the line and then Anna heard shuffling sounds. The voice came back on. "I don't know anything about art. It's kind of big. It's a picture of a kid; I think it's a girl. Kind of blond curly hair. She's standing on a chair by a window. Is that what you need to know?"

Anna's ears rang. She saw the painting in front of her as clearly as when she had held it in her hands in the basement of the villa. She calmed her voice. "I see. And can you tell me if there are any marks on the back? That's also important."

"OK, hold on. Yeah, there's part of a sticker. It's hard to read. I think it says 'Darmstadt.' The rest is torn off."

Anna picked up the pencil and poised it over the paper. "Yes, I think we can help you. Could you please leave your information with me? I will ask the appraiser to call you back and arrange an appointment."

"Sure. You can just have them called Major Philips' office in Frankfurt. I'll answer." She recited the number. Anna wrote it down with a shaking hand.

"Thank you. Is there anything else I can do?"

"No, that's all. Thank you. I thought I was going to have to call around all day. You've been very helpful. What is your name?"

"I am Frau Klein. I am the translator."

"Great. I'll tell the Major when he gets back. He's on leave for a few days. This was one of the things he left for me to take care of. Thank you again," she trilled.

"It was my pleasure," Anna said and cradled the receiver.

"What was that all about?" the clerk asked.

"Oh nothing, just some paperwork that got lost. I'll get this to the right person." Anna took the paper and put it in her pocket. "Thank you."

"Good you showed up when you did," the clerk said. "Don't tell them I let you go in there."

"Not a word," Anna replied.

Anna's head ached. She could not keep her mind on her work and had made several mistakes already that morning. Her eyes wandered out the window to the spot where she thought she had seen Oskar the day before. The pounding of the typewriters punched at the inside of her skull and she thought she might actually vomit. After her pretense yesterday it was unlikely Frau Obersdorfer would have much sympathy. She glanced at her watch and saw with amazement that it had only been five minutes since she last checked the time.

Since the big shipments from Frankfurt had arrived, the typing pool was besieged with custody cards that that corresponded to each piece. A photographer took a photo of each item, which was stapled to a card that described it in detail—whether the item was signed, who the artist was, and any other relevant information. That day alone Anna had typed up custody cards for several masterpieces and felt a twinge of resentment return. Only four days ago she had been out in the courtyard with the others, surrounded by hundreds of paintings she had only ever seen in photographs. Now they were covered in dust and housed unceremoniously in shabby coverings, like a royal family in political exile. And she was trapped in the typing pool, privy only to the inventory and its accompanying bureaucracy. Her mind wandered and landed on Cooper again. She could only imagine his frustration, logging shipments at the airfield. Her fingers rubbed the keys of the typewriter and she followed her thoughts as she pretended to try to decipher the scribbles on the notes she was typing. She wondered if she might never see Cooper again.

"Frau Klein, more typing, less dreaming," Frau Obersdorfer growled. Anna jumped. The woman was some kind of psychic. Anna began typing again and sent her thoughts elsewhere. But the one that she had tried hardest to submerge finally floated into her consciousness and she looked at it straight on. Oskar. She had seen him the day before after all. She was sure of it. He had been looking for her. She looked out the window again, instinctively, as if he might reappear, but her view was blocked by the hips of Frau Obersdorfer, who stepped between her and the window. Anna could smell the stale sweat on her dress as she leaned down, her face close.

"After lunch, you trade places with Fraulein Walter." She pointed a finger toward the young woman at the desk closest to the wall, far from the window and its cooling breeze. "You'll be able to concentrate better."

Anna clenched her teeth and poked at the keys. Frau Obersdorfer straightened and clapped her hands. "*Meine Damen*, it's lunch time. See you in one hour. Enjoy your lunch."

Anna picked up her bag and made her way into he hall and down the stairs. Instead of falling into step with the others going toward the canteen across the street, she turned the other direction, toward the courtyard. There were no trucks and not much activity, so she pulled herself onto the side of the loading dock, the same spot where she and Cooper had conspired together. She pulled the papers she had taken from the file room from her bag. With a cautious glance to check her surroundings, she shuffled the list of gallery owners and pulled the last memo to the top and began to read. It was from the Military Headquarters in Frankfurt, addressed to the regional military government in Darmstadt, which had questioned the lack of reporting on the villa's stash. Dated 20 August, the same day the large Merkers mine shipment had arrived at the Collecting Point, it described the pieces of art at the villa as insignificant and not important enough to be classified as a major find of art objects. In addition, the memo continued, the collection had been claimed as the holdings of the gallery owned by the deceased wife of Ludwig Schneider. It was just as Cooper had said.

Anna looked up and stared into the distance. Schneider had already claimed the stash at the villa. She had been right. Schenk and Schneider knew exactly where the painting she tried to sell them had come from because it was Schneider's own painting. She shook her head. How stupid. She returned to the memo, which went on to exonerate Schneider from any wartime crimes, per careful review of his *Fragebogen* and other documents. He had moved the stash to the villa to protect it from Allied bombs, under the permission of the local

Gauleiter. The memo concluded with the claim that he would supply a full list of the inventory, at which time all the art should be returned to him, pending his finding a more suitable storage place.

Anna gripped the paper between clenched fists. Of course, that list would not include the Runge painting. That had been Phillips' payment in exchange for holding his nose to avoid Schneider's stench. Her thumb rested on top of the signature and name of the memo's author, but she almost didn't need to look. She lifted her thumb and there it was: James E. Phillips, Major, Military Government, Frankfurt.

Anna paused and tried to catch up with her thoughts. Maybe the Americans who had questioned her were after Schneider and not Cooper. Were they one step ahead of her already? Or had Phillips sent the MPs to turn her against Cooper? Schneider was brazenly claiming ownership of the stash at the villa based on nothing but his word and Phillips was backing him up.

She scanned the courtyard. Most of the workers had left for lunch. The few that remained stood around smoking and talking or resting in the shade. A jeep sat near the entry gate, its nose pointed toward the opening in the fence like the getaway car in a bank robbery. Anna stared at it. She chewed on the inside of her cheek and looked around again, her heart accelerating alongside the idea hatching in her head. There were no Americans anywhere that she could see. Maybe the jeep was one assigned to the Collecting Point, or maybe it belonged to a visiting colonel—there was no way of knowing. She slid off the loading dock and began walking, slowly at first, then fast, as if her legs knew they had only a few seconds before her mind started slowing them down. She pulled her papers from her bag and tried to see inside the sentry booth but could only see the guard's back. He was busy flirting with a mousy young German woman who was standing on the sidewalk laughing too loudly and twirling her dirty hair between her fingers.

Without breaking stride, Anna slid into the jeep's driver's side. She had not driven a car since the truck she and Amalia had driven to Wiesbaden had broken down. She tested the gear shift and pushed it into what she hoped was neutral. Her left foot found the start button and she put all her weight behind it. As the jeep rumbled awake, she stomped on the clutch, grasped the wheel with one hand, and pushed the gear shift forward with the other. Releasing the clutch, she felt the jeep lurch forward. A small part of her brain introduced the notion that stealing a United States Army jeep might be a terrible idea, one that should be reconsidered before she went much further. Anna silenced it with a press to the gas pedal that sent the jeep careening toward the entry. She held her breath. As the jeep passed the sentry, the guard did not turn his head, instead waving his arm in her direction in a casual salute. Anna turned the jeep to the right, away from his view, and shifted gears. Her fingers choked the steering wheel and she did not dare look back.

Her heart pounded in her chest as she turned onto the Rheinstrasse, heading west out of town. She focused on the road ahead and marveled at how easy the jeep was to drive compared to the lumbering truck she had driven the three hundred kilometers from Kappellendorf. The wind whipped through her hair and whorled into her ears. She loved driving and all that it represented. For a moment she wished she could push the gas pedal to the floor and never let up. Instead she slowed to a sensible speed, so as not to draw more attention to herself.

At the intersection with the Schwalbacherstrasse, an MP directed the meager traffic with earnest authority. Anna willed him not to notice her, but her own psychic powers were lacking. She could not have been more obviously out of place if she had been wearing a Russian Army uniform. As the MP waved the cross traffic though with one hand, he turned his head and stared, as if to sort out what he was seeing. In three steps he was next to the jeep.

"What the hell, lady? What do you think you're doing? Do you speak English?" His fleshy face glistened with sweat and his hooded eyes darted from side to side. One hand moved toward the holster on his hip.

She cleared her throat. "Yes, hello, officer. I am on official business, for the Collecting Point." She pulled her translator papers from her bag and presented them with a steady hand. "I am doing work for Captain Henry Cooper. He needs a dignitary to be escorted back to the Collecting Point. I am just on my way to fetch him."

The MP looked skeptical. "You shouldn't be driving. There should be a driver."

Anna nodded her head as if to agree with him. "Yes, of course you are correct, but it was a bit of an emergency and no one else was available. He told me I might have some trouble, so he suggested that you please be in contact with his office directly. Back at the Collecting Point. I can give you the telephone number." She pretended to dig around in her bag. Behind her, another jeep's horn protested and made her jump. The MP shot an angry look at the car and then returned to examining her papers.

"Anna Klein. You're a translator?"

"Yes. The translator. For the officers." Funny how the lies became liquid, flowing easily and filling the space once you let them loose.

The MP stared at her and seemed to be considering his options. Anna made a show of being in a hurry, placing one hand back on the gear shift, ready to drive on. Finally, he stepped back. "Okay, fine."

He handed the papers back to her. "You're free to go. Drive on." He waved her through with irritation. Anna stepped on the gas and smiled to herself. Cooper had definitely rubbed off on her.

Anna slowed the jeep near the entrance of the displaced persons camp and pulled over to the curb. Somehow she had to get Oskar to talk this time, to tell her about the art in the villa and what he was really doing there. He was the only other witness.

On her right was a two-story, stone-front building that was mostly intact. The large entry door was still in one piece and was closed. The building looked like the kind of place where an *Ami* might have official business. She decided to leave the jeep parked there rather than risk driving it into the camp and being questioned a second time. She jumped from the jeep and crossed the street in a quick jog, Otto's old boots making her strides long and easy. When she arrived at the gate, she showed her papers again and revised her story about official business for the Collecting Point. This time she was there to question a resident on an urgent matter. She threw out Cooper's name again and was waved through with no questions.

Maria was clearing tables in the dining room. The air was damp and hot and smelled of body odor and grease. Women picked up stacks of metal plates from the ends of the long tables and talked loudly amongst themselves. Anna picked up a stack near her and caught up with Maria as she walked to the kitchen window to deposit them with the dishwashers. The women greeted each other warmly and Anna asked where she could find Oskar.

Maria's face darkened. "He's run away. I didn't know how to find you. I wanted to tell you," she said, wiping her hands on her dress.

Anna's heart sank. "When?"

"Yesterday morning, I think. He wasn't at breakfast and no one saw him in the morning, except for one boy, who thinks he saw him sneak from his bed at dawn. I can't imagine where he could have gone, especially since he had good news the day before."

"What good news? Did someone come for him?"

Maria nodded and gestured for Anna to sit down.

"Day before yesterday, a man appeared. In the morning. I had taken all the linens to the laundry and was helping with the washing when it happened, so I wasn't there, but the other women told me about the visit. A man came to see Oskar, said he was the boy's family, and they talked for a while out in the play yard. Then the man went off to file the paperwork to take Oskar home. That usually takes a few days, so he would have had to come back for him. But after that, something wasn't right with Oskar. He wasn't happy at all. I tried to talk to him but he fell silent again, like he was when he first came. I thought maybe the reality of everything was sinking in, finally. But it was odd. He had been happier before the visit, if you could say that. I was concerned, but I never thought he would run away. I mean, where could he possibly go?"

"You didn't see this man?"

Maria shook her head. "No. But they said he was quite friendly, looked like an upstanding fellow. Seemed very eager to help the boy."

"Did he fill out any papers here?"

Maria shrugged. "I don't think so, not here. But you could check."

Anna stood. Now she was sure she had seen Oskar on the street the day before.

"Do you think you could check? I have to go right now, but I'll be back soon."

"Of course. I'll go to the administrative office later today." Maria tilted her head. "Where is your Captain? Did he bring you?"

Anna reddened. "No. I came alone. I just wanted to be sure Oskar was all right. I was worried for him." She looked at the floor by her feet. "And he's not my Captain. Not anymore," she added and then wondered why she had mentioned it.

Maria let the words lie, pushing herself to her feet and picking up another stack of plates. "If you say so." She smiled a tired smile that did not take hold on her face, gone as quickly as it had appeared.

Anna walked back to the jeep as fast as she could. Lunchtime at the Collecting Point was well over and the typing pool would be back in business by now. She sat in the driver's seat and considered her next step. If she didn't go back, Frau Obersdorfer would have her fired for sure. Then again, if she did go back, the result would be the same. Either way, she was in trouble. What was interesting was that she didn't much care. It was an entirely new feeling. A fly buzzed around her head and she swatted at it, squinting into the sky as she considered this change in herself. A warm breeze tickled the back of her neck and she smiled. She might as well make the most of her shrinking autonomy while she could. She put the jeep into gear and pulled out into the sparse traffic. Two hands firmly on the steering wheel, she accelerated and continued heading west, away from the city.

chapter twenty-one

The gravel crunched under the tires as Anna drove up the long lane toward the front door of the villa. The place looked as deserted as the day she and Cooper had found it, unsuspecting of what the visit would bring. Nothing had changed; there still wasn't even a lock on the door. She left the jeep in the drive in front and pushed her way into the house. Inside the hall, she stood for a moment, listening. The house was dead and silent, the air thick and stale. She wanted to throw open the windows, to clean the coating of dust from the surfaces, to bring the place back to life. The downstairs rooms seemed untouched since her last visit and she turned her attention to the upstairs. She and Cooper had not made it much past the bedroom at the end of the hall, the one where they had found Oskar. Now she climbed the stairs slowly, allowing them to creak under her feet, waiting between steps for any other sounds. At the top, she turned right and tried each of the four doorways leading up to the room at the end. All the rooms had been stripped of their valuables. They were like empty cardboard boxes, their contents removed and only the packing material left. Here a bed frame, there a dresser of drawers. Anna pulled open wardrobe doors, looked under beds and peeked behind curtains. The place revealed nothing, as if it had been scrubbed clean of its identity.

The room at the far end, overlooking the back garden, was much larger than the others. The shutters were closed and the curtains drawn. Anna held her breath as she crossed to the window to let light in. The curtains released a shower of grit when she pulled at them, then she cracked the shutters open. The dusty sunlight revealed a room full of white metal bed frames stacked along the far wall. A large cabinet with drawers and a glass front with several shelves stood near the window. She tugged at its small knob and opened the door. Inside were bandages and bottles of tinctures and other medical items. The drawers revealed more of the same, as well as tablets for pain and others for fever. Anna opened up a box full of tins of arnica cream. She put two into her pocket, then closed the box. The top was marked with a stamp: *Lebensborn Kinderheim*. The orphanage. Anna clenched her teeth as she rummaged though the box and pocketed all she could fit: aspirin, bandages, even a small thermometer. The sensation of something nipping at her heels made her jump, but when she looked at her feet, nothing was there. She scanned the room again. *A sickbay or clinic, maybe*, she thought. She tried to picture the small faces of the children who had lived here. She could see a smaller version of Oskar, his short pants and knee socks, hair standing in every direction. Had he been here, then, too?

She paced the room and tried to think. Why did Oskar run away from the camp when the man came for him? The boy had told her he had no one. Surely he would have known this person? But why not be happy to see him? And where had Oskar run to? She was surprised to find herself a little angry with him for not coming to her. She thought she had made more progress and that he had begun to trust her. But, then again, he still thought of her as the enemy. Still, she knew for sure that she had seen him outside the fence at the Collecting Point, and a small part of her knew he would turn up again, somewhere. She worried he was scared and hungry and she wanted to will him to come to her. She wanted to keep him safe. But, for now, she felt useless. Her pacing took her back into the hall and to the other end—to the room where they had found Oskar. Its contents seemed much the same: the rumpled bed, the dirty bath, and the open wardrobe. Even Oskar's piles of rocks in the corner were still there. She studied the footprints in the dusty floor, reliving their meeting. The small smudges must have been Oskar, and the medium ones with the small heel print were hers. Cooper's prints were unique—American Army issue boots with their rubber soles, and were in a clear line from the wardrobe to the window and back to the door. A fourth set of footprints was visible in the corner and near the wardrobe. They were large, a man's shoe, but not a rugged army boot—something more refined. Neither she nor Cooper had ventured by the far wall and Anna knew with near perfect certainty that the prints had not been there before. Still, that meant nothing. She shook her head. The front door was still unlocked; anyone could have come inside.

Walking around the room, she slid the dust around under her feet and was about to close the wardrobe door when something inside caught her eye. A small package, like a brick wrapped in newspaper, had been pushed to the back corner of the wardrobe floor. When she picked it up, the weight in her hands told her immediately what must be inside. She slid a finger under the seam of the wrapping. When the newspaper unfolded, she saw her hunch had been correct. Inside was a stack of American dollar bills, all different denominations. She flipped through the bills and then counted them out deliberately. There were fives and tens and many one dollar bills, crumpled and dirty. They added up to exactly three hundred dollars. Anna sat back and to spread the newspaper out on the floor and saw it was the front page of the *Stars and Stripes*. An earnest General MacArthur stared at her from the photo, awaiting Japan's capitulation. The paper was dated 13 August, the day before the Japanese had surrendered, ten days ago. She scanned her memory to put all the events in the proper order. It was the day after the Japanese surrender that Cooper had come back out to the villa, alone, in the night. Was this money the reason Cooper had been attacked? Or—something tickled her conscience—had he put it there himself, as a bribe? But for whom? She stared at the money and fanned it out on the floor in front of her. American presidents she had never heard of stared up, daring her. Three hundred dollars. So much money. Her mind focused on another possibility. Three hundred was the exact amount Schenk had quoted her for the travel papers, either for Thomas to come to Wiesbaden, or for Anna and Amalia to return home. He had made a point to say the amount more than once. Was this money put here for her to find? Who had put it there? And what if she did take it? Thomas could come, she could quit the job, and get Schenk off her back. She could get on with putting her life back together and return to being a wife and mother.

They would disappear and build their new life somewhere far away. She closed her eyes to imagine the scene: the smell of food cooking in a kitchen in a small house; flowers in the garden; Thomas working in his office; the sounds of children playing outside the window. She imagined herself grabbing the money and getting in the jeep and driving away, fetching Amalia from Frieda's house and disappearing with no explanation and no reason. Just dissolving into the ether or into another life, one with no politics or sides to choose, just her and Thomas and Amalia. But she knew this was just a dream. In this world there were always sides to choose and Thomas had chosen his. Soon she would have to choose hers, too.

The sound of a revving engine speeding up the drive startled her back to reality. She wadded the newspaper around the money and shoved it back into the wardrobe. At the top of the stairs, she hunkered down and peered at the front door from behind the balustrade. Scanning her surroundings for anything that could be used as a weapon, she tried to quiet her breathing. *Don't be ridiculous,* she thought. *You are here on official business. There's no reason to be afraid.* She pulled herself upright and began to descend the stairs. She gripped the railing hard and went slowly, waiting for the next sound. *This kind of thing never happens to people who stay put in the typing pool.*

The car pulled to a stop in front, probably next to where she had parked the jeep. She waited for the door to open but nothing happened. After several moments of silence she heard the footsteps crunch toward the side of the house toward the basement door. Anna took the stairs two at a time and ran toward the entry foyer. Peeking out the small window next to the door, she saw the other car, another jeep, parked at an angle in front of hers, blocking an easy escape.

Steadying herself, she pulled the door open and walked calmly toward the jeep, her eyes focused on the driver's seat as if it were the last lifeboat on the Titanic.

"Well, Frau Klein," a voice sang. Anna didn't recognize it, and for an instant she realized that she had held out a small hope that the visitor might be Cooper. But it wasn't. She stopped and turned.

"Fancy meeting you here," Corporal Miller said. Anna's brain took a moment to place him, but his pancake face and sneer quickly reminded her of their ride to the supply store. He walked around from the side of the house, gun in hand and cigarette hanging from his lips.

"Corporal. You scared me." Anna tried to blanket her fear, patting her chest in mock surprise and putting on a strained smile. She waited for his next move, but he just stood there, daring her to misstep.

"I was just leaving," she volunteered, taking several steps toward the jeep. She was close enough now to put a hand on it, which helped steady her weak knees. "I'm afraid I'm in a hurry."

Miller snorted. "I'll say. What are you doing out here anyway? All alone."

"Just checking up on something for the Captain. He wanted to be sure the property had been secured." She could not think of anything else to say. "Everything looks good to me, so I'll be going." She turned to get into the jeep but Miller pulled her arm toward him. She stifled a gasp and forced herself to look him in the eye.

"You ain't got no business here," he snorted. "You stole that jeep. You're not here for Cooper. He's counting pencil shipments out in Erbenheim. You think I'm stupid?" He tugged on her arm, pulling her closer.

Anna resisted the urge to answer truthfully. She stayed quiet and waited for the next volley.

Miller took a drag on his cigarette and blew the smoke into her hair. "Look, I know why you're here. There was a lot of good stuff out here, I know, I saw it. You're not the first one to think that way. But I'll tell you what. I'll overlook the fact that I saw you out here, trespassing on U.S. government property, driving a stolen jeep. You're in a heap of trouble already. But I'll do you this favor, and you can just owe me, okay? I'll think of some way you can repay me and I'll let you know." He smiled, pleased with the plan he had worked out. His eyes slid from her face downwards and pulled on her arm again so that she was pressed against him. For a moment they stood in the twisted embrace, face to face, eyes locked. With his free hand Miller began to grab at her pants, digging into her pockets and tossing out the medicines. He groped along her legs and back up under her blouse, his hands clawing and grabbing her breasts and along her shoulder. She heard the fabric of her blouse tear under her arm. Anna tensed and tried to shift her weight so she could kick him but he held her arm tight enough to keep her off balance. Finally she got enough traction to lean her shoulder into him as hard as she could. He stepped back and let go of her arm.

"Don't you touch me," she spat. Her voice was an angry growl. "Don't you ever touch me again."

Miller raised his hands in mock innocence. "Hey, doll, don't flatter yourself. I was just making sure you didn't take something that didn't belong to you. Besides all that." He kicked at the medical supplies he had pulled from her pockets. He laughed. "Just for that, I should have you arrested." He threw his cigarette at her. "In fact, I still might."

Anna backed up without taking her eyes off him.

"You could do that," she said. "But I don't know what I might tell people about all the things I *did* find here." She rubbed her arm and looked up to the bedroom window.

Miller lit another cigarette and inhaled, squinting through the smoke.

"Just get the hell out of here," he said as he waved her away. "Stupid *Kraut*."

Anna climbed into the jeep and stomped on the starter. She backed up and then stopped to put the car into first gear. Miller stepped next to the driver's side and pushed his head next to hers.

"But you do still owe me," he said.

She turned to look him in the eye. "Actually, I think we are even, Corporal," she said. "I won't tell if you don't."

As she stepped on the gas and released the clutch, she turned the jeep down the long drive. As the dust cloud separated her from the American, she could feel the adrenaline leave her body, like water from a sieve. She felt every bump on the dirt lane, each one asking, "Why didn't you just take the money?" She could imagine the smile on Miller's face as he reached inside the wardrobe and found the reward she was sure he had come for. His payoff for selling Cooper up the river, for helping Schneider get his job, for spying on her. *Greed, betrayal, power.* Same old song, just in a different language.

Anna pulled the jeep into the parking spot outside the sprawling supply barracks. She had waved her papers and batted her eyes at the guard and succeeded in getting into the airfield. The exchange with Miller had thrown her off and she felt lightheaded. Her empty stomach could not absorb the anxiety. She leaned back against the seat and rubbed her temples with the flat of her hand, considering which of the barracks she should try first. The barracks to the right seemed as good as any. She went inside and was relieved to recognize the gum-chewing receptionist at her post. Anna was sweating through her blouse and her hair had come loose from its clip. She felt like a castaway wandering from the wilderness.

"I'm here to see Corporal Bender," she announced, trying to preempt any questions. "It's urgent." She held up her papers.

The woman smacked the chewing gum between her teeth and surveyed the papers, then Anna's face. She paused.

"An urgent supply matter?" she said, with dripping sarcasm.

Anna nodded.

The *Ami* shook her head. "Okay then, sign here and here." She pushed the ledger at Anna, who signed her name as illegibly as she could manage, which was easy, given her shaking hands. The woman pointed her down the hall and Anna nodded her thanks before walking away as quickly as she could. *Please, please be here*, she thought.

Inside the supply room, Bender sat with his head over a large inventory book, chewing on a pencil. He looked pleased to see her.

"Anna Klein. You did come to see me again." He straightened and held out a hand.

Anna smiled and shook his hand. She felt stupid and sure that she had made a mistake coming here.

Bender's face darkened. "Are you okay? You look like you've been gone with the wind. Have seat." He walked around the counter and placed a stool next to her. "What can I do for you?"

Anna exhaled and tried to formulate a reasonable answer.

"I need to speak to Captain Cooper."

Bender nodded. "I figured." He picked up the receiver of the big black phone on his desk, dialed some numbers and instructed the person who answered to send Cooper over immediately.

"He'll be in here in a few minutes. Poor guy, he's busy dealing with supplies inventory out at the hangar." He smiled. "So what's going on?"

Anna shifted uncomfortably and pulled her bag to her chest. "I'm in some trouble and I need help."

Bender grinned. "Hmmm."

Anna rolled her eyes. "No, not like that. I am, at this moment, supposed to be sitting in the typing pool at the Collecting Point. I have been missing since lunchtime."

"You don't look missing to me," Bender said.

"I spent the afternoon sneaking around a secured property outside of town. And, well, I took a jeep to get there," Anna said.

Bender let a slow smile spread over his face. "I'm sorry, say again? You stole a jeep?"

Anna nodded. "Borrowed, really. But now I don't know how to return it. I know I'll lose my job. But I don't want to be arrested, too."

"What on earth possessed you to take a jeep?"

"I had to." Anna straightened. "I was trapped in that damn typing pool and I knew something was wrong. With the boy—that's another story. And I was right, he had run away from the camp, and so I decided to go out to where we found him to see if he was there, but he wasn't. And then I got caught and now I don't know what to do next. So I came here." She slumped back down, elbows on the counter, head in her hands.

Bender rubbed his forehead. "I gotta say, you and Cooper make quite the pair. This sounds just like some crap he'd pull." He shook his head. "You people just have to break the rules, don't you?"

Anna looked at him. "I was never like this before. I was a good German."

"Well, you see where that got you," Bender snorted and stood. "Sit tight. Cooper will be here soon."

Anna said nothing as Bender walked around the counter and began sorting stacks of papers. They were silent as Anna ran over the events in her mind.

When Cooper arrived ten minutes later, Anna was surprised at how glad she was to see him. He smiled, but his face was drawn and his skin was sallow and gray, as if he had been deflated.

"How are you?" he asked. *Amis* always had to know how you were.

"I am all right," she replied. "And you? You look terrible, if I may say so."

Cooper pulled up a stool and sat down. "You may. Now tell me what's going on. How the hell did you get here?"

"How much time do you have?" Anna said.

"For you, I've got all day," Cooper said. "Now, go ahead."

She didn't get very far into the story before Cooper jumped in. "Major Phillips? You took a call from Phillips?"

He leaned in close and lowered his voice. Anna could smell coffee on his breath. "And you're telling me that the Runge, *our Runge* is somehow in Frankfurt in Major Phillips' office?"

Anna pursed her lips and nodded slowly. "*And*, he wants it appraised. Just that painting, nothing else. *And*, someone's removed the gallery label."

"The Runge was taken that night when I was out at the villa, remember?" he said rubbing the back of his neck. "I'm sure of it now because it hasn't turned up on the inventory list of the stash, not that it's been officially catalogued and all."

"Maybe Phillips was the one that took it," Anna said.

"Yeah, not likely. I think I'd know if I was getting the crap kicked out of me by my own superior. Anyway, Phillips is not the breaking-and-entering type. He's more the lying down and napping type."

"The painting could have landed on the black market. He could have bought it. Maybe it was a bribe. Or he confiscated it," Anna said.

"We don't even know who took the painting in the first place."

"Maybe it was Schenk," Anna said. "Or his friends. He's not the breaking-and-entering type either, but he seems like he has friends who are."

"Why do you say that? It could have been anyone."

"Because, like I told you, Schenk told me yesterday that by trying to sell him that landscape I showed him our hand. As if to say he knows for sure we have the art from the basement. And remember how Schneider asked how I knew about the Gallerie Breuer when I brought it up that first day? If they knew about the art in the villa and the Runge, then that would have raised alarms for them. The painting you gave me came from the stash, so now they know for sure we have what was at the villa."

"But we had already marked the repository when Schneider came here. He must have known we had the art then."

"No, you hadn't done it yet, remember? Someone took the Runge the next night when you were there. That means only you and I for sure saw the Runge in the villa, as part of that repository. It was never registered because it never made it to the Collecting Point with the rest of the pieces. And you didn't mention what happened that night to anyone, did you?"

Cooper bit his lip. "Nope."

"Did you report the stash or not?"

Cooper looked sheepish. "I didn't at first. I told you, I wanted to buy some time. It was about three or four days after."

"Your report isn't in the file. Or I should say there's no record of it having been received. Who did you report it to?"

"I reported it to Farmer, of course, the director. He runs this show."

"Well, who does he report it to?" Anna was impatient.

Cooper's face slackened. "Frankfurt. Phillips. Shit."

Anna nodded. "So why is Darmstadt asking why you didn't report it if Frankfurt has the, what do you call it?"

"Jurisdiction. I have no idea. Listen, we have another problem. Darmstadt has called a hearing."

Bender, who had been following the conversation like volleys in a tennis match, let out a loud whistle. "Uh oh," he said.

"Now don't worry. It will be fine. It's just Anna and me, and a panel, asking questions about this case. They know something's fishy too. I think it's a good thing, if you ask me." He shot a look at Bender.

"If you say so," Bender said. He turned his attention to his clipboard and pretended not to listen. Anna and Cooper sat on their stools face to face, their knees almost intertwined.

"When is this hearing?" Anna asked, clearing her throat.

"Day after tomorrow. The Army will send a car for you. I guess if you had been at the Collecting Point they would have let you know."

"I'm sure I won't be at the Collecting Point anymore, not after today." Anna felt remorse, only in that she would have to find another job, something more suitable to a wife and mother. Telephone operator. Sales clerk. Doctor's wife. But isn't that what she wanted?

"Was it worth it? Taking the jeep? Did you find out anything more? You know you just need to tell them the truth at the hearing. You've done nothing wrong except not follow procedure. That, they can hang on me. I'll take that hit. But you probably will lose your job."

Anna nodded. "I just wish I could find the damn camera. I know you took a photo of the Runge painting in the basement. Without that photo, we have no proof that it was there." She sighed. "And then there's Oskar," she added.

Cooper groaned. "What about Oskar?"

"He's run away. Someone came to the camp to claim him and he ran away."

Cooper smirked. "That little dickens. God, he's a handful." He looked at his watch.

"Don't you worry at all about what will happen to him?"

Cooper sighed. Anna could tell Oskar's future was not occupying a large space in Cooper's mind. "Sure I do, but look, I gotta get back. I can only deal with one thing at a time," he said. "The kid will be fine. Someone did come for him after all. He'll turn up. It will all get straightened out."

"But he ran away," Anna said.

"He'll be fine. He's just a little skittish. Doesn't have his bearings yet. He'll get straightened out." Cooper nodded to himself, moving on to a checklist running in his head. "You said Phillips was out of town, right? That buys us a day at least before he figures out that we know about his painting."

"Do you think you'll get your job back?" Anna asked before she could stop herself.

"Let's not worry about that now. We'll get you back to the camp first so you can face Frau what's-her-name."

"Obersdorfer. I am sure I've already been fired. I just need to get my bicycle. And tomorrow I'll look for another job."

"Look, let's just get through the hearing and then we'll see. Things may sort themselves out."

"Yes, they may. But in the meantime I need to feed my daughter. And for that I need a job."

Bender spoke up. "Okay, look, the way I figure it, the immediate problem we have is getting the lady back home and getting the jeep back to the Collecting Point. So, here's what we do: I'll give her a ride and drop the jeep off. Coop, you come get me from the Collecting Point. If anyone asks, I'll make a stink about them screwing up their paperwork. After five minutes they won't care anyway, as long as the vehicle is back. And I'll bring the typing madam some ribbon and extra carbon paper. Tell her it was ordered special for her. That'll make her happy, right?" He smiled. "I'll say you were called away on last-minute translating business for Frankfurt. It couldn't be helped." He waved his arms around his head. "It was all a big screw up and such a mess. But you'll be back in the morning. At least that'll soften her up."

Cooper leaned forward and slapped him on the back. "Bender, you are a king among men. Your talents are wasted in the supply store."

Bender shook his head. "I'm much more dangerous this way. I told you I'd pay you back."

Anna sat up. "I forgot about Miller."

"What about him?"

"I found money at the villa. Three hundred dollars wrapped in newspaper and hidden in the wardrobe. I thought maybe it was there for me to find, so I could get myself in worse trouble, but then Miller showed up and he was angry. I know the money was for him. And he knows that I saw it there."

"Miller is full of shit and everyone knows it," Cooper said. "For him to tell that he saw you out there means he'd have to admit he was there too, which he had no business being. He'll have figured that out by now. He's just a stupid opportunist, thinks he can play all the angles, but, fortunately for us, he's always one step behind everyone. He's not a bad guy, he's just here for the wrong reason."

"What reason is that?" Anna asked.

"Himself," Cooper replied. "Now, let's get you home to your girl, and let's get this jeep back. I want to hear more about Schenk and the travel papers. How much did you say he wanted?"

"Three hundred dollars." Anna picked up her bag and stood. She felt heavy and was tired of talking.

"That seems to be the going rate for a lot of things today," Cooper said. "Do you have that kind of money?"

"No, of course not," Anna snapped. She looked into Cooper's face. "Where would I get money like that?"

Cooper shrugged. "Sounds to me like you could have just had three hundred bucks pretty easily. It's good to know you didn't take the bait."

"I would never."

"I know that." Cooper stood and offered a hand to help her off the stool. "Let's get going."

Anna dropped her bicycle on the ground outside the Schilling house and pushed the gate open. Cooper had left her at the Collecting Point gate and tried to reassure her that all would be fine. Still, she avoided confronting Frau Obersdorfer, deciding instead to ride up the Gustav-Freitag-Strasse and fetch Amalia, even though there was still more than an hour left in the workday. They could take the afternoon to tidy up the house and maybe go for a walk. Being with Amalia forced her to think about something else, even if it was just *The Snow Queen* or what was for dinner.

She let herself into the cool foyer of the house. The door to Emil's apartment stood open, the darkness of the long hallway receding inside like a tunnel that glowed with the light from the living room window at its end. Calling for him, she knocked on the door and waited for an answer. She called out again and stepped into the apartment, peeking first into the kitchen, then the bedroom and then following the hallway into the living room at the end. Everything was tidy and clean, his few belongings put away. Even the handful of books on the small shelf was perfectly lined up. As she turned to go, she paused again to listen for any sounds. Her eyes fell on a painting hanging by the door, hung very low in a spot much too small for its size. She blinked. The painting was a large landscape, with a forested plain, mountains, and impossibly blue sky. In the foreground were sheep painted in bright white that made them look like overgrown dandelions. A small figure of a shepherd sat hunkered in the shadows. The flat sky, the evenly weighted strokes—it was the same style and subject as the painting she had taken to the Nassauer Hof. She looked closely at the illegible signature, which looked to be the exact same scrawl as the one on her painting: all up-and-down strokes in heavy black paint. She lifted the painting and tilted it away from the wall with both hands. She wedged her head underneath and peered at the back. In the bottom left-hand corner, there was a small white label.

Gallerie Neustadt, Mainz. The same artist and the same gallery. It seemed an impossible coincidence. Perhaps Emil could shed some light on the artist, and, more importantly, who owned the gallery. She made a note to remember to ask him as she stepped out into the foyer.

With one foot already on the stairs going up to Frieda's apartment, she stopped. Voices rose from underneath the stairs, from behind the basement door. Raised, tense exclamations were followed by shouts, voices arguing back and forth, and then words stepping all over each other. Anna pulled open the heavy basement door and was struck by the moldy damp air that now always reminded her of bombing raids and nights spent underground. The inside was dark except for a weak circle of light seeping toward her from the right, where one of the storage stalls was illuminated. Anna's view was blocked by stacks of crates and furniture and the voices were quieter. She could not understand what was being said, or who was doing the talking. She walked in the direction of the light. "Hello?" she called out. "Frieda, is that you?"

"Mama?" Amalia's voice flew through the air.

"Maus?" Anna stepped into the light as Frieda's and Emil's heads swung in her direction.

"Mama!" Amalia cried again. She was standing at the far end near the back wall. Frieda clamped a hand on the girl's shoulder when she saw Anna.

"What is going on here?" Anna asked. "Come along, Maus. Let's go home." She held out a hand, but the girl didn't move.

"Amalia?" Anna stepped forward but she saw that Frieda held the girl back. "Frieda? Let her go." Anna grabbed the girl's hand and then saw the gun that Emil held in an unsteady hand. He pointed it at her and she gasped. "Emil, what's...what are you doing?"

Emil's face was slack and his eyes floated, unfocused. He licked his lips and blinked slowly. "I'm just trying to help," he said. "I'm not a bad guy." He waved the gun in an argumentative gesture. "Really, I–"

"Emil! Oh my God, are you drunk?"

"Of course he's drunk," Frieda hissed, still holding Amalia with a firm hand on her shoulder.

"You let her go," Emil mumbled. "Her mother's here, so now you let Amalia go, Frieda. Did you her me? Her *mother* is here."

Anna gave a cautious smile to reassure Emil. "Yes, let her go Frieda." But Frieda and Amalia didn't move. Anna looked at her daughter and saw the fear on her face.

"Let her go, dammit," Anna shouted, the panic rising now. "Have you all gone crazy?"

Emil snorted. "I'm just drunk. It's Frieda who's gone crazy. Why don't you give Anna a tour of the little playroom you have down here? I don't think she's seen it yet. I only found it myself last week. Really, go on," he laughed.

Anna scanned the small space for the first time. Between the old boxes and dirty trunks lay a stack of old newspapers. She squinted and saw they were all copies of the *Voelkischer Beobachter*, the vile racist newspaper that was the staple of the Nazi diet. On top, scattered every which way, lay small toy soldiers in the uniform of the SA, giving little Hitler salutes and carrying tiny banners. They had been the staple of every good German boy's toy box. A doll wore a red dress like the one on the doll Frieda had given Amalia. Only this one's dress clearly showed part of the white circle and black swastika of the fabric's original purpose as a Nazi flag. Next to Emil stood a large trunk, its lid open, spilling over with uniforms and other pieces of clothing, their familiar insignia giving them away. Anna wanted only to run. She held out her hand for her daughter. "We are leaving."

"No, wait, you don't understand," Emil slurred. "Don't you know who my sister was? What she did for the glory of the Reich?"

Anna stood rooted to her spot, silent.

"She told you she was a *Schwester*, a nurse, didn't she? But it's not what you think. She wasn't any nurse. She was a *sister*. In the Lebensborn. Do you know what that is ?"

"Yes, of course," Anna said. "Who cares about that now? So what?" She reached her hand toward Amalia but Frieda wrapped an arm around the girl's body, pinning her arms.

Anna stared at Frieda and their eyes met. Amalia began to cry and Anna felt the panic seize her with such force that her ears rang. *What the hell is going on?*

Emil kept up his slurred soliloquy. "She made babies. To give to the Führer. Only pedigreed SS men need apply. No entanglements, no responsibilities, just the honor of fathering another child for the master race. Isn't that right, sister? How much cannon fodder did you supply? Three, or was it four?" He looked at Anna, as if he was just remembering she was in the room. "That's how you become a *Schwester* in Lebensborn. Tell her, sister, about what you did. And then I'll tell her what I did in Russia. Then she can decide which one of us is worse. Or better, I guess, depending on how you look at these things." He chuckled and wiped his mouth with the back of his hand.

"Emil put the gun down," Anna said. "This is not the way. Just put the gun down, please."

"This gun? Oh, it's not mine. It belongs to your *Ami*, that Captain Cooper. It was his." He nodded to underscore the fact. "I took it from him."

"What?" Nothing was making sense to Anna, but she didn't want to hear Emil's confession. She reached again for Amalia, but Frieda pulled her away.

Emil continued nodding and bit his lip. "*Ja*. It was me. Why was he out there at the villa that night anyway? He wasn't supposed to be there. I was just trying to help you..."

"Of course you were," Anna said. She had no idea what he was trying to say. "And you did. Now, just give me the gun. We can talk about it later after you've had a rest." It occurred to her that's just what Thomas would have said.

"No, no, it's okay," he said, slowly wrapping his lips around the American word. "I'll just tell you now."

"Emil, just shut up, why don't you?" Frieda barked and made them all jump. Amalia let out a frightened cry.

Emil raised the gun and aimed at his sister. "You shut up now. So, listen to me, Anna, this is important. I went out there, to the villa, because I had to take the painting. Because I knew what they were going to do with all the art. They were going to use it for bribes. But then you and the *Ami* found it and I knew they would come back for it, you see?"

Anna didn't see anything except that Amalia was still crying and that Frieda had a firm grip on her. She was barely listening to Emil.

"And that stupid Cooper showed up and he was going to mess up my plan. But I got the painting anyway."

"You stole the Runge painting from the villa? Why?"

"I told you. I needed it to prove the truth about the art. I was going to bring it to the *Amis*. Because it's all stolen, and Schneider was going to use it to pay off anyone who got close to finding out where it really came from. So he could be a big important somebody. Right Frieda?

And now they lie and say it's not stolen. But it is. Took it from the Jewish families and then kept it all for themselves. Pretended it was theirs. I think the *Amis* will like to know the truth. I am going to tell them, Anna, don't worry. And I will tell them about her too." He waved his empty arm around his head. "You must have told some good lies on your *Fragebogen*, sister. You were always such a better liar than me."

"Shut up, Emil. No one cares about what you have to say. They should have left you in Stalingrad. Then you'd at least be a real hero, instead of the disgrace you are. *Feigling*," she spat. "Coward." She looked at Anna. "Listen, you. I don't want you pillow talking to your American about me or about any of this. Don't you want to have a better future for you and your daughter? Have a nice house, more children? Not have to work for the *Amis* like some whore? How can you allow yourself to be so degraded? After everything we fought for? You are a traitor to the Reich."

"Stop!" Anna screamed. "You are crazy, both of you." She could make no sense of anything Emil or Frieda were saying. Her vision was focused only on Amalia's little face, twisted in fear. *Why is she not coming to me?*

Frieda shook her head. "No. If you go to the *Amis* and tell them about me, I will tell Ludwig. He can make it so you lose your job. The *Amis* love him. And Schenk, he can make it so you lose a lot more. You understand?" She squeezed Amalia's shoulder and the girl cried out.

Anna felt something powerful take over where her mind and her muscles had collapsed from fear. She lunged forward and pushed Frieda backward as she rammed her shoulder into the woman's rib cage. With her other hand she pushed Amalia out of the way, sending her stumbling onto her hands and knees. "Run, Maus!" she shouted as she tried to regain her balance, but Frieda scratched and punched, arms flailing as Anna tried to reach around to get to Amalia.

"Mama!" Amalia screamed as Emil grabbed her. Anna only saw him drag her into the darkness of the cellar, but before she could react, Frieda struck her across the face with the heel of her hand, sending her jaw painfully out of joint. Anna swung back, landing a punch that drew blood at the top of Frieda's cheekbone. Frieda clawed at Anna's face as Anna swung both fists wildly, blind with fury and terror. Frieda grabbed Anna's hair and pulled her head toward the floor. Anna threw a fist upwards that connected with Frieda's throat. Coughing, Frieda lost her footing and pulled Anna with her as she fell to the ground. Her head struck the back wall behind her with a flat thud and she screamed as she slid. Anna felt herself being pulled down, but then she was grabbed from behind and yanked backward, her hair still in Frieda's hand.

"Stop, Anna!" Emil held her around the arms as she kicked at Frieda. "You have to get out of here." He pushed her toward the door. "Get out," he shouted. "Both of you."

"I did nothing wrong," Frieda yelled after them. "Any one of your *Amis* comes after me, you know what will happen to you."

Anna barely registered the threat as she scrambled toward Amalia, who was standing at the basement door. "Run, Maus," she cried again, but the girl stood firm with her hand held out, waiting for her mother. When their hands connected, they ran out into the foyer and then the brightness of the sunshine.

"Mama?" Amalia stopped.

"Not now, Maus. Get on, and let's go," Anna panted as she struggled to right the bicycle. She looked back at the front door, expecting to see Frieda emerge from the darkness.

"But Mama, this is heavy." Amalia held up her arm. The gun dangled from her sagging wrist.

Anna snatched it from her. "How did you get this?"

"Emil told me to take it. To give it to you," Amalia whispered. "Mama your mouth is bleeding."

Not knowing what else to do with the gun, Anna laid the gun in the basket attached to the handlebars. She leaned the bike against her thigh and lifted her daughter on to the back. "I'm all right," she said. "Let's go now." She pushed off and pedaled down the hill. Once she had put some distance between them and the house, she became aware of the warm metallic taste filling her mouth. She spat a dark red splatter onto the street. It was her tongue that found the source. Her tooth was finally gone.

chapter twenty-two

While everyone slept, Anna stood in the bathroom and finished washing Amalia's clothes. She was too agitated to sleep and needed quiet to think. The art, Emil, Cooper's missing gun, Frieda and Schneider—now this was all connected, too. It made her head hurt. She hung the little dress on the line above the bathtub and slid down against the tile wall to stretch her legs on the cool floor. She lit a cigarette and watched the paper burn around the edges. The silence of the night rang in her ears. She closed her eyes and considered the bigger problem of what she would do now that her job at the Collecting Point was over. She would go back to the *Arbeitsamt* to apply for another job and this time she would tell them she spoke English. Surely some colonel somewhere needed a secretary. She would say good-bye to Cooper and wish him well. She would wait for Thomas, who was probably on his way already. And if not, then, well she would cross that bridge when the time came.

"Mama?" Amalia's voice made her jump.

"Maus? What is it?"

"Mama, I can't sleep." Amalia padded over to her mother and folded herself into her mother's lap.

"Are you feeling sick?"

The girl shook her head. "No, I just can't stay asleep."

Anna stroked her daughter's hair. "Are you worried about something? About what happened today?"

Amalia nodded. "I'm sorry I took the pin."

Anna gently pushed Amalia away so she could look at her. "What pin, Maus?"

"The pin I found at Fraulein Schilling's house. In the basement where she kept all those toys. I've been keeping it in my box."

"And?"

"And Fraulein was looking for it today and she couldn't find it. So she got really angry. And then I told her I took it and she got even more angry. I said I would give it back, but she was too mad already. And that's when Herr Schilling found us in the basement. Because I think he heard her yelling."

"I think you had better tell me everything. Go on."

"The basement is where she keeps the special toys. If you were really good she would take them upstairs to play with. You saw it, Mama. She had dress up clothes down there, too. She said they were old uniforms, from the war. That's where I found the pin. I took it for my collection. I am very sorry. I will give it back."

Anna took a deep breath and set the information aside for the moment. "Oh don't worry about a silly pin. Tell me why you were in the basement today."

"That's what I am trying to tell you. Fraulein was looking for the pin and she was making me help her and then I told her I took it. And then she asked me lots of questions about you. And about Captain Cooper. And when I didn't know, she hit me. She just kept yelling and yelling. I was so scared, Mama."

A blind rage filled every space inside Anna's body. "She hit you? Where?"

"Just here." Amalia pointed to her cheek as she looked at the floor. "She was really mad. She never hit me before; she was always so nice and sweet and pretty. I am sorry I was bad," Amalia said, tugging at the hem of her dress. "And then Emil came in and he was acting all strange. And then they got into a fight and Emil shouted at me to leave, to go home, but Fraulein Schilling grabbed me and wouldn't let me go. She was holding my arm so tight and she kept yelling at me that I had to do what she said or you would be in trouble. That you would get hurt. And that's when he pulled the gun from his pocket. And he scared me so bad. And they yelled at each other and he called her bad names and said he would kill her if she didn't let me go. But she held on to me. And then I saw you. I am sorry, Mama."

Anna's fury tumbled in her core, ricocheting off her insides like a rubber ball. When she didn't let it out, it turned on her. How could she have been so stupid? To trust her child to people she didn't know at all? "You did nothing wrong, Maus. Not even taking the pin. It was good you took the pin, you understand?" *You did nothing wrong.* These words applied only to children now.

"I will give it back," Amalia whispered.

"Can you show the pin to me?" Anna asked.

Amalia padded into the living room and returned with her treasure box. She put it on the floor at Anna's feet and sat down, legs splayed on either side. As she rummaged, Anna caught glimpses of her many finds: various buttons, the piece of ribbon Madeleine had given her and the postcards from Anna's mother. Small, dirty, once shiny objects slid around between her little fingers until she pulled out what she had been looking for. "Here," she said as she pressed the pin into Anna's outstretched hand. It was a long, thin rectangle framing a set of leaves. The word *Helferin* was spaced evenly across the length of the strip. It was the two lighting bolts in the center that left no doubt. Frieda was an SS *Helferin*, a helper. Emil's story was holding up. "It was in the dress up clothes, Fraulein's old uniforms. She said the lightning bolts meant she was important. That she did important work for Germany."

Anna put the pin on the floor. "She did?"

"And she told us that the Americans are nothing but monsters and that no good German would work with them. And she said the Americans were going to steal everything from us. Is that true, Mama?"

Anna shook her head. "No, Maus. That is not true."

"Are you mad at me, Mama?"

"No. I am just glad you are safe now." Anna began to cry. "And I am sorry about everything. I am so sorry." She pulled Amalia close. "Fraulein Schilling has some very bad ideas about how things should be. And I didn't know about her, otherwise I would never have let you stay with her. I don't think I'll ever let you out of my sight again, Maus, I swear it."

"Is Herr Schilling a bad man too?"

"I don't know if he is a bad man. I don't think so. I think he is very mad about things that happened in the war, but he doesn't know how to feel better. Sometimes when very bad things happen to people it takes a long time for them to heal. Even when the hurt is all on the inside where you can't see it. Do you understand?"

Amalia nodded. "Papa could make Herr Schilling feel better." She paused. "But Mama? I am scared. Why is Papa not coming?"

Anna closed her eyes. "Why do you think Papa isn't coming?"

Amalia shrugged. "I don't know. Because he's taking too long. And because he is mad at us for leaving."

"Well, you know, it takes a long time to travel now. Things are complicated. But he will come."

"But what if he doesn't? Lots of papas never came back."

"I know, but ours will."

"You don't know that for sure."

Anna decided to give her daughter the credit she deserved. The weight of the unfounded optimism was beginning to crush them both. "You are right. I don't know anything for sure. But until we know different we are going to look forward to him coming, right?" She rested her cheek on her daughter's head. They sat this way, without talking, for a long time. Amalia's body felt heavy and Anna thought she had fallen asleep, but then the girl said, "Is Oskar all right?"

"What makes you ask about Oskar?" Anna said.

"I don't know. I just miss him a little bit."

"Yes, I think so," Anna lied. "I think he wants to find his family." Another lie.

"But Mama?" Amalia turned her head toward Anna and put her lips close to Anna's ear. "He already has a family person. I am not supposed to tell you." She pulled her head back to wait for Anna's reaction.

Anna acted as if the news was not important, knowing that a big reaction would make Amalia rethink sharing her secret.

"Oh, really?" she said. "Well, that's good news. Who is it?"

Amalia considered her answer. "His uncle," she said. "His uncle came to visit him."

"How do you know this?"

"He told me his uncle came to the camp a long time ago. To talk to him. And he said his uncle would take him away."

Anna pushed her hands on the floor to straighten herself. "Oh?" she said, smiling. "But that's a good thing isn't it? For Oskar to have a family?"

Amalia shook her head. "Oskar said he's not very nice. He said he would run away rather than live with his uncle. But I am not supposed to tell you. He made me promise." She closed her lips and shook her head.

"I know Maus, I won't tell, I promise. Can you tell me his uncle's name?"

Amalia shook her head harder. "He didn't tell me."

The two of them sat on the floor, their limbs interlocked. The tile was cold and Anna felt ready to finally crawl into bed. She tried to think of how to extract more information from her daughter but sensed that Amalia had decided she had spilled too many beans already. She gave it one more try. "Did his uncle hurt him?"

"I don't know, Mama. I told you, he didn't say." She set her jaw. "Tell me again about Papa. Does he still love us?"

Anna pulled her close and wrapped her arms around her daughter. "Of course Papa loves us. And he will come, you'll see. Now, let's go to bed." She got to her feet, Amalia still cradled in her arms. The two of them crawled into bed next to Madeleine who was breathing steadily into her pillow. Anna laid back and inhaled, holding back a wave of emotion that attacked from out of nowhere. She stifled a sob.

Amalia wrapped a small hand around her mother's neck and pushed her head into Anna's shoulder. The girl's breathing slowed again and Anna sensed her daughter was working on a thought. After a long silence Amalia whispered, "Mama, do you know what is my favorite part in the *Snow Queen*?"

Anna shook her head. "Tell me."

"When the rose bushes talk to the little girl."

"Yes? What do they say to her?"

Amalia rubbed her eyes. "The roses grow when her tears make the dirt wet. The girl is crying because she can't find her friend and she thinks he is dead, you remember? And then the roses bloom and tell her that they have come from underneath the ground where all the dead people are. But he's not there. So he is still alive and she must never give up on finding him."

"I see," Anna said. "And does she find him?"

"Of course she does. You know the story, Mama."

"I know. I just wanted to make sure the story ends the same way every time. You never know."

"Yes, you do. Stories always end the same." Amalia pushed the full weight of her body against her mother's. "Just in life, it's different. Right?"

"Yes. In life it's different." Anna stroked her daughter's hair. She felt their fate nipping at her heels, as if she was keeping only one step ahead. That was yet to be settled and her sacrifice had not yet come. She wondered how their story would end.

◆ ◆ ◆

Anna did not sleep. As the night deepened she replayed the events of the day in her mind and wondered what had happened after she had run from the Schilling house. Then her thoughts turned to Frieda. A familiar fear gripped her, the same one she had gotten used to carrying with her daily. She thought she left it behind in Kappellendorf and that when the Americans took over she could relinquish it, like an old passport. She wondered how many more like Frieda there were, still clinging to their twisted *Weltanschauung*, their world view that was growing even more hideous in the bright light of its own demise. Finally, just before sunrise, Anna got up and began to write a report of sorts, using Madeleine's old stationery and the stub of a pencil. It took more than five pages to retell everything she had found out. She wanted to clear her thoughts before the hearing in Darmstadt and provide her own account of the events. She would give the report directly to Captain Farmer.

After the sun rose, she rinsed Madeleine's teacup in the sink and then sat for a long time, staring out the kitchen windows as the day came to life. After she cobbled together a breakfast for Amalia and Madeleine, she felt the need to get away from the tiny apartment. Maybe if her legs got moving, her thoughts would settle and steady her nerves for what was coming. The hearing in Darmstadt would put her in the spotlight—her and her communist husband. She had heard that people committed suicide during their interrogations and that some *Ami* officers had beaten women or threatened them with dogs—and worse. She pulled on her boots and stomped her foot on the ground to gather her strength. No sense in worrying about it now.

She left Amalia and Madeleine chewing on their breakfast bread crusts and looking through Amalia's box of treasures. She had put Frieda's pin away in the kitchen drawer, unsure what to do with it. She wanted to hurl it out the window, but, of course, that was ridiculous. She would figure something out later. For now, she walked the streets, half hoping to find Oskar on this quiet morning. The sun was still low in the east, casting the streets in cool, damp shade that smelled of clean night air. She walked up and down, back and forth, for more than an hour. People emerged from their homes and began sweeping the sidewalks as if it mattered. Children climbed the piles of rubble. Old men took up seats on chairs by doorways to wait for something better to come along. Anna picked up the pace and turned back into the Rheinstrasse where she bumped straight into Frau Hermann, dressed in her Sunday finery: black dress with little pleats and mother of pearl buttons on the bodice. It was the same dress nearly every woman in Germany owned. The funeral dress.

"Oh, excuse me," Anna sputtered. "I didn't see you coming."

"Good morning, Frau Klein. I am glad to see you."

"Are you?" Anna heard herself say. She shifted her weight to keep walking but then stopped. "I want to thank you for the eggs and the jam you brought for Auntie. I know she is very grateful. And she is feeling much better."

But Frau Hermann surprised her. "Don't mention it, my dear. We do have to look out for each other don't we? And I am so glad to see you safe and well, especially after what happened yesterday. How is Amalia holding up?"

Anna was shocked. Did the woman really know everything? "I'm sorry?" she said by way of stalling.

Frau Hermann was prepared. "The Schilling house yesterday. I heard about the attack."

"I wouldn't say it was an attack, really it was more of, well, I don't know, really. It was very unfortunate."

"Well, I would certainly call it an attack if one of you ends up in the hospital and the other one in jail." Frau Hermann was clearly pleased to be able to break the news.

"What do you mean?"

"The woman, the sister, whatever her name is. She's in the hospital, near death. Her brother attacked her."

"I don't understand."

Frau Hermann stepped in closer out of habit, as if there was anyone on the street who might overhear. "Yes, my sister-in-law's neighbor told me at church this morning. I go to the early service. She knows the woman who lives next door to the Schillings. Apparently they had an argument and you know the boy—he came to see you the other day—he's not quite right in the head anymore. Anyway, the neighbor heard some shouting but didn't think much of it. There was always a lot of that, what with all the children they keep. The *Amis* came and took the boy away last night. He must have turned himself in because the police just came from nowhere. The sister, she's in bad shape up at the hospital. They don't think she will survive." She sucked on her teeth. "*Furchtbar*. Just terrible."

Anna deflected. "Did he have a weapon?"

"She said she heard it was a letter opener, one of those silver kind. Stabbed her in the throat with it. Can you imagine? It's a wonder she wasn't killed instantly. Poor girl."

Anna regarded Frau Hermann's flushed face. She was breathing hard and the heat was creating little beads of sweat that lined her upper lip between the wispy dark hairs of her mustache. "You know she was SS don't you?" Anna said, as if she had just declared Frieda to have brown eyes instead of blue ones. "Lebensborn," she added. Perhaps Frau Hermann would be willing to spill a few more of her beans.

"*Ach, ja,* Lebensborn, but that was hardly regular SS was it? Taking care of little babies? Doing such womanly work? You can't accuse her of being one of them just for that. You know she was alone and had to fend for herself. She needed a job. What was she going to do?" Frau Hermann dismissed the notion with a roll of the eyes.

Anna was unmoved. "I don't think she just took care of babies. I think she was in the business of having babies. And there were other jobs she could have done," she said, her voice flat. "SS is SS, no matter how pretty you try to make it look."

Frau Hermann waved her away. "Sure it's easy now to point fingers. Anyway, the *Amis* must have already cleared her. She's really just a child herself. If you ask me, it was the brother who was always trouble. And when he came back from the front it was even worse."

"What do you mean?"

"Oh, just different little things. They add up, you know. He was always running around with this woman. Some friend of the family. Tall and blonde, a real beauty. He bought her things and they went places. We all saw them around, and people talked about them. She was much too old for him, and married anyway. I don't know what their relationship was, but it wasn't right. He was just a boy and she should have known better. Then he got shipped off and when he came back from Russia he wasn't the same, always lurking on the black market, looking secretive."

"What happened to the woman?" Anna asked.

"Who knows? Dead, probably. Or moved away, or what do they call it, *verschleppt*? Displaced."

Having lightened her gossip load, Frau Hermann was finished talking and ready to move on. "Anyway, I thought you would want to know. And, I am sure your American will know more. You can always ask him."

"And what about the Schilling boy, where is he?"

"Probably in the jail in the Albrechtstrasse. Just back there." She pointed in the direction Anna had come from. "That's where they take everybody first."

The courts and jail complex in the Albrechtstrasse was only one street over and around the corner from Madeleine's apartment, and Anna looped around on the way back from her walk. She debated the whole way whether or not to go there, but in the end she knew it was the only thing to do. The sprawling building took up the entire block between the Moritzstrasse and the Oranienstrasse and threatened to swallow the people who disappeared inside, swimming like minnows into the shark's mouth. When its heavy door slammed closed behind her, Anna felt claustrophobic immediately. Its black marble floors and white vaulted ceilings were grand, but the air was stale and heavy. A flight of stairs split at the landing, leading off to the left and right. She took the stairs up and approached an old man sitting at the desk and asked for directions to the visitation rooms. He gruffly pointed her back downstairs and instructed her to follow the signs along the corridor.

Anna followed the narrow hallway, turning first one way and then back again. When she felt she had been completely swallowed into the building's bowels of cramped passages, she arrived at the visitation room. She completed the paperwork, produced her own papers for the American guard and sat down to wait. The room was large, but the ceiling was low and the air thick with cigarette smoke. There were no windows and three long tables with attached benches stood in the faint glow of the room's exposed bulbs. The walls closed in on Anna even more.

After a long wait, the door opened and Emil appeared with another guard. Emil looked slight and fragile, as if he had withered overnight. Anna stood, but he motioned for her to stay seated as he sidled onto the bench across the table from her. The guard, who was almost as tall as the door and thin as a broomstick, closed the door and took up his position, close enough to eavesdrop on their conversation.

"Anna. How are you? How is Amalia?" Emil smiled.

"Emil." Anna was so relieved to see him that she had to fight to keep control of her rising emotions.

He rested his shackled hands on the table. "Tell me how Amalia is doing. I hope she was not too scared."

"She is doing well." Anna leaned forward. "How is Frieda?

Emil looked at his hands. "I don't know. They took her to the hospital."

Anna looked at the guard before whispering, "Why did you do this? What on earth–"

"I was so hoping you would come. I need to tell you things. I am glad you are here," he said. "Please, just let me speak, will you?"

Anna closed her mouth and offered him a Lucky Strike from the packet he had given her.

Emil shook his head. "You know the painting I told you I took from the villa, the picture of the little girl standing on the chair?"

Anna nodded.

"It's disappeared. I took it because it was one of the only ones there that still had the original label on it. Schneider had gotten busy tearing the labels off and putting fake ones on. And Breuer's was a well-known gallery in this area, so I figured that was probably the most famous painting in that whole lot. And now it's gone. I was going to give it to you and that *Ami* of yours, but then it got taken."

Anna nodded and turned the cigarette packet over in her hands as she waited for more.

"I took it to my house and was going to explain the whole thing to you. I left you a note at your desk. But you didn't come, and then I lost my head and we fought. In the alleyway, you remember? And then the painting was gone. So it's all a big mess now."

"Yes, I remember. But, Emil, how did you even know about the art at the villa?" Anna tried to piece the story together.

"Because my sister worked there when it was a home for children—the Lebensborn home. And she let Schneider hide it there. He gave her a cut, of course. The Gestapo caught him, but they never caught her or found the art. And he kept his mouth shut so she'd keep his secret."

Anna shook her head. "Frieda and Schneider? But how do they even know each other?"

"I'm getting to that," Emil said. "But now that the painting is gone, I can't prove any of this."

"Actually, I know where the painting is, don't worry," Anna said.

"You do?"

"Yes, it's safe. So the fake labels were supposed to throw the *Amis* off the path when they tried to return the paintings to their owners?"

"Yes, but it was a stupid idea, I thought. The *Amis* would have figured it out pretty soon. But maybe not if Schneider was the one processing the art the Collecting Point. Do you see?"

Anna nodded. "But why didn't you tell the Monuments Men all this?"

"I didn't know at first that's what their job at the Collecting Point was. No one ever explained it to me. I was just fixing the plumbing. When I figured out that they were in charge of returning stolen art, I saw my chance to do the right thing. I took the painting and had it in my apartment. I swear, I was going to take it to the *Amis*. But it's large and not so easy to smuggle around. So before I could get it out of the house, Frieda must have found it and given it back to Schneider."

Anna remembered following Schneider with the package. "And he gave it to Schenk." She paused. "And they used it to bribe the Major in Frankfurt. So he would push Schneider through. Pretty clever. But what about Schenk? Who is he anyway?"

Emil smiled. "There is no Schenk. He took that name from one of Schneider's friends who died years ago. His real name is Gerhardt Heinrich."

Anna's mind began to focus as Emil continued. "Heinrich owned a gallery in Mainz before the war. I met him because he was the brother of a close friend who was a painter and whose work he sold. I bought one or two paintings, just for fun. But then he began working at the Reichskulturkammer in Frankfurt with Schneider before he got promoted to the ERR. The Einsatzstab Reichsleiter Rosenberg. They were nothing more than art thieves. Not that I gave a damn about some stolen pieces of art. There was so much else to worry about. But Heinrich was one of the best looters and as ruthless as any SS *Sturmbannführer* to hear him tell it. Went to Vienna, Paris, God knows where, and came back with art that was worth millions. Took from all of the big Jewish collectors, sent a lot of people to concentration camps, left a lot of corpses in his wake. All for a few paintings. He was too high-profile to disappear back into the swamp. So he changed his name."

Anna had a flash of recognition. "He's on my list of gallery owners, Heinrich is. He's marked deceased."

Emil nodded. He shot a look at the guard and rubbed the frostbitten stumps of his fingers. "That's right. He got himself a fake death certificate. And all that stuff at the villa? Schneider stole from Jewish families too. He was supposed to give it to his bosses, but he kept it for himself. They found out and sent him to Dachau, but they never found the stash, thanks to my sister. She helped him hide it at the villa. She met him through Gerhard Heinrich. I think she was sort of sweet on Heinrich, even though he was much to old for her. They met at a Party rally and then she wanted to prove herself as a true believer so he would like her. She was pretty and she had the right look, she knew that, but it wasn't enough. You had to prove your commitment. He knew it, too—that she would do anything for him. So when he asked her to help his good friend Schneider, of course she did. By then she was up to her waist in the SS—literally—and had become a bigger believer than Heinrich and Himmler put together. Heinrich gave her paintings to keep her cooperative, even though he didn't need to anymore. She would have done anything for him.

"I thought those two cretins had vanished and that she would come to her senses, but first Schneider and then Heinrich turned up again, like they are indestructible. It turned out the art was all still down there in the basement, but now they saw the *Amis* taking all the stuff and wanted to make sure they stayed in business. When you found the stash at the villa I had already told the police—the Americans—about it. Somehow it got all turned around and they thought Captain Cooper was to blame. Also, there was a rat in the larder." Emil lowered his voice. "Someone was keeping tabs on what you and Cooper were doing and reporting it back to Schneider."

"Let me guess. That Corporal. Miller," Anna said.

"That's right. He tried to incriminate you to the police. It was Miller who gave Schneider your address so he could bribe you. That was their first try to get to you. How did you know?"

"I think I found Miller's payment. From Schneider. At the villa."

"It was all small-time stuff until I heard all about your meeting at the Nassauer Hof. Heinrich—the one you know as Schenk—and Frieda talked about it later that night after you met him. Heinrich was furious. I knew you had stepped into something you didn't understand. And when you mentioned to me that you were looking to buy travel papers, I knew the offer must have come from him. He was going to set you up, to get to you somehow. And that's how Frieda saw her chance to help him again. She was going to use Amalia to get to you. I was trying to tell you, but I didn't know how."

Anna sank into her chair feeling angry and stupid and furious. *How could you have been so trusting?* "I'm sorry Emil. I really misunderstood you."

"Don't. It doesn't matter now. I didn't know what she was doing. I thought she was done with all that like I am. Otherwise I never would have let her keep Amalia. Never. You have to believe me. She is my sister. I wanted to believe she was not one of them, like the crazies I dealt with at the front. That she was not like that. But then I found that room in the basement. And I heard what she told the children. She was always asking Amalia about you and what you were doing. She would give her treats in exchange for a promise not to tell you about it. I was an idiot. The whole country is full of idiots like me."

"But why did you do it Emil? Why did you try to kill her? Your own sister."

Emil said nothing for a long time. When he finally began to speak, he looked Anna directly in the eye, as if to imprint the words. "Sometimes, before I went to the front, I would go to the Lebensborn home and play with the children. I was a bit of a true believer myself. We all thought the war would be over in a year, and then there would be a glorious future for Germany. It was all so bright and shiny and clean, with happy little babies and families coming to take them to nice homes. I didn't know what it all meant, not until I went to Russia and saw what we were really doing."

Anna tried again. "But why didn't you just tell the *Amis* about Frieda? There are processes to deal with people like her. Why not just report her?"

"Because no one would listen to me. Who believes a nobody like me? A crazy soldier? Not about the painting, not about her. The *Amis* had cleared her. They didn't know anything about Lebensborn. She said she was a nurse, they believed her and there we are. So I dealt with it myself. Because she is not sorry, not at all, not for anything she did." He rubbed his palms as his shoulders slumped and his head tilted to one side, as if he had no more strength to hold it up. "I don't deserve to be out there. And neither does she. I didn't do the right thing so many times when I should have. So I am doing it now."

"Oh, Emil. I am sorry. But this is not the way to go about it. Don't you know that?"

"Anna, you have no idea. So many times I wanted to do the right thing. Every day I had the chance. But I never did. I was too scared of what they would do to me. And now I have nightmares, every night. Always they are the same."

"Tell me," Anna said. "It will help if you talk about it. Really."

Emil stared into the distance. When he spoke it was so quiet that Anna had to lean forward to hear. "I saw her one day, standing in the middle of a field. It was in the Ukraine. We had been marching all day and the weather was hot. We were so tired. We came over the hill and saw the troop of the *Einsatzgruppe*, you know, the special killing squads, that was ahead of us pulled over on the side of the road. They were supposed to have been hours ahead of us, to the next town. But these guys had pulled over and were running around in the field, scaring the women working there. They'd run at them with fixed bayonets and scream and carry on. One of them was taking photographs." He turned his head and looked at the guard who stared straight ahead.

"Then I saw one of them," Emil continued. "He was pointing his K98 right at a woman. She was carrying a small child, a baby. He had already shot her cow, it was lying on the ground mooing and snorting. She tried to shield the baby from him with her shoulder, turning her body away from him. As if that would do any good. And the only thing I could think was, which one is he going to shoot first? The baby or the mother? If he shoots the baby first, the mother will live the horror of watching her child die. But she knows if he shoots her first, she can't protect her baby. And then his friend came with the camera. To take a picture, can you imagine? I couldn't believe what had become of us. Were we all animals? Why were we acting like this?" He paused and stared into empty space behind Anna.

"And there wasn't a damn thing I could do. They kept us full of vodka and threatened to kill our families if we didn't follow orders. And they would have shot me if I stepped out of line and then shot her anyway. Now I wish I had done it, then none of this would be happening. But then, we didn't know up from down anymore, we were so tired and scared. We all just kept marching like nothing was happening. And then he shot her. She fell, and dropped the baby. It started crying." He looked at Anna. "And then he shot the baby. Just like that." He snapped his fingers.

Anna pressed her lips together. She slid her hand across the table and took hold of Emil's. It was ice cold. As she squeezed his fingers he moved his eyes to meet hers. They held only despair and anguish in their dark blue pools. His easy smile and sweet nature had been destroyed. He was completely broken.

He cocked his head. "I see her every day. Her skirt blowing in the wind, her hand over the baby's head. The last thing she saw in this life was us, German soldiers, marching past her, watching the show. No one could help her." He wiped his nose with the back of his hand and exhaled. "Don't you wonder what's going to become of us? After all this?"

Anna closed her eyes. The war may have been over but now the world seemed full of people acting out their own internal conflicts. Keeping the cause going, making amends, giving up, whatever it was. When you empty the world of all its goodness, people will fill it with anything that makes them feel better.

"Emil, I wish I could take your pain from you."

"All right, time's up, Schilling. Say your good-byes," the guard said flatly. He jingled his keys to make his point.

Emil stood and pulled Anna to her feet. "Now I've told you everything. And I do feel better." He held her hand against his cheek and closed his eyes. Anna smiled and felt a small spark of hope surge in her chest. As the guard pushed Emil through the door, he turned to look at her. As their eyes met, Anna felt a panic take hold of her and she grabbed his shoulder. "Emil, you must tell them everything you know," she said. "You did a good thing with the painting. They will show you mercy. And I will tell them too. I have a hearing tomorrow. I will tell them everything you've told me. It will be all right, I know it." She knew no such thing but could think of nothing else to say.

He smiled at her as if she were a child. Taking her hand again, he put it to his mouth for a kiss. In that moment, she could feel his torment for herself.

"Goodbye, Anna. Don't cry, please," he said. "I do feel better that you came. Thank you." He let go of her hand, nodded at the guard, and was gone.

chapter twenty-three

Anna tugged at the belt that was attempting to keep Otto's pants from sliding down over her hips. Either the belt was stretching or she had lost more weight. The room was hot and the air smelled of food cooking—or maybe it was body odor, it was hard to tell. The chair the *Amis* had given her had one leg shorter than the others, causing it to wobble and make a scraping sound on the wood floor. She rocked in her seat, back and forth, as she stared at the green metal door at the other end of the room. "Wait here. Someone will be here to escort you shortly," the little corporal with the oily face and thick waist had told her. That had been a while ago. Footsteps on the other side of the door came and went and voices murmured, but the door never moved. It was like waiting for the doctor, Anna thought.

She reviewed her planned testimony in her head. Cooper suggested she stick to just the pertinent facts: stolen art found in villa, plot to infiltrate the Collecting Point to influence the restitution of those paintings, bribing an American officer and lying on the *Fragebogen* that had failed to be processed before offering Schneider the plum job. Anna felt uneasy about implicating any *Amis* in the wrongdoing, but she knew she would have to speak up if she was going to tell the truth.

"Frau Klein?" An American soldier with the crisp look of fresh laundry stood in the open door. "Please come with me. They are ready for you." He held an arm out to usher her through the door and led the way down the long hallway. Anna could feel her stomach lurch upward, then downward, not sure of which direction to issue its protest. She could not help letting out a small gasp when the GI pushed open another, bigger door and she saw the panel of American officers sitting along a long table raised up on a pedestal. Their five heads turned toward her, expressionless and dull-eyed, before returning to the paperwork in front of them. Anna scanned the room. There was a small table with two chairs, both facing the panel. An MP stood, legs splayed, in front of an open window at the corner of the room and a stenographer—an older woman with a tight blond bun and wrinkles like rivulets—sat in the other corner.

"Take a seat, Frau Klein," the American head in the middle of the panel said. He wore thick glasses and a tired expression, both sitting on his face uncomfortably like a bad disguise. "We'll get started shortly, just as soon as—" He stopped speaking when the door opened.

Anna turned, expecting to see Cooper, but instead found herself looking at Major Phillips, who strode toward the *Amis* without looking in her direction.

"Jim, so good to see you. Thanks for coming on short notice." The middle one stood and extended a hand. "This won't take long. Sorry for all the formality, but we need to get the book closed on this nonsense once and for all so we can get on with our lives." He gestured to an empty chair at the end of the table. "Have a seat and we'll get started." He turned his face to Anna as Phillips lowered himself into the seat.

"Now, Frau Klein, let's start with the basics. State your full name and present address for the record. I trust you have brought all your papers with you?" He looked at her, eyebrows raised with expectation.

Anna was unprepared for things proceeding without Cooper. She thought they would have sat at the table together, providing corroboration for each other's stories, he helping her understand the strange way *Amis* talked when doing official business. Where was he this time?

"Frau Klein?" The American tapped his pencil.

"Yes, sir, I just want to ask, I thought Captain Cooper would be here as well?"

"We can start without him, I'm sure he won't miss anything important."

Phillips cleared his throat. "Actually, I'm also waiting on someone myself, but we can go ahead and get started. He should be here soon, and I need to get back to Frankfurt before lunch."

All eyes turned to Anna and she felt the blood rise in her cheeks. She willed her voice to steady as she stated her particulars in reply to the middle one's questions. As she spoke she scanned the other members of the panel. They were various incarnations of tired, gray men who seemed disinterested in her existence, much less her reason for being there.

The one on the right, a balding, thin man with a nearly square face, cleared his throat as he straightened his papers. He did not look at her when he spoke.

"Frau Klein, please state your case as clearly and succinctly as you can."

Anna nodded and began recounting the events of the day when she and Cooper found the stash of art. She was unsure how much detail to go into without confusing the main points of her report. It was like trying to tell the plot of a novel—you always felt like you had to go back and explain things you left out. She began to sweat. Before she could get to the part about the missing Runge painting, the middle *Ami* held up a hand.

"Just a moment. You are telling me that you and Captain Cooper found this hidden stash of art in a basement in this abandoned villa. So it was taken to the Collecting Point, yes? What exactly is the problem? Please get to the point."

"Sir, if you'll let me continue, I will tell you the problem." Anna controlled the irritation seeping into her voice.

The *Ami* on the right sighed. Phillips crossed his arms in front of his chest and looked at Anna as if to dare her to go on.

"What I am saying is that by the time the art came to the Collecting Point, one of the pieces was missing. It was at about this time that Herr Ludwig Schneider was referred to us, to Captain Cooper, by Major Phillips for a position at the Collecting Point."

"So?" a new *Ami*, the one on the left, spoke. "How do you know one of the pieces was missing? And what does Herr Schneider have to do with it?"

"I am getting to that, sir. I know one of the pieces was missing because I remember it from the villa. When the art arrived at the Collecting Point we saw right away that a particular painting was not among them. I know this for sure." Now she was lying. The only reason she knew the Runge was missing was because Emil had stolen it after beating up Cooper in the middle of the night. She licked her lips. "And then the very same painting turned up in the possession of Major Phillips."

"I fail to see how any of this ridiculous story is even provable," Major Phillips snorted. "I don't have any painting. I sent Schneider over to the CP because they needed qualified people. He's a restorer and knowledgable about art. Doesn't he deserve a job as much as you do, Frau Klein?"

Anna paused and considered her options. She decided to go all in before they could interrupt her again. "Herr Schneider is working with Konrad Schenk to bribe American officials in order to receive favorable treatment and gain access to the art at the Collecting Point and influence its restitution. The art from the villa, which Herr Schneider claims is his, was stolen from Jewish collectors and gallery owners by him and the man you know as Herr Schenk. They should have turned it over to the Reichskulturkammer but they didn't. They kept it for themselves. It's all stolen. And Konrad Schenk is not really who he says he is anyway. His real name is Gerhart Heinrich. He was one of the most prolific art thieves in the Third Reich." She had blurted out the whole story almost in one breath.

A smile appeared on the middle one's face just before he let out a lengthy chuckle. "Well, Frau Klein, that's quite a story. Why don't you slow down and tell us how you intend to prove any of this. These are very serious charges. Are you aware of the consequences of making false accusations against an American officer?"

Anna looked at Phillips who wore a bemused expression. She remembered his yelling at Cooper the day she overheard them from the bottom of the stairs. Then he had seemed like a man under pressure. Now he was a man in total control. He had them all in his pocket. He knew something she didn't know.

The middle Ami looked at his watch. "Let me ask you again, Frau Klein. How can you prove that one of the paintings is missing, not to mention any of the other accusations you are making?"

A scraping sound announced the door opening, and Anna swung around hoping finally to see Cooper's face. Instead, this time it was Konrad Schenk. He strode into the room, his hand extended toward Major Phillips, who stood and returned the greeting with a smile as if seeing an old school friend.

"I am sorry to have kept you all waiting, I hope it's not an inconvenience," Schenk said in clear English. He slid into the chair next to Phillips and faced Anna. "Frau Klein." He cocked his head in her direction and then spoke in English. "Good morning, Frau Klein."

The American spoke, loudly this time, as if to sound more insistent. "Frau Klein is just telling us about how you, Herr Schenk, are not really you, and that along with Ludwig Schneider, you are conspiring to steal from the United States Army just as you stole from the Nazis and the Jews, apparently. She claims you gave Major Phillips a painting in order to earn his support, and, was there anything else you wanted to add Frau Klein?"

Anna squared her shoulders and sat up. "And there's a boy involved too. He was living at the villa and—"

"Oh, yes, a boy, living in an abandoned house," Schenk interrupted. "You want to blame that on me too? Anything else you'd like to blame on me? Hunger? Bombings? Genocide? I mean, we're all guilty now aren't we?" He laughed and Anna was surprised to see the *Amis* join in, as if Schenk was the floor show at a dinner theater.

When the chuckling had dissipated, the middle one spoke again. "Let me ask you, Herr Schenk, do you know of a—what was the name—Gerhart Heinrich?"

"Of course I know him. He had a small gallery in Mainz. He was well-known in the business. But he's passed away. He was rather on in years."

"So would you say that people in Wiesbaden would know if you were Gerhart Heinrich?"

Schenk laughed. "It's a joke, no? Everyone knew Heinrich. What a stupid idea."

"Do you have any idea why Frau Klein would make such an accusation against you?"

Schenk turned the corners of his mouth downward and rocked his head from side to side to ponder the possibilities. He shrugged. "I can't honestly say. I do know that Frau Klein has been asking around for travel papers for her husband, the good Doctor Thomas Klein of Thuringia. Perhaps she thinks implicating me in some imaginary scheme will get her in your good graces. She even asked me for assistance by trying to sell me a painting, which is, of course, in clear violation of your laws. I refused to help her, so perhaps this is her retribution. It's possible her husband has abandoned her and her little girl—no doubt it's a terrifying thought for a woman alone. She is desperate." He paused and turned directly to the Americans, who seemed more interested now. "Her husband is a communist, you know. He was well known to have participated in an underground movement to overthrow the government. I can only assume her political convictions are similar. Rather than question my credentials, I would perhaps ask you why the United States Army would have a communist in their employ." He smiled as the Americans shifted in their seats. The square-faced one cleared his throat. None of them looked at Schenk.

Anna reeled from the assault and tried to comprehend what she had just heard. She, a communist? This was the second time he had made this insinuation. Had she walked into a trap? Had Emil lied to her? Had she jumped to conclusions, wanting to believe Emil's story to explain everything that had happened? Had he really set her up instead, to face this moment?

"Frau Klein, answer the question," the middle *Ami* barked. Now he was interested in her.

"I'm sorry?" Anna stammered.

"I said, are you a communist?"

"No, I am not. I was never a communist. I was never a Nazi either. I never…" she sputtered, angry now. How dare these men turn on her this way? "I am just a German, a mother, trying to rebuild my life. I came here to tell the truth and that is what I am doing. I stand by everything I said."

"I'll ask one more time. How do you intend to prove your story? It is your word against that of Major Phillips."

"Captain Cooper will support my story. You should ask him. And why don't you ask Major Phillips how the obtained the painting that he has in his office. The one his secretary is trying to get appraised for him," Anna replied, but she knew she had already lost.

Phillips leaned forward. "Young lady, what paintings I do or do not have in my office is hardly any of your concern. I resent very strongly your implication that I am guilty of any wrongdoing. How dare you impugn my reputation? Who the hell do you think you are?" he snarled, spitting the words at her.

The American on the panel who had not yet spoken finally cleared his throat. "Frau Klein, we cannot accept your accusations based on nothing but your opinion. We require some kind of documentation about the painting, about Herr Schenk. A photograph, an inventory, even a witness. Anything that will support the story you have told us. Unless you can produce some proof, I'm afraid there's nothing we can do. All we know is that you and Captain Cooper have been running amok in the Collecting Point and we have to put a stop to that."

Anna sank back in her chair. She was being ambushed. Cooper had thrown her to the wolves. Was he on their side, too? When the middle *Ami* spoke again she barely heard him over the rush of voices in her head.

"And under no circumstances can we have a communist among our civilian workforce. Frau Klein, is it your wish to be reunited with your husband in Thuringia? It can be arranged for you to return to him in the Russian sector. In fact, that is my recommendation. That would be preferable for all involved, would it not?"

"No, I do not wish to go back," Anna said. "My husband is coming here to be with us. I have done nothing wrong. I am not a communist." A bilious panic rose in her throat. *Damn that Cooper.*

The square-faced *Ami* spoke. "Am I to understand that you are living here with your daughter?"

"Yes, she—"

"And you are the sole caretaker for her, is that right?"

"Yes."

"That's not true. She lives with her aunt, a Frau Wolf. In the Adolfsallee," Schenk volunteered.

The *Ami* ignored him and turned to the panel. "I suggest we look into her case further, but as the sole caretaker of a small child we cannot remand her into custody without creating even more work for ourselves. However, I recommend that Frau Klein be officially removed from her position at the Collecting Point and be prohibited from taking any work with the Occupation Forces, pending further investigation into her case."

The middle one did not waste a second to advance this idea. "Agreed. Frau Klein, you are no longer employed at the Collecting Point, effective immediately. Your status is pending and you are forbidden to leave the city of Wiesbaden. You may go now, but expect to hear from us in the next few days. You might prepare yourself and your daughter for a return journey to Thuringia."

The panel stood, gathered their papers, and made their way to the door, followed by Phillips. Schenk lingered until the others had filed out of the room and shot a quick glance at the MP as he approached Anna.

"I told you to watch yourself, you stupid girl," he said. "Not even your *Ami* can help you now. Where is he anyway? He's in as much hot water as you are."

Anna regarded him with a cool look that belied her fear. "Don't worry about me, Herr Heinrich. No matter what, I will be *okay*, I promise you." She pushed past him and walked out the door.

Anna lay on the bed, listening to Amalia playing with Lulu on the floor. Madeleine lay next to Anna in a restless sleep, her breathing shallow. Anna turned over the damp compress on the woman's forehead to keep her cool. Anna had not slept for a second night, her subconscious mind working on something that she didn't yet comprehend. A revelation was buried deep, where she could not access it. It churned under every thought and action like something waiting for the outlet to erupt.

The unease from the events of the past few days sat with Anna but she ignored it, putting it in a corner of her mind like a troublesome child. Only the anger at Emil kept boiling over. If he had lied to her, why? Was he really working with Schenk? If the idea was to get rid of her, he had certainly done a good job of letting her hang herself. Anna still had not told Amalia about Emil's attack on Frieda. She hadn't told anyone about anything that had happened. The girl seemed content to distract herself. She had gotten very good at not asking questions.

Anna dipped into her mind's vortex and pulled out a thought. Up came the name Gerhard Heinrich. Konrad Schenk's real name. She rolled over, reached into her bag, and pulled out the list she had taken from the file room. Sitting up and crossing her legs, she flattened the page onto the bed. Her finger ran down the list of known gallery owners and found what she was looking for. There he was, Gerhart Heinrich, as a gallery owner in Mainz, marked deceased, just as Schenk had said. But there was something else that she could not remember about him. Something Emil had said that seemed to want to attach itself to the name, but just she couldn't catch it.

She stood and pulled the drapes closed to keep the light from Madeleine's face, then pulled on her shoes. "Maus you stay here. I'll only be gone a little while," Anna said, patting Amalia on the head. "If you need anything, go and tell Frau Hermann, don't bother Auntie, all right?"

"Yes, Mama," Amalia said, distracted.

Anna slung her bag over her shoulder and rode the bicycle to the Albrechstrasse as quickly as she could. It took only a few minutes to get there; her urge to confront Emil about the story he had fed her kept her moving against some invisible deadline. By the time she arrived at the end of the warren of corridors, she was sweating and out of breath. The visitor line was long and the close quarters made her feel sick to her stomach. She would ask Emil directly if he was lying, if he had set her up all along. She also suspected it was Emil who knew where the missing camera and its film with the photos of the art had gone. Why steal the painting if he knew there were photos? Without the photo, the story was impossible to prove. He must have taken the camera from Cooper's office in order to make his story work. Anna raged silently as she waited.

When she finally got to the small window at the front, the American sitting behind the desk looked at her papers. Despite his earnest demeanor, he was very young, his cheeks betraying the remnants of baby fat.

He looked up. "You are here to see who?"

"Emil Schilling," Anna said. "I was here yesterday. I should be on his list."

The guard held up her papers. "Just a minute, ma'am." He walked to the back of the office and conferred with another *Ami*, this one of higher rank. After a lengthy exchange, the second man nodded, took her papers and walked back to the window.

"You're Anna Klein?" he asked.

Anna nodded.

"Come with me, please," he said, and unlocked the door next to the window. He ushered her through to a small office and closed the door behind them.

"Please, have a seat." The *Ami* pulled out a chair for her, then sat down across the desk. He was older and had a kind face. His black hair was greased back and his large ears stood out from his head. When he spoke, his voice was soft—like a kindly priest or doctor sent to reassure her. Anna's thoughts had already gotten away from her but she didn't dare follow them.

"Are you Emil Schilling's next of kin? Are you his family?" he asked.

Anna shook her head. "No. I am just a friend.

"Well, Frau Klein, I am only supposed to talk to his family, but we haven't been able to find anyone aside from his sister, who is too incapacitated. Since you are here I will tell you." He folded his hands on the desk and waited several seconds before continuing. "I am very sorry to tell you this. Emil Schilling was found dead in his cell this morning."

Anna felt the air go very still. Her skin prickled. She blinked at the American.

"Excuse me?"

"He took his own life. I am very sorry."

Anna shook her head. "I don't understand. It's not—"

"He hanged himself with his own shirt. It was...torn into strips and then, well, never mind." He said. "I am very sorry to have to give you this news."

Anna nodded. She didn't know what to do or say.

The American cleared his throat. "And there's one more thing." He pulled a piece of paper from his breast pocket and pushed it across the desk. "He left this specifically for you. Since he named you in this letter, I feel comfortable that I am not breaking protocol in telling you the news." He stood. "I'll leave you alone. Take your time. I am very sorry for your loss, ma'am."

When he had closed the door, Anna sat motionless for several minutes. Maybe if she didn't move none of this would be real. Maybe it hadn't really happened. If she could stop time, then she'd never have to leave the room and try to absorb what she had just learned. She could not let herself feel anything for fear of losing control.

After a long while, when she could no longer endure the questions that needled her, she pulled the letter toward her and focused her eyes on the uneven script. At the top Emil had printed the words "my last will and testament" in capital letters. Underneath were five lines written in a schoolboy's careful hand, followed by his signature:

> *I have only one meaningful worldly possession: the painting of the Rhein that hangs in my apartment. It is not valuable, but it reminds me of my happiest days. The artist was my friend. She and her family are dead, so I bequeath the painting to my friend Anna Klein and her daughter Amalia, who showed me compassion and grace. I wish them a long and happy life together. I hope they remember me fondly.*

When she had finished reading Emil's words a second time, Anna laid her head on the desk, resting her cheek on top of the paper. A searing ache started inside her hands and flowed up her arms until it filled her entire body. She closed her eyes and let it submerge her. There was nothing else she could do.

Anna stepped out into the street and shaded her eyes with a hand that had only just begun to stop shaking. She stared at her feet on the ground and waited for her eyes to adjust as she gave silent thanks that at least she was out of the building. The vision of Emil refused to go away—his body swinging from the rafters, the rags of his torn up shirt around his broken neck. It was so strong and clear that it was as if she had to look past it to see where she was going. She pushed his letter into her pocket, picked up her bicycle and began pedaling hard and fast away from the jail—but the image kept pace. She could not shake it. Before she realized where she was going she turned the corner into the Gustav-Freitag-Strasse.

Anna felt as if she was being pulled on an invisible string controlled by something much larger than herself. She was without fear or sadness or even anger as she pushed open the gate and walked around to the back of the house, then down the stairs to the basement entry. She pulled hard on the door with both hands, each tug growing stronger, as if her life depended on it. After several tries it came off the frame altogether, thanks to the wood rot from some long-ago flood. Anna went ahead into the darkness, feeling her way along the brick wall until she found the light switch and the door to the house.

Emil's apartment was unlocked, and inside it was still as tidy as when Anna had seen it last, except now the air felt stifling and old. Not sure what she was looking for, she began pulling open drawers and wardrobe doors, rifling through clothing and papers with increasing force and speed. Something had to give her an answer, to explain Emil's story. In the living room she lifted the sofa cushions and threw them across the room and pulled books from the shelf. She dug through the drawers of the little desk in the corner, finding only old stamps, ration books, and a few letters. Sweating now, she lay on the floor and reached a hand under the sofa, running it along the floor, groping at nothing. In the back corner, her fingers bumped over something. She stretched her arm, wedging her head under the couch, but she couldn't reach it. She peered into the darkness and could only make out a little boxy shape. Pushing herself to her feet, she yanked the sofa away from the wall and kneeled on the seat to look over its back. In the dusty corner lay a small metal camera. She almost let out a cheer as she pulled the camera up into her lap to examine it. It was American, for sure. The Kodak 35 insignia across the top proved that. *Made in the USA*. She turned it over and popped up the viewfinder. The crack was unmistakable. It was Cooper's camera.

Elated, she peered though the viewfinder and pressed the shutter, but it did not respond. She turned the winding wheel with her thumb and groaned when it kept turning without hitting a stop. There was no film inside.

She hurled the camera at the wall and fell forward, holding her head in her hands. A scream forced itself from her lungs and she pushed it out with the force of the rage that finally overtook her. Of course, Schenk had the film. Emil probably gave it to him. They had all set her up. She had walked right into it. She buried her head in her hands and began to weep, not just for herself or for Cooper or for the damn Runge painting, but for having failed at this little, miserable attempt to do right. To fix this one thing that meant nothing in the bigger scheme, in the story that would be told of what happened in the war, of all the horrors that had been perpetrated. Not even this one stupid little story about a stolen painting would have a happy end. They had won. She was absolutely useless after all.

"Forget it," Anna said out loud when she finally stood up. "I am finished. We will just go home to Kappellendorf. I am tired. I give up."

She crossed the room to pick up the camera and wiped her eyes with the back of her sleeve. It wasn't until she walked past the landscape painting that hung near the door that she remembered Emil's letter. Anna blinked at the picture. '*The painting of the Rhein that hangs in my apartment.*' Was this the painting Emil had left to her? The one she had noticed the day she found Amalia in the basement with Frieda? She looked around. There was no other landscape painting anywhere, only portraits and old photos. It was surely by the same artist as the one she had tried to sell to Schneider. And now Emil, who had known the artist, was gone. No Emil, no film, no way to prove anything. She stared at the painting. Not knowing what else to do, she lifted it from the wall and closed the door as she left the apartment.

In the foyer, she paused, looking up the stairs to Frieda's apartment. Broken glass from the door above trailed down to the ground floor, probably from the ambulance drivers who carried her, or from the men who arrested Emil. Anna imagined the final scene that took place just upstairs between brother and sister: Emil drunk and enraged, stabbing his sister in the throat with a letter opener. Frieda staggering and falling, Emil calmly going to telephone the police and confessing. She wondered how they had ended up in the living room, when the fight had begun in the basement. Had he followed her upstairs with the intent of attacking her? Had he come up for the letter opener and she followed? Anna remembered sitting on the sofa eating *Apfelstrudel*, the tour of the playroom and Frieda's first kindnesses. Anna thought she had found a friend, someone to rely on. Instead she had walked into her own demise. She hoisted the painting under her arm. Maybe she could take it back to Kappellendorf as souvenir of her brief taste of freedom. As a reminder of what could have been.

chapter twenty-four

Madeleine and Amalia were listening to the American radio station as Anna sat on the kitchen stool leafing through the list of gallery owners and staring at the SS pin laying on the table, almost afraid to touch it. How had Frieda gotten past the *Amis*? Were they checking anyone at all? Everyone walking around Germany now had a past full of secrets and Anna felt stupid for ever having thought otherwise. She unfolded Oskar's papers and searched the form again for any clues. She had no doubt that he must have spent time at the children's home at the villa. Had he been one of the children borne by the young women doing their duty for the Reich? He certainly had the perfect Aryan look and the attitude to go along with it.

A loud knock on the door made her jump. She looked out the window. The sun had set and the curfew was nearly in effect. She wondered if she should get the gun resting on her toilet tank. The knock came again. After sliding the SS pin and the papers into the kitchen drawer, she stepped into the hall. "Who's there?" she asked into the door frame.

"It's me, Frau Klein. Oskar."

Anna pulled the door open and saw Cooper's smiling face. His hands rested on Oskar's shoulders.

"Guess who I found?" He pushed Oskar toward her.

"Oskar!" Anna said, making her voice bright. "Where have you been?"

"I caught him digging through the trash behind the mess hall after dinner. One of the guys chased him off, but I grabbed him."

Anna opened the door wide and motioned them both inside. "He ran away from the camp. Didn't you?" she said. She wanted to yell at the boy and throw the blame for everything that had happened that day at his feet. Of course that was unfair, but it was easy. He was dirty and his legs were bloodied and scraped. A large bruise circled his right eye.

"Oh my God, Oskar, you poor boy. What's happened?" She reached out to him, but Oskar winced and jerked away.

"So, you want him? Or should I take him back to the DP camp?" Cooper asked.

Oskar crossed his arms but kept his eyes locked on Anna.

"Oskar, it's you!" Amalia ran toward him and nearly knocked him off his feet. "Mama can he stay?" She wrapped her little arms around his shoulders and squeezed.

"He can stay," Anna said. "Let's get him cleaned up." She ushered the boy into the living room and got him situated on the sofa. "Maus, introduce Oskar to Auntie and you all stay here while I talk to Captain Cooper."

Cooper stood by the door as if to make an easy escape. Before Anna could speak, he held up a finger. "I know. I am just as mad as you are about the hearing. Believe me, there was no way for me to get there. I got called to a meeting in Frankfurt and I had to be there. Phillips set me up, I swear. And I know you want to tell me all about it, but let's do that tomorrow. I—" He stopped as Anna brushed past him into the bathroom, ignoring him. When she re-emerged she presented Cooper's Colt to him on the palms of her hands as if it were a special dessert.

"I believe this is yours," she said.

Cooper drew a sharp breath and shook his head. Taking the gun, he turned it over in his hand, inspecting it from all angles. "Do I want to know where you got this?" he asked without meeting her eyes.

"From Emil Schilling. He was the one who took it from you from you that night at the villa."

"Your *Wehrmacht* friend? Well, shit. You've got to be kidding me. How do you figure that?"

"He told me. He also told me that he saw the Runge painting there. He's our witness. Except he's dead."

"Say again?"

"I'll have to tell you the whole story another time," Anna said.

"Emil? Is dead? But how is it that you have my gun now?" Cooper asked, tilting his head sideways, the same way he had the first day they met in the hallway outside the typing pool.

"I don't have your gun. You do." Anna said. "And you should probably go now." She walked to the door and pulled the handle.

Cooper holstered the weapon but made no move to the door. "You're really not going to tell me?"

"Not tonight," Anna said. "I am too tired."

"Okay," Cooper said. "Sure thing." He stepped out onto the landing but couldn't resist one final attempt. "There's nothing at all you want to tell me?"

"There is a lot I want to tell you, but it will have to wait. You will receive my report tomorrow. I will bring it to the Collecting Point."

"Oh, good, so you are coming back to work? Everything turned out okay?"

"No, it didn't. It didn't turn out *okay*,"Anna sneered. "Now, please just go."

Cooper tried one more time but Anna opened the door and waited.

"Okay, I'm going," he said. "But this isn't the end of the story."

"No it's not. It's not the end of your story," Anna said, and closed the door before he could see her tears. *But it might be the end of ours.*

"Start from the beginning," Madeleine said as she stroked Anna's hair. "Tell me everything."

Anna sank into the bed and began recounting the events of the past few days. The children were downstairs playing in the courtyard. Oskar had barely tolerated Anna cleaning him up, but he had not lashed out at her as he usually did. Their laughter floated through the open window and Anna thought it made life seem almost normal. It had been a long time since she had heard the sounds of children playing outside her window. But as she told Madeleine about Emil and Frieda and the disastrous hearing, the familiar anger rose up in her. She felt helpless and used, like she was a pawn in someone else's game. She had felt that way for as long as she could remember.

When Anna had finished, Madeleine squeezed her hand. "That poor Schilling girl. And the boy too. It's just terrible, even after all that's happened. May God rest his soul. When will you tell Amalia?"

"Oh I don't know. I suppose I'll need to tell her soon enough. It depends on what happens with the *Amis*. Maybe we'll be gone and I won't have to tell her."

"Now stop that. You aren't going anywhere. Look, this not as bad as you think. If this Schenk person's name is really Gerhard Heinrich that won't be hard to prove. You've planted the seed that you are on to them. The Americans just need to check the records. You can get your American to do that for you. It will just take some time."

"Yes, exactly, "Anna said. "I just don't know how much time I have."

"There must be someone who knew this Heinrich from the war, or from before. He must have some family somewhere. He didn't just hatch from a chicken egg yesterday. Now, why don't you make me some tea and then show me these paintings?" She gave Anna a push off the bed.

While the tea steeped, Anna brought Emil's painting and its Collecting Point sibling to show Madeleine. "Emil said the artist of his painting was a friend of his. And look, this one is clearly by the same hand wouldn't you say?"

"Hmm," Madeleine nodded. "A bit amateurish. But I guess they have a certain charm. What will you do with it?"

"I haven't any idea," Anna replied. She leaned the paintings against the wall and sat down on the bed. "Schenk recognized the one I brought to the Nassauer Hof, so he must know the artist too. Somehow it's all connected but I can't figure out how. I'm not going to ask Schenk and it's too late to ask Emil. I can't prove anything Emil told me, either." She sighed.

The door opened and Oskar and Amalia thundered into the living room, arms and legs flying and voices bright with laughter. They tumbled onto the sofa, their smell of sweat and dirt filling the room. Amalia lay back, her head on Oskar's chest. Lulu peeked out from under his arm. They were both out of breath.

"Oskar, you need to put some cold water on your eye," Anna said. "It's starting to swell up. I'll get you a washcloth, and then you and I are going to have a talk." She went into the bathroom and ran a cloth under the tap. The water was nice and cool on her hands as she wrung it out. She liked having Oskar with her. It felt more like a family and it was nice for Amalia to have someone to play with and to look out for her. If she could just get the truth out of him, she could decide what to do next.

When she came back in the living room, Amalia was playing with Lulu and Oskar was staring at the paintings, which where she had left them leaning against the wall. He had turned as white as his hair, which seemed to stand even more on edge than usual.

"What's the matter?" Anna asked.

"Where did you get those pictures?" He looked at her, confusion and fear swirling in his eyes."Why do you have them?"

"Do you recognize that one from the villa?" She pointed at the smaller landscape Cooper had provided for the failed Nassauer Hof sale. "That's where it came from. You probably saw it there. This other one, I—"

"Why do you have it?" Oskar shouted. He was angry, back to his defiant self. Now blood rose in his cheeks and his eyes glistened. He looked at her accusingly. "Those are my pictures."

Anna looked at him and then at the paintings. Something was shifting inside her brain, a piece of the puzzle inched its way closer to its rightful spot, spinning and twirling around. She took a step toward him and reached out her hand. "What do you mean these are yours? Oskar, it's very important that you tell me the truth now."

Oskar shook his head, hard. "No. I can't."

"Yes, you can. Nothing bad will happen. Are you scared of your uncle? He can't hurt you anymore. You are safe with me. Now, tell me the truth."

"How do you know about my uncle?"

"Never mind that now. Why are you so afraid of him?"

He jerked his arm out of Anna's grip. "Because he said he would hurt me if I told anyone. And that he would hurt you too."

"Me? How does your uncle know me?"

"You met him at that hotel. He told me. You had a picture of mine that you tried to sell him. A picture of my Mama's. He thought I had something to do with you going there to see him."

Anna threw the wet towel on the sofa and sat down. "Listen, that's enough of all this intrigue. You will tell me the truth now, Oskar, all of it. I am fed up with these guessing games." She took his chin into her hand and turned his face toward hers. "Tell me everything, now. Nothing bad will happen, I promise. But you have to talk."

He stared at her for a long time, his jaw working. "All right, I'll tell you. It was my job to guard the paintings at the villa. After my mama died, I had to go live with him, with my Uncle Gerhart. But he didn't want me, so he made me stay at the villa so I could tell him if the *Amis* found his paintings. But when you came with the *Ami*, you found me too, and you took me away. That made him even more mad at me. When he found me at the camp he was really angry."

Anna slid to the floor and stared at the boy. "Your uncle Gerhart? Gerhart who?"

"Gerhart Heinrich." Oskar said. "He is my mother's brother."

Anna's gaze focused on the boy and she spoke very slowly as she tried to follow the trail. "And your uncle, Gerhart Heinrich, was at the hotel when I tried to sell him this painting?" She pointed to the smaller landscape.

Oskar nodded. "You can't tell him I told you. He can hurt you. And Amalia, too. That's why I didn't tell you anything. I was too scared. I am sorry that I messed things up."

Anna pulled herself to her feet, only half-listening. She went into the kitchen and came back with the papers she had been studying. The lists of gallery owners, Oskar's parents' death certificates. Something had finally clicked. She shuffled though the papers until she found the one she wanted. The death certificate. The one thing she had paid no attention to had been what she'd needed all along. Oskar's mother's name: Magda Grünewald, *geborene* Heinrich. Her maiden name. Oskar was telling the truth.

Anna went back to the boy and pulled him toward her. "You have nothing to be sorry for, Oskar. You are safe now." She wrapped her arms around him and sat in the revelation as if a light was shining on both of them. Schenk really *was* Gerhart Heinrich. And someone could prove it. Emil had told her the truth. She was relieved and elated and horrified all at once.

After a while, Oskar spoke. "But Frau Klein? How did you get my Mama's pictures?"

"These pictures belonged to your Mama?" Anna asked. "Really?"

"No." Oskar shook his head and sniffed. "My Mama painted them. We would go together when she painted, down by the river. This was my favorite painting because I am in it. See?" He pointed to the small shepherd tending his flock on Emil's painting, his eyes bright and the color rising in his cheeks. "But then she put it in my uncle's gallery to be sold. She wanted to make extra money for herself. For us."

"And I knew the man who bought it." Anna said. Emil's story was coming into the light. "His name was Emil Schilling. And I think he was your mothers friend?"

Oskar nodded. "Yes," he said. "Emil. You knew him too? But how did you get the picture?"

Anna inhaled. "I think Emil wanted you to have this painting, only he didn't know you how to find you. He must have thought you died in the bombs too. If your uncle was keeping you a secret, then he wouldn't have known you were alive."

"You saw Emil? When?" Oskar's face smoothed and his eyes widened.

"He lives at the house with Fraulein Schilling," Amalia said. "Where I go during the day. You can come with me and see him."

Oskar looked confused, his brow furrowed over eyes that darted between Anna and the painting.

Anna steadied herself. "I have to tell you something." She took one child's hand in each of hers. "Now listen, both of you. It is important that you know that Emil was a good man. He suffered a lot though, and he had a lot of pain inside him."

Amalia looked liked she wanted to say something, but stopped herself. Anna looked at Oskar. His expression was dense, his eyes locked into hers. She took a deep breath.

"I am very sad to tell you that Emil is dead."

Amalia crawled to Madeleine who folded her arms around her. Oskar looked at Anna, the earnestness back on his face like a mask.

"Yes, I know. He died. At Stalingrad. That's what my uncle told me."

Anna kneeled forward and stroked his cheek.

"No, he didn't die there. He came home. He was here. He even helped take care of Amalia, and he worked for the Americans, like me. But then he got very sick, from the war."

"He was here all this time? In Wiesbaden?"

Anna nodded. She picked up the painting. "Before he died he said he wanted me to have this painting, but I know it's only because he thought you were dead. If he had known you were alive, he would have given it to you," she said. "Emil was your mother's friend, wasn't he?"

Oskar nodded. "Emil Schilling was *my* friend. He sometimes came to the orphanage to see his sister while I was there, to play with us. That's what he told me, but I don't remember because I was too small. But when I went with my Mama and Papa, he still came to visit. And my Mama always made him food and took care of him, because he didn't really have anyone. He was like my big brother. But then he had to go to Russia to fight. And my uncle told me he died there."

Anna stroked his cheek. "And Emil thought you had died with your mother in the bombs. If he had known you were here, he would have given the painting to you himself." *If he had known, he would be alive now*, she thought.

"But why didn't you tell him about me?" Oskar asked.

"He didn't know that I knew you. And I didn't know any of this until just now. And now it's too late." She sat back onto the floor and rubbed her face. "I am so sorry, Oskar. I really am."

Oskar chewed the inside of his cheek to keep from crying. "Did the *Amis* kill him?" he finally asked.

"No. The war just made him too sick. He couldn't go on living and so he died."

Amalia curled into a little ball in Madeleine's lap. Oskar sat frozen, staring into a void between his knees and the floor. The anger he had worn for so long was replaced by a sadness that seemed to compress him into the floor. Anna regarded their pitiable little tableau, each of them trying to find a way to live with the new knowledge. For a long time no one moved. Anna felt the full weight of the last years finally strike her down. The cost had been tallied and no one had come out unscathed.

"Now I have no one at all who wants me," Oskar said to the floor. "Not in the whole world."

"That's not true, Oskar. You have me. You have us." Anna pulled him close and felt his presence, solid and real. She was still here. She had survived. Maybe things would be all right, in their way. "Do you want to stay with us, here at this house?" she whispered in his ear. "If I can arrange it?"

Oskar nodded.

"And do you promise to be good and not to run away?"

He nodded again. "But what if my uncle comes after me? He will hurt you."

"No, he won't. I won't let him. We will tell the Americans all about him, you and me. And then he won't be able to hurt you any more. Will you help me?"

"What do I have to do?"

"Just tell me everything you know. I will write it down. And then we will tell the *Amis*. And they will do the rest."

"And what about the paintings?"

"You get to keep those. They are yours after all."

He nodded again. "I will help you." He raised his face to hers. "And Frau Klein? I am sorry I lied."

Anna tousled his hair. "Just don't do it any more. Now, come and help me."

The two of them stayed up well after Madeleine and Amalia had fallen asleep, Oskar telling Anna what he knew about Gerhart Heinrich, which, in the end was not all that much, but it was enough to prove the Schenk was not who he said he was. Anna's suspicions had been right. Heinrich had owned the Gallerie Neustadt in Mainz until the war took him away, stealing art from collectors under the guise of the Reichskulturkammer. As the boy's only living relative, he had been given custody of Oskar after his parents died in the bombing of Darmstadt in September of 1944, and had sent him to live in the villa, alone and in charge of guarding his stolen art. He would send food some weeks, but mostly Oskar fended for himself, stealing food from nearby farms or simply going hungry. His rewards were either beatings or negligence, both of which he accepted as his fate. But he was mostly a scared, lonely little boy who missed his mother and couldn't understand what had happened to the promise of his gilded childhood. His hatred for the Americans was understandable, and he knew nothing else of the true horrors committed by the Nazis. There would be time for that conversation another day. It wasn't until well after midnight that he began to fade. Anna made him a bed on the sofa and he lay down, half asleep already.

She tucked the blanket under his chin. "Good night, sweet boy," she whispered. "I hope you sleep well. Tomorrow we will go tell the *Amis* your story. And then we will go to the camp and I will tell them you are staying with me."

"And then what happens?"

"And then we will see. But now you sleep."

Back in the kitchen, now her new office, the little lamp she had set up on the table cast a sickly yellow glow onto the floor and oozed up the walls to create shadowy angles. Emil's painting leaned against the table leg. Anna and Oskar had looked at it together as the boy told her about his friend: Emil, who came to the orphanage to visit his sister and play with the children, especially Oskar. Emil, who had been a big brother to Oskar, and after he had been adopted had been taken in by Magda as well. Emil, who came to dinner and went on picnics with them, who brought Oskar little presents and liked eating ice cream and reading Winnetou stories. Emil, who put on a uniform and went off to glorious war and then never came back.

She picked up the painting and turned it over. The label from the Gallerie Neustadt was still intact on this one, but there were no other markings on the back. There had been only one buyer, and the painting had hung in his apartment in the Gustav-Freytag-Strasse ever since. There was no war-time adventure for this painting. The canvas was only slightly torn at the back in one corner, and the stretchers were in good shape. She held it up to the light and ran her hand across the back of the canvas. A large piece of tape was wrapped around the big center stretcher and Anna ran her hand underneath to feel for any damage. She felt something on the underside of the wood, something like a folded piece of paper. She picked at the ends of the tape, and after several tries, managed to peel off one end. The tape made a scraping sound as she unraveled it from the back of the wood. With it came the small piece of paper. It was folded inward on itself lengthwise and Anna could see it was a photo. Peeling the tape off, she unfolded the picture and pulled the lamp toward her. It was a dark photo, but its subject was very clear. Among a row of paintings, leaning against a table on a dirty basement floor, was the painting of the little girl in a yellow dress. It was the photo Cooper had taken, the only one that proved the Runge had been with the others in the basement that day. Anna turned the photo over. On the back, in what she knew to be Emil's handwriting, he had written *Viel Glück, Anna*. Good luck.

chapter twenty-five

Anna laid the photo down in front of Captain Farmer. He stood on one side of the big metal desk in the director's office at the Collecting Point; she and Cooper stood on the other. "And there's this, too," she said, taking a stack of loose papers from her bag. She sorted through them as she spoke. "I made a report, but it's not typed, I'm sorry. This is the list of known gallery owners with Gerhart Heinrich's name and, this here is the boy's parents' death certificate. See, here, this is his mother's maiden name." She pointed to Magda's Grünewald's particulars on the form. "The boy is right outside if you wish to speak to him directly." She straightened and waited as Captain Farmer flipped through the pages.

"This photo was taken by you, Cooper?"

Cooper cleared his throat. "Yes, the day after we found the stash, before this painting was stolen."

"And you say you found this, where?" Farmer asked Anna.

"That's a long story," Cooper answered.

"I guess Emil knew the photo was the key to the story. He must have had the film developed and then tried to figure out how to give it to me."

"I could have thought of a few easier ways," Cooper said.

Farmer smiled. "Good work, Frau Klein. I'm sorry about the run-in you had with the tribunal. I'll prepare a report for the regional command in Darmstadt. They are looking into it and this whole mess. They've been on to Schneider for a while, too. Believe me, they were none too happy to hear about the treatment you received, and I apologize also. We are lucky to have you with us."

Anna nodded her thanks and fidgeted with her purse strap. She was anxious to be done with the meeting.

"So she gets her job back?" Cooper asked.

"I'm working on that," Farmer answered. "I just got you back in here Cooper, give me a chance, will you? I just hope you'll both toe the line for a while. I don't need all this scrutiny. We have too much work to do and the State Department is making all kinds of noise back home about where all this art we have should go now. Lots of folks stateside want to get their hands on this stuff, too. I have enough to deal with."

"Yes sir," Anna and Cooper said in unison.

"One more thing. Tell me again: How did this painting get in Phillips' hands exactly?"

"It's all in my report, Captain, but it was Emil Schilling who was onto Schneider's scheme from the beginning. He took it from the villa because it still had the original gallery labels on it. Those labels proved the painting's true provenance—that it had been part of the collection of a Jewish gallery owner in Darmstadt. Schneider was removing the labels of the paintings in order to be able to claim they were his. But before Emil could get the Runge painting to us, Schneider got his hands on it anyway—thanks to the Schilling woman—and used it to bribe Phillips in exchange for his position here."

"And the other fellow, this Schenk? You are sure he's not who he claims to be?"

"Yes, turns out he was one of the better art thieves the Nazis had," Cooper said. "He's going by the name of a deceased art dealer from Mainz. But the boy, his nephew, can prove his identity. And, sir, I think you might want to take a look at what Corporal Miller has been up to."

Farmer sighed. "Yes, I know all about his side businesses. We'll shut him down too. He's got some real capitalist skills. Too bad they are wasted in the army."

Cooper elbowed Anna in the ribs. She felt as if they were two school children turning homework in to the teacher, but she couldn't help giving him a smile.

"It will take me a while to go through all of this," Farmer muttered as he sat down. "The kids are waiting outside? Your daughter and the boy?"

Anna nodded. "I'm sorry. I thought maybe you'd want to talk to Oskar, and Amalia, well, she couldn't be dissuaded from coming along. I can send them home."

"Not at all," Farmer said. "You know, we are working on setting up a place for the children of our workers. Frau Obersdorfer gave me an earful about women needing a safe place for their children to go during the day. It might take a few days yet, but not much longer. Now if you'll excuse me. I don't think I'll be too long." He nodded toward the door and turned his attention to the papers in front of him.

Cooper ushered Anna out of the office.

In the foyer, Oskar and Amalia sat on a rickety bench along the wall, their legs swinging in tandem.

"Hey there, duchess," Cooper said.

"Hey there, Captain," Amalia giggled.

"If her English gets any better we can give her a job," he laughed. His demeanor turned serious as he pulled Anna aside. "Listen, I'm so sorry about your friend, about Emil. I wish I could have done something."

"I don't think there's anything you could have done, Captain. He was suffering. He couldn't see a place for himself in the world anymore. He didn't believe he deserved to go on."

"There's a lot of that going on," Cooper said. "Suicides, murders. A lot of desperate people out there."

"That's been going on for quite some time," Anna said. "But at least Oskar got his mother's paintings back."

"Your first restitution. That's something to celebrate."

"It's hardly like returning a Rembrandt to its owner." Anna tapped her foot and looked at the door to Farmer's office.

"I'll bet it is to Oskar." A grin spread over his face. "Look, Farmer will be a while. Since you're all here, why don't you come with me for a minute? It won't take long."

The three of them followed Cooper into the small hallways at the back of the museum. He pulled a set of keys from his pocket, unlocked one door, and then, after they had gone through several rooms filled with crates, he stopped at a metal door and produced another set of keys. He winked and put his finger to his lips. The door gave way under the push of his shoulder and revealed a darkened room. He waved them inside and closed the door. A damp cool wrapped itself around them. Cooper turned on the light, which revealed a labyrinth of dirty wooden crates. Amalia sneezed into her hand.

"Hurry," Cooper said and disappeared around a corner. They followed him between the crates until they hit a dead end. A large rectangular crate sat alone against the back wall. They stood around it and Anna let Cooper indulge in the theatrics he had planned for so long. Cooper knelt in front of the crate and pulled on the front panel.

"The brass is coming from Frankfurt tonight to see this, so they've rigged the crate for easy viewing. Now, you can't tell anyone I did this. Are you ready? She's been buried underground for a long time, but now she's ready to see you."

Anna nodded and pulled Amalia and Oskar close, sharing in their anticipation.

Cooper pulled the panel off and placed it to the side. Anna bent down to get a better look.

"What is it, Mama?" Amalia whispered.

Inside the shadows of its cocoon, she saw the famous silhouette, the long neck and the flare of the headpiece. The eyes gazed out at them, unperturbed and unaltered by the centuries. It seemed so unlikely, so heroic in a way, that inside this box this statue would exist completely untouched and unmarred. For her, the horrors of the past ten years were only a blip. Anna blinked to clear her eyes.

"She is so beautiful!" Amalia exclaimed.

"That is Nefertiti. The painted queen—the most beautiful woman who ever lived. She's more than 2,000 years old," Cooper said triumphantly. "You like her?"

"I've seen her in a book." Oskar's eyes were wide. "In one of my

Mama's books." He was finally impressed.

Anna smiled at Cooper. She still admired his unwavering optimism. In spite of everything, he really believed everything would be all right in the end.

They looked at the face for a long time, the four of them paying their respects to the ancient bust. It would be around long after they were all gone and Anna considered the effort that it had taken to keep her safe for just the last handful of years. She wondered once more how humans could be so barbaric and so magnificent at the same moment in history. Was it possible one trait needed the other to exist?

Amalia slipped a hand into Anna's and squeezed it tight. "She is the most beautiful thing I have ever seen," she said.

"We had better go," Cooper said, pulling the crate closed. He ushered them out of the room and turned off the light before closing and locking the door.

"Thank you, Captain," Anna said, as they walked back to the office. "They will never forget this."

"I thought they'd like that." He took her arm and waited until the children had run ahead into the open foyer. Anna stiffened.

"You okay? You seem distracted. You'll get your job back, you know that right? There's a place for you here. If you want it."

Anna stepped back and adjusted the strap of her bag on her shoulder. "I'm just a little tired after all that's happened."

"And? There's something else, I can tell. I know you better than you think. Is it something to do with your husband?"

"No, it's not that. Well, yes it is actually. I am worried about what the tribunal brought up about him. What they know..."

"You mean about him being a Red?"

"Yes. That hasn't changed. What am I to do about that?"

"Don't worry about that now. We will get that sorted out. You never know, maybe he's come to his senses. Times are changing." He softened. "You're not convinced. What is it that's really bothering you?"

"It's nothing. Just feeling a bit out of sorts that's all." Anna smiled. "I am so happy you got your job back. They are lucky to have you." She repeated the words Farmer had said to her earlier. "I know you will do a lot of good." She shifted her bag again. It felt heavier than ever. "If you'll excuse me, I just need to step outside and get a bit of air."

Cooper looked concerned, but relented. "Okay. Take your time. I'll wait here with the kiddos."

Anna sat on the loading dock, which was quiet for the moment. A few GIs milled around, but there was very little activity outside now that the full shipment from the Merkers mine had been secured inside the building. There were more guards at the fence, and things seemed more formal than they had when she had first started working there—when there had been no running water and no desks or even electricity. All the windows were repaired but tiny glass shards still remained here and there. They still crunched under foot like pebbles, even inside the building, as they were slowly ground into dust with every step.

Anna took a deep breath and reached into her bag for the envelope that Frau Hermann had pushed under her door early that morning. She had not had the nerve to open it, even though the handwriting was as familiar as her own. Instead she had put it in her bag. She wanted to find the right moment to read it, but the letter's weight on her shoulder had become too much and she could not wait any longer. She held the little envelope up to her nose and took a deep breath, then ran a finger over the return address, the familiar name conjuring a picture of her old house, in her old town, in her old life. The sun shining in an unknowing sky, the trees blowing in the oblivious wind. She saw her little garden and remembered how, in the morning, the sun would make the leaves of her marigolds glow like little golden nuggets. Amalia took her first wobbly steps there next to the lilac bush, and Anna thought it would be her home forever because, maybe, if she was lucky and very quiet, the world would pass her by. She pressed her lips together and peeled the edge of the flap upward, then stuck her finger into the hole and split open the top of the envelope. The paper inside was thin and mismatched, taken from different writing pads. She steadied her hands.

My darling Anna,

I hope and pray that this letter finds you and Amalia and that you are safe. Since you did not arrive in Landstuhl as planned, I am hoping you made contact with Madeleine and that perhaps your messages have been delayed. I could not wait any longer to hear from you so I am sending this to her address on blind faith.

Things here are not the same without you. Life is slowly getting better and back to normal. The new Russian Kommandant was in touch with me two weeks ago and has given me a position running the hospital. I am able to help a lot of people, mostly from the area but also those who are just passing through. Now that there is more medicine, things are easier. The communists are setting up the town leadership and I hope to earn a position of some kind. Surely a doctor can contribute something?

I wonder what you are hearing about the Russian sector? I can tell you it's not nearly as bad here as maybe other places, Berlin and such. Things here are very calm and the soldiers can be quite friendly. Just yesterday one came to the house with fresh horsemeat for the patients at the hospital. Once you understand the Russian temperament, you will get along well. I want you both to come home. You can help me with the hospital and Amalia can start school. Everything is getting organized. There is nothing to be afraid of anymore. I am sending some money to help you on your way.

Please come back to me. I am waiting for my beautiful girls.

With all my love,

Thomas

Anna fingered the money he had put inside the folded paper and re-read the letter. The realization was slow to wash over her, but when it did she felt like she had sunk to the bottom of the ocean. He wasn't coming. There would be no new life here, no future for them, no happy ending. She thought of Amalia and her heart ached. She could not sentence her daughter to a life that would kill everything unique and vibrant about her. She knew their only future was on this side of the border. Why couldn't Thomas see it, too? She wanted to scream at him to come to his senses, that the Russians had nothing for him, that he was stepping out of one oppression into another. That it was no longer enough for her to simply survive on someone else's terms. She looked up at the sky, clear, with only a few smudges of clouds high in the east beyond the hills. She loved her husband more than ever, she needed him, and their daughter deserved to have her family together. But they were here now. They had made it this far. Amalia was safe. They were free.

Anna sat for a long time, letting her thoughts steep, and feeling caught between moments, as if time had stopped as it waited for her. There would be a before and there would be an after. This was the dividing line. She had to decide.

She had not moved when a jeep pulled up to the Collecting Point's rear entrance and two MPs jumped out and ran inside, their guns in hand. She put the letter back in the bag and followed them into the foyer. They had disappeared into the offices in the side wing where the restorers had set up their workshop.

"What is going on?" she asked when she found Cooper sitting on the bench with Oskar and Amalia. "What are they doing?"

Cooper shrugged. "I guess we'll find out. Have a seat. You feeling better?"

"Not really," Anna said as she pulled Amalia into her lap.

They heard shouting and then the shuffle of a physical struggle from the workshop. American voices yelled and a woman shrieked. Amalia's body tensed, and she buried her head into Anna's shoulder. People stopped what they were doing and looked in the direction of the noise, which was now coming toward them. Captain Farmer came out of his office just as the white helmets of the MPs appeared at the far end of the foyer, surrounded by other GIs and a handful of workers. The clump of people approached the main entry and Farmer stepped in to hold the door open as officiously as the bellman at the Hansa Hotel. As they descended the stairs, Anna stood up on tiptoe to see the sweating head of Ludwig Schneider in between the shoulders of the two MPs. The door slammed shut with finality, and the people who had gathered to watch the show now hurried to look busy again. Farmer motioned to Cooper to follow him, and the two of them squeaked into his office and closed the door.

"What happened, Mama?" Amalia asked.

"I guess they've arrested Herr Schneider," Anna replied.

"That was because of you, Frau Klein," Oskar said. "Because you told the *Amis* the truth. And they believed you. Because you figured it out." He nodded to himself.

"That was so smart, Mama," Amalia chimed in.

Anna chuckled. "That's all very good. Now, why don't you two run along and go check on Auntie? I don't think you need to wait anymore. I'll come home when I am finished here." She put Amalia down and gave her a little push. "Oskar, you are in charge. You go straight home, no monkeying around."

"Yes, Frau Klein." Oskar took Amalia's hand and pulled her toward the door. Amalia was happy to go along and they both stopped to wave before leaving the building. Amalia stood, framed in the doorway, looking over her shoulder at Anna, then turning to step into the bright world. The light from the open door raked across the stone floor at Annas's feet, catching the fragments of crystal embedded in it. They sparkled against the dull gray like stars in the sky—tiny mirror fragments in the darknes—until the door closed and they disappeared.

"Hey, I've got great news." Cooper startled her. "Oh, are you okay?"

Anna wiped her eye with the back of her hand and straightened her back. "Yes, I'm all right. Just thinking." She pulled her bag onto her lap. "What's your good news?"

He grinned like a boy with a secret and sat down next to her. "Not only did you get your job back, but Farmer got you reclassified.

You, Anna Klein, are now a level-two employee of the United States Military Government. That means you get housing assistance and a little bit more money. How about that?"

Anna was taken aback. "But don't they know about my husband? What about my 'status,' or whatever the men on the tribunal called it? Am I even allowed to stay?"

Cooper waved her off. "Don't worry about that. Farmer was impressed with your report and your dedication; he wants to make sure you stick around. We need good people like you. And not just in the typing pool either. I know the little old Monuments Fine Arts and Archives unit may not be as glamorous as working for some brass in Frankfurt, but I like to think it has its perks. And there's a lot of work to be done. Things are about to get even more interesting around here." He leaned forward and rested his forearms on his knees. He looked at her over his shoulder, his gaze direct. "So, what do you say?"

Anna flushed. "I don't know what to say, Captain. That is too kind. Really." The blood rising in her cheeks warmed her scalp. She touched her hair, embarrassed.

Cooper looked disappointed. "Well, that's not very enthusiastic. I am going to need a little bit more than that." He sat up, palms on his knees. "So tell me you won't leave us, even after all this mess. You're here to stay, right?"

Anna looked at the ground. Now she knew what would be taken from her. All this time she had eluded the unspeakable horror that ruled the world around her. It had swirled close, once or twice grazing her enough to draw blood but not enough to knock her down. She had known all along that she had not yet paid the full price for her own survival. But now fate had finally come for her and taken her husband, as it had done to millions of women like her. It was not the bombs or a death camp, or even the guillotine or firing squad that took him. It had not even been the war. It was the peace that had taken Thomas away. There was no place for Anna with him any more. She had to pick a side. *Please forgive me, Amalia. One day, maybe you will understand.*

She looked to Cooper, who was studying her the same way he had done the day they first met, his eyes connecting with hers, waiting.

"Well?" he said.

"Yes, I am," she said, pushing a big American smile through her tears. "I am here to stay."

acknowledgements

I owe many debts of gratitude to the sources and people who made this book possible. Among the numerous works of non-fiction dealing with the Third Reich I consulted for research, the ones I returned to repeatedly were Allison Owings' *Frauen: German Women Recall the Third Reich*, *Die Brandnacht* by Klaus Schmidt and *Of Pure Blood* by Marc Hillel and Clarissa Henry. The exhibition catalog *Hitler und die Deutschen* was another invaluable resource, as were countless documentaries, photo archives, and classic films dealing with the immediate aftermath of the war, most notably *A Foreign Affair, The Third Man and The Search.*

Much of my understanding about the achievements of the MFAA came through the work of Robert Edsel and his books, *Rescuing da Vinci* and *The Monuments Men*, as well as *The Rape of Europa* by Lynn H. Nicholas and the *Safekeepers* by Walter I. Farmer. I was also known to disappear for days inside Fold3.com, which contains the entirety of the Monuments Men archives, and provided a great deal of detail of the Collecting Points' day-to-day operations.

In Germany I am grateful for the extremely generous assistance and support of Hans-Werner and Ursula Schmidt in Frankfurt, and for Georg Habs at the Wiesbaden *Stadtarchiv*, who was a goldmine of photographic material and historic insight. *Die Herren* Samuel Weinberger and Majer Szanckower of Frankfurt very kindly spent an afternoon sharing their stories when the plot of this book was headed in a very different direction. I am very thankful to them and intend to incorporate that important research into the next book.

Closer to home, there are many people who are directly—and some perhaps unwittingly—responsible for the existence of this book. At the Iowa Summer Writing Festival Kelly Dwyer taught me twice about the *whats* of plotting, and Susan Taylor Chehak taught me the *whys*. Thank you both for inspiring and motivating me with humor and joy. My friends Kelly Lyons and Susan Schultz let me flesh out ideas, listened, and reassured me for all these years, and Kelly Roberson convinced me I could write a book in the first place. Linda Sullivan: thank you for your support and enthusiasm, and Sally Fly: thank you for your generosity and the quiet conference room. John Son was wise enough to tell me two years ago that the book wasn't ready when I was sure it was (and he was so right). Connie Levy patiently marked up an early draft and reminded me over monthly lunches why we write, and my editor Caroline Tolley provided a steadfast voice that saved me in the final rounds of writing. Emily Kristen Anderson was a joy to work with as is the patient and indefatigable Stephanie Barko. Thank you also to the many friends, colleagues, and clients who asked me in passing, "how's the book coming?" and cheerfully endured the subsequent tirades; your interest and encouragement kept me going. And, very special thanks to the genius and genial Adam Fortner who put the perfect images where there were only words, turned the manuscript into a real-life book, and is my collaborator and friend from beginning to end.

I am immensely grateful to my family, who tolerated the fallout of this project far longer than is reasonable or even advisable. Katie, who read, listened, and counseled on long walks, and Mark who patiently answered questions about German Romantic painters and other art-related particulars. To Frank and Jessie: thanks for the moral support and ample cocktails at crucial junctures. And, to my parents, without whom this book simply *would not be:* my mother for her unwavering support and encouragement, her insight and invaluable memory, and my father for believing in the project and unquestioningly supporting it from its very earliest days. Thank you for everything, always.

Finally, to Lee and E: thank you for your monumental patience and your faith in my dream, and for talking me off the ledge more than once. You let me disappear into a faraway place many times, and you were always there when I came back. You are my safe harbor and I love you both.

Made in the USA
Coppell, TX
09 May 2021

55354035R00246